I0789029

Vampocalypse
vendetta

A Novel By

E.S. Brown

Copyright ©2024 Line By Lion Publications
www.pixelandpen.studio
ISBN 978-1-948807-52-4
Cover Design by Thomas Lamkin Jr.
Editing by Dani J. Caile

For more information, email www.linebylionpublications.com

Also by ES Brown

Starphoenix

Vampocalypse

Codename: Scarlett

Once Killed, Twice Dead: A Codename Scarlett Prequel

NEW WORLD
NORTHWEST OUTSKIRTS
DA
RE
PACIFIC WASTELANDS
C
B

TERRITORIES
KOTA
ACHES
ENTRAL
BARRENS
ATLANTIC
BADLANDS
SOUTH GULF
COAST LANDS

Vampocalypse

vendetta

A Novel By

E.S. Brown

"We are the only true Gods."

From "The Vampire Scriptures: Book of the Immortal"

Z

I fucking love vampires.

I love how they fight to the end, only to become cowards and beg for their lives when they know their time is done. I love the look in their eyes when they realize they've lost to a "filthy human." I love how they die.

In this world full of vampires, they are the reason I exist. If not for them, I would be weak and without purpose. But all that changed when they killed my entire family in front of my four-year old eyes in that New York hotel so many years ago. Now I live my days as master-at-arms of Camp Expectation, a large community of humans hiding in plain sight in the barrens of an area that used to be known as central Oregon, and keep keen eyes over our small part of this world – a world forever under the mustard glow of the ever-ecliptic sun and its unique brand of darkness.

Darkness.

Sometimes I'm afraid to open my eyes…afraid of what I might see.

Sometimes I'm afraid to keep my eyes shut…afraid of what I do see.

I remember my mother, my father, and my brother, but it's more of just their essence. While I still clearly see their deaths, their faces have faded over the years. Being orphaned at the age of four taught me that life isn't fair, life hurts, life's a bastard. But in my loss I came upon a new "family": the man who saved me as my blood family perished, the man who calls himself Judge. He took me in, raised me, and showed me how to fight and how to survive in this Vampocalyptic world.

I wish vampires would have perished during the three-year cold and radiation spell like so many humans did following the initial nuclear blasts. But as vampires appeared to be completely immune to the harsh conditions, pockets of humans adapted and somehow survived in the barrens and wastelands of the New World. And so I have lived my life working tirelessly to avenge my family against the dark filth that plagues the Earth like blackened scabs that never heal. Each kill works towards ridding the world of the scourge of undead that have taken over. But I am never satisfied. Each kill does nothing to appease the loss of my loved ones. Or my thirst to kill more.

My duties as master-at-arms often resulted in many long, uneventful days making rounds of Camp Expectation's defenses and occasionally assisting with policing the two thousand residents that lived behind its tall, ultra-fortified walls. But I would leave when I could – despite appeals from both Judge and the town governor. Fuck them. Fuck all of them. Judge doesn't own me, and the governor certainly doesn't, either. I am my own person and no one was going to hold me back from what I wanted to do – what little there was to do in this crazy world.

My motorcycle was a rebuilt and customized 1981 Honda CM400 Hondamatic. It had a purple fairing with tall windscreen, high handlebars, and even a rear passenger seat with what was known as a 'sissy bar.' I remember reading on a placard next to where I found the bike in a museum showroom years ago that it used to belong to some 1980s music icon. It was no one I had ever heard of, though word was that he also regularly "shredded" it on guitar.

My bike was one of my three prized possessions, the others being the Japanese sai that were strapped to each of my hips. The custom-made weapons had center blades – or "monouchi" – longer than what was typical even for the trident-like armaments. I would spend hours crafting and sharpening the blades to have fine points and razor sharp edges that would provide for easier kills and decapitations. Fighting with sai against the oversized talons of the vampires almost made me feel as if I had claws of my own.

I loved the feeling of the warm air as it splashed against my face and whipped through my long, dark hair that I always made sure to have down for these solo rides. The feeling was liberating, journeying out on long roads with not a care in the world. When I was alone and riding, there was no pain or sorrow, no loneliness or bitterness. There was just the road, the wind, the hum of my bike, and me.

And the explosion that suddenly destroyed the road directly ahead.

My bike went spinning and I went flying, landing face down hard on the almost cement-like dry dirt of the barrens that extended for miles on either side of the road. I coughed as the air fought to come back into my lungs. Slowly, the fog in my eyes dissipated and the cloud of dust around me cleared. I pushed up onto my hands and knees and found myself on one side of the two-lane road while my bike lay on the opposite side. Sonofabitch. My bike better be fine or someone was gonna pay. I was alone, about thirty miles outside of Camp Expectation, and possibly – though hopefully not – without my bike. Fucking hell.

I did a quick check of my hips and was relieved that both sai were still strapped into their holsters. Looking ahead a good part of the road was gone, replaced by a crater with heavy debris surrounding the blast zone. It was a miracle I wasn't killed by the explosion. If Judge was here he would find a way to admonish me and remind me that one day my luck was going to run out.

But not today, bitches.

That's when the movement caught my attention. My eyes darted over to the right while the rest of me remained still. On the far side of the road, not far from my bike, a shape rose out of the sand. It was humanoid and dressed head-to-toe in loose fabrics bound at the neck, arms, legs, and all major joints with wraps of wide bandages like the ones wrapped around its head. No skin was visible and I couldn't make out how it was seeing through the thick fabric that covered its eyes. I had never seen anyone – or anything – like this odd combination of mummy and scarecrow. I quickly leapt to my feet while my arms made an "X" in front of me as I drew both sai from their cross-draw hip holsters. I carefully watched the…creature…as it stood unmoving, slightly slouched with its wrapped up arms and bandaged hands cocked forward and fingers spread like some sort of reptilian claws, as it "stared" at me.

More movement on my left somehow surprised me. It was another of the sand-humanoids rising up from seemingly nothing but hard, crumbling dirt. I turned and saw another and another and another – until their numbers finally stopped at fifteen and they surrounded me. None of them advanced forward, instead they all just stood and watched me. I turned in tight, slow circles as I held my weapons up, ready to defend…or strike.

Two of the sand-humans stood shoulder-to-shoulder, which was different as none of the rest were even close to touching each other. I watched curiously as the two parted and a third that stood hidden behind them stepped forward. The two bowed their heads as the third, an apparent leader, presented itself. While all the others were dressed in grays and taupe and other decidedly desert tones, this one had sashes of dark blue and red as overlaid accents. It stood noticeably more upright, though still not fully, and walked with an air of confidence that the rest did not exhibit. I maintained my guard and watched this one keenly as it stopped little more than an arm's length away from me.

"I've killed many more vampires at once under much more dire circumstances." Having been raised and surrounded by American-English speakers for thirty years, my native Russian accent was almost completely gone, only occasionally hinting through.

The sand-human leader held up its bandaged hands with palms showing as if in a gesture of peace.

"You... have nothing to fear... with us, valla." The voice was distinctly male and sounded hushed and dry, yet unusually authoritative despite an odd diction and misplaced pauses.

"If I have nothing to fear then I have no quarrel with you." That's just me playing into his verbal game but knowing better.

His head turned as he "looked" at each of his hands — I still didn't understand how he could see through all the bandages — before his "gaze" settled back on me. The featureless face hidden behind the loose cloth bits and bandages was admittedly somewhat unnerving.

"Allow me to intro...duce myself. My...name is Hobart. Hobart Issaquah. But please... call... me Issaquah." The sand-human splayed his hands out to his sides and bowed. "It's my pleasure... to... meet you."

"Interesting name."

"I... have inter...esting beginnings."

I remained stoic and unwavering, staying acutely aware of the others that were around me. I had no reason to trust these things, especially after they wrecked my ride. Issaquah raised his hands upwards again. It seemed as though he wanted to hold his hands high in the air but there was something restricting him, perhaps a physical condition of some sort from the looks of how his upper body quivered as he strained to lift his hands any higher than the sides of his head.

"We… are… peaceful roamers of this… land."

"'Peaceful' isn't a word that comes to mind. Especially not after you caused me to crash my bike." I wasn't sure I liked where this was going. I shifted the weight of my stance to be more nimble if attacked from any direction.

Issaquah held a hand up dismissively. "We… have a… statement. Would… you care to hear it?"

My danger radar was reaching peak levels. I started to shake my head. "I don't think —"

Issaquah tilted his head back and stretched his arms out to his sides. It was almost messianic. "For every… child life should… be fulfilling."

As he spoke, more and more of his "people" came up out of the ground. They were all faceless, genderless, and ageless under their coverings but it did seem that some were younger than others from their size and the way they moved. Most disturbing was that they were all moaning the same deep, chant-like moan. I continuously adjusted my footing and constantly reassessed my surroundings.

"We… pray that each… and every heartbeat… lives and… loves… and develops beyond the… walls of… poverty and… injustice. For this… we… all pray, amen."

The group around me echoed the word in unison: "Amen."

"God is here…between you… and me. He is everywhere. And… he commands us… guides us and… delivers us rewards for… our prayers."

"Rewards?" My eyes continued to dart around me, ever vigilant.

"Yes, valla… we prayed… for you to come."

"Valla. Why do you keep calling me that?"

"It's… a term of respect… Valla, the great nourisher." Issaquah lowered his arms and tilted his head back towards me. "God… God has delivered you."

"Delivered? I think you're forgetting about the bike you blew me off of."

Issaquah extended his right hand towards me. The low moaning from the cult-like sand-humans around me grew steadily louder. With his left hand he pulled away the loose bandages from around his right forearm. What was underneath was barely human – the forearm was ashen gray and skeletal from malnourishment combined with the pockmarks and bruises of whatever horrors of sickness he may be enduring.

"All... of us suffer... from the Sickness. God brought it to... us... the Sickness from the Sky. And we are... also starved. Our... young ones... must have nourishment." Issaquah *"looked"* upwards again towards the yellow-gray sky. *"We asked... for nourishment... this valla... and God delivered you... the great nourishment."*

Of course. They're going to try and fucking eat me. Shoulda seen that coming.

Issaquah curled most of his fingers to leave only his first finger pointing at me. He emitted his own throaty tone, though his was much louder and more commanding than the others. I spun around and saw that nearly three dozen wrapped bodies were converging upon me from all sides. Their arms were stretched outwards while their moaning turned to a high pitched screeching – a screeching I instantly recognized:

Vampires.

Stories of vampire mutations permeated the lands but I never fully believed them, having never come across any personally, let alone knowing anyone who had either. These *"strains"* were known as wasteland clans that lived lawlessly outside the structure of the modern vampire mecca-cities. Yet even though the existence of these mutants around me came as somewhat of a surprise, there was one thing about me these vampires didn't know:

I'm always ready for surprises.

I made swift broad arcs with both of my weapons, cutting down the three sandvampires closest to me. As the screeches from others around me continued, the bandages around their mouths began to pull and tear away, revealing bits of ashen skin and long pointed teeth. Fingernails tore through the tips of their hand wraps to expose sharp talons looking for flesh to tear into. Thankfully none of them could fly – at least none of them showed that they could – but they were fast. For every blade strike of mine that landed true, there were five or more strikes that met open air.

Two large sandvampires came at me from my left. I dropped low and spun while swiping my sai in a low flat arc – cleanly separating them at their knees. Their unholy shrieks joined those of a dozen others that lay wounded and no longer able to fight. For what the creatures lacked in fighting prowess, however, they more than made up in numbers. Every one I maimed or killed was replaced twofold by fresh bodies out of the ground. Through the melee I did not see Issaquah – he was leaving the attacks to his soldiers.

I rushed forward with a shoulder leading the way and burst through a wall of the monsters. I skirted the edge of the crater in the road and stopped behind my crashed motorcycle. For the first time I was not completely surrounded, instead having open space around most of me and facing a line of the creatures that stood ready to strike.

But then they didn't.

Instead, the wall of sandvampires separated down the middle and parted like the Biblical Red Sea. And there stood Issaquah. He sauntered forward, in no hurry, the tips of his outstretched fingers touching the hands of nearby clan members as he passed them by. He stopped walking once he was beyond the line of monsters and the "sea" of vampires closed the gap they had created for him to pass through. The guttural tones and screeching stopped and the air was quiet. Not even a slight breeze whispered through the silence as this creature and I "stared" each other down.

"You are… relentless… and solid prey. But… we can no… longer wait for this fight to… end."

"Then let me go."

Issaquah shook his head. "Not that simple. But… I do have a proposal… for you."

My eyes narrowed and surveyed the line of bandaged creatures standing before me. They had remained still and unmoving during my interaction with Issaquah but now there was motion among them as three of the mummy-like monsters in pre-teenaged bodies came forward. Issaquah waved his hands in the direction of the small beings.

"These... are prizes of mine... each turned... when they were just seven years of age." Issaquah took a deep breath. "I ...consider them my ...children. Dispose of... them and you... may go. But I... warn that it will... not be easy."

"What kind of mad creature turns a child into a vampire? Then commands it to fight?"

Laughter came from behind the bandaged face gazing at me. It was a laugh that quickly dissolved into something deep, dark, and undecipherable.

"Are you really going to make me fight these kids?" This was my one final plea.

An answer came in the form of an attack as the "children" (they may have been turned at age seven but who knows how long ago that was) leapt at me, arms raised, with talons like spikes nearly the lengths of their forearms. I crouched and prepared to leap backwards and away from the attack but the little fuckers were fast and the razor-edged tips of a vampire claw snagged my left sleeve. As I jumped my sleeve ripped and tore away, leaving a gash that ran from my bicep down to my forearm. The cut wasn't extremely deep but still made for a red stream that ran and dripped away as I somersaulted backwards and landed on my feet.

A moment later I was surrounded by three sandvampires that barely stood as tall as my hip. Their inhuman sounds were loud and pierced the air as their fingertips took endless stabs at me. I made a quick turn, using the tri-pronged steel in my grasp to parry away certain death. I twisted around and dropped in time to come face-to-bandaged face with one of the children. The swipe from its talons would have stabbed my face if I hadn't dropped low in time. The deadly spikes from another assailant were about to enter my right side but I rolled away and the creature's claw struck nothing but hard ground.

A sudden kick into my side stopped my momentum. I ended on my back, face up, staring into the bandaged "face" of the third sandvampire child as it stood over me. Superhuman I am not and special powers I do not possess so it was with extreme luck that I brought my sai together in an "X" in front of my face just in time to stop the creature's sharp fingertips just a few hairs-widths away from gouging into my eyes. I kicked the child away then rolled to the side, barely evading a deadly onslaught of stabs and swipes from the razor-edged spikes of another of my attackers. I managed to kick one of the hands away which provided an opening for me to roll up onto my feet. My back was to the line of vampires watching the fight and their hisses and jeers made it obvious they were anxious for this fight to end.

The little creatures fighting me rushed at me all at once. As I took a step backwards, I tripped among some debris from the blast that crashed my bike and I stumbled into the line of vampires watching the fight. One of the adult vampires grabbed my left arm and I could feel its warm breath on my exposed skin as it went to take a bite. I yanked my arm away just before its teeth punctured my arm. I was then shoved violently away from the line and towards the oncoming tiny attackers. Screeches and shouts from the crowd made it obvious that this was not going to stop until they saw me dead.

They made my mind up for me, then. I tried to play nice. I tried to not kill their children in front of them.

So much for trying.

The three vampire children attacked simultaneously. I jumped and completed a spinning side kick, knocking the nearest of the three across its face. The sandvampire child dropped and I thought I heard a slight whimper. The other two emitted their high-pitched, blook-curdling screams as they rushed in. I dropped down, spun around, and sliced the nearest child's feet off at its ankles. The creature cried out and fell, unable to stand or walk. I plunged the long center blade of one of my sai into its forehead and the screaming ceased as the creature stopped moving.

There was no time to relish in the kill as a strong kick in my back knocked me forward and I stumbled once again into the arms of the baiting crowd. They thrust me back into the fight. I turned to face the two remaining vampire children and felt a sudden pain across the left side of my face. I dropped the weapon in my left hand from the instant intense agony and put my hand to the side of my face. Warm blood pulsed from between my fingers from the deep cut. It felt like the entire side of my face was on fire. I couldn't make out the entire wound, but the stinging and pain went from my forehead, over my left eye, and down to my cheek. The taste of warm, wet iron filled my mouth.

The sandvampire child before me laughed from behind its ghoulish coverings. It held up one of its claws and fresh blood – my blood – dripped down its arm. My face throbbed and ached and blood obscured the vision in my left eye. The fight was not at its end and I could afford no time to tend to my wounds. I wiped the streaming blood out of my eye as I twisted away to avoid another near-death swipe from another talon, this one nearly grazing the side of my throat.

The two remaining sandvampire children were leaping rapidly around me, thrusting and swiping their talons as they bounced in a deadly and dizzying display of athleticism and prowess. I spent the next several moments, and way too much time, avoiding their strikes to initiate any of my own. My face ached and I was growing tired of this fight – it was time for this to end. Now.

There was a sudden lull in the battle. Each of the half- sized assailants was about ten feet away and I stood between them. At least twice that distance in front of me and posing no immediate threat was the line of vampires urging the battle to continue as if this was some sort of gladiatorial arena fight. Issaquah stood in front of them – silent and commanding with his presence.

The two child sandvampires rushed in together. I landed a hard jumping side kick into the creature on my right, knocking it onto its back. I swiped my loose sai from off the ground near my feet and held it up just in time to block a deadly strike from the creature on my left. My weapon and the monster's claws were locked in a hard battle as we each tried to overpower each other – me pushing with all my might with my left hand while the vampire pressed with all its strength with both hands. We stared at each other for an intense moment – at least we seemed to despite the bandages – and that's when I brought my other sai up from underneath, severing both of the sandvampire child's hands at the forearms. The inhumane cries from the creature pierced the air…until a quick swipe of my sai blade took off the top half of the monster's head.

The third and final child assailant was upon me with a fury and flurry of nonstop stabs and swipes. I performed one parry, then a second, then a third, then I lost count. The child darted left then right then easily evaded two quick attacks from me. There was a crash as the steel of my weapons met with the razor-like talons of my aggressor, then a clang, and another crash before the fight finally ended…with a thrust of my sai up into the chin and through the top of the head of the small but dangerous assailant. I yanked my blade down and away and blood sprayed from the wound as the lifeless child body crumbled to the ground.

A stunned silence fell upon the crowd. I'm guessing they'd never figured on their warrior children being disposed of. I'm also guessing they'd never come across anyone like me.

The crowd slowly began to slither and seethe prompting Issaquah to raise a fist into the air, which immediately silenced the rabid onlookers. He lowered his arm then stepped forward. A slight breeze began to waft through the barrens and I could feel tiny grains of sand hitting the still bleeding gash on my face. A sandvampire rushed up to Issaquah from the crowd behind him and whispered something I could not hear. Issaquah stepped forward and the gap between us narrowed to just a few feet. He stretched his arms out far to his sides and struck a pose that only fed into the religious-like fanaticism running through these creatures.

"I am… the… great Hobart Issaquah!" he exclaimed in an oddly triumphant shout. "And… I shall not… be vanquished!"

"And I am Zarina Ismagilova…" I said, calmly and poised.

My next movement was sudden and definitely unexpected by Issaquah as I thrust forward and up hard and fast at an angle with both sai together in both hands. A deep, diagonal gash appeared at Issaquah's right hip, continued up and across his stomach and chest, and stopped at his right shoulder. The look on his face echoed the surprised gasps that came from the crowd – gasps that became screams as I brought one of my weapons around and with a clean swipe removed Issaquah's head from his body.

I went and stood over the head, which had rolled off and stopped face up a few feet away. The bandages around his right eye had moved, exposing part of the creature's face, and I could see what looked like dark, charred skin underneath. His eye flickered as life of the undead still coursed through his head. I looked down, coldly.

"...and I'm a vampire killer," were the last words he heard before I stabbed the tip of a sai into his eye.

Wails and cries from the shocked and shattered sandvampires filled the air. I glared at the line of them and raised my weapon high with Issaquah's unmoving, dead head spiked to its tip.

"Who's next?" I shouted.

The sandvampires scattered away and their screeching diminished as they dropped down and disappeared into any number of invisible holes in the desert wastes around me. I let Issaquah's head slide off the end of my weapon then shook away as much vampire blood off the steel as I could.

I let out a long exhale as I felt my adrenaline finally begin to normalize. The ground around me was not an uncommon scene – parts of dead vampires, destruction, and beyond it all, endless desolation. But this time my face hurt, bad. The stinging returned in a fury as my breathing slowed, my heartbeat stabilized, and I became aware once again of the realities surrounding me. I touched the left side of my face, delicately, and didn't quite recoil despite the bite from the touch. The bleeding had slowed but I needed to get back to Camp Expectation and have the wound tended to ASAP.

But first I had to get my bike.

I walked over and stared at my fallen ride. Finally feeling a modicum of security I sheathed my weapons then stood my bike up and looked it over. The windscreen was cracked and broken, the fairing was terribly scratched, and the sissy bar was bent backwards, but other than that and a fair amount of dust and dirt covering where it had fallen and rested, the bike seemed fine. I mounted the motorcycle, turned the key to unlock the starter, and it fired-up on the first kick. The sound of the engine as it roared to life was simultaneously relieving and soothing.

I twisted the accelerator and kicked dirt and debris as I spun the back end of the bike around to face away from the crater and back down the road from which I originally came. The filtered sun was beginning to drop lower in the sky and the grainy haze of the day was getting darker as nighttime drew near. As long as I started now I would be back to Camp Expectation well before sunset, and well before even more dangerous desert dwellers *crawled or flew out from the darkness. I released the brake and smoked the back tire as I stared down the long, straight road ahead. The engine roared then screamed as I sped back towards the direction of some sort of salvation, ahead of the approaching night.*

JUDGE

I didn't sign up for this shit.

Of course, if I had never signed up, I'd probably be dead. Just like the rest of my family.

I still clearly remember getting the call that fateful afternoon decades ago. I knew from watching the news that there was a shitshow going on. And I was getting sent right into the heart of it. I remember telling my beloved Beth not to worry, that everything was going to be fine. If I could survive being sent to Iraq and Afghanistan, going to Times Square New York was going to be a fucking vacation. I remember hugging my daughters tight and telling them to be good and that I'd be home soon. Their smiling faces in the living room window as I pulled away in my 4x4 are burned into my mind.

It was the last time I saw any of them alive.

When I was finally able to return after the horror of Times Square, I came home to…I can't describe the scene I came home to. My wife and daughters…what was left of them anyway…forever gone to the war on humans. Forever lost to the Vampocalypse.

After realizing there was no one left for me at home, I knew I wanted to get us as far away from the scene as possible. We, that is, Zarina and me, packed what we could into my wife's Range Rover – including a cache of weapons I had stowed in the MRAP I commandeered as we fled Times Square – and headed towards Portland, Oregon. I didn't know anyone in Portland. I think I just wanted to get far, far away from New York and the gruesome memories, and the West Coast seemed like a viable destination for lack of nowhere else to go.

As we headed out with an uncertainty of what the fuel situation was going to be, the Range Rover proved to be the more economical and wiser choice over the MRAP as operational gas stations were not as plentiful as I would have liked. Occasional use of the two spare gas jugs I kept filled with us got us where I wanted with just one close call of nearly running completely out of fuel. The drive across the country was long, taking more than a week. The days and nights were filled with uncertainty but were ultimately, thankfully, uneventful. I avoided the major cities, which added to the drive, but after experiencing the terror firsthand in New York, I didn't want to take the chance of coming across a situation like that again. Each small town we came upon and drove through was completely desecrated – it was obvious that battles for survival were waged in every area, each with its own tale of travesty and destruction, and each ending with the transformation of most of the humans into vampires and the remaining humans scattering in fear.

I only drove during the safety of sunlight, while at night we would find refuge in empty or deserted buildings as they often seemed safer than sleeping in the Range Rover where it felt like we were more exposed and could easily be snuck upon. We kept watch over each other in short shifts as the other would sleep. It wasn't easy putting my trust in a four-year old but seeing how she handled herself in New York after witnessing the brutal murder of her family garnered a level of respect I didn't have even for some of my fallen fellow Marines.

During the journey I first taught Zarina how to use a handgun then several types of guns and rifles that were taken from the MRAP. I was surprised at how easily she picked up on the weaponry, even at four-years-old. Granted, I had to help her when it came to shooting some of the larger weapons otherwise the recoil could have done some real harm. But she was a trooper and a soldier in every sense of the word and I was so very proud of her for it.

With both of our families gone, we adopted each other as our new family. At some point, I don't recall exactly when, Zarina started calling herself "Z" and almost always insisted others refer to her by that instead of her full name. I think it was her way of taking ownership of her life from a world that was ruthless and cold and had taken everything from her. Of course, almost everyone had everything taken away from them. We were no different. Now, typically, the only ones who refer to her as Zarina other than me are her enemies before they die. If she provides them the opportunity, that is.

I had also altered my name to better personify who I was in this shell of my former self, and to better identify the man who had grown hardened and callous in this cruel and darkened world. So much that made me who I was – my family, my Marine brothers – had been wiped away, extinguished. As such, "Dave Judge" no longer existed. I was the one who determined the fate of those who would cross or threaten me. I now simply called myself Judge.

I wish I more clearly remembered the days before the bombs fell and the sun went out. The happy moments. Those images are fleeting – just ghosts of what they once were. My most vivid memories of faces long gone were from the days leading up to Times Square. Recollections of routine training and hazing with and among my fire teammates – Torres, Heath, Knowles, Dugan, Kirkpatrick – somehow remain in the forefront of my mind. They were all good people who didn't deserve to die like they did. I wish I could have at least taken their legacy back to their loved ones but I had no hopes of finding survivors once I realized most of humanity had been wiped out.

My team was all dead. I was the only one of them to survive. And even though it had been thirty years, their faces were still the freshest in my memories. I can still see them all, young and full of life. I sometimes wonder what they would look like today, and if any of them would be like me: a fifty-five year-old man with thinning, graying hair who had packed on a few extra pounds, but not too many to bog me down in a fight. Yes, I'm older, but also wiser. Don't get me wrong – I'm still a badass, but I sometimes tread more cautiously. I'm not always so eager to enter the fray when it's not absolutely necessary. I realize more, now, that not every fight needs to be fought. And not every fight is mine.

In this world, it's not a matter of if you become a victim in a fight, but a matter of when. My left arm – or lack thereof – is evidence of that. But what I lost below the elbow became my gain as I now could interchange the prosthetic with a multitude of weaponry: though my preferred weapon of choice was a razor-edged pointed trident. Not only did it look fucking cool, but it more than did the job needed in a fight. In addition, when I do go out for a fight I wear part of a vampire skull face as a mask – a little treasure from an early kill. It looks fucking mean as hell with its oversized jowls and elongated fangs and has done its job of striking fear in many of my opponents.

For thirty years I watched over Zarina, as her protector and adoptive father, shielding her the best I could from the dangers of not only the vampires themselves but secrets they possessed. There were mysteries in this world Zarina did not need to know – such as why our paths were forced to cross in the first place. She had been identified in the early days of the Great Turn for a reason and I was going to do whatever I could to always protect her. This post-apocalyptic wasteland was not one for the weak and I did everything in my power to teach Zarina to be strong, independent, and resilient. And goddammit, I think I did a good job.

It was somewhat of a surprise to me, then, the day she returned to Camp Expectation on her damaged bike with a much too deep vertical slice on the left side of her face. It was a shock to everyone how she was able to drive safely back as she did considering the amount of blood loss she must have suffered. She was immediately taken to the infirmary – a large, old, two-story townhouse that had been expanded and renovated into a medical care facility – where I rushed to meet her after receiving word of her arrival and condition. I came into the room where she was being mended to hear her refusing an anesthetic injection from the chief doctor. She was instead demanding a bottle of tequila.

"Goddamn, you, Zarina!" I was incensed at her stubbornness. "You know the doctor doesn't have tequila on hand."

"Actually..."

I looked at Dr. Cleary, who only shrugged. "She came dangerously close to losing that eye."

"Just stitch me up," Zarina said wearily.

Doc Cleary looked at his assistant who sat on the other side of the gurney where Zarina sat holding a thick compress that covered the entire left half of her face.

"Lisa," the doctor said as he nodded toward a corner of the room, "the good stuff under the cabinet."

Lisa spun around on her padded stool, stood up, and walked to a nearby wooden cabinet. She crouched down and opened the middle set of cabinet doors. Inside were several higher-end bottles of liquor. She selected one particular bottle then walked back and stood in front of Zarina. After removing the cork stopper, she held the bottle out to the one-eyed patient.

Zarina mustered a half-smile and yanked the crystal bottle out of the woman's hand, wasting no time putting it to her mouth and guzzling much of its contents. She let out a half-yelp, half-cry then exhaled sharply as she fought back a cough. We made eye contact and I shook my head and couldn't help but laugh.

"Fuck off, old man," Zarina spat out. To the unknowing, the insult would have sounded genuine but to me, years of banter with one another told me that this was just another in a long line of times she's told me to fuck off. I chuckled and waved it off.

The doctor leaned in close to Zarina and asked, "Are you ready?"

Zarina looked at the man then nodded. The look in the one eye of hers not hidden behind the compress was wide with anxiety and apprehension. She pulled the pad slowly away from her wound, revealing a still fresh-looking cut surrounded by a fair amount of dried and crusted blood. Zarina sucked on her lower lip then bit it hard – almost hard enough to break the skin.

"This is gonna hurt." The doctor was blunt, providing the statement as a certainty.

"Yeah, yeah," Zarina replied as she took another swig from the bottle. "Just get it over with."

I've seen a lot of horrors in combat. Some of those horrors involved people torturing people, others involved vampires tearing and dismembering humans right in front of me – some of those men I loved as brothers. But for some reason I couldn't watch as the doctor cleaned and stitched the side of Zarina's face back together. It took several drinks of tequila but Zarina endured the pain – every poke, every suture, every pull of the string.

I left the hospital before the procedure was complete and paid a visit to the town garage to check on Zarina's prized purple motorcycle. She'd be happy to know the bike was gonna be fine.

It wasn't long before I received a call on my walkie talkie from Doc Cleary. Zarina was all ready to go. I didn't even have to meet her inside as she was standing on the covered front patio when I arrived back at the townhouse hospital. She was decidedly drunk and had unsurprisingly refused to remain inside for any recovery. The black vertical stitching running down the left side of her face made me sad — it was going to leave one hell of a scar. I felt bad that I wasn't there to protect her when it happened.

"Don't give me that look," Zarina said disapprovingly as she shook a finger at me. She was holding herself up against one of the vertical posts supporting the patio overhang. The porch was awash in a gauzy shadow as the sun had started to touch the distant horizon.

"What look?"

"The 'I wish I could have protected you' look."

I closed my eyes and shook my head as I said "Fuck off, Zarina." She knew that was as good as an "I love you" on any day.

"You shouldn't be out here," I went on as I walked up the three steps to the porch. "Let's get you back inside and laying down to recover."

I went to put a supportive arm around her but she pushed it away.

"No. I want to get to my own bed."

"Fine," I said as I allowed her some space. "But I'm going to make sure you get there alright — or should I say 'stumble there' alright."

"Ha, ha, Judge."

Zarina had grown to become one of the strongest women I'd ever known. In all my years with her I had never seen her cry. I faintly recall her eyes welling when her family was killed but ever since then she has been like stone, even now when the doctor was stitching her up without a true anesthetic. The tequila did seem to help, though. Despite seeming to nearly fall over while standing on the porch, once she got away from the hospital, her steps were strong and surefooted, and she walked straight with no issues. It would be just a few short blocks to her apartment. During our walk I insisted she tell me about how she earned her wound.

I couldn't help but laugh.

"Children, huh? Just kids? You mean, like, crayon-coloring, just learning to read, standing no more than hip-high kids?"

Zarina stopped in the middle of the dirt street and looked at me. The finger she wagged at me from the porch was back, this time poking into my chest.

"Not 'just kids,' Judge." Her tone was low and serious.

I held my hands up defensively as if I was under arrest. "Easy, Zarina. I'm just giving you shit. Relax."

Her finger slowly dropped but the stern look in her face didn't relax as I got her to her apartment and her bedroom. Maybe it was the stitches. Or maybe she was thoroughly pissed. Or maybe she was just drunk. Probably all three. As I looked at her, my longtime adoptive daughter, with the fresh scar on her face, I promised myself to do whatever I could to prevent anything like that from ever happening to her again.

Since then, Zarina would still go out on her own beyond the walls at times but she agreed to do it less often and less late in the day. I had been sorry I wasn't there to protect her when the wound occurred, and in the four years since she received her horrible scar, no other encounter or altercation left any sort of mark on either her or me, leaving us healthy to do our duties as required of Camp Expectation.

Camp Expectation. When we first arrived after countless days of a nomadic lifestyle, the town was nothing more than a tiny out-of-the-way sanctuary for humans seeking safety in the wastes. But as it grew, a feeling of solidarity and strength it didn't possess before came to be under the leadership of its governor, a woman named Kylee Haddock. Still, the feeling living here under constant threat of discovery and death was far from the days of the Old World, before the days of the ever-constant sepia-toned skies that were the product of the periodic nuclear detonations feeding the neverending nuclear winter designed to block out direct sunlight forever.

The community was nestled among the hills that surrounded an area known in the Old World as Prineville in the State of Oregon, though the population of Camp Expectation was only about a quarter of what Prineville's was before the Vampocalypse. "States," let alone the United States of America as a whole, no longer existed. Rather, the entirety of North America was a single body governed under vampire rule. Known as the North America New World Territories, the continent was divided into six primary regions: the Northwest Outskirts, Dakota Reaches, Pacific Wastelands, Central Barrens, Atlantic Badlands, and the South Gulf Coastlands. As much of the land was desolate, barren, and unusable following the war, most of the vampire population resided in what were known as "meccas," immense modern metropolitan areas full of vampires living their daily lives in the New World, in many ways like humans lived their lives in the days of old. There were economies, jobs, and recreation. There were "good" vampires and "bad" vampires just as there were good humans and bad humans. At the end of the day, though, few vampires had any care or love for humans as their brains and consciousnesses were forever corrupted by the virus that changed them. If there were vampires who were friendly towards humans, I've never met one, though I'd like to believe they do exist.

At Camp Expectation everyone had their own place. Zarina's was master-at-arms. Mine was commander of the security forces. The nature of our positions often seemed interchangeable and sometimes would require the governor to call upon us for special missions. We enjoyed these missions the most as it broke up the monotony that was the norm of many days. When called, we would meet the governor in her private office, located off the main council chamber of the town hall. This circumstance was no different.

Governor Haddock was around my age and had short gray-blonde hair. Each wrinkle around her eyes and her sunken cheeks had a hardened story to tell – a warrior's story to go with the warrior's life that she had lived. She wasted no time jumping right into the matters at hand.

"There's word of a community about one hundred and fifty miles northeast from here. A smaller place, estimated about a thousand residents, but we don't know its true nature." The governor's voice was always calm and smooth and could lull the most brutish to sleep if saying the right words.

Zarina's eyes widened a bit. The scar over her left eye did nothing to hinder her expressions. "How are we just now finding this? A hundred and fifty miles is pretty close for us never to have known about this place."

I looked at Zarina. "It's like using a telescope to monitor the entire night sky. We can only find things if we're looking practically right at them. Despite the expeditions we send out, there's still a lot of uncharted territory."

The governor nodded. "I want you two to check it out and see what's going on there."

I looked back at the governor. "Does the place have a name?"

"It's called Escape Town. Initial reports are that it's a neutral human encampment but we need to make sure. Report your findings directly to me. I expect to hear something within the week."

"We'll check this place out right away, Governor Haddock," I said.

Zarina's brow furrowed. "We'll get the answers you seek. And if there are vampires involved, we'll see to their extermination. This I promise you."

EPISODE 1

ESCAPE TOWN
PACIFIC WASTELANDS

THE area started as a simple farmhouse on a large plot of land in the middle of central Oregon. Over the years, Escape Town grew into something reminiscent of an old country town, self-sustaining and thus far eluding discovery by the undead creatures that would seek to destroy its residents or use them for food. They had few automobiles and no electricity, but they had access to fresh water and the land provided for their animals and produce to allow them to thrive.

While Escape Town started small with just a few families, it had grown over time to house nearly a thousand residents. As the populace grew, walls were built and continuously jockeyed outward to accommodate the growth. For nearly thirty years – the number of years that had passed since the Vampocalypse – Escape Town thrived within its twenty-foot tall perimeter wall. The wall was comprised of wooden braces with plywood and steel panels and had a single wooden gate made of thick logs as tall as the wall itself. The gate was operated by a mechanical pulley system and provided the only way in or out. Several guard towers were positioned unevenly along the wall perimeter to provide around-the-clock security watch. Each tower was accessed by a ladder that came up from underneath and opened onto a small platform just large enough to accommodate a single guard. The guard had a full view over the top of the wall and had full use of the automated *atlatl,* or spear launcher, mounted to the tower.

Within the reinforced steel and wood walls, life continued almost as if the threat of vampires and death didn't exist. There was a school that accommodated all ages. Every person in the community had their own role – whether that was to farm food, make clothing, construct homes and other structures, work as security within and on the wall, or any number of other jobs or tasks that it took to ensure a thriving, fully functioning society. There was recreation for both adults and children, with the most popular sport being small-sided soccer or any variation where a ball was kicked around.

It was a "sunny" summer afternoon, or as sunny as the polluted skies would allow. Though many of the distinct seasons around the globe had become an amalgamation of weather that remained mostly stagnant year-round, people still kept track of the time of year based on old-style calendars. Days in the "fall and winter" were still shorter than those during "spring and summer." Other than that, though, most days were nearly the same with overcast skies shining a constant mustard-colored hue upon the Earth.

Kasper Nilsen sat forward in his chair at the table of the town council meeting. The monthly gathering was held in the conference room of the town library. Two eight-foot long rectangular tables were set next to each other to accommodate the thirteen board members. Twelve sets of eyes stared hard at him, as they did every meeting when it was his turn to raise topics of discussion. His topics were always the same and they always elicited the same reactions.

"If we don't do something this town is going to be dead soon," Kasper said. His impassioned expression and fervent tone underlined his arguments. But they always seemed to fall on deaf ears.

"Please stop with your fearmongering and doom-and-gloom rhetoric, Kasper." It was Caren – "with a 'C'," as she liked to always remind everyone – Banks who exhaled the initial retort. The thirty-three-year-old mother of four had been a member of the board for just seven months and demonstrated from day one that she was not shy about speaking whatever was on her mind. She pointed a hard finger at Kasper as she spoke.

Kasper blinked several times as he stared blankly at Caren, pondering on his response. He looked away without saying anything and scratched his chin through the scruffy, gray beard that made him look older than the late forties father of two he actually was.

"Come now, Caren, Kasper here is just doing what he's been appointed to do," said Jim Elliott from his place at head of the table as he leaned forward on one elbow. His voice was thin and airy yet still managed to exude the charm of a used car salesperson.

Jim Elliott was the original owner of Escape Town back when it was just a modest farm. It was through his efforts and direction over several years that the town grew to become a cozy yet thriving community. Escape Town had only ever had one mayor and that was the self-appointed and never-challenged Jim Elliott.

Jim was in his mid-seventies, pale, and near-skeletal in appearance, with thin white hair that touched his shoulders. For the last several years, if not perhaps decades, he wore nearly identical black suits every day along with a wide-brimmed flat-topped hat. Kasper felt Jim's "undertaker attire" was fitting for the state of the town. Jim looked at Kasper and smiled what had become his trademark toothy smile. It wasn't a smile of agreement nor acceptance but, from Kasper's experience, it was one born more from condescendence.

"I have to say, though, Kasper, that every meeting as of late you bring up the same points." Jim's face turned exasperated. "Haven't you realized yet that the board as a whole isn't interested in your concerns?"

Kasper turned his attention to the mayor and said, "Like you said, I'm only doing what I've been appointed to do," before refocusing on Caren. "I was appointed as the town's chief structural security engineer and in that role I'm responsible for the maintenance and functionality of the wall and any structures connected to it."

He stared coldly from board member to board member as he continued to speak.

"I know none of you want to hear the truth but I'm going to give it to you. Our security wall is in disrepair. Much of the wooden framework and panels are rotting out and need to be replaced –"

"Resources have been scarce as of late," Jim interjected. "You know this, Kasper."

Kasper took a pause and let out a quick breath. "What about the lack of weapons maintenance? I've done checks of the tower atlatls and," Kasper looked down as he rummaged through a short stack of papers on the table in front of him. He licked his thumb and a finger then quickly leafed through several loose pages.

"Here," he said as he pulled out a page and set it down on the table. He turned the paper around to face Jim, who sat three seats away from him, and slid it in the mayor's direction. "Over half have failing timing chains. Seventeen have bad rotors and need full bearing replacements. Thirteen need targeting calibrations. Do you know how many are considered to be one hundred percent functional?"

Kasper's eyes scanned the table and was met with empty stares.

"Three," he answered without waiting for a response. He knew he'd be waiting a while if he relied on anyone on the council to hazard a guess. He poked a finger hard against the paperwork. "Out of fifty."

He let the words hang in the air to punctuate his point. No one immediately responded. Several of the councilmembers used the opportunity to break their stares from him and look away – some seemed embarrassed, others looked indifferent.

"Let me say this again." Kasper leaned forward on the table and bore his glare into the hollow eyes of the mayor. "With only three functioning atlatls our primary defense against vampire attacks is practically nonexistent and we have no plan or timeline in place for repairing the rest. Hell, we don't have a plan to repair even *one*."

Mini conversations erupted around the table. Many were concerned about Kasper's "tone" and "true intentions" behind releasing such dire news. A few voices, too few, seemed actually concerned about the state of the weapons, which made Kasper happy but provided no relief. Others had no concerns at all, much to Kasper's chagrin. Voices were loud, overtalked each other (especially those few on Kasper's side), and failed to display any sense of decorum.

"He's just trying to scare us. There's nothing really wrong with the wall defenses..."

"He's only doing this to better position himself in the eyes of the townspeople..."

"He's always wanted to be the mayor..."

The room quickly silenced as Jim smacked his gavel onto a small pad sitting on the table. He stood from his chair, straightened his black suit, and adjusted his hat. The mayor spread his arms out before him.

"Ten years, Kasper. *Ten years!*" Jim exclaimed. "Do you know what that represents?"

Kasper knew but refused to respond.

"That's how long it's been since we've been attacked by vampires here. Should I say that again, son? *Ten years.*"

"I know that, Jim. But that tells me that we should be more vigilant than ever. It's not a matter of *when* we'll get attacked again, it's a question of *how soon.*"

"Well it tells me something completely different." Jim's words were hard and decidedly pronounced. "It tells me that the vampires have decided to leave us alone and in peace under terms of the truce I forged."

Kasper shook his head and ran a hand over the thin hair on top of his head.

"I can't believe you're still holding onto that. Do you really believe the vampires are going to honor that? It's a fragile truce at best."

Quiet chuckles and whispers circled the table.

"Did I mention it's been *ten years* since the last attack on our community?" Jim's voice was low and more patronizing than ever as he again repeated his facts and shot Kasper that condescending smile once more. Kasper's shoulders dropped and he cocked his head and sighed as he looked back at the mayor.

"Just making sure." With that, Jim sat back into his chair and folded his fingers across his chest.

Kasper scooped his papers up off the table.

"Leave those," said Jim. "I promise you I'll review your assessments and take them all under advisement."

Kasper scanned the faces of the other board members before settling on Caren.

"It's not 'doom and gloom,' Caren. This is a serious issue. But I'll tell you what. I hope I'm wrong and just crying for no reason. I truly hope an attack never comes and that you're able to look down on me from your pedestal knowing that you're right, that you've always been right. But if *I* end up being right, and nothing can be done about it, then I want to be there to see your face when you realize it."

Kasper looked again around the table and pointed at each councilmember.

"I hope each of you can laugh at me for as long as you live. If the price I pay for being wrong is each of you looking down on me, then so be it. I'll take that all day long over being right and the horrors that would come along with that."

Kasper stood from the table and looked at the mayor.

"Take a look at those assessments. Fix the problems or not. I'm tired of wasting my breath on trying."

Kasper turned and headed toward the conference room door.

"Kasper, I –" started Jim but was cut off as Kasper waved a dismissive hand.

"Let him go, Jim," said Caren, mockingly. "Let him keep walking right out the door and right off the council. He should be replaced. There's no place for people like him here."

Kasper stopped as he got to the door and turned and looked back at Caren. He started to say something and clenched a fist almost as hard as he clenched his jaw, biting words. After one final cursory glance at the council he left the conference room.

KASPER made the 15-minute walk from the library to the nearby community soccer pitch, which was about a quarter of the size of a full-sized field, where his wife Helena was taking her players through warm-up drills as they prepared for the upcoming match set to begin within the half-hour. The 5-person team was coed and comprised of 7 to 9-year-olds and was part of a tiny rec league within Escape Town. It was Helena's idea to formulate the soccer league for the children of the community. She managed the league and also coached two of its four teams.

The day was muggy, like most, but the players were used to it as none of them were alive during the days before the Vampocalypse. Those born into the New World were accustomed to the weather, thick air, and constant overcast skies. Kasper sidled up to Helena as she studied her team tapping soccer balls around cones and shooting into makeshift "goals" comprised of rectangular wooden framework about six feet wide and four feet high.

"You made it," Helena said as Kasper gave her a quick 'hello' kiss on the cheek.

"I had to get outta there," Kasper said. "Too many talking heads have zero concerns over the safety of our town. They think I'm blowing things out of proportion, as usual."

Helena smirked. "Let me guess. Caren 'with a C' had to throw in her two cents?"

Kasper stammered for a moment. "More like her two dollars!"

"You know she does that to get under your skin. You can't let her get to you like that."

Kasper rubbed his forehead and sighed. "I know, I know. I just get so frustrated with all of them. Jim, especially, since he's the one who holds the keys to getting anything done around here. He's too content with how things have been. He believes the vampires are going to leave us alone indefinitely. Just because we haven't been attacked in ten years doesn't mean it's not going to happen again."

"That guy's always been an idiot. If it weren't so dangerous trying to find someplace else to stay we would've been out of here a long time ago."

"At the rate it's going it's not going to make much difference between being here or out navigating the Wastelands. We've all seen how Jim's slowly decreased our security over the last five years. There's hardly anyone left who knows how to even use an atlatl turret. Though I suppose with only three of them working we only need three people who need to know."

Having seen enough of the foot drill, Helena gave her whistle a short tweet then called the team off the pitch for a water break. She handed plastic water bottles to two players while the rest grabbed their own off the ground. Loud chatter from the players overtook Kasper and Helena's conversation. Kasper quickly surveyed the area and the parents lined up on the sidelines preparing to watch the game.

"Where's Haley?" Kasper asked as he took another look around.

"When I reached her on our walkie she said she was deeply involved with studying blood cells from the dead vampire body they've got on ice at the lab."

"Sounds interesting," Kasper commented.

"Sounds gross." Helena wrinkled her nose then turned her attention to her team. "If you have to use the bathroom, now's the time."

The entire team ran off, many of them laughing, to the restroom building next to where the parents were sitting, leaving Kasper and Helena alone. The sounds of the opposing team warming up could be heard from the opposite side of the pitch. Helena pulled her long, brown hair back and tied it into a ponytail. She threw on a nondescript blue-gray baseball cap from her coach's bag, pulling her ponytail through the opening in the back, and started picking up the cones from the foot drill. Kasper joined her.

"I don't understand why they just don't let you do what you were selected to do."

Kasper shook his head. "You know how Jim and the others are."

Helena rolled her eyes. "You're the one who should be in charge. Jim says he allows the Escape Town council to run things but he actually makes all the decisions."

Kasper grunted. "I'm surprised anything gets done at all."

All the cones were picked up and Kasper handed his stack to Helena who put them all into a large mesh bag.

"You're right about it only being a matter of time until the next attack," Helena said. "Maybe we'll be lucky and be long gone before it actually happens."

Kasper's face grew stoic. "I'm not counting on that. And I don't like relying on luck."

"Me, neither, but at this point luck is all we have."

The other team was called over by their coach as Helena's team began to filter back. Kasper surveyed the area again.

"Shouldn't Annika be here by now?"

"Running late from her archery lesson."

"Typical," said Kasper, shaking his head in jest. "That girl's never on time for anything."

"A sixteen-year-old's going to do what they're going to do. She'll be here."

THE engine screamed as the RPMs on the dirt bike were pushed to their limit. Dropping sideways, the bike came precariously close to being parallel with the ground as it slid towards the inside of the steel wall. A staccato of rocks and pebbles spat against the steel, pinging like machine gun fire as it cut through the high-pitched whine of the bike's engine. Righting itself just before smacking into the panel, the motorcycle sped away from the tall steel barrier, the final maneuver in the bike's out of the way detour across an undeveloped portion of Escape Town's grounds. The bike wobbled a little as it transitioned from the choppy dirt lot and onto the hard ground of one of the small town's roads.

Annika shook her head to get her loosely flowing, long, dirty-blonde hair out of her face. She smiled as she smelled the odor of the gasoline burning through the engine. Increasing her speed, she rode across a small courtyard with brick walkways that channeled through oases of short grasses before cutting through a small alleyway between two buildings. She turned her head away as she sped past the recreational soccer fields, noting a game with elementary aged children was in progress and hoping no one noticed her despite her bike's engine broadcasting her presence. After crossing a spacious commons area, she pulled into a small lot outside a large brick building. The four-story tall structure was oversized by the town's standards and housed the town's infirmary, laboratories, and places of higher learning. She threw a leg over the bike as she dismounted the parked vehicle then tossed her hair before heading inside.

AT just 20-years-old, Haley Nilsen, Kasper and Helena's oldest daughter, was Escape Town's leading cell biology and genetics scientist (though to be fair, she was Escape Town's *only* cell biology and genetics scientist). In all its years, Escape Town never had a scientist who had taken as much interest in the field as Haley. Having been born in the post-Vampocalyptic New World, Haley never knew what life was like before the particle bombs were deployed and the virus was unleashed. But she knew that the world she grew up in wasn't like how things should be and refused to accept when people referred to it as "the new normal." She was convinced there had to be a way to change things back to the way they were – after all, the world was changed in just a matter of hours by something created by human scientists; it only made sense to Haley that it was going to be human scientists that were going to change the world back.

With such ardent beliefs taking hold at a very young age, Haley took every opportunity to read whatever scientific journals she could get her hands on in the Escape Town library (many of the books of which had been collected over the years by adventurers who journeyed beyond the perimeter wall in the interest of gathering materials, goods, and items that could be taken back to help life feel more "normal"). And while the books provided good baseline understanding, it was the subsequent hands-on study that allowed Haley to increase her knowledge at an almost exponential rate.

So when one of the outer excursions produced a dead vampire body a few days ago, Haley was giddy at the prospect of being able to dissect and study the corpse in the controlled environment of the sterilized laboratory she established in the back rooms of the town infirmary. The group had happened across the vampire wandering alone and while it was more feral, it seemed weak from hunger and was thankfully easily overcome. Haley was happy to see the body had very little damage to it save for the gash in the side of its head – clearly from the axe blow that brought the vampire down.

Haley stared intently into the microscope on the desk in front of her. The images weren't as clear as she needed, so she rotated the revolving nosepiece to line up the objective lens with the most power then relocated one of the small tabletop oil lamps closer to provide better lighting. The blood sample on the slide showed a mosaic of cell patterns the likes of which she had never encountered prior to her studies on the vampire body. There was something vaguely human about them while at the same time something animalistic and almost bacteria-like. She picked up a pen and jotted several notes into her notebook on the table. Within reach on the desk were two dozen eyedroppers resting upright in a stand with their points downward, each with a different blood type inside. Some were human, others primate; there were even some that ranged from reptile to rodent to feline, along with a score of others.

Haley took a dropper from the middle of the stand – it was marked as number "17" and labeled as containing human blood type O-positive, the most common human blood type – and expelled a single drop onto the vampire blood on the slide. Then she waited.

At first the human and vampire cells seemed to repel each other like oil and water. But then almost immediately the vampire blood surrounded the human cells, squeezing them, breaking them down, then effectively consuming them until they no longer existed. The entire sample on the slide looked as if there was never any human blood on it in the first place. She took her pen and wrote down some more notes before throwing the pen across the room in frustration.

She slumped back in her chair and rubbed her eyes. She had been at this for nearly five hours straight, viewing various cell samples from different tissues extracted from the vampire body. This was in addition to performing similar experiments, each time changing conditions of the test slightly, and studying nearly ten hours a day each of the last three days. Every result was the same, meaning she was getting nowhere fast. But she wasn't going to give up.

She let out a loud sigh and looked around the small room that was part private office and part laboratory. She had one assistant but they had left for the day, leaving her alone to her studies and experiments. The shrill sound of a dirt bike motorcycle engine pulling up outside and not far from her second-story laboratory window caught her attention. Glancing at the analog clock on the wall she realized she was running late to get to her mom's soccer match. While she knew her studies were important, she also knew that overworking while overtired was a sure way to make mistakes and get nowhere even faster.

There's time for just one more experiment…

"I knew you'd still be here."

Haley turned and faced the source of the voice with a look of annoyance. The tone of her voice did nothing to disguise her irritation.

"What're you doing here? Shouldn't you be at mom's soccer match?" Haley looked her sister up and down.

Annika stood at the entrance to the lab, leaning sideways against the doorframe.

"I had something I needed to do after my archery lesson," replied Annika. She turned her head purposefully to the side in an obvious gesture.

Haley narrowed her eyes as she focused on her younger sister.

"That's new," said Haley.

"Oh, this?" Annika asked. She smiled as she touched her nose next to the golden ring protruding from her left nostril.

"Is that the 'something' you needed to do?" asked Haley.

"Maybe," Annika answered, coyly.

"Mom's not gonna think that's more important than her games and your lessons."

Annika twisted her lip as she walked over to a chair in the corner of the room and collapsed into it. "It's all getting boring."

"I thought you liked archery."

"I do but I'm just getting tired of it. It's the same routine every day. At this point I don't feel like practice is making me any better. My archery coach says he believes I'm shooting at Olympic-class levels, whatever that's worth since the Olympics no longer exist. I mean, where do you go from there?"

Haley rolled her eyes. "Must be tough being the best at everything you do."

"It is," Annika responded, coming across only half-joking.

Haley turned back to her table and her experiments. "Well I'm busy right now. I'm trying to get these last few samples processed before we run out of daylight completely."

Annika slid down in her chair. She thoughtlessly picked at one of the fingernails on her right hand.

"You ever wonder what it was like?" Annika asked without looking up. "I mean, like, really wonder almost to where you feel like you're going to burst from wanting life to be like it was back then?"

Haley stopped what she was doing and stared at Annika. "It's strange, but yeah, I know what you mean."

Annika's expression dropped. "Even though we weren't around…I wish the world was bright with blue skies and clean oceans and that vampires were truly just a myth."

Haley placed the dropper she was holding back into its vertical stand. She walked over and stood in front of her sister.

"For what it's worth, it's not exactly like they said it would be. In my reading and research from the days before the Great Turn, they made it sound like life in a nuclear winter would be impossible. But trees and vegetation are still able to grow in many areas and radiation hot spots are few and far between, thankfully."

Annika looked up at her older sister. Haley had always seemed generations wiser than her despite just a four-year difference in their ages.

"I just wish we could see and feel direct sun," said Annika. "I hope I get to experience that some day before I die."

Haley crossed her arms. "Don't sound so hopeless. If a cure can be found then we can put a stop to the nuclear winter and you'll get that sun." She smiled and softened her tone. "At least we don't know how warm the sun used to feel so we don't know what we're really missing, right?"

Annika scowled as she didn't find that very reassuring.

A loud *BOOM!* followed by screams and commotion suddenly sounded from outside. The high-pitched wail of a siren rose in the air.

"What the hell is that?" Annika asked as she bolted upright in her chair.

"I think that's the vampire attack alarm," replied Haley. "It's been so long since I've heard it I almost forgot what it sounded like."

Annika's eyes grew wide. "Are we under attack?"

"I don't know. Maybe it's a drill?"

The sisters rushed to the large laboratory window and looked out across the adjacent lot where Annika's dirt bike was parked. A column of smoke was rising just beyond two rows of single-story buildings. They immediately realized that it was from the direction of Escape Town's entrance gate. People flooded the courtyard, running in all directions. Loud bangs could be heard from indistinct sources in the distance. But the sounds that were the most terrifying were the shrieks that filled the air like unfettered wailing banshees, while the sounds that were the most worrisome were the screams from those in fear – or worse.

"Mom and dad!" Annika exclaimed.

Barely a moment later Annika was trailing Haley out the front door of the building as they rushed through the commotion and towards the nearby soccer field in hopes of finding their parents safe amid whatever terror disrupted the town.

EPISODE 2

ESCAPE TOWN
PACIFIC WASTELANDS

KASPER and Helena shot each other a confused look when they heard the boom from the direction of the gate.

"What was that?" Helena asked, the edges of her words crisp with concern.

"I'm not sure. It didn't sound good, though."

"Kasper. Look!"

Kasper's eyes followed where Helena was pointing. Her finger was aimed at the sky, over the tops of the nearby buildings, towards the west and the glow of the sun behind the particle haze filtering the late afternoon. The ever-present gray mist of the unending manufactured nuclear winter wasn't the only thing obscuring the strained sunlight.

"Oh my fucking…" Helena's words trailed off.

"I'm going to go check on the gate." Kasper sounded frantic. "Get hold of the girls and get home."

Helena grabbed the two-way radio hanging from her hip as Kasper ran off.

"Holy shit, Kasper, be careful!" she shouted. She looked up at the swelling shadow of vampires in the sky over the town, and tried not to panic as she called out over the radio. "Haley? Are you there? Haley?"

"MOM!" Haley called back through her radio as she ran.

"Is Annika with you?" Helena's voice crackled through.

"She's right here," Haley answered before she lowered her walkie and looked ahead.

They were running across an expansive concrete commons area that marked the center of town. Just on the other side were the recreation areas, starting with a playground and half-sized basketball court. Beyond that were larger playfields, including the soccer pitch. Helena had already seen her daughters and was running towards them. The mother and her girls ran to each other, avoiding the panicked townspeople crisscrossing through the plaza. They embraced and Helena held her girls tighter than she ever had before.

"Where's Dad?" Annika asked as she pulled away from the hug.

"He went to the gate."

"Oh my god," exclaimed Haley. "What good is he going to do there?"

"It's his job, Haley. He'll do whatever he needs to do." Helena's words were certain even if her tone wasn't convincing. Her eyes shot back and forth between her daughters. "We need to get out of here."

The sounds from the terrified town residents suddenly noticeably shifted and Helena's gaze drifted upwards. When she first saw the vampires in the skies above the town moments earlier, there looked to be a couple hundred of the creatures flying in a spiral high overhead. Now, though, the monsters were swooping from the sky and plucking townspeople as they ran. Talons as long as fingers and as sharp as knives dug into the chests, shoulders, and midsections of the fleeing with strength and a ferocity that made it impossible for anyone to break free. Within moments dozens of people were being carried high into the sky, away from Escape Town and to destinations and horrors unknown. Helena realized the town would be devastated in a matter of minutes. None of them would stand a chance.

"We need to get under cover," said Helena as she put an arm around each of her daughters. The three of them crouched and ran as fast as they could out of the courtyard and towards a nearby row of buildings.

KASPER had a visual on the gate about two hundred feet ahead – and the situation was worse than he feared. The heavy, thick logs that made up the gate had been blown away from their hinges, and the mechanical pulleys laid in broken, burning pieces. He ran to the nearest section of wall and scrambled up the ladder to the platform of the guard tower. Upon reaching the top, Kasper took hold of the 360-degree automated spear launcher. He pivoted the large weapon on its swivel mount and aimed it down and in the direction of the vampires rushing in through the open gate. He couldn't fathom how many of the creatures were flooding the town on foot. Sounds from vampires above suddenly caught his attention. Whether by air or by foot, all of the creatures were dressed alike in near formfitting, black, special ops-style uniforms. It was obvious this was a coordinated attack by the governing vampire colony. But why they felt the need to send so many was beyond Kasper's understanding. A hundred could have easily decimated the town – the numbers being witnessed would result in complete annihilation.

Kasper turned his attention back to the ground. With so many targets to choose from, aiming the fully-automated atlatl wasn't going to be an issue. The weapon was made up of a large open-topped launch chute with a spring-loaded speed-feeder that filled from a trough full of deadly spears. It took two hands to operate the mechanism via the dual-joystick controller mounted at the rear of the weapon. Squeezing the left controller launched one long, pointed, wooden spear at a time whereas squeezing both controllers simultaneously activated the automated speed-feeder. Kasper squeezed both controllers.

The weapon went to work and deadly meter-long wooden spears pumped out of the launcher at a rate of four per second. The feeder trough was mounted high above Kasper and connected adjacent to the launcher. It used a gravity feed and spring system to load the spears as fast as the weapon could expel them. A shot to the head or heart with a wooden spear easily eliminated any of the creatures. Many of the spears met a mark resulting in the truncated screech of a vampire as the spear struck true. Vampire chests and heads burst all around Kasper from the deadly projectiles he rained down upon them.

Through the shrieks and cries and mayhem of it all, Kasper noticed a single, unmoving figure standing in the fiery opening of the demolished gateway. He guessed it was the attacking colony's leader but there was something different about this vampire. Unlike the others, this one was like a statue, silent and motionless save for a billowing dark cloak and cowl. Kasper turned the spear launcher towards the figure and fired.

The atlatl shot just two spears before it clanked and sputtered to a stop with a loud squeal. The mysterious cloaked vampire effortlessly knocked both spears away with its left hand and turned its head in Kasper's direction. Kasper had never known of a vampire with such speed and precision timing to block an attack so casually. He cursed to himself as he smacked his hand against the side of the broken launch chute. Then he realized that the screech of the failed automated launcher got the attention of two vampires running underneath his atlatl tower. The creatures were already scrambling up the ladder to his platform. He used a foot to slam shut the access panel at the top of the ladder. That would do little to slow the vampires down.

"Fuck."

Kasper looked at the spear gravity feeder and began kicking the mounts that attached it to the platform with the bottom of his foot. After four swift, hard kicks the brace gave way. The open-topped feeder tipped toward him and wooden spears spilled out. He grabbed two, turned, and slammed the tip of one clean through the face of a vampire as it leapt over one of the wooden guardrails and onto the platform right next to him. The floor panel slammed open and the second vampire clambered up and onto the tiny platform. Kasper pulled the bloodied spear from the dead vampire and caught the second creature with both wooden weapons through its chin and out the top of its head.

Kasper pushed the freshly killed vampire to the side then grabbed two unused spears from those that had spilt out of the feeder. He dropped them through the open floor hatch to the ground below then stepped onto the ladder. After going down a couple of rungs, he swung his feet to the outsides of the side rails then, loosely holding the rails with his hands, allowed himself to slide quickly down the ladder rather than scrambling down one rung at a time. He exerted just enough friction with his grip and feet to keep from slamming against the ground. He grabbed the two spears off the ground and ran towards his home – where he hoped Helena and his girls would be waiting.

Sheer panic ruled the town as people ran with seemingly no destination in mind other than to get away from vampires anywhere they could. As Kasper ran into the town square he was surrounded by the deathly screams of those either being slaughtered or plucked from the ground and carried away to who-knows-what fate. Somehow unsurprisingly, there was one person in the square who was not running. The man stood on top of a wooden crate with his hands cupped around his mouth like a megaphone. Even among the chaos and pandemonium, Jim Elliott's delusions took hold of him.

"There is nothing to fear!" Jim shouted out, straining to be heard over the cries and screams. "Just do as they say and they won't hurt you!"

Kasper ran up to the mayor and pointed an angry finger at his face.

"You son-of-a-bitch!" Kasper shouted. "This is all your fault! You goddamn motherfucker!"

The old man ignored Kasper's tirade like he was some insignificant heckler. Kasper squeezed his fists with unfocused anger. The fool wouldn't listen to him at the town council meetings, why would this be any different?

"You've brought death to us all!" Kasper turned away from the mayor with angry tears in his eyes. And in a moment that admittedly filled Kasper with more pleasure than guilt, he hoped Jim Elliott would meet his maker this day in the most unpleasant way possible.

Kasper was about to continue across the courtyard when he saw a woman run up to Jim and crying as she grabbed at his legs and midsection. Blood pulsed from several deep gashes in her face and one of her eyes was completely missing, leaving just a hollowed, bloodied socket.

"Jim! Jim! You need to save us, Jim!" Her voice was garbled but familiar.

And in that moment Kasper realized the woman behind the ghastly bloodied face was that of Caren Banks. Jim Elliott didn't pay her any more attention than he did to Kasper. Kasper shook his head and turned away when Caren suddenly grabbed him by his shirt and spun him back around. She pulled him close and their faces were barely an inch apart.

"Help me, Kasper! Save me!"

Bloodied spit particles spattered against Kasper's face as she screamed at him. Kasper recoiled and shoved the hideous woman away.

"Get off of me!"

Caren stumbled sideways and fell onto the concrete pathway beneath her. She waved an enraged fist at Kasper.

"This is your fault, you asshole!" the delirious woman screamed. "You're the one in charge of the security and you failed! You failed, you son-of-a-cocksucker! I hope you die! I hope you –"

A vampire swooped in out of nowhere, sunk its long talons into the already open wounds on Caren's face, and carried her straight up into the air by her head. The woman's high-pitched screams blended with the shrieks of the monster carrying her, creating a chorus born from the depths of hell. Kasper stared, transfixed, as a second vampire latched onto the screeching woman. The two vampires hissed and snarled at each other. The second vampire wrapped its arms around Caren and thrust its claws deep into her midsection. The creatures continued to growl aggressively at one another as they each lay claim to the prey while they twisted and pulled in opposite directions.

Caren's cries stopped as her body was torn in two. Kasper had to jump back to avoid being splattered by blood and entrails that rained from above. Having experienced much more of Caren's demise than he ever intended, Kasper turned and ran in the direction of his home on the far side of the courtyard. He was nearly to the edge of the open plaza when he spotted his family sprinting towards him. He ran towards his loved ones with a renewed vigor. Helena raced forward and the two of them embraced – and in that moment Kasper was lost in the arms of the woman he had known and loved for twenty-five years.

"Thank god you're okay!" Kasper exclaimed. Haley and Annika rushed in and the four of them held each other tight. Kasper quickly pulled away not allowing any of them to get much if any solace in the huddle.

"We've got to go now," said Kasper.

"We can't get to the apartment," Helena said. "There are too many vampires in that direction. Can we get to the gate?"

Kasper shook his head. "They've blown the gate and cut off…"

His words faded as he looked past his wife and at the figure in the dark cloak and cowl. Whoever this was had made their way to the town square and was standing at the edge of the courtyard. Helena's eyes followed Kasper's gaze.

"Who is that?" asked Helena.

"I don't know." Kasper shook his head. "But I don't think I want to find out." He turned his head frantically from side-to-side as he scanned for an escape route. "There." He pointed with one of the spears towards a break in a line of nearby buildings. "Follow me. There's an old bomb shelter under the library. If we can get there hopefully there's room for us to hide out."

In a thin attempt to avoid any vampires attacking from above, Kasper crouched as low as he could while still rushing forward. Helena and their daughters followed closely behind, copying Kasper's stance as they headed towards the buildings. Haley grabbed hold of Annika's hand and practically dragged her along. Annika didn't need the help but the warmth of her sister's hand was comforting among the surrounding bedlam. Annika watched in part-horror, part-glee as a vampire that landed directly in front of her father met a quick death as Kasper simultaneously jabbed the points of both of his spears into the monster, one through its face and the other through its heart. The creature dropped straight down, dead. Kasper looked back at Haley and Annika – his face freshly splattered with vampire blood – and shot his daughters an expression that was part smile, part relief.

"You girls okay?"

Haley nodded her head rapidly while Annika gave a simple, "Mm-hmm."

Kasper gave his girls a quick wink – then was yanked up into the air by a vampire. The abrupt motion caught Kasper by surprise and he dropped the bloody spears he was carrying. A second vampire flew close behind, grabbed Helena, and pulled her up and followed in the direction Kasper was being carried.

"Mom! Dad!" Annika screamed and frantic tears shot out like pipes that suddenly burst.

"Shhh!" Haley cautioned as she grabbed her younger sister by her upper arms. She shook her sister lightly as she stared into her eyes. "There's nothing we can do for them right now. We need to stay focused. We won't be any good to them if we're dead." Haley said the words out loud as much for her own benefit as Annika's. It felt like a placebo of a sentiment.

Annika's eyes were darting about but finally met with Haley's just as her sister finished speaking. Tears were streaming down her face but she managed to retain most of her composure as she nodded briskly. Haley wiped some of the tears from the younger girl's cheeks while Annika sniffled. Annika brushed Haley's hands away.

"I'm okay! I'm okay," Annika said, unconvincingly.

Haley picked up the spears dropped by their father and handed one to Annika.

"We need to get to the library like Dad said," said Haley. The confidence in her voice surprised herself. How she managed to hold herself together amazed even her. "It's just three buildings down this way."

The sisters continued in the direction their father was originally taking them and towards a break in the nearby line of brick buildings. They crept around the corner of the closest building without garnering the attention of any of the creatures invading their community. A sudden realization overtook Haley. She stopped and pressed herself against the wall.

"What is it?" Annika asked in a hushed tone.

"It's getting really quiet."

"Yeah, so?"

"Listen."

The two remained unmoving and barely breathing as what sounded like the screams of no more than five people dropped to that of three, two, then one. The final scream lingered for several blood-curdling moments before coming to an abrupt halt. There were a few lingering sounds of faint whimpers and cries, distant yet still foreboding. Then everything fell eerily silent.

"Follow me," whispered Haley.

Haley rushed quietly to the next corner of the building and peered carefully into the courtyard. Annika copied the gesture and the sisters found themselves witnessing the horrors of an unknown drama that unfolded before them.

Dozens of vampires formed a large, loose circle in the courtyard while others flew and kept watch from high overhead. The circle was two or three vampires deep in some places but had broken gaps that Haley and Annika were able to use to see through the crowd and to whatever was happening within. In the middle of the circle was a line of twenty people on their knees with their hands behind their heads. A line of vampires stood immediately behind the kneeling humans with the tips of their razor-like talons lightly pressing into the necks of the prisoners. Even from the distance, it was easy for Haley and Annika to make out at least two of the people held captive.

"Mom and Dad! They're alive!" Annika exclaimed in a loud whisper that was well beyond Haley's liking.

Haley strongly shoved her sister back against the wall and placed a hand over her mouth.

"You need to keep quiet," Haley said in a hushed but firm tone as she looked sternly into Annika's eyes. "You're going to get us killed. And you might get Mom and Dad killed, too, in the process."

Annika failed to fight back tears that were conceived from a concoction of anger, fear, and anxiety as she nodded her head. Haley took her hand away and Annika let out a heavy breath.

"Sorry if I overreacted," muttered Haley.

"Sorry for almost getting us killed."

Haley looked cautiously back around the corner of the building. Annika carefully peeked around her sister's shoulder.

"Is that all the people left?" Annika asked quietly.

"I hope not. I'm hoping a lot of them are hiding in their homes."

A voice unlike any that either sister had ever heard suddenly came from the center of the gathering. They looked at each other in bewilderment as it startled and stunned them. Haley could only give a slight shrug before their collective gaze returned to the courtyard and focused on the mysterious vampire in the center of the circle.

THE vampire was already tall and the thick-heeled boots it wore only made its height and presence even more menacing. It was dressed all in black and wore a cloak that nipped at its heels and a cowl that kept its facial features shrouded under a veil of shadow.

A black fingerless-gloved right hand with inch-long talons reached up from the darkness of the cloak, gingerly grabbed the front edge of the dark hood and laid it back, finally exposing the face of the mysterious intruder. The visage was both beautiful and grotesque, drawing gasps from the captive townspeople. The face was that of a man in his mid-thirties, with sharp, chiseled features outlined in a halo of short blonde hair…more accurately, this described the right half of his face. The entire left side of the face was no longer skin and flesh. In its place were several dark gray steel plates intricately interconnected that allowed for movement and chilling expressions.

The man brought his left hand up – a gesture that elicited a fresh round of gasps as the left arm was not human nor vampire. Rather, the entire arm down to its fingertips was a series of metal plates, rods, pulleys, wires, and servomotors. The monstrosity removed its wraparound sunglasses and surveyed the helpless humans before it through mismatched eyes. Its right eye was gray and "human" while its left was a marble-sized glowing red sphere floating in a cold black void of an eye socket.

The cyborg-vampire brought dread to all those in its presence, including vampires under its command though none of them would dare to reveal their cowardice out of fear of reprisal. The creature stood silently for a few long, anxiety-inducing moments, slowly pulling its half-human, half-robot lips back and revealing a set of black-chrome teeth, long and sharp like those of any other vampire though these had permanent dark crimson tips. When the monster finally spoke, an underlying electronic tone in its voice made every syllable more pronounced and ominous. It was the voice out of the darkest of nightmares and from the deepest of netherworlds.

"My name is Ryder Sloane. I seek the one known as Prater Saxon."

PRATER

THE dampened midafternoon sunlight filtered through the crisscrossing branches of the forest canopy. Water rushed along in a wide stream that ran nearby but out of view from where I stood. The scents of grasses and trees and freshness of Earth after a gentle rain surrounded me. Even the soot hanging in the air couldn't completely extinguish such vibrant richness from my senses. I looked up and the winds high above blustered along clouds that suddenly obscured the already dimmed sun. Within moments the rain returned with light droplets like the spring shower that passed just minutes earlier. I held the bundle of sticks I carried in my arms close as the drops rapidly grew larger and fell faster. My dark, shoulder-length hair quickly matted against my face and I hastened my stride as I headed in the direction of the trickling stream.

I broke through the trees and looked up and down the gravelly shoreline as the water flowed swiftly by. The rain became a straight downpour and even with my keen vampire eyesight I had to strain to make out the shapes beckoning to me down the shore. The hazy figures were distant and one was clearly larger than the other. The rain grew stronger still and at least there was little wind to listen through as I picked up on the voice calling my name. The woman waved me along and I could hear light laughter from a second voice. The child at the woman's feet frolicked along the stream and splashed in ankle-high water in the rain. I smiled and pulled the sticks tight against my body with one arm while I raised my other hand in acknowledgement.

I rushed towards the woman and child and my footsteps on the shifting rocks quickly became drowned out by the sound of thunder almost directly overhead. A rumble resonated through the ground, shaking the trees. The woman continued to call to me even though the thunder and pounding rain prevented me from hearing her. I finally reached her and she scooped up the laughing child before we ran together to an alcove in a rocky hillside nearby.

The alcove was spacious, about one and a half stories high and several stories deep – more than enough to accommodate the three of us as a functional living space. I dropped the sticks and had barely wiped the long hair out of my eyes and away from my face when I felt the warm embrace and Jeanne's lips on mine. She never seemed to mind my moustache or the beard that never grew beyond thick stubble. I gasped for a breath and my vampire teeth, always exposed as I no longer felt a need to hide their true nature behind false sets, grew half an inch as a euphoria began to take hold of my desires. For several long, unending moments I was lost in her taste and her essence as her arms held me tight and I welcomed the comfort of another body against mine.

So there we were. The world of vampires didn't exist. The threat of the undead tearing us apart or taking us away to one of the blood banks was a distant, almost untouchable reality. We not only survived in this world but we actually lived. *It was just the three of us: me; the love of my life, my Jeanne, my one and only; and our three-year-old daughter, Dahlia.*

I looked down and the little girl had her tiny arms around my leg and she was looking up at me, beaming. She had the beauty of her mother, the brightness of the persevering sun, and an innocence that was admirable in a world that was often cruel and unforgiving. I can't even remember the last time I heard her fuss or cry. Already at such a young age she had the strength of her mother. I already felt there was so much I could learn from this young person – she had so much to give to this world and I was a better person myself because of her.

I couldn't wait to get a fire going and for my wet clothes to dry. My black waist length tactical-style jacket was great for being out and exposed to the elements but provided no comfort soaking wet. I continued to look into Jeanne's eyes as we separated from our embrace. This woman was my world and I was forever lost in those amazing eyes…eyes that suddenly turned to shock and surprise. With my back to the alcove entrance, I wasn't immediately aware of what she saw, but I heard them – the splashes of feet landing on wet ground. I turned to face our unwanted, undesired, and uninvited visitors.

There were three of them – two females and a male – dressed in long black overcoats open over red button-down suits. With the downpour of rain unavoidable, the vampires stood there facing us while dripping wet, doing nothing to hide their snarling jowls and flexing their long talons. I glanced to my far right to where my twin swords leaned against the alcove wall sheathed in their X-shaped shoulder strap holster. I cursed myself for not having been wearing the weapons this entire time. I looked back at the monsters who stood silhouetted as lightning flashed brightly behind them. Thunder echoed through the alcove and the vampires rushed in.

I sprinted towards my weapons and glanced back to see Jeanne shielding Dahlia from the incoming creatures. To my dismay only one of the vampires, the male, came after me while the other two sprinted at Jeanne and Dahlia. Reaching my weapons, I grabbed one of the sword handles and unsheathed the sharp steel as I turned to face my oncoming attacker. I stabbed just as the vampire was upon me but the creature suddenly flipped upside-down and planted its feet on the alcove ceiling. It evaded every slice, swipe, and stab I made. Deciding on a different tactic, I feigned a sweeping strike and as the creature lurched sideways I instead performed a spinning back kick that landed squarely in the monster's chest, knocking it backwards away from the ceiling and onto the dirt floor.

The other two vampires stalked Jeanne and Dahlia slowly and menacingly in a wide circle with their hand-razors outstretched. Their monstrous hissing echoed off the rocky walls. Dahlia pressed herself against the back of Jeanne's legs, covering her ears with her little hands to block out the unholy sounds. Jeanne – ever the warrior that I loved so dearly – stood with her right hand on our daughter and her left hand brandishing her signature silver metallic baton that had seen so much action and killed many a vampire. I was sure Jeanne expected today to be no different.

But this was not an easy fight.

The vampire facing Jeanne most directly charged at her, flipping upside-down and running along the rock ceiling. Jeanne adjusted her stance and released a flurry of defensive movements in the air with her baton to try and keep the vampire at bay. She risked stealing a quick glance behind her and saw that the other vampire was also running along the alcove ceiling and was just about to grab Dahlia.

Our daughter screamed as Jeanne spun around and managed to clock the vampire across the side of its head just before it grabbed Dahlia. The monster fell sideways screeching a horrific sound that could have caused oversensitive ears to bleed. It held the side of its head as blood rushed out from the opening in its skull left by Jeanne's strike. Jeanne had no time to take solace in having felled the creature before she was grabbed from behind by her first attacker.

I would have hurried to help if not for having to deal with my own assailant. The vampire I knocked to the ground was already scrambling to its feet. I grabbed my other sword by the handle and snapped my wrist to fling the cumbersome X-shaped holster away. The vampire launched itself at me, flying through the air with a ferocity I had not witnessed in a very long time. I brought both my blades up in an X in front of me, slicing outwards just as the vampire reached for me.

The vampire's hands went flying in two different directions as they were cut off at their forearms. I dropped low and rolled away as the creature flew over me, panicked, and slammed into the alcove wall. Without paying it any further attention I ran towards Jeanne who had dropped her baton and was struggling to keep the vampire on her back from digging its claws into her or from sinking its teeth into her neck. I could hear Jeanne's cries from her efforts stemming from the rapid realization that she would not be able to fend off the creature much longer. Dahlia managed to not get trapped in the fight and ran towards one of the alcove walls. The vampire opened its mouth wide and bore its mouthful of vampire-venom dripping daggers onto Jeanne's neck...

...just as my sword sliced the monster's head in two, splaying it cleanly in half right down the middle. My swipe was true and accurate and ensured Jeanne herself was never in any danger. The vampire didn't even have time to cry out before falling off Jeanne in a bloody, dead clump.

Immediately our attention was on Dahlia. To our horror, she was crouched low and screaming as the vampire with the cracked skull was lumbering towards her. The blow from Jeanne's baton didn't kill the creature but it was having trouble fully functioning as it limped and staggered towards our little girl. Jeanne scooped her baton off the floor of the alcove and ran towards Dahlia as my attention was directed back at my original assailant. He was flying straight at me with bloody trails streaming from handless forearms. I raised both of my swords preparing to strike as the creature began spinning in the air like some bizarrely grotesque missile.

I crouched low, planning to thrust upward as the vampire flew over me. But just as I prepared to attack, the creature drastically altered its course and instead shot towards Jeanne. I leapt onto my feet and called out to warn her but it was too late. The vampire snatched Jeanne under her arms from behind. She didn't see it coming. Her cries rapidly diminished as the monster again altered its course and flew out of the alcove and into the dark thundering storm.

Before I could react to Jeanne's sudden abduction, Dahlia's screams diverted my attention back to her. I turned to see the vampire woman whose partially crushed skull still oozed blood grab my daughter and pull her in tight before also flying away and out of the alcove. I sprinted out into the pouring rain, screaming Dahlia and Jeanne's names alternately. The flying vampires were much faster than me and when I burst into the rainstorm they were already gone.

I continued to scream, scanning the skies and grounds around me without a clue as to where any of them were. Tears were washed away by the downpour that flooded upon me from the gray sky. Lightning illuminated the surroundings but provided no clues. My loves were lost.

I took a deep breath and tried to regain some composure when a pain like I've never felt tore through me. I looked down and saw the bloody hand of a vampire bursting out of my chest. All breath escaped me and I immediately began to gurgle and cough as blood filled my lungs and throat. There was a sickening slosh as the hand pulled out of me and I fell onto my knees then collapsed onto my back. Looking up I expected to see the face of my attacker but what I saw instead was a head horrifically sliced down the middle – the vampire I thought I had left for dead after saving Jeanne was somehow still alive.

My labored breathing grew more wet and shallow and I struggled to keep my eyes open. Normal blinks turned into long blinks that turned into seemingly endless stretches of darkness…

"Prater…"

Jeanne?

No. Not Jeanne. Jeanne's dead. She's been dead for years.

"Prater…"

A woman's voice…but young. Where did it come from? Who was it?

I opened my eyes and sat up straight with a heave. I looked around me, my vampire eyesight piercing the darkness of the alcove. It was the middle of the night and I was alone – as I had been for years. My Jeanne was long dead along with our unborn child. A light rain, not nearly a storm, pattered outside the cave entrance and I could hear the rushing stream not far away. But there was that voice that sometimes calls to me – sometimes in dreams, sometimes in nightmares like this one.

And sometimes when I'm awake.

The voice, distinctly female…yet unrecognizable. Younger, older, it's hard to tell. It's distant but my name is clearly distinguishable. Or maybe I'm just going crazy in this crazy world.

No one even knows I'm alive. No one who cares, anyway. Who would even be interested in finding me?

EPISODE 3

ESCAPE TOWN OUTSKIRTS
PACIFIC WASTELANDS

"WHO'S Prater Saxon?" Z and Judge asked almost in unison as they turned their heads and looked at each other. Their voices were low with Judge's voice muffled further still through the black neck gaiter and overlaying mask of vampire jaws he wore when on missions. Neither of them knew who the mysterious robotic vampire inside Escape Town was or why it was after someone named Prater Saxon.

After being dispatched to investigate Escape Town by the governor, Judge and Z traversed the approximate one hundred and fifty mile trip from Camp Expectation on their motorcycles: Z on her trusty purple Hondamatic and Judge on his less flashy yet powerful Harley-Davidson Fat Boy 114. His was modified with the throttle and clutch on the right handlebar, along with a brake pedal adapted to operate both brakes, to allow him to drive with one hand. It took a little over two hours across the Wastelands to get to their destination based on directions provided by the scouts who had reported the initial information to the governor. Their journey ended on a plateau about four miles away from Escape Town where they were able to stop and discreetly view the town from an elevated distance. Before they began their reconnaissance, they refueled their motorcycles from spare tanks they brought with them to ensure having enough for the journey home.

The two of them laid on their stomachs as they surveyed the town from the ridge – Judge through a small set of binoculars while Z preferred a retractable spyglass. Their electronically enhanced equipment provided clear hi-definition images. Between them was a pen-shaped device set on a small A-frame stand and pointed at the town. The governor called it an "audio micro-transfer device" that operated on what she referred to as "laser-sound technology" and transmitted a signal to discreet earpieces that Judge and Z each wore in one of their ears. They knew the governor maintained a private research and development team but rarely did much come to fruition. These devices made it out, though, and provided Judge and Z quality audio and visual surveillance for the town despite their distance away. The governor was always cryptic about how such cutting edge technology came from what on the surface appeared to be underdeveloped facilities operating with sparse resources.

When they first arrived, the attack on Escape Town had yet to occur and they took time to observe and take notes of the town from afar. The landscape from the plateau cliff's edge to Escape Town was mostly hard brown and gray ground with sporadic green brush that had overcome all odds to somehow thrive in the desolate terrain. Rising from the ground was the wood and steel twenty-foot tall wall that encircled the town. The seemingly haphazardly spaced guard towers did little to provide any assurance that the community was well-defended.

"Those walls are pretty pathetic," murmured Judge. "There's no way they'd do any good against a decent vampire attack."

"And their air defenses look abysmal," Z added. "Look at those decrepit atlatl turrets. For some reason only two of them are occupied."

"Considering the condition of their fence I'd be surprised if even those two work."

They continued to survey the grounds silently for several moments. The round walls of Escape Town looked like a gigantic misshapen crown bursting up from the desert ground surrounding it. Everything seemed quiet, calm, and normal – or as normal as a post-apocalyptic town struggling to survive could be.

Despite the sad state of its defenses, Escape Town conveyed a simplicity and wholesomeness that Judge hadn't recognized in a while. Life at Camp Expectation never seemed simple and nothing in this world could ever truly be wholesome again, at least not in Judge's estimation. People at Camp Expectation always seemed to be slightly on edge despite their calm demeanor. In many ways it made Judge long for a life simpler than the ones he and Z had come to know there. With nothing else really to distract him, Judge had thrown himself fully into his role as security force commander, a responsibility that occupied him 24/7. But it was a very impersonal and at times high-stress position. With the constant threat of vampire attacks a neverending reality, maintaining hypersensitivity and keenness to his surroundings at all times was paramount – but also exhausting. The stress of being responsible for the safety of two thousand residents at times felt overwhelming but Judge handled it well. Serene moments such as these allowed the U.S. Marine to take pause and, at times, cope with memories that flooded him without warning.

One of those memories trembled through him as they witnessed the sudden attack by vampires on Escape Town. The vampire colony approached from the west, most of them on the ground in rolling transports and people carriers of various shapes that kicked up rooster tails of dust while others flew overhead of their own power through the air. Once the gate was blown apart and several barriers breached, Judge and Z became privy to the horrors within the walls. They watched, helpless from afar, each with the aching inner struggle of what to do: Do we help and fight? Do we continue as witnesses only? No two situations were ever the same and the emotions involved were always strong.

This attack was larger and more vicious than any they had ever witnessed on a group of survivors. As a result, the fight didn't last long before it was reduced to relative calm and silence as those residents unable to somehow successfully hide were effectively annihilated or taken away into transports, leaving just the few captives in the town courtyard. It was when they heard the strange cyborg-vampire leader – something else neither of them had ever seen – looking for a specific individual that Judge was struck by the memory…and a pang of guilt.

Z lowered her spyglass and retracted it with a whir and a click. "We need to get down there," she said decisively.

Judge picked up on the slight Russian accent that despite all the years that had passed only tended to come out when she was most serious. He put a hand on top of Z's as she started to put her spyglass away.

"Wait."

"What is it?" Z asked with an air of impatience. "I've seen enough. We need to go help."

"Hold on, Zarina." He lowered the vampire jaws mask and gaiter covering his face. "There's something I've been wanting to tell you."

Z blinked as she stared at Judge then cocked her head to the side as confusion swept over her face.

"Is everything okay?" Her trepidation was evident. Z could tell there was something different about Judge's tone…something she had never heard in him before.

Judge sighed as his eyes dropped.

"You're making me nervous, Judge. What is it?"

Judge slowly brought his eyes back up to meet those of his adoptive daughter.

"I never told you why your family was targeted for rescue."

Z's eyes narrowed as she processed what Judge just said. This was an odd subject to bring up at an even odder time.

"Yes, you did," she said. "You said your team identified us as survivors in the hotel and came for us. Doesn't sound like there was much else to it." She paused before adding, "This is a strange thing to bring up now."

"I know, I know." Judge shook his head.

Judge scuttled back from the ridge and stood up. Z turned sideways and watched him silently face their motorcycles that were parked several feet away from the edge of the plateau. She scooted away from the edge before standing up a few feet behind him, uncertain of what was happening and why Judge was suddenly acting the way he was.

"What's going on?" Z asked. "What is it you're trying to say?"

Judge turned and faced the woman he had raised as his daughter with a melancholy in his eyes that Z didn't recognize.

"That's not all there was to it," said Judge. "There's more."

JUDGE

THE rumble of the MTVR resonated through the tight cabin where my fellow Marines and I prepared for our Times Square mission. Tensions weren't any higher than if we were holed up somewhere in the Middle East, though the feeling in the air was different. Maybe it was the fact that this mission was on U.S. soil. Or perhaps it was the unusual nature of what we were facing. We raised our voices when we spoke to be heard over the engines and road noise — and perhaps to help disguise any anxiety any of us might have felt.

I remember PFC Barry Dugan looking shocked when I told him, "You better hold onto your ass. We're fighting vampires."

Our fire team leader Sergeant Steven Knowles downplayed it all. He thought it was just an epidemic of motherfuckers high on some new drug. In some ways, technically, I suppose that was true. But I can't help but wonder if the sergeant's dismissal of the true nature of the threat didn't somehow later play into the deaths of my fellow Marines.

"These things may no longer act entirely human, but like I said, there's no such thing as vampires," the sergeant told us. If he only fucking knew.

At the time, even I couldn't help but play into the sergeant's casual approach. I remember smacking Dugan on the back of the helmet and assuring him, "There ain't nothing too big for this squad to handle. You pump enough lead into anything and they muthafuckin' die!"

If I only fucking knew. That cavalier attitude didn't save anyone. It's an attitude I've long since shed. I can still clearly see the looks on everyone's faces as the sergeant laid out details of the mission.

"Our main focus is to extract any survivors. This is a rescue mission. We will not leave emptyhanded."

Those words have stuck with me all these years...probably because they weren't entirely true. I didn't learn the true purpose of the mission until after it was too late, after all my team was dead…and after all my family was dead.

The first clue that this wasn't simply a group of drugged-out crazies was that the intersection of Broadway and Seventh Avenue was covered in blood and body parts. There was no life to be seen anywhere. The famed Times Square intersection was quiet with the only sign of "life" coming from the unending flashing of neon and LED signs that gave the gory intersection a gruesome glow that I'll never forget.

Armed with my M16 with its M203 40mm grenade launcher, I was way too cocky for my own good — the price paid by youth and a headstrong attitude unbefitting of the actual dangers at hand. We donned our gas masks and followed the sergeant into the hotel, searching for our target: the family that I would come to know as the Ismagilovas. Finding the family hiding in the hotel ballroom was a relief at first as they were mostly alive, only the father had already perished. I don't know how it was they lived when the ballroom was filled with the bodies and body parts of thousands of the hotel guests. Relief turned into horrors I had never before seen as one by one my fellow Marines Torres, Heath, and Dugan were picked off in front of me. Sergeant Knowles fought valiantly and died a hero like the rest of them. It was his actions in particular that helped with Zarina's and my escape. But those horrors paled to those experienced by Zarina herself: she witnessed her mother and brother literally get torn apart in front of her, their blood showering her in the process. Yet she never flinched, let alone fully cried. Her silent strength was only reinforced as she watched me with wide eyes as I cut off my own left forearm after getting bit by a vampire during the rescue operation for her and her family.

As I limped out of the hotel to face the New World with Zarina by my side for the first time, I knew everything was going to be different. Not just for Zarina and me, but for everyone, forever. I didn't know, though, about Zarina being specially sought out until about eighteen months later and in a most unusual circumstance.

We lived much of our time as nomads, as was the norm for many of the Vampocalypse survivors at the time, sometimes staying with small groups of other survivors we would come across, other times fending for ourselves. I had long since abandoned the Range Rover. It became increasingly difficult to find gasoline in the earlier days following the Vampocalypse (unlike now where power and gasoline weren't a particular problem in some of the larger survivor towns, Camp Expectation being among them). After several months we simply ran out of fuel and instead spent our days on foot. We kept what supplies we could in our backpacks, along with each of us carrying a handgun (I carried two) and hunting knives. I also had my M16.

We mostly stayed in the western half of what used to be the United States, in the Pacific Wastelands, near the Cascade Mountains. We kept clear of any perceived or known vampire hotspots. Living day-to-day was never easy. Many of the days were long and uneventful but any uneventful day was a good day that kept us alive. 'Excitement' always involved vampires and vampires always led to death. Thankfully, Zarina and I had so far not been on the receiving end of death's touch, but in this world, you never knew when your number was up.

Many long days were also hungry and thirsty days. You got used to the hunger, though, and we learned to be especially thankful for life as much on the days when sustenance was lean as we were on the rare occasions when we had more than enough. There was that time, then, eighteen months after Times Square, when we had gone over a week without food and while that wasn't necessarily a point of complete desperation, it was a point where any potential salvation needed to be exploited.

Traveling on foot opened me up to moving about day or night as our whims took us. It was the middle of one night in our endless, destinationless travels when we saw a twinkle of fire as we traversed one of the forested areas of the Wastelands. The light was in the distance, flickering between the remains of once majestic trees that used to be lush and green and stretch into the sky but were now just boney fingers grasping at a bright, new dawn that never came.

I motioned to Zarina silently and we steadied our breathing and stepped cautiously to reduce any sounds as we crept towards the fire. I led the way as Zarina followed close behind. There were three khaki military-style shelter tents sandwiched between the trees along the far edge of the encampment. As we snuck closer I could make out seven adult-sized humanoids sitting around the fire on large rocks, logs, and even a couple of old, tattered folding lawn chairs. Though we were still a good hundred feet away, even with just the glow of the campfire, it looked like they each wore a dark head and face covering and had some sort of mask across the lower part of their faces. It took just a few moments for me to realize the masks were actually made up of the lower parts of skulls – specifically, cheekbones, mandibles, and sets of inch-long vampire teeth. Zarina and I glanced at each other and exchanged a look of uncertainty. Why would vampires wear the skulls of vampires? Unless, of course, these were humans and not vampires. If that was the case then maybe there wouldn't be a fight after all.

The voices that came from behind their masks were a combination of male and female though I couldn't make out how many of each. They were loud and boisterous and the way they spoke of a recent hunt where they slaughtered an unsuspecting group of humans and stole their supplies settled the question of what they were: indisputably vampires. And there were only seven of them. At this point in my life I'd already fought against and defeated more – I could easily take out these. Truth told we could have avoided the conflict altogether but we needed supplies – especially food – and there may not have been a better opportunity in the near enough future.

I took Zarina and dropped back several yards, far enough back to hopefully take advantage of the forest in the dark, while close enough to maximize my kill shots between the trees. Slowly and silently, I set my rifle down and removed my backpack. I opened the bag and removed a metallic U-shaped bracket that clipped onto the end of the hard plastic covering that shielded the stump of my left forearm. I fastened the bracket to the hand guard on the barrel of the M16, working around the sound suppressor already attached to the rifle, then nudged the bottom of the loaded magazine that was already in place to ensure it was securely affixed.

Then I went to work. Three muffled bangs quickly sounded and three of the aberrations fell before the rest scattered into the dark.

I looked at Zarina and whispered, "Stay down and stay here."

I stuck low to the ground as I shuffled away from Zarina, wanting any attention to be on me solely. A rustling to my left drew my attention and

I whipped the rifle in that direction but only saw the near pitch blackness of the night among the dead forest. Another sound, this one to my right and I turned again but this time I caught some movement in nearby brush and I fired my weapon. The demonic screeching I heard in the next moment didn't come from the brush but rather from behind me. It was the last thing I heard before the hard knock on the back of my head immediately shut all my senses down…

I don't believe I was out for very long, but when I came to there was a moment of surprise when I realized I was still alive, though for what reason I didn't know. I quickly assessed my surroundings. I was sitting on a metallic folding chair with my arms behind me and wrapped around a two-inch thick pole that served as the center support for one of the military-style tents I spied earlier. A thick rope was wrapped around me several times, immobilizing my arms behind me and securing me to the pole. I sat facing the entrance to the tent and counted three battery-powered lanterns that emitted a gray-white glow from their LED bulbs. I guessed the space around me to be about the size of a two-car garage. I couldn't see behind me but I had the sense that I was alone. Zarina was nowhere to be seen. There were two single-wide empty cots on my left, while on my right were two long trunks sitting on folding stands with their lids open. One looked to hold an assortment of swords, spears, and knives, while the other had some guns and rifles, including my M16, and even a few grenades. My prosthetic bracket was still clipped to the rifle's hand guard.

I wasn't sure what vampires would want with collecting so many weapons. Perhaps they found some sort of efficiency in their use. Or maybe they figured every weapon in their possession was one less in the hands of their enemy. None of it mattered for my current predicament.

I shuffled and wiggled to try and work the ropes loose but they were too tight. The lump on the back of my head throbbed and I momentarily shut my eyes to block out a quick pulse of pain. I looked up to where the pole I was tied to terminated at the center of the tent ceiling but that didn't spark any ideas for escape. I looked back at the closer of the two weapons chests, the one with swords and blades. Maybe I could work myself around the pole and kick the chest with an outstretched leg. If I could knock the trunk off its stand then maybe I could use a foot to slide something over that could be used to cut my ropes...

The rustling of the canvas door being yanked aside interrupted my plans. Two of the four remaining vampires walked in. One of the creatures walked right up to me with determination in its step. It put its face right in front of mine and I could see the vampire jaws it wore as a mask had streaks of dried blood on them. Dark fabric wrapped around the rest of the monster's head left just the tiniest of gaps for it to see through. I was sure, though, the creature's augmented vision helped it see just fine.

"Where is the girl?" the monster asked in a low, gravelly voice.

The lower mandible of the mask moved up and down when the creature spoke, adding a chilling animation to an already gruesome image. Despite this I found I could still smirk at the face that I knew could easily spell my death. In this insane world I'd learned that death could come any day, at any moment, and without warning. The fact I was even still alive was beyond my comprehension at times, especially now. Facing these things so close, even as it tried to strike fear into me, did nothing but increase my resolve.

"What girl?" I asked.

The punch came hard and out of nowhere and my head recoiled back – the bump on the back of my head struck the pole I was tied to and that pain was second only to what I felt cutting my own arm off.

"Fuck!" I shouted. "Fuck, fuck, fuck!"

The monster was back in my face but this time it held an electronic tablet in one hand with a photo pulled up on its display. To my shock it was a photo of Zarina and her family, the Ismagilovas.

"You know these people," the vampire stated more than asked. Despite my best efforts to hide the surprise, a subtleness in my expression must have betrayed me.

Still, I shook my head as I replied, "I've never seen these people before."

You would have thought the next punch and slam of the back of my head against the pole would have hurt even more that the last, perhaps even done me in for any resistance I had remaining. Actually, my head was feeling numb from the first strike so this somehow didn't seem to hurt as bad.

That said, it still hurt like a motherfucker.

The vampire stepped away and looked to be completing inputs on the tablet. After a few quiet moments it came back to me and showed me a new picture on the display: a closeup picture of me taken from security footage inside the Marriott Marquis Hotel shortly after we found Zarina and her family.

"Corporal David Judge of the United States Marines," the vampire hissed from behind its death mask. "It's truly luck that you came upon us. There's been a notice out for you, or more precisely your little associate, for some time."

"What do you want with her?" I growled as the pain slowly seeped away from the throbbing on the back of my head.

The creature tossed the electronic tablet into the trunk with the rifles and guns. The vampire glanced back at me then the two vampires left me alone in the tent. My heart was in the back of my throat as I hurriedly hobbled myself and my chair around the pole just far enough to give my plan of kicking an outstretched foot towards the trunk filled with blades a go.

It was all in vain. There was still almost a foot of space between my extended leg and the trunk. I let out a heavy breath and squeezed my eyes tight.

Think, think, think…

A sudden "pssst" from the far side of the tent caught me off guard. I looked over and peeking out from under the fabric of the tent wall was Zarina.

"Hey," I whispered. "Get out of here before they come back."

The young girl, always headstrong, scrambled into the tent. Arguing with her at this point would only waste time.

"Get a knife from that trunk. Cut my ropes."

Zarina rushed across the tent and grabbed a six-inch knife with an ornate handle from the top of the pile in the open chest and tore into the ropes behind me.

"Hurry," I urged. "They can be back any moment."

Voices approaching the canvas door spiked the tension in the tent.

"They're back. Get out of here. Go, now!"

I watched Zarina's feet disappear back under the left tent wall just as two vampires reentered. The one with the red marks on its mask stood over me. It ignored the fact that I had moved partway around the pole.

"You have one final opportunity to tell us what we want to know. Where is the girl?"

I shook my head and sneered at my captor. "You're going to kill me either way so why would I tell you shit?"

The vampire stooped to be closer to eye level with me. Oddly, there was a softness in its gruff tone this time when it spoke.

"What you tell me will decide how you die. Quick and painless or, my preference, slow and painfully drawn out."

"Well, I choose quick and painless…"

The creature's head tilted. I took it as a sign of disappointment.

"…for you," I added as I brought my right hand around from behind my back and the freshly cut ropes that once bound me fell loosely away. I plunged the knife Zarina left in my hand before she fled the tent into the vampire's left temple all the way to its gilded hilt. I twisted the blade like I was rolling the throttle on a motorcycle to a satisfying, though sickening, crunch then pulled it out as the dead creature dropped to the ground.

Adrenaline drove me as I leapt off the chair and rushed around the pole to place it between the other vampire and me. The two of us squared off on opposite sides of the pole, feigning attacks and strikes – me with my knife, the vampire with its deadly talons. As we shuffled and worked each other in this dangerous death dance, I found myself in front of the two chests of weapons. I shot quick glances at the open trunks, assessing the odds of upgrading to a larger and more dangerous weapon before the vampire could get to me, then decided to stick with my knife. I focused my attention on my attacker and prepared to strike.

The vampire struck first. The creature launched at me with its superhuman speed and narrowly avoided hitting the pole as it reached with its claws and screeched its murderous cry. I sprang to my left as fast and as far as I could as the vampire just missed grabbing me and crashed into the trunk of swords and blades and onto the floor. The trunk and its folding stand toppled and swords and cutting weapons of various types and sizes spilt out…the most prominent of which was a shiny, silver trident with a foot-long handle. I wondered, very briefly, how it was the vampires came into possession of that particular weapon before I struck.

I plunged my knife into the base of the vampire's skull as it was getting onto its hands and knees. The creature let out a final cry then slumped onto its stomach, dead. I took a moment to let my adrenaline ease through me, taking a few deep breaths as I felt my heart beating in the back of my throat.

I was about to stand when I heard the now familiar sound of the tent door pull back. Rolling off the dead vampire and grabbing the first thing within reach, I turned and stabbed forward with the trident just as the vampire was on me. The three points punctured the creature's face diagonally, plunging deep as the sharp points and razor-edges sliced through the monster's head. Inertia drove the vampire's body onto me and I fell flat onto the ground, pinned under the heavy creature. As the bloody head of the vampire flopped next to me, I was lucky that the handle of the trident didn't in turn puncture me in the face, instead driving into the dirt next to my head.

My heavy breathing was like a windstorm in a tunnel in the otherwise deadly quiet that followed. After struggling for a few moments with the heavy body on top of me, I was finally able to get the creature off as I rolled us both to the side. But as I rolled back and looked up, the last remaining vampire was suddenly on top of me. Its face was close enough to where I could smell its decaying breath through its mask and the inhuman screech that emitted from the depths of its throat would be a sound I would never forget. I thought I was as good as dead –

– if not for the pointed tip of the slender weapon that abruptly burst forth from the area of fabric between the creature's eyes and spraying cold, dead vampire blood onto my face before stopping less than an inch from between my own eyes. I found myself holding my breath, unmoving on the outside but shaking like mad on the inside. The monster fell to the side, next to its deceased brethren, and as it did the tip of the weapon of its demise withdrew, disappearing into the creature's face. My eyes moved up to see my rescuer.

Zarina stood there with a look of deadly determination on her face unlike any expression I had ever seen on her before. In her hands she held a Japanese sai. She must have picked the three-pronged steel weapon up off the floor…and just in the nick of time. She stood silent and still and her breathing looked steadier than mine. Our eyes met and for a moment we stared at each other, unblinking, before she finally stepped away to allow me some space. I wiped blood off my face and got to my feet. Looking at Zarina I felt relieved that the cold gaze she gave her victim had finally softened. There was an expression of satisfaction in her face that stopped just short of a smile. Despite her youth – she was barely six years old – she already had a lifetime behind her eyes. She held the sai out to her side and admired it.

"I think I'll keep this," she said. Her voice was soft but her tone was determined. She bent down and grabbed a second sai that matched the one in her hands. It wasn't unusual for the weapon to come in matching pairs. "And this one, too."

"Yeah, you should," I told her.

I looked around the tent, pondering our next move. Now that I was up and mobile and not involved in a fight, I realized there were two additional trunks along the back wall of the tent.

"Hey, go check those out. See what's inside."

As Zarina went to the chests, I grabbed the electronic tablet off the pile of guns in the trunk near me. I pressed a button on its side and the screen glowed to life with the image of me inside the hotel. I tapped the "back" button on the screen and the picture of the Ismagilovas appeared. A single red dot flashed on the body of each of the family members except Zarina: hers was white with a glowing blue halo. I tapped this dot and Zarina's image enlarged to fill the screen while those of her family members faded away. A pulsing yellow icon in the shape of a file folder appeared next to Zarina's face.

I looked up at Zarina across the tent just as she opened the first of the trunks.

"What do you see?" I asked. "Anything we can use?"

Zarina was rummaging through whatever was inside.

"A few cans of food."

"Probably left over from whatever humans they took these camping goods from. Lucky for us, vampires wouldn't have much to do with canned goods. Check the other trunk."

I returned my attention to the tablet and tapped on the file folder. The virtual file opened and showed:

CLEANSING LIST | | TARGET BLOOD TYPE: AB NEGATIVE

Those words flashed briefly before the words TARGET LIST *appeared, followed by a list of names in gray text with a horizontal black line through them. I didn't have to scroll far, though, before the names turned to red text with no line crossing them out. And at the top of that portion of the list:*

ZARINA ISMAGILOVA

This didn't say much but Zarina obviously had the attention of the vampires and seemingly for having a specific blood type. I had no idea exactly what this all meant. It was enough to know, though, that I had to keep Zarina safe against all the odds the world would throw at her. It was up to me to ensure she slept soundly at night knowing I would always be there for her.

"It's just a bunch of junk," Zarina said about the other trunk, breaking my concentration on the tablet.

"Okay, we'll at least take the food and some weapons."

I looked back at the list on the tablet and scrolled up. There was nothing to see beyond the short list of names in red. I tapped the "back" button again but this time when I did the tablet blanked out, leaving just a black screen. I repeatedly tapped the screen and pressed buttons on the sides of the device but it didn't reactivate. I couldn't afford to waste any more time with it and dropped it to the ground. I slammed a heel onto it, shattering the screen.

We had no desire to keep camp among the dead so I made haste to get our backpacks and bring them to the tent. We loaded what food there was along with a few knives, a handgun, a few grenades, and as much ammunition as we could handle without weighing us down too much. I also picked up my M16 along with its prosthetic bracket.

Then something else caught my attention: the trident. I went and pulled it from the vampire's head and was surprised at how easily it slid out.

Its edges and points were extremely sharp and the weapon could surely do some solid damage in a battle. With Zarina's help I found a way to strap the trident to the side of my backpack – I'd figure out later how to make best use of it. Between that, my M16, and the additional weapons, I was more than set as we prepared to venture out once again into the demonic world. Z was perfectly happy with her sai.

"It's like we both have tridents," Z said in fun, alluding to the three-pronged nature of both types of weapons after I explained to her what the trident was.

"It's like we both have sai," I replied.

It was just before dawn of the grainy sunrise when we were ready to leave the tent. I made sure Zarina was set with her backpack and that it wasn't too heavy. She looked at the sai she gripped in each hand before looking up at me and her expression showed a maturity far beyond her very young age. Just before we left the tent I looked down at one of the dead vampires and, in particular, the set of vampire skull jaws it wore as a mask. I reached down and yanked the bone mask off the creature, breaking the straps securing it behind the monster's head. I held it up in front of my face and looked at Zarina.

"What do you think?

Zarina smiled and gave me a thumbs-up.

I dropped my pack and shoved the mask into the top of it before slinging the bag again around my shoulders. I nodded at Zarina then pulled the tent door aside. We headed out into the early morning and back into the dead forest.

Zarina never inquired about the questions the vampire had asked me and never acted as if there was anything she wanted or needed to know. Perhaps she hadn't heard anything they said or maybe she thought she knew all there was to know. I knew, though, it was inevitable that someday I would tell her – someday far from this night when this evening would be a distant memory. My hope was that whenever I did tell her that she would be understanding as to why I waited and that she'll be able to forgive me.

I managed to "forget" to bring it up for thirty years which was both too long yet not long enough.

EPISODE 4

ESCAPE TOWN OUTSKIRTS
PACIFIC WASTELANDS

"THEY'VE been after me all this time? Because of my blood type? And you didn't fucking tell me?"

Judge watched Zarina as she marched up to him with a finger pointed at his face. She had taken the news about as well as he had feared.

"What I'm saying, Zarina, is I don't know if they've been after you or not. I actually almost believe they haven't. We've never come across any vampires looking for someone specific since then until now." Judge paused before adding, "And it's got me freaked out."

Z's nostrils flared as she stared into her pseudo-adoptive father's eyes. All Judge saw in her was anger. All Zarina saw in Judge was pity. She turned and took a few steps away as she rubbed her forehead.

"All these years? I'm fucking thirty-four years old for god's sake! At what point are you going to stop treating me like a child?"

"I'm not treating you like a child." Judge didn't hide the pleading in his voice. "I just couldn't find a good way to bring this up to you before."

"You certainly have poor timing bringing this up now." Zarina turned and looked back at the man. She didn't mean to cause the sadness in his eyes but the hurt she felt couldn't provide him any consolation.

"There would have never been a good time," Judge said quietly. Then he straightened himself and pointed in the direction of Escape Town. "But that thing out there, that thing isn't a normal vampire," he said, more authoritative. "And I don't know, it's giving me a bad fucking feeling how it's looking for someone specific. It made me think you aren't actually out of danger at all."

The thousand thoughts that went through Zarina's head all fought to be said at once. Ultimately, ironically, she didn't know what to say at all. Instead she walked to her bike.

"I'm not talking about this bullshit right now," Z grumbled as she mounted her motorcycle. "I'm going down there to help those people."

Judge went and stood beside Z as she prepared to start the bike.

"Wait," he said. "This isn't our fight. Whatever that thing is down there isn't like anything we've ever seen. I don't want to take the chance that it could be looking for you, too. We should take this back to the governor."

Z huffed and shook her head. "You've grown soft, old man."

Judge reached out and put his hand on top of Zarina's that she had rested on the bike throttle.

"You're going to get yourself killed, Zarina."

Z found the pleading in Judge's voice almost laughable. "I never think about death heading into a fight."

"What if death thinks about you? I don't know what I'd do if I lost you, Zarina."

Z looked at Judge's hand on hers with disdain then looked back up at his somber face. Judge pulled his hand away and she started the motorcycle with a kick.

"Z, please…" Judge begged.

Z spat on the ground near Judge's feet.

"You never call me 'Z'. Now's not the time to start."

"You're my daughter," Judge implored over the rumble of the bike motor. "I've always tried to do right by you."

Z looked at Judge and when their eyes met, for the first time in his life, Judge felt he didn't know the woman staring back at him. Her next words hurt worse than anything he had felt since the death of his family.

"You're not my father."

Without another word, Z sped away on her bike – away from an anger she had never before felt and didn't know how to disseminate – and down the side of the plateau, on a direct course to Escape Town. Judge spared no time mounting his own bike and following his daughter at high speed towards the town and the mysterious vampire that commanded the raid. His every instinct betrayed his actions and screamed for him to stop but there was no way he was going to let Zarina go into the battle alone.

He had promised to always protect her and that's what he was going to do…despite whatever price that would need to be paid.

EPISODE 5

ESCAPE TOWN
PACIFIC WASTELANDS

THE half-vampire, half-robot cybernetic aberration that called itself Ryder Sloane paced slowly in front of the captive townspeople as they kneeled helpless before him. Each step had a purpose as the creature looked down upon each of his prisoners, though none dared to glance up into the monster's eyes. With their hands behind their heads and being held in place by the vampires that stood behind each of them, the twenty remaining townspeople were powerless to do anything but watch and listen to their malformed captor.

"I seek the one known as Prater Saxon." The words were meticulously spoken and punctuated each step the creature took. A flange in the creature's electronically enhanced voice became more noticeable the longer it spoke. "I know he's been here. I've been tracking him."

Sloane stopped and looked skyward. The part-vampire, part-mechanical nostrils flared as he sniffed the air before dropping his eyes – one vampire and the other mechanical – back on the line of prisoners.

"He is of great interest to us." The creature's steady pace resumed. "Your people are destroyed, either dead or taken captive. There is no escape. Your only hope is to tell me what I need to know."

The monstrosity stopped in front of Helena Nilsen and grabbed her by the chin, forcing her to look up at him. Kasper was kneeling beside her and snuck sideways glances of his terrified wife. He couldn't let her be subject to violence or torture by this creature and was about to say something when another voice broke the tension.

"He's been through here but left some time ago."

Jim Elliott looked up at the cyborg vampire from under the wide rim of his black hat from where he knelt at the far end of the line of prisoners. The airiness of his voice did little to invoke authority in the presence of the creature. He tried to make up for this by relying on his charm and non-threatening nature. He definitely caught the creature's attention as the vampire leader walked determinedly down the line and stood in front of him.

"Who are you?" the cyborg vampire asked. "You know Prater Saxon?"

The mayor looked up into the eyes of the monster staring down at him and smiled thinly.

"My name's Jim Elliott, but please, call me Jim. I'm the mayor of this community. I'd like to see what we can do about salvaging whatever is left of it, if that's okay with you."

Kasper glanced down the line at Jim, surprised at how calm he sounded despite the circumstances. He never figured on the man being one of character to bargain for the safety of the town or others.

Sloane looked at the vampire holding the mayor captive and gave a subtle nod. The creature pulled up on Jim's neck from behind, forcing him to stand. The cyborg vampire stepped back and put several paces between himself and the mayor. Jim glanced cursedly back at the vampire behind him, who had released hold of his neck after he stood. He looked at the vampire leader and ever so slowly lowered his hands from behind his head, making sure to keep his palms out and facing towards the robotic creature.

"Tell me what you know about Prater Saxon...Jim Elliott," Sloane commanded.

Jim straightened his black suit jacket. "We actually tried to talk him into staying but he wouldn't have it." He took a cautious step towards the vampire leader. "Ryder Sloane, is it? May I call you

Ryder?" He cracked a larger smile and offered a hand to shake as he laid on his thick charm.

Sloane made no gesture in response other than to ask, "How long was he here?"

Jim cleared his throat as he took another soft step forward. "He allowed us to accommodate him for just one night before he left."

"How long has it been?"

"A little over a week." A couple more steps and Jim drew ever closer to the vampire monster. He gently clasped his hands in front of himself. "Don't know where he was going. He didn't say. That's all I know."

Kasper stole glances of the interaction, not wanting to draw any attention to himself or Helena, especially after the creature had put his hands on his wife once already.

Sloane took a deep breath. "If that's all you know then I have no further use for you," he said as he twitched his head to the side as a signal to the vampire that had held on to the mayor. The creature was on the town leader in a blink with its claws prepared to inflict unspeakable horrors upon the man.

"Wait!" Jim exclaimed and held his hands up again as if in surrender.

The mayor stood just a few feet in front of the vampire leader. To his relief Sloane raised a palm and the vampire behind him stopped just as the tips of its claws pressed lightly into his neck. He squinted his eyes more from shock than pain but quickly composed a withered smile.

"There's got to be something we can do to save the town." The flutter in Jim's voice was slight but there. "You've done enough, yes? Killed enough and taken enough of us? Let the rest of us go. We are obviously of no harm."

Kasper and Helena exchanged a subtle glance. They were both surprised by Jim's attempt at a negotiation. Despite ensuring the townspeople's general health and happiness, he always seemed to do so with an undercutting air of self-interest and self-preservation. They watched the vampire leader step to within an arm's length of the mayor. Jim looked into the eyes of the creature that stood before him and somehow mustered his full, broad smile.

"You attempt to bargain yet have nothing to bargain with," said Sloane as he raised his robotic left hand high.

Jim suddenly dropped to his knees and put his hands together, pleading.

"No, no, you can't! There's a deal. I made a deal with the vampires. We're supposed to be left alone."

"I know of no deal."

"Not with you but with another of your kind. I'm telling you, it's true!"

"All humans are forfeit." Sloane's body tightened as he prepared to unleash upon the pathetic human before him.

"Please, please, I beg you." The smile was gone – as was the confidence and charm – and now Jim's voice wavered. "Don't do this. I can be of use. I can help in other ways. As their leader I know how these humans act and think. I'm more valuable than any of the others. Spare me, please, I'll do anything you say."

Kasper scowled and kept from muttering in anger under his breath. There it was. That self-serving snake was never interested in saving the townspeople. As usual the repulsive serpent was only looking out for himself.

Sloane brought his robot hand down hard onto the mayor's head, crushing the top of his black hat as he administered an iron grip. The wide brim of the hat pushed down and covered most of the mayor's face, leaving only his thin lips showing. The cyborg said nothing as he effortlessly crushed the mayor's skull as if squeezing a raw egg. The sickening crunch solicited more gasps and screams from the captive humans than the sight of blood and brain running down from under the brim of the black hat. The body sank away as the cyborg vampire loosened his grip and what was left of the mayor slid out from under the bloody hat that remained in the creature's grasp.

The robotic vampire looked up and down the line of remaining humans as they quivered on their knees.

"If any of you have any information to add about Prater Saxon, say it now."

Each of the prisoners looked wordlessly at the ground. A few whimpers and sniffles escaped some of the captives despite efforts to stifle themselves. Sloane walked down the line and stopped in front of Kasper. He placed Jim's bloody hat on top of Kasper's head. Kasper fought reacting in disgust as blood with bits of brain and bone trickled down his face.

"You," said Sloane. "You can save yourself and these people. I'm asking this for the last time." He leaned forward and put his half-robot, half-vampire face so close to Kasper their noses almost touched. "Where did Prater Saxon go?"

HALEY and Annika listened intently as their mayor did his best to square off against the vampire leader. They each held their wooden spears close to their bodies as they peered discreetly around the corner of the building and at the proceedings in the courtyard.

"What are they saying?" Annika whispered. "I'm having trouble hearing."

"I can't make it all out," Haley said, quietly. "I think the mayor's trying to keep the vampires from killing all of them."

"I don't care about all of them. I only care about Mom and Dad."

"Me, too."

Suddenly to the girls' horror the vampire leader crushed the mayor's skull. Annika's breath quickened and Haley was swift to put a free hand over her sister's mouth as she pulled her away from the view of the courtyard.

"Calm down, Annika," Haley whispered. "Hold it together."

Annika did her best to stay quiet as she took several long, deep breaths.

"What if, what if he does that to Dad? Or Mom?" The words came with a quiver as Annika's hands began to shake.

"That is *not* going to happen," Haley asserted, unblinking. "Do you hear me? We have to believe it. It's not going to happen. Okay?"

Annika reached up and wiped her tears away as she sniffled and nodded.

"Okay," Haley repeated but this time her tone was softer and more reassuring. "Remember, we have to hold onto hope."

Annika nodded and watched as Haley peeked back around the corner of the building. She took a step to follow when a pain like nothing she had ever experienced shot through her shoulders – from where the inch-long talons of a vampire grabbed her and yanked her suddenly skyward. Struggling as she fought through the agony, Annika tried to stab at the creature with her spear that she had miraculously managed to cling to but the creature easily knocked it out of her hand. She screamed for her sister only to see the blur of a vampire streak down and snatch Haley and pull her into the air as well.

The jarring attack knocked Haley's weapon loose from her grasp. The sisters screamed as they were flown to the center of the courtyard and dropped to the ground from about ten feet in the air. It was a wonder how neither of them suffered in the fall beyond sore bodies and getting the wind knocked out of them. Vampires rushed in and grabbed the girls as they gasped for breath and brought them to kneel in front of their half-robot leader. Neither Kasper nor Helena could contain their shock at seeing their daughters suddenly deposited in the circle.

"Ohmigod!" Helena shouted. "The girls!"

"Haley! Annika!" Kasper exclaimed as he struggled futilely to break away from the steel grip of the vampire holding the back of his neck.

Sloane's gaze moved from the girls to Kasper and Helena then back to the girls. Haley stared up with the curiosity of a scientist at the cyborg creature glaring down at her. Annika barely kept her tears and nervous trembling at bay as she stole glimpses of the monster. The younger sister shuddered as the creature gave her a cold look before abruptly grabbing Haley by the throat with his robot hand and lifting her high into the air. Exclamations and gasps erupted from the captive townspeople. Helena and Annika screamed while Kasper cried out to his daughter. Haley was the only one who was quiet as the tight grasp around her throat prevented any sounds from escaping or a breath from being taken. She clawed at the cold steel hand but was futile in loosening the monster's grip.

"No, no!" Kasper called out. "Stop! Let her go!"

The cyborg slowly turned his head towards Kasper. "No more games. Just answers."

Kasper nodded his head furiously. "Anything! Anything. Just don't hurt my Haley."

Sloane alternated his looks between the captive father and the girl in his grip whose struggles rapidly decreased as her windpipe slowly began to crush. Haley's eyes started to roll back as the last ounce of fight was about to escape her when the robot hand suddenly released its hold and she slumped to the ground coughing and gasping and silently thanking the stars she was still alive. The vampire standing guard next to Haley let her be as she fought to recover from the trauma she just suffered. Annika helplessly watched her sister on the ground wheezing for air and grimaced as tears once again seeped from her eyes.

The cyborg vampire snarled and looked at Kasper…

"Fine. I won't hurt *your Haley*."

…then looked at Annika, whose scream barely drowned out the cries and protests of her parents. The grip on the top of her head by the robot hand was like iron and the pressure it exerted was immediate and painful while not yet damaging. Annika clawed fruitlessly at the steel arm holding her in place like an anvil.

"Last chance," Sloane said to Kasper. "Tell me what you know."

"He said he was going to Camp Expectation," Kasper blurted without hesitation. "But, but I don't know where that is and I got the sense that he didn't either."

A tense silence between Kasper and Sloane followed while Annika continued to sob and grab at the vice grip holding her down.

"Anything else?" Sloane asked with an underlying impatience.

"I don't, I can't…" Kasper's eyes squeezed tight…then popped opened wide. "South! He said he was headed south."

The cyborg creature addressed one of the vampires standing nearby.

"Canvas the town. Search every corner of every building and every home. Gather all remaining humans for the blood banks in Alcatraz."

Kasper shook his head vigorously. "No, wait! You know everything now and have already destroyed the town. Let us go. Please let my daughter go."

Sloane ignored the appeals, instead keeping his attention on the vampire nearest him. "Carry out the order."

Before the vampire could respond, a new sound cut through the air. It was a hum at first, then a loud purr, then a rumble – then *two* distinct rumbles.

"What is that?" the vampire asked its leader.

Sloane listened intently as he turned his attention in the direction of the main gate. With both vampire and cybernetic-enhanced eyesight, the creature focused on the destroyed entrance in the distance as he tried to determine the source of the distant sounds.

BLINDED by the anger stemming from the recent revelation by Judge, Z drove her motorcycle with the rage and determination of a suicide mission. She wanted nothing more than to kill some vampires. Wind whipped relentlessly by as she sped her bike in the direction of the gate. She guessed there to be about a hundred vampires maintaining watch around Escape Town with many perched on top of the wall while others were on the ground guarding holes in the flimsy steel panels. Leading up to the gate was a convoy of vehicles of what looked like ground troop transports interspersed with several large doublewide mobile shipping container carriers with their tops cranked open. Vampires flew overhead and dropped human survivors from the town screaming and flailing into the open containers. Z guessed these prisoners would be taken to the blood banks in one of the vampire meccas if not face other unknown horrors. Just outside the gate sat a single tank-like vehicle with a large cannon mounted to its front. This looked to be what was used to blow the gate open at the start of the siege.

Z zipped past the convoy at such high speed that the stunned vampires did little but watch her zoom by. Some met their end as Z held a strong arm outward with a sai extended – puncturing clean through a few of the creatures heads as she approached the gate. She glanced into her side view mirror and saw Judge not far behind and causing his own carnage with the sharp edges of his trident.

The two motorcycles entered Escape Town fast and their engines roared like attacking lions as they raced into the courtyard. The bikes cut through the outer rings of vampires – literally – as creature heads, hands, and arms flew from slicing steel wielded by their riders. Z poised to add the cyborg vampire to her kill count. Her cycle screamed down the line of kneeling townspeople as she went to make the deadly strike when Sloane took his hand off Annika and sidestepped, bringing his robot arm around and into Z's upper chest. Grabbing quick hold of her throat, the cybernetic vampire lifted Z up and, as her bike crashed uncontrollably to the ground, slammed her hard onto her back.

Annika took quick advantage of her newfound freedom and dropped to Haley's side who had finally regained her breath and was moving slowly to sit up. Their parents and the other kneeling townspeople were still held tight by their vampire guards and remained helpless to assist in any fight.

A second motorcycle suddenly barreled into the area as Judge launched himself off his bike and at the cybernetic monster that held Z pinned to the ground by her throat. As Judge's bike fell to the side, the robotic vampire released his grip of Z and landed a hard backhanded swipe with his mechanical arm against the side of Judge's head just as the Marine was about to drive his trident into the monster's chest.

Sloane took a moment to assess the two humans laying before him – Z was still gasping for air and holding her throat – then grabbed Judge's trident prosthesis with his own metallic hand. It didn't take much for the steel blades of the trident to crush under pressure as the cyborg squeezed. The vampire leader then put his robotic left leg onto Judge's chest and pulled the man's arm up straight. Judge looked up into the seemingly lifeless eyes of the monster holding him captive and stifled a scream as he felt his left arm straining from pressure on the socket at his shoulder. Finally the clamps holding the crushed trident in place on Judge's left forearm stump broke away and the vampire tossed the appendage aside.

"Primitive," the low electronic-toned voice said callously.

Z coughed and struggled to regain her composure as she rolled to her side and saw one of her sai laying just out of reach. She went to make a grab for it when she was unexpectedly yanked to her feet by one arm by a vampire she didn't realize was standing over her. A second vampire grabbed her other arm and the two creatures held her captive and she was forced to watch the ensuing exchange between the cyborg vampire and her defenseless, adoptive father.

Judge gasped for breath as the heavy steel of the robotic foot applied more pressure on his chest. He tried to push and knock the black booted foot away with his right hand but to no avail. The monster looked down at him then reached down and snatched the vampire skull mask off his face. The vampire leader held the mask above Judge's face then easily crushed it with its robot hand. Broken bits of bone and skull dust dropped onto Judge's face despite his efforts to look away. With superhuman swiftness the cyborg vampire took hold of Judge's left upper arm and squeezed tight as the creature leaned in towards Judge's face.

"Tell me what you know about Prater Saxon," the robotic-flanged voice said.

Sloane moved in even closer to Judge's face and narrowed his mismatched demonic eyes. Judge was repulsed by the smell of decay mixed with iron that emanated from the creature's breath. He spat into the monster's face without hesitation. Saliva slid down the black-chrome plates making up the monster's left cheek.

"Who the *fuck* is Prater Saxon?" Judge raged at the creature.

Sloane then stood more upright while still holding Judge's left arm stump and keeping his heavy foot on Judge's chest. The real pressure – and the real pain – began as the vampire pulled on Judge's left arm. Judge couldn't contain his screams as he felt his left shoulder instantly dislocate. Z's cries for mercy for her adoptive father went unheeded. Sloane looked back at the screeching woman and smirked before turning his attention back at Judge. The creature looked down at the face contorting in expressions of anguish. Amplified cries filled the courtyard as Sloane tore what remained of Judge's left arm completely out of its socket and tossed it aside to the shock of the onlooking townspeople. The bloody appendage landed at Z's feet.

Z's cries were second only to the shouts from Judge himself as he shuddered in pain. Exposed and torn muscles, veins, and sinew pumped blood from his shoulder and onto the ground. Z tried frantically to tear herself away from the two vampires holding her by her arms but couldn't break from their firm grips. She looked down at Judge who looked back with tears in his eyes – but his were more like tears of love lost rather than physical pain. Judge unexpectedly forced a smile at his daughter before looking up at the vampire still pinning him down.

"I will never understand human behavior," Sloane said as he studied Judge's grin.

Judge coughed as he reached inside his leather jacket then quickly put his hand to his mouth – to bite the safety pin of the hand grenade he removed from his inside pocket. With a quick yank the grenade pin was pulled. In the next instant the safety lever was released. Judge spat aside the pin and held the grenade up high as he looked at Z and said his final words.

"I love you, Zarina."

Z didn't have time to feel any anguish as her reflexes immediately kicked in the moment she heard her father speak those words. Taking advantage of the sudden shock resonating through everyone at the sight of the grenade, Z dropped herself like dead weight and slipped from the grasp of the vampires holding her. At the same time, several of the vampires holding humans captives in front of them abruptly took to the skies, taking their prisoners with them. Among those suddenly swept skyward were Kasper and Helena. Just as their parents were being flown away, Annika grabbed onto Haley and the two rolled on the ground away from Judge as a vampire dove to make a grab for them.

As the blast from the detonated grenade reverberated through the courtyard, Z reached out and grabbed her sai from her position lying flat on her stomach, twisted around, and swiped it in a wide arc just inches above the ground. The two vampires who had hold of her just moments before found themselves on the ground as the sharp tip of one of the side prongs of her weapon sliced through the tendons behind their ankles.

Haley looked down at Annika's face from her position lying prone on top of her sister after the two finished their roll away from the blast. The vampire who had tried to grab the girls just as the grenade exploded had luckily absorbed much of the explosion and was now scattered through the area in a thousand pieces.

"Are you okay?" Haley asked as tears of relief filled her eyes. She couldn't hear herself through the ringing in her ears and figured Annika's hearing was probably also temporarily gone from the sound of the blast. Despite this, Annika nodded in the affirmative, much to Haley's relief.

Z brought herself to look through the haze left from the explosion that permeated the area and in the direction of Judge and the cyborg vampire. The man who had raised her all these years – her *father* – was gone. Yet the creature who was the target of her father's sacrifice survived. Like a demon from an undiscovered level of hell, the cyborg vampire stood defiant, burning as fire engulfed the vampire half of the monster while the robotic half just gleamed its metallic surfaces through the flames. Then without warning the vampire cyborg jetted into the sky with a horror-inducing screech and sailed away from Escape Town. The remaining vampires abruptly began to leave – those that could fly did so while the rest scattered on foot.

Annika and Haley looked at each other with an ease in their eyes as some relief had finally come. Something out of Annika's view caught Haley's attention and Annika watched as her sister reached over then bring an item between them: it was the blue-gray baseball cap her mother had been wearing as she was being taken away. With the cap so close between their faces, Annika could smell her mother's essence in the fabric and she shared a look of hope with her sister – then Haley was yanked into the air by one of the last remaining vampires as it made its escape.

"Haley!" Annika shouted as she watched her sister become a distant speck in the sky in a matter of moments.

Just like that, her entire family was gone...lost to horrors constrained only by the limits of the imagination. A warm hand suddenly took hold of hers and she looked up into the eyes of the person she only knew up until now as "the woman on the bike."

"Let's get you out of here."

Z pulled a hysterical Annika to her feet then went and stood up her bike. She climbed on and had a crying and shaking Annika get seated behind her. With her sai sheathed and her passenger secure, Z started the motorcycle. The warm rumble of the engine was a welcome change from the sounds left by the devastation. The few townspeople who remained were slowly being joined by those who had managed to hide and elude capture. Only a few dozen survived. One of the people limped his way towards Z and outstretched a hand. Z could see that the man was holding onto his side, suppressing a wound that was bleeding profusely despite the pressure he exerted to stop it.

"Help…please."

Z looked at the man knowing there was nothing she could do for him or for the town at all. There were mostly likely still vampires out front with the convoy and they would undoubtedly not want to lose any potential contributions to their blood banks. And with the town already lost, sending help from Camp Expectation would surely only be sending people to a slaughter.

Z revved her engine as she took one final look at the smoldering remains of her father. A single tear fell from her left eye, hugging the four-year-old scar on her face as it rolled down her cheek before falling away.

Dirt spit out from behind the bike as Z and Annika sped away from the courtyard. Opting to avoid the main gate and potential altercation with any of the convoy that was left out front, Z headed for one of the openings that had been knocked through a weak point in the wall during the initial siege. The purple-hooded motorcycle burst through the gap, garnering no attention from the remaining vampires that had already begun converging on the few surviving townspeople, and sped into the desolation of the wastelands before them.

EPISODE 6

SAN FRANCISCO MECCA BLOOD BANKS
ALCATRAZ ISLAND

RAIN came less frequently but wasn't completely unusual in the post-Vampocalyptic world. In San Francisco the average number of rainy days per year went from seventy-two during the Old World to under fifty – none of it was ever refreshing, doing little more than to wash down some of the dirt and residue that lingered in the air 365-days a year. The skies were especially dark and heavy with this particular weather pattern. What began as gentle showers were steadily growing stronger and the clouds all but extinguished the faded light from the dipping sun on the horizon.

Alcatraz Island rested on the northern edge of the weather system, away from the heaviest precipitation, but the incessant drizzle was already being whipped by a steadily increasing breeze. Completely refurbished, the main cell house on the island was now entirely a modern construction that left no visible reminders of its former self. The renovated building was a black and soulless structure, with no windows and no outstanding architectural design.

The island dock was expanded and upgraded to accommodate larger boats and deliveries. Large floodlights affixed to the dock's four tall guard towers filled the area with a bright white glow, accentuating the increasing rain. Two large vessels were nestled into place, side by side, with their sterns open to the receiving port. Each of the boats held large, double-wide shipping containers. One set of the containers was standard height while the other was twice as tall. Vampire workers on the dock made sure the tail ramp of each boat was completely lowered and secure before they prepared to open the end doors of the broad, steel containers.

Jonathan Stirling stood at the edge of the black rooftop of the renovated main cell house overlooking the loading docks far below. His hands were in the pockets of his black overcoat as rain dripped from the edges of the umbrella held over him by the aide standing nearby. He was not disguised – in this post-Vampocalypse world there was no reason for any vampire to hide – and the whites of his eyes were blood red surrounding dark blue irises, making his eyes look purple from some angles and in certain lighting. Some other features of his had noticeably changed over the decades following the Great Turn. His jowls were extended outward not enough to look quite animalistic but still added an unnatural attribute to the president's face. His fangs were clearly visible though not fully extended, a trait reserved for only when necessary. Adding to his feral nature was Stirling's newfound habit of occasionally silently snapping or gnawing at the air, sometimes in large exaggerated movements that seemed to be providing some sort of comfort or relief from some invisible pain. No one dared mention the new physical changes or mannerisms but whispers in some circles had some wondering about the president's unusual afflictions.

"These are the last of the transports from Vegas," Stirling said as thunder crackled in the distance from beyond the Golden Gate. Without looking at his companion he added, "Is that right, Mr. Titus?"

"On one boat, yes. The other contains recent acquisitions from the recent raid in the interior Wastelands." Titus held an umbrella over himself that kept his dark suit and overcoat dry and overlapped one of Stirling's shoulders.

"Appamattox and his family are among them?"

"They are," Titus replied. He gave Stirling a curious look. "If you don't mind me asking, what's your concern with this man, Mr. President? What makes him so important?"

Stirling still called himself "president" after assuming the title following the slaughter of the human prior President Warren Harrison on Air Force One thirty years ago. Still looking every bit the young and healthy mid-thirties man as he had over the last three thousand years, Stirling ruled as the dictator he was, instilling just enough fear into his "people" to keep everyone in line with his wishes.

"Professor Appamattox played a vital role in crafting the world we know today. In a way, he's the father to billions of our vampire brothers and sisters."

Titus cocked his head slightly. "I don't understand your meaning."

"He created the virus that brought forth the Great Turn. Our kind owes everything to him. I told him I would ensure his family's comfort and I'm a man of my word."

Stirling and Titus watched as the two-story tall double steel doors were opened on the larger of the two shipping containers. Two electric heavy towing vehicles the size of forklifts backed up side-by-side to the dark opening. Vampires worked in and out of the shadows as the vehicles were connected to something unseen. It didn't take long before one of the vehicles pulled forward, towing out a tall, rectangular, glass case on wheels that was as wide and as long as a single shipping container itself. Several rows of medical cots stacked on top of each other could be seen through the glass. Each held a human kept barely alive since being imprisoned in the blood banks prior to the Vampocalypse. Dozens of needles and tubes punctured various parts of their bodies from their temples, down through their necks, arms, chest, and stomach, and through their groins and legs, and ran to banks of processors and temporary life support systems mounted at the foot of each set of cots. Their bodies had visibly aged over the last thirty years while blood was steadily extracted from their owners. Stirling didn't know where Appamattox was among them but it was enough for the president to know he was there.

"He deserves better than this, I suppose." Stirling sighed. He looked up and bit gently at the falling rain. "I hope he knows how much good has come from his creation."

Stirling and Titus continued to watch as the glass container was driven away while the other tow vehicle followed suit with the second, and final, case. The vehicles towed their cargo up a short road and disappeared into another dark building. Titus beamed a look of triumph.

"That's it, sir. With those being the final bodies from Vegas, the old banks are no more. All of those facilities have been officially decommissioned and these bodies will be transferred to the new processing mechanisms."

"Once again, I must commend you on your work, Mr. Titus. You're certain the new banks will outperform the old as you say?"

Titus nodded enthusiastically. "Without question, Mr. President. We originally had ten blood farms that we've successfully reduced to seven megafarms, each one adjacent to a North America New World Territory mecca-city. Each megafarm has the capacity to house at least ten times as many bodies as the largest of the old farms."

"My understanding is that this couldn't have come at a better time, is that right?"

Thunder popped in the distance followed by a faint flash of lightning.

"Correct, Mr. President. Initial projected shelf life for a donor was twenty-five years. By implementing new technologies and reducing extraction flow over the last few years we managed to stretch the donor life by five years. The new processes took over just in time. In the last two weeks we lost nearly three hundred donors. Their bodies just simply expired. But that was nothing compared to the tens of thousands we've preserved."

Stirling smiled and placed a hand on Titus' shoulder. The claws on his hand were nearly two inches long, and that was while the president was in a docile state. They could easily grow to more than twice the length if needed under the right circumstances.

"You have done so very well for us all these years, Mr. Titus. I cannot thank you enough for your efforts."

Titus nodded. "I appreciate that, sir. It's taken a lot of effort designing and developing the new extraction and preservation processes. I'm happy to say that the new cocooning phases devised by myself and Dr. Deuteronicus can increase the shelf life of each donor to nearly a thousand years."

A delighted smugness flashed across Stirling's face. "With nearly ninety percent of the human race either transformed or wiped out during the Great Turn, I applaud you and the good doctor's ability to triumph over what could have been a real tragedy. Your knowledge and creations are truly a gift, Mr. Titus." He gave Titus' shoulder a final squeeze then pulled his hand away. He snarled quietly and took another large bite at the air.

Titus smiled but maintained a look of humility. "Much appreciated, Mr. President." He paused before continuing, "I wonder if our global partners have taken such precautions. I don't understand why they won't accept our help with the technology we create."

Stirling turned his gaze back to the work happening on the dock. "Our kind can carry too much pride, Mr. Titus. This is a matter I will be sure to address at our upcoming summit."

Titus narrowed his eyes. "Are you sure having the summit here is a good idea, Mr. President? I know I'm no advisor and politics is far from my wheelhouse, but with this summit being the first of its kind, I would have thought it better to let another territory do the test run to ensure matters go…smoothly."

Stirling grinned. "You underestimate the impact of holding the first summit here. We have the opportunity to show the world what we are truly capable of, that we are the best to ensure a prosperous future for all vampirekind. The eyes of the world will be on us and I shall deliver on the promise of being the best to host the gathering."

"Of course, sir," Titus said, sounding more at ease. "I meant no disrespect."

"None taken, Mr. Titus. None taken."

The large shipping container that carried the blood bank transports to the island was closed and the ramp to the boat raised. As this occurred, several dozen vampires lined the dock from the ramp of the second boat, forming two lines that created a pathway to yet another black building. This building was smaller than the others and was triangular in shape with its roof angled down until it touched the ground, seeming to indicate there was a passageway inside that must lead underground. Dark storm clouds were rapidly rolling in and the rain began to fall harder as the most recent thunder sounded closer than ever.

A phone beeped in the pocket of the aide holding the umbrella over Stirling. Councilor Marques Wright answered it without saying a word. The black, 20-something-looking vampire was a White House intern in the pre-Vampocalypse days. Stirling recognized both talent and hustle in the young man and elevated him to the role of his personal aide following the Great Turn. After listening for a few moments, the call silently ended, and Marques put the phone back into his pocket before addressing the president.

"Sir, General Sloane is due to arrive shortly."

Stirling smiled thinly. "Good. I'm eager to learn of his progress in the hunt for Prater Saxon."

DARKNESS. People were packed into the steel container shoulder-to-shoulder, pressed front and back against those around them. And they were all enclosed in complete and utter darkness. No one said a word as they were uncertain of where they were or exactly what was happening…not to mention the sheer fear and panic coursing through everyone's spines. For a while it felt by the sounds and movement like they were on a boat, and now that boat had seemingly docked.

Helena Nilsen was one of those pressed tight facing the doors and by some miracle Kasper and Haley managed to be by her side. They had quickly found each other when they were dropped into the container outside Escape Town. Vampires pushed and organized them like cattle as the container filled. The family remained together as the container made its way to its final destination of Alcatraz

Island. Almost unbearable heat from being packed together in the container had everyone dripping with sweat.

Voices and sounds could be heard from immediately outside the doors. The loud clanging of the steel latches of the door being unlocked echoed through the container. The captives pressed back what little they could as the double doors opened. Helena squinted and held up a hand as lightning flashed almost directly over the island, briefly overpowering the dock spotlights. Cold wind rushed in, drawing the breath from some of those immediately facing the doors, including Helena. Rain pelted her face as she put her arms around her family members on either side of her and held them tight. She could hear Kasper whispering reassurances that she knew were empty. She could feel Haley shuddering inside as she worked through her fear of whatever was to come. Helena, forever a face of strength in the family, remained stoic as she stared forward and fought her insides from shaking themselves apart as anxiousness swelled to almost unbearable levels.

Two lines of vampires formed a pathway from the open doors to a destiny Helena didn't want to discover yet was surely inevitable. A voice from unseen overhead loudspeakers on the dock ordered the people to exit in a single file line. The two lines of vampires advanced in, narrowing the walkway ahead and Helena could see all their fangs and claws to the fullest, further adding to the fear coursing through her. Their red eyes pierced through her very consciousness as their hisses and growls mixed with the sounds of the strengthening storm. A vampire pulled one of the men in the front row and forced him to be the first down the path despite his protests. The vampire then grabbed Helena – she was second.

Helena recognized the man ahead of her from Escape Town. His name was Charles and he was a father to one of the girls who trained with Annika's archery coach.

Annika – Annika – oh my god I hope Annika's okay wherever she is...

They walked slowly down the path between the rows of snapping and snarling vampires. Helena reached back casually with one hand and felt Haley right behind her. She stole a quick glance over her shoulder and saw Kasper was right behind Haley. Charles continued his objections as vampires on both sides grabbed and pulled him by his arms and forced him further down the line. As they moved along Helena realized Charles' cries steadily changed from sounding fearful to become more defiant and angry.

Lightning flashed again and Charles was suddenly fighting with one of the vampires. Helena stepped back to stay clear as Charles threw a vampire to the ground as he screamed and shook with the look of a man who had lost all hope. Through the cries she heard him yell his daughter's name and how she was murdered in front of him during the raid with no remorse. This was a man whose soul had been torn from him. This was a man who had nothing to lose.

This was a man whose head and limbs were simultaneously ripped away by creatures that swarmed him and flew him up just a few feet over everyone's heads as they completed the task. Blood from the dismembered body momentarily turned the rain red. Helena felt the warm, red spray cover her face and she didn't have time to wipe her eyes clear or even react before a vampire grabbed her and forced her to move along. She stepped shakily over the mangled torso of Charles that had dropped into a clump in the path in front of her.

They continued to walk, single file as directed to the black building ahead. Haley had gotten close enough behind her mother to grab her from behind and hold on, seeking comfort, but was pulled away, forced to maintain a few feet of distance between them. The dark opening to the structure loomed ahead and even a bright flash of lightning couldn't provide any clue as to what awaited.

Almost immediately upon entering the building, the captives were forced into rows and loaded onto a large freight elevator. Dull lighting cast a grayish hue on everyone. Every face looked sick with fear as their eyes darted nervously around in an effort to assess surroundings and comprehend what was happening. A steel gate slid down from the top and locked into place. Loud, sharp clanging sounds prefaced the steady hum of motors as the elevator began to descend not straight down but at a sharp angle. Helena guessed they had gone seven stories before the elevator stopped and the steel gates opened to another corridor where the lighting wasn't much better than that of the freight elevator. They were ushered back into a single file line and as they were led further along the passageway, Helena had trouble imagining where they were in relation to the old prison on the surface above and the water that surrounded the island. Was this part of the facility located underground? Were they walking through an underwater passage of some sort?

Before long they were forced to stop and turn to their left. The prisoners were instructed to remain where they stood and the vampire guards surrounding them stepped back. A bevy of bright spotlights turned on, blinding the captives. Helena held her arms up to block the light and while she looked away and down the line, she exchanged quick panicked looks with Haley and Kasper who were in line next to her.

Twenty of the prisoners, including Helena, Kasper, and Haley, stood side-by-side about five feet apart from each other on a long and shallow black stage. The rest of the line was instructed to wait and stay back. With the lights in her eyes, Helena couldn't see anything beyond the edge of the platform they were on, but the sound of distant generators whined and echoed, and the room felt large. A putrid, musty odor hung in the air. Helena could see traces of her breath, while the cool crispness of the room touched her skin.

Five spindly, black appendages rose from the darkness of the floor and surrounded her, just as similar spider-like limbs encircled each person on the stage, eliciting gasps and screams from up and down the line. Helena couldn't tell if the "legs" were mechanical or organic, a distinction probably best left out of the minds of those helpless to experience the horror of it all. The sounds of the generators were immediately drowned by cries from the prisoners as the appendages shot silky gray strands from their tips. Helena suddenly lost control of her body as the appendages began to jostle and spin her around, their tips moving up and down as they continued to spray their web-like strands. Moving with the precision of a spider encasing its prey, the legs carefully cocooned Helena just as the other captives under the spotlights were similarly wrapped. The screams that echoed through the large room quickly became muted as the gray silk covered people's heads – including their noses and mouths. Helena felt her body shudder and convulse as her air supply was cut off. She remained upright, as did all the prisoners, held in place by the spidery legs that cocooned them.

What happened next – what Helena and those on the stage couldn't see – were several large open shells resembling sets of giant bat wings descend from the ceiling. Attached to multiple hoses and chains that guided them, the shells lowered and surrounded each cocoon. The spider-like legs retreated back into the floor as the "wings" folded inward, overlapping as they enveloped the prisoners in a nightmare that added to the abyss of the thick silk strands already encasing them.

With the wings closed and in place, no one could see the tubes that snaked within, puncturing a hole in the casing around each prisoner's mouth before forcing themselves down their throats and stopping near vital organs. Spines erupted from within the tubes and penetrated various tissues, anchoring life support systems. Next, hundreds of needles shot out from within the wings like a futuristic iron maiden torture chamber, piercing the prisoners through their mummy-like cocoons from their temples to their ankles – a combination of mechanisms set to track vitals and steadily draw blood over the next thousand years.

Each newly formed life support pod was lifted in the air by its chains and, as the horrified eyes of the waiting prisoners watched, additional lights turned on in the facility. The freshly cocooned captives had been on a staging area for the damned. Looking out, a large depot revealed itself in the new light – an immense cavern carved in the black rock ten stories deep and a thousand feet from the stage to its back wall. Countless rows of similar black pods were suspended from a web of rails that ran from the staging area to the far end of the enormous space.

As the horror and panic of her situation increased, for a brief moment Helena thought of her parents who were living in Boston at the time of the Vampocalypse. She never heard from them after the Great Turn and she could only hope they died quickly and painlessly. Then her husband Kasper entered her mind. He was always a good man and so good to…

Their daughters. Haley and Annika. Helena wanted to scream knowing Haley was enduring the same horrors she was, and the tears that came from that knowledge mixed with those from knowing Annika was facing an uncertain future alone. Helena tried to take a deep breath but found her breathing was no longer her own and was instead being controlled by whatever vile vital systems that both ravaged and managed her body.

Anxiety flooded through her as the thoughts of her family intensified…then retreated as a fogginess crept through her brain. The screams she wanted to scream and the tears she wanted to cry rapidly faded. The anxiety dissipated and any memories were tucked away as the files within her mind closed one at a time. A brightness and warmth washed over her then everything inside her head went dark. She didn't feel a thing as her pod was locked into place: just another featureless and faceless blood bag in the depths far below San Francisco Bay.

EPISODE 7

CAMP EXPECTATION
PACIFIC WASTELANDS

THE studio apartment was long and narrow and cloaked mostly in shadow. Barely four hours had passed since the downfall of Escape Town and night had crept across the Wastelands. The soft incandescent glow from outdoor lamps that lit Camp Expectation at night filtered in through half-closed window blinds. The lone window provided a small glimpse to the outside world three stories below while a single door on the opposite wall was the only way in or out. Thin swaths of light cut through the air, illuminating dust particles floating in the room. The room was bare – a single chair with side table were in the back left corner; a twin-sized bed ran along the right wall; there was a kitchenette just inside the door and to the left; and a small bathroom with toilet and shower stall like what could be found in an RV was hidden in a closet on the left wall. A small dresser sat outside the bathroom. The room was neat and tidy and the bare walls gave no indication from first look that anyone lived there.

Z stood in front of the dresser, staring at its barren top. She closed her eyes and took a deep breath and held it for several seconds before exhaling. Slowly she reached up and pulled open the top drawer. The drawer was half-filled with stacks of folded T-shirts mostly black or gray in color. She rummaged through the drawer lightly before closing it and opening the next drawer below. This drawer had folded undergarments and socks – along with a black cardboard box the size of a cigar box. She pulled the box out of the drawer and went and sat on the edge of the bed.

The box rested on Z's lap. She looked at it and took another long deep breath while she ran her fingers along the edges of the lid. Closing her eyes, she slowly exhaled. Her hands trembled ever so slightly as she reopened her eyes. With gentle fingers she removed the top of the box and set it aside. Inside the box was a dark green handkerchief that covered everything beneath it. She took the kerchief out of the box and put it on top of the box lid. There wasn't much inside the box. She pushed aside two blue buttons, a black ballpoint pen, a sunshine smiley face sticker, and two dice – she could only guess as to the relevance of each of the assorted items – before she touched what sat flat beneath them.

Z sat for a moment, contemplative. Her eyes blinked several times rapidly and one would have almost thought there was a tear in the corner of one of them. The glimpse was fleeting and probably a trick of the light. She pulled the flat, square item out of the box then set the box on the bed. She held the item with both of her hands as she stared up at the ceiling. Another deep breath. Slowly she looked down as she turned the item over.

It was a photograph. Judge, his wife, and daughters. They were smiling and the sun was shining bright in a clear blue sky. It was a family photo taken at a place Judge had told Z about called "Disneyland" – an almost mystical, if not at this time *mythical*, place that existed in a world of the distant past. Judge was so happy in this photo. He had shown it to her before – it was the only photo he had of his family, and it was the only photo Z knew that existed of Judge himself.

Her eyes narrowed as she stared at the man who was her adoptive father and protector for so many years – decades, even. Then she couldn't help the anger that surged through her. Anger at herself, at the circumstances, at Judge himself. How could he leave her like this? She always assumed their time together was numbered – in the post-Vampocalyptic world it was a wonder they had survived together as long as they did. But it was still so sudden, without warning.

And goddammit – why did he have to leave while they were angry at each other? Or, more accurately, while she was angry at him?

"You're not my father."

Z shook her head, slowly, then vigorously as her final words to him echoed through her head – bouncing off the walls of the small studio apartment, somehow growing louder in intensity as the words repeated over and over and over...

Goddamn you, Judge, for leaving me like this. Goddamn you for leaving me angry.

She knew, though, her anger wasn't really with him – it was mostly, if not entirely, with herself. She felt sorrow and regret and remorse and deep, deep sadness...but the right words wouldn't come. The sadness was different than what she remembered from when her family was slaughtered by vampires when she was four. Even though that happened so very long ago, somehow, it seemed to almost not be real. In many ways it was nothing more than a distant memory that felt like it could have belonged to someone else. This – Judge's death – was very real. Though it didn't shatter her, it made her feel more cold and disconnected to this world.

A knock on the door and a voice displaced her thoughts, the anger, and the grief. "The governor is ready to see you."

Z looked at the photo one more time before folding it in half and slipping it into a small pocket of her black tactical vest. She zippered the pocket then pressed down on its overlapping flap. She stood up from the bed and went to the door and gave the apartment one last, long look before opening it. On the outside of the door was a nameplate with "D. Judge" inscribed into it. She slid the nameplate out of its holder leaving a blank placard under room number 319.

Z barely glanced at the guard waiting outside the door as she said, "You can dispose of the rest. I have everything I need."

She walked down the indoor apartment hallway and dropped the nameplate into an open trash receptacle without a second glance. She passed by the elevator, opting instead to take the nearby stairs down to the ground floor and exit. The negative energy she was experiencing forced her to move, and taking the three flights down would help.

BEING out in the open air further helped Z clear her head and better compartmentalize her feelings surrounding Judge. As she walked across an open square between concrete and brick buildings, it struck Z how different life was here compared to what she saw at Escape Town despite some of the internal structures being similar. With approximately two thousand residents, Camp Expectation was about twice the size of Escape Town. There was the availability of electricity, a luxury not afforded by many human survivalist communities, and one not evidenced to have existed at the smaller town. Camp Expectation's walls were more fortified and its defense weaponry was clean, up-to-date, and functional. The entire town was surrounded by low foothills on all sides that provided a natural barrier and helped hide Camp Expectation from those who would spy from a distance.

Even though the sun had dipped away hours earlier, activity within Camp Expectation still thrived. Lights at night were reduced to a third of their usual glow, but that didn't stop some members of the community from organizing an outside gathering of several families. Other folks walked along the streets or rode bicycles while small electric golfcart-style vehicles transported those who preferred to be shuttled to their destinations. Life moved on – no one around her knew of Judge's sacrifice, no one knew the fresh pain she was going through.

Z approached the town hall and governor's council chamber, a large white structure that looked like it could have been built in the 1700s. A set of wide inclined steps led to a vast concrete landing with a smaller set of stairs leading up to a portico supported by four concrete pillars overhanging a set of doublewide entrance doors. Two guards stood out front, one on either side of the entrance, facing forward at full attention. Z stopped at the bottom of the stairs leading to the entrance and looked up. Even in the dark, low storm clouds could be seen floating in the night sky. She sniffed the air – the smell of oncoming rain was undeniable. Z guessed the outdoor community activities wouldn't be taking place much longer with rain coming in soon. As the town's master-at-arms, there was no need for Z to identify herself to the guards when she reached the top of the stairs. Each of the guards pulled open one of the heavy wooden doors, providing her immediate access, closing them right behind her as she entered the building.

"HE – it – was like nothing I'd ever seen." There was a slight apprehension in Z's words that surprised even Z herself.

Kylee Haddock, Governor of Camp Expectation, sat back in her tall leather chair and Z was settled into one of the two seats on the other side of her desk across from her. The governor's office was located off a hall adjacent to the main council chamber. There were no guards in this room – none were considered necessary – not that there was space to accommodate them. The office was small and barely fit the furniture, Kylee had described it in the past as "cozy," and had subdued lighting that sharpened both women's features. Gray and white tones filled the room and highlighted the geometric patterns carved into the concrete walls. There were no windows due to the space being located in the interior of the building itself.

Kylee ran her hand over her slicked-back gray-blonde hair, the tips of which barely touched the top of the collar of her gray jacket. She picked up a printout off a short stack of papers sitting in an open file folder on her desk and quickly looked it over.

"I've read your preliminary statement and report," Kylee said as she dropped the page back onto the desk. She looked at Z and squinted slightly. "Half-robot, half-vampire? I have no reason to doubt you, Z, you're my most trusted agent, but are you sure of what you saw? By your own account you were ripped off your motorcycle and the wind was knocked out of you. You probably have a concussion but you're too stubborn to have the doctor check you out." She leaned forward as far as she could with her elbows on her desk. "Within moments of being knocked off the bike you witnessed your father's –"

"*Adopted* father," Z corrected.

Kylee inhaled sharply through her nostrils. "Within moments you witnessed your *adopted* father commit suicide to save you. That's a lot of stress to go through."

Z stared blankly without any reaction. Kylee sighed and her features softened – a rare occurrence – as she looked deep into Z's eyes.

"I'm sorry about Judge. I truly am."

"I appreciate that." Z's tone was subdued but not sad.

"If you need some time –"

Z held up a hand to interrupt. "I've been through worse. I'll get through this." She preferred to avoid the subject altogether.

Kylee paused then put her fingertips together as the edges of her lips turned down. Her eyes focused on the bruises on Z's neck.

"Looks like you've been left with quite the souvenir."

The reminder flashed the image of Ryder Sloane through her mind – the monster snatching her by her throat off her motorcycle then slamming her to the ground so effortlessly. This quickly flipped to her final images of Judge as he…

"I said I'll be fine," Z stated sharply.

"Okay, okay," breathed Kylee, resigning herself to Z's unwillingness to discuss anything affecting her personally. *As usual.*

"This cybernetic vampire, where do you suppose it came from? And there was just the one?"

"Just the one, yes. He, it, was rounding people up for the blood banks and specifically mentioned the banks in San Francisco. My guess is it's based out of the mecca there."

Kylee sat back. "Most likely a creation of Stirling's. Who knows what freaks of nature he's developing to unleash upon this world."

Z sat upright in her chair. She looked down at the floor where she held her gaze for a couple of moments before slowly bringing her eyes up to Kylee.

"There's something else. Something I didn't put in the report." Z's words came out slowly as she selected her words carefully. Her eyes dropped again. "Something Judge told me."

Kylee cocked her head slightly, a nuance not unnoticed by Z.

"What is it?" Kylee asked. "What couldn't you possibly put in the report?"

Z's body language remained stiff as she moved to the edge of her seat. "He told me…" Trailing off, she paused and swallowed hard. Judge's words rattled in her head as much as they rattled her soul. This time when the words came out they were rapid fire – Z could barely contain them. "He said that the vampires have been after me because of my blood type, possibly for decades."

Kylee let the slightest beat pass before reacting. "I know."

Z bolted upright and could barely keep herself from leaping out her seat. "What?" she exclaimed. "You know? You've known this and never told me?"

Kylee blinked a long, lingering blink and slowly let out a deep breath before opening her eyes and finally answering.

"There was no good to come from you knowing. You'd have been in a constant paranoia, always looking over your shoulder. And for what? In the last thirty years no one has come knocking on the door for you. You would have spent your entire life worrying about nothing."

For every response that came to mind, Z thought twice and better about actually saying it. Her eyes were wide, staring in disbelief at the woman across the desk.

"You're a soldier, Zarina. You know that paranoia leads to mistakes, and mistakes lead to tombstones. I'm not ready to write your epitaph yet."

The tension in Z continued to rise. "What's so special about my blood type? Tell me everything you know."

Kylee shook her head. "I'm not sure." She tried to get a read through the anger in Z's eyes. "All we know is that vampires had been targeting those with AB negative blood since the Great Turn, but as to exactly why, there's been no real clue."

Z shook her head. She jumped up angrily and walked behind her seat. She leaned forward onto the back of the chair as she hung her head and breathed heavily. Kylee was right – nothing good would have come from her knowing. But, *dammit*, people she trusted knew this secret yet never made the effort to tell her. The anger building within her was rooted in an unshaking feeling of betrayal. All the while a conflicting logic tried to tell her this was just her loved ones trying to keep her safe. Still, sentiments to the contrary took up more of her consciousness than she cared to fight.

"You've always been my best." Kylee stood up but didn't move from behind her desk. Her posture eased in an effort to come across non-threatening and help Z relax. "I've always held you in the highest regard. That's why you're second to me here. I trust you in every way."

"Just not enough to trust me with the truth," Z seethed.

Now Kylee walked around the desk and chairs and stood next to her master-at-arms. She put a hand on Z's shoulder and gripped it tight.

"I recognized a strength and potential in you that I had not seen in anyone in a very long time. You've built a reputation of being ruthless and quick to the fight. You are a serious badass, Z. And I need you alive and alert."

The Russian woman looked slyly at the governor and Kylee thought there was a hint of a smile...a very, tiny, subtle hint, but it was there. They exchanged a knowing look and Kylee nodded.

"I understand, governor. No distractions."

Kylee pulled her hand away from Z's shoulder and went and sat back behind her desk while Z settled again into her own seat.

"Getting back to the matter at hand, there was a lot to glean from your report," Kylee said as she flipped through the loose papers in the folder in front of her before stopping on a specific page and holding it up. "This in particular. The cyborg-vampire was looking for someone."

"Yes, someone named Prater Saxon."

A slightly flushed look fell over Kylee, an expression Z had never seen on the governor before.

"Do you know who that is?" Z asked.

Kylee glanced through a few more of the pages then closed the folder.

"Maybe our new guest can help answer some of these questions," Kylee replied without answering the question.

"You mean the girl, Annika?"

"Yes, I haven't heard any recent updates. Do you know how she's doing?"

"I had left her with Dr. Cleary."

"We should pay her a visit."

"It's late, governor, and she's been through a lot. Don't you think we should let her get some rest? We can meet up with her in the morning."

"The wicked never sleep, Z. Every moment we wait is a moment lost to the fight."

Z slid to the edge of her chair and leaned forward with her elbows on her knees.

"She's sixteen-years-old and just lost her entire family. Excuse me for being protective but if anyone has any idea what she's going through, it's me. She needs to rest."

Kylee studied Z's expression. She could see the sincerity in the woman's eyes and understood in ways that Z had no way of knowing.

"You have an affinity for the girl. Good. For the time being you're going to be the girl's caretaker. You've both lost a lot – I understand that. I think it'll be good for you to have each other."

Z's eyes relaxed and she sat back. She was not in any way opposed to the idea. The girl had no one, and really, neither did she. They would be good to have each other, at least for now. Her face sharpened again.

"As her caretaker, then, I'm going to insist we wait until tomorrow to meet with her. She's no good to us if she isn't allowed to recover and be healthy."

Kylee picked a silver pen up from her desk and twirled it meticulously between her fingers.

"Understood," Kylee said. "Get with her in the morning. Be sure she's cleaned up and comfortable and get her some breakfast. I'll meet with the two of you once she's good and ready."

"Thank you."

"It's been a long day. You take care of yourself as well."

Z stood up. The two women exchanged final niceties before Z left the office, closing the door behind her, leaving Kylee alone.

Kylee held the pen in her hand upright just a few inches from the center of her eyes. She focused on it and her forehead wrinkled a little. The room was intensely quiet with the only sound being that of her light breathing. She stood up and turned to face the concrete wall behind her. The three-dimensional geometric designs cut into the wall overlapped and seemed randomly placed yet managed to all work together like a hundred instruments in a large orchestra creating a singular harmonious sound.

Kylee ran a finger along the wall until she found a small hole located just off center of the middle. She inserted the pen into the hole until it stopped, leaving half of it sticking out. She turned it three times and as she did a tiny metallic clicking could be heard faintly from within the wall. After the third turn the pen stopped and instead of a "click" there was more of a "clang" and she removed the pen from the wall. The heavy sound of concrete scraping against concrete filled the office as a section in the center of the wall the size of a door slid back and away, revealing a dark opening. Kylee slipped into the darkness just as the concrete access moved back into place, leaving the gray and white office silent and empty.

PRATER

FIFTEEN years. Half my life. That's how long I spent under Kylee's care before I left. For fifteen years I was under her guardianship and tutelage. Kylee's the one who raised me — teaching me, training and preparing me for this world. Some would call it a "cruel" world; to me, though, it's simply the only world I've ever known. Ky — the name I called her as an infant and the one that remained as our special connection (I was the only one to ever call her that) — was herself versed in survivalist ways before the days of the Great Turn. She taught me how to hunt (like a human, that is, as there were plenty of opportunities that allowed me to give in to a more feral animal side out in the Wastelands), and how to survive alone in the wild.

After being taken to a holding facility on Joint-Base Lewis McChord following the days the bombs dropped, Ky spent little time allowing us to be shuffled from one shelter to the next before finally giving up on whatever shoestring government claimed to have jurisdiction of the area. The reality at the time was that there was no coordinated government. There was no infrastructure in place to support the various pockets of survivors to communicate, let alone providing any way to organize into any unified body. The truth was that it was every person, every group for themselves. Any local leaders were fooling themselves if they felt their ways were the only ways, let alone the "right" ways. Following the Vampocalypse, Ky grew weary of the either disorganization or narcissism of whichever group we were shuttled to next. It wasn't long before she took off on her own with a two-year old me in her care, to fend for ourselves in the Wastelands.

It was during our time alone that my real education began as Ky prepared me to not simply survive, but actually live in this world. She maintained her teachings as we filled the role, like so many disparate others, of nomads in the Pacific Wastelands. Ky always remained wary and distrusting of others, even when we were taken in by friendly groups of strangers. Her cautiousness and way of not staying in one place for long became ingrained into me. It wasn't just her teachings, though, that prepared me for survival as a loner in the desolate wastes. That's why I had no qualms the day I decided to leave at age fifteen.

Even though Ky taught me how to shoot a gun, I always felt more comfortable fighting with swords – knowing I never needed to reload was comforting. The man who gave me my first katana and taught me how to use them was one of very few people I ever called a friend. Up until the time I went out on my own, there were only two people I ever considered to be true friends. Ky, who of course was also my adoptive mother, was my best friend in the post-Vampocalypse world. The other was Master Rin Miyamoto.

I was seven-years old when we came across a small community of about three hundred called Expanse Village. This was by far the largest group we had encountered and we did our best to be covert as we monitored the open camp from afar. Ky insisted on being extra cautious as a group this size could obviously easily overwhelm us. She wanted to do her best to ensure they weren't hostile, as well as to formulate the best way for us to show we also didn't pose any danger. Our intentions to initiate an approach were cut short as a scouting team discovered us and brought us into the encampment under guard after taking our weapons.

The first person we met once inside was the leader of the camp and the man who would become my master, Rin Miyamoto. It didn't take long for Master Miyamoto and Ky to strike up a strong rapport. We were accepted as members of the camp and our weapons were returned to us. It also didn't take too long for Ky to decide our nomadic life was through, having found this group of welcoming, likeminded survivors. I can't say I didn't really mind.

Master Miyamoto always had a genuinely kind smile – the kind that opened you up to instantly trusting the face behind the expression. Ky taught me to always be careful around such smiles, but in this case, Master Miyamoto proved time and again to be honest and sincere in everything he said and everything he did. I spent many years learning under Miyamoto, increasing not only my skills but my discipline as a student of the blade. We would spar with our swords – sometimes each of us wielding single blades, other times with two – and my efforts were always feeble. I could never best *my master during any of my trials. There were times, when I was especially young, when I would get mad and actually ask, at times practically beg, my master to just let me win. Just once. But he always refused, telling me, "If I allow you to win, you learn nothing, earning only the emptiness of an imaginary victory."*

The fire that Ky instilled into me that drove me to survive was the other side to the calm and coolness Master Miyamoto taught me. It was because of the friendship and trust we built over the years that led me to one day when I was thirteen, with Ky's blessing, confide in Master Miyamoto the fact of my being part-vampire. I'll never forget the look he gave me – an almost knowing with an underlying curiosity. He vowed to never repeat this truth about me and the honor he demonstrated through the years affirmed my belief that my secret would always be safe with him.

It was our deep friendship and trust in one another that made it so hard for Miyamoto to tell me that Kylee was dead.

I was fifteen when the attack came, in the middle of the night, nearly eight years to the day from when we first came upon the camp. The attack was as brutal as it was fast. The people fought valiantly but were no match for the might of the bloodsuckers and their enhanced abilities. When the dust settled, all hope for Expanse Village was lost. Most of its residents were gone, having presumably been taken away to the blood banks to become sustenance for the undead.

Some of us, myself included, had scattered into a heavier wooded area nearby in an effort to escape from the invaders. I sheathed my katana into the X-shaped holder strapped to my back and ran as fast as my legs would carry me. In the darkness and mayhem I got separated from Ky and Master Miyamoto. I could only hope they were safe as I sprinted through the trees, my enhanced vampire eyesight allowing me to see in the dark of the night as I created my own path through the until then undisturbed dirt and shrubs of the forested grounds.

A sharp pain shot through my chest every time I inhaled as my body fought to press forward despite exhaustion fighting to take hold. I would occasionally steal glances behind me to reassure myself that no one was following. Several looks later and still no one appeared to be coming for me. I kept telling myself "Just one more look back, just one more look back…" as I tried to talk myself into feeling safe so I could finally slow down. As I looked behind me for what I told myself was going to be the final time, my feet suddenly felt nothing but air. In the millisecond that followed I realized I had come out of the trees and stepped off a cliffside and into a fathom of nothingness. What I didn't know, though, was that Master Miyamoto had been running through the trees as well in a path almost parallel to mine. His strong hand grabbed me by the collar and yanked me away from the cliff and certain death. We tumbled together to the ground. I laid there with my heart pounding deafeningly in my ears and my breathing more shallow and quicker than ever.

It was in the light of the next morning, as we searched for any fellow survivors, Master Miyamoto told me Ky was dead. The emotional hopelessness that came from hearing those words was worse than the physical helplessness I felt when I stepped unknowingly off the cliff.

"How did it happen?" I asked. My words were barely finished when Master Miyamoto was nodding with his eyes down.

"She was impaled and carried away." He paused, still looking down. "She wasn't moving."

Grief. Shock. Emptiness. All at once. I couldn't help but cry in front of the group. Despite the best efforts of Master Miyamoto, I was inconsolable. I was like this, off and on, over the next few hours as the emptiness inside was eventually replaced by a thick fog of blind anger. Master Miyamoto immediately cautioned me from allowing strong emotions to take control. I could have easily allowed hate to consume me but with Master Miyamoto's help I was able to refocus myself to stay present and control the pain.

After the revelation of Ky's death, we located a handful of other survivors. All told there were just fourteen of us remaining. We were all grieving in our own ways but knew our lives were meant to go on, at least in those moments. So we trudged forward, meandering in the wastes with little rhyme or reason other than to just try and stay alive. In the end I was left stronger by the loss of my mother – the woman had not given birth to me but was my mother nonetheless – though sorting through the emotions afterwards left me quiet and distant. I was never the overly extroverted type but Ky's death forever changed me.

It was then, after a week of returning to the nomad life with the other Expanse Village survivors, that I knew it was time for me to go. Master Miyamoto took the news with a stern face, showing no indications of remorse. He did nothing to try and stop me – he respected me too much for that. He said he understood my decision, even at my relatively young age, and made sure there wasn't anything I needed. So I left, quietly and unceremoniously sneaking away as the group prepared to setup camp for the evening.

It would not be the first time I would walk away from something in my life without looking back.

*** Priority Brief ***

NORTH AMERICAN FREEDOM ALLIANCE
DEPARTMENT OF HUMAN RESOURCES COMMAND

*** CLASSIFIED DOCUMENTATION: *EYES ONLY* ***

FROM THE DESK OF: GENERAL OLIVER KAUR
SUBJECT: OPERATION TWILIGHT FURY

The following report was collected from a variety of sources including live monitoring via audio/visual body transmitters, high altitude drone footage, long-range infrared heat scanners, and periodic reports from members of Special Ops Team Bloodforce Four involved with Operation Twilight Fury.

ACTION: Members of Special Ops Team Bloodforce Four infiltrated the vampire submarine base at former Naval Base Point Loma in San Diego, in the former State of California, officially initiating Operation Twilight Fury, and effectively taking control of the nuclear *Annihilator*-class vampire submarine *Harbinger One*.

BACKGROUND: The sole, ongoing mission of the global fleet of *Annihilator*-class vessels is to periodically deploy nuclear devices either in the atmosphere or in areas unpopulated by vampires to ensure the ongoing nuclear winter does not break and allow direct sunlight to reach the Earth. The *Harbinger One* was in preparations for imminent deployment to perform these routine detonations which provided a prime opportunity to commandeer the vessel.

The order of events that occurred during the acquisition of the *Harbinger One* was as follows:

At approximately 0300: The 17-member Special Ops Team Bloodforce Four reached the entrance to the sub base. Security was comprised of just two vampire guards in each of the two guard towers, along with two additional guards on the ground at the chain link fence gate entrance itself. The grounds were otherwise empty during this time of the morning.

Four members of Special Ops Team Bloodforce Four were lost while fighting to gain entrance through the gate. Two vampire guards were stationed at the entrance to the dock walkway leading to the *Harbinger One* itself and were disposed of by the Special Ops Team upon approach.

By 0313: The team boarded the submarine through its forward hatch then divided into four small teams. Teams Bravo and Charlie secured the radio and sonar rooms while Delta and Echo secured control and navigation rooms. From then, missile control along with the crew and officer areas were secured.

Vampire resistance was minimal as the Team worked through various parts of the vessel. Despite this, two additional members of Bloodforce Four were lost to the fighting that occurred while commandeering the submarine.

By 0350: The vessel was under full control of Special Ops Team Bloodforce Four and headed to sea towards its target destination of San Francisco Bay.

NOTATIONS: The submarine's missile control systems were irreparably damaged during the fight that ensued for control of the vessel. As a result, use of **Directive AA-17** was authorized.

Directive AA-17 permits manual detonation of nuclear devices on board the *Harbinger One* while in closest achievable proximity to the *target*. Manual detonation is accomplished via use of the programming datapad brought aboard the vessel by Special Ops Team Bloodforce Four. This datapad contains specially designed applications that allow the team to locally access and initiate the detonation commands.

The *Harbinger One* is currently *enroute* to San Francisco Bay with an ETA of 2100 hours this evening. Detonation is set to occur once the *Harbinger One* reaches specified target points in the Bay. Additional details will follow pending further developments.

*** End Brief ***

EPISODE 8

SAN FRANCISCO MECCA
NORTH AMERICA NEW WORLD TERRITORIES VAMPIRE CAPITOL

OF all the vampire mecca-cities in the North America New World Territories, San Francisco Mecca was the largest. The mecca-cities were where vampires congregated and lived on each of the continents after the Great Turn. Initially beginning as sanctuaries for the masses who were distraught or confused (or both) by what they had suddenly become, over time those in charge under the will of the new vampire leadership quickly organized the areas into what became highly modernized, thriving communities tens of millions strong. Each mecca-city was largely self-contained when it came to resources and supplies – each city had its own blood bank megafarm located just adjacent – negating most of the need for vampires to move or travel between cities. Personal automobiles were abolished, and public transportation systems were utilized in all areas except for those in prominence. Most vampires kept to their own mecca, though airplanes and railways did exist for those who still had a necessity for traveling to other places. While many vampires could fly of their own volition, that was a limited ability best served for short distances.

In many ways, vampires lived the types of lives humans used to: there were jobs and commerce and recreation. Most were civilized – working to maintain any sense of normalcy despite their newfound immortalities – while those that were feral to the point of unproductivity were quietly rounded up and "handled." There were the vampire equivalent of families with, not too infrequently, multiple partnerships that crossed genders. Some families had vampire children: many used to be human prior to the Great Turn but were now forever trapped in a child's body no matter what their age. And while vampires could not breed, there were legalized adoption centers that provided human children conceived and raised on farms just for the purpose of being sold and, when the vampire parents were ready, turned.

What many considered to be the classic San Francisco skyline was mostly gone. The buildings were there but many had been renovated by vampire architects providing for a contrasting patchwork of glistening chrome-covered towers mixed with structures covered in dark glass. The Transamerica Pyramid and the Salesforce Tower – the two tallest buildings in the city – were now barely shadows of their former respective magnificence. Their once unique and inviting designs now stood like two dark monoliths encompassed in black glass and puncturing the burnt skies in a way their original human architects could never have envisioned.

The buildings were connected by a passageway that itself was a marvel of engineering. Suspended five hundred feet in the air, the corridor was as wide as each building and spanned the near mile distance between the two structures, supported on its direct path by half a dozen immense black columns. It had a curved ceiling with hidden recessed lighting that ran the length of the hall, providing an ambient glow to the faces of those who made their way between the skyscrapers. Travelators, or moving sidewalks, ran along the outer sides as well as down the middle of the wide hallway while there were pathways for small electric vehicles that could carry up to four passengers. Those who could fly drifted overhead as the high ceiling allowed for four "lanes" of sky traffic. Altogether, the large, imposing structure of the connected dark towers provided the seat of government as the capitol building for the North American New World Territories.

IT was early morning following the storm. The rains had cleared, leaving San Francisco Mecca under a blanket of fog not uncharacteristic of the Bay Area even in the post-Vampocalypse. President Jonathan Stirling and his advisors walked steadily down the middle travelator, though the smooth-moving motorized sidewalk did most of the work getting them towards the Transamerica Pyramid tower portion of the capitol building. The corridor wasn't terribly busy so early in the morning and Stirling set a purposeful pace. Passersby at most would provide a polite smile and nod, knowing better than to approach their president unless initially summoned. Stirling almost always made sure to at the very least smile in return, when not involuntarily gnashing or biting at the air, acting very much still the politician that he – even in this world – needed to be.

"President Yaromir Volkov of the USVR and King Mbarek Zewde of the Africa Vampire Alliance finally confirmed their attendance early this morning," said Vice President Andrea McCullough. The former secretary of state relished the new role appointed to her thirty years ago by Stirling. "Nothing like waiting until the last minute. They need to be on a plane already to make it in time."

Unfortunately, not everyone was as thrilled with the vice president's promotion.

"I wouldn't sound so proud of this meeting you've put together, Andrea," said Senator Elite Samuel Ellis. The title of "senator elite" was a position created as successor to the presidency behind the vice president following the dissolution of the House and Senate as part of the government restructuring after the Vampocalypse. Samuel was never fully satisfied with the title, figuring full well he had little to no chance of increasing his position of power since there were no term limits or – in the case of vampires – life expectancies.

"These leaders can be contentious," Samuel went on. "They are strong personalities each with their own opinions and sometimes their emotions get the better of them. Do we really want such a power play all together in one room?" The senator elite, in contrast to the fit and forever 37-year-old vice president, had added some substantial weight to his "middle aged" body over the last thirty years. He lumbered on with the group without protest though each labored step did take him some additional effort.

Andrea continued to look forward as she addressed the senator elite. "Really, Samuel, I'm growing tired of your constant bashing of this summit. There's nothing to be concerned with and you know it. This in-person meeting is sorely needed to not only maintain but strengthen relations between the global territories." She shifted her eternally bloodshot green eyes to her fellow politician, "I think you're just jealous of how well this project of mine is going."

Samuel stammered as he tried to formulate what to say next. "You don't know what you're talking about. Regardless of your position, you're always going to exist in my shadow."

Andrea put no effort into stifling a laugh. "That's not hard considering how well fed you're staying. It's a good thing Mr. Titus found a way to increase our blood supplies."

Samuel let out a loud huff as his large body turned to face the vice president. He snarled as he raised a threatening talon high in the air. President Stirling stopped walking and held up a hand. The small group continued to move down the corridor as the travelator did its work. The president looked back and forth at his companions with a sneer of disgust – Andrea on his left and Samuel on his right. His personal aide, Councilor Marques Wright, stood just behind him.

"That's enough," Stirling commanded. "This constant bickering between the two of you has grown beyond tiresome through the ages." His eyes rested on Andrea. "You've done a fine job putting this meeting together." Then he looked at Samuel. "I agree it's a meeting long overdue. I'll hear nothing else to the contrary."

Samuel stifled a grumble and simply nodded. Stirling resumed his stride and the group once again followed along.

"Thank you, Jonathan," said Andrea as she shot a triumphant glance past Stirling and at the senator elite. Samuel shot back an incensed expression. Andrea smiled as she continued, "Everything is set. Soon the entire world will be watching as we come together in a display of unity never demonstrated, not even by humans in their time. Councilor Wright, do you have an update on the itinerary?"

"Yes, thank you, Madame Vice President," said the councilor. "The delegates are all due to arrive over the next eight hours. All the details along with full itineraries have been downloaded to your datapads."

Stirling turned and looked Andrea straight on. "It has taken a long time, over two decades, to get the populations in line and under control since the Great Turn. I'm thrilled this summit is finally coming together and you have been an integral part of that process." He faced forward again as he continued to lead the group down the still moving travelator. "There was so much turmoil following the Vampocalypse. Far too many fought against their newfound existence and instead became vicious and feral and needed to be brought in line. So many lost their lives because of it." He shook his head in disgust. "Cold, senseless deaths. For that," now he glanced back at the senator elite, "I have you to thank."

"It wasn't an easy feat," Samuel said with a glimmer of pride. "After the Great Turn it was difficult restructuring the DoD squads to being an all-vampire faction –"

Andrea couldn't keep herself from letting out another chuckle.

"Do you have something to add?" Samuel frothed at the vice president, clearly annoyed at the interruption.

"Nothing, Samuel, nothing at all other than I remember you being so fond of your little kill division. It was just a pity their relevance went away as quickly as humanity turned."

Samuel was about to reply to the vice president's quip when a sharp look from Stirling made him think better of it.

"As I was saying," Samuel continued as he chose to move on from Andrea's taunts. "There needed to be a new way to bring the population of savages under control. It turned out to not be too difficult getting a vampire military in line with us as most of the generals were loyal to you, Jonathan, before the Great Turn. The matter assimilating the newturns as part of the new vampire society took some time. Thankfully, the wills and minds of most were open to their newfound existences and brought themselves in line."

"This still took considerable time," Stirling added. He gnawed at the air and had a look of fire in his eyes. "Over two decades of guidance, prodding, and action, we finally are close to realizing the vampire vision I have held for millennia. The upcoming summit will be where I solidify my vision into a global state."

The group continued and the end of the travelator was finally coming near.

"Something I've remained unsure about, Jonathan," Samuel said after some silence. "I've always wondered why we abandoned our pursuit of the AB negatives? You had a portion of my DoD squads looking for those humans for some time only to abandon the orders without warning. I thought the ABs were needed as part of your daybreak initiative?"

Stirling's eyes maintained straight ahead. "According to Dr. Deuteronicus decades of research on those humans and development of the AB negatives have led nowhere. As of now, capturing Prater Saxon is the only way."

"And you have a way of tracking this Saxon down?"

One side of Stirling's jowls twitched. "I've sent my personal enforcer to capture and bring him to me."

Samuel couldn't contain a sardonic tone. "I can't say I'm very confident in this pet of yours you've created, Jonathan. Its results so far have been uneven at best. You expect this to be any different?"

Stirling finally looked at the senator elite. "He will get the job done."

The look the president shot Samuel meant the conversation was closed.

The group reached the end of the travelator, and they were deposited off the moving walkway and under a large gold arch that spanned the width of the wide passage. As they entered the former Transamerica Pyramid portion of the capitol building, Stirling led the group to a set of nearby elevators and pressed the "down" button on one of the control panels.

"There are still many specifics to discuss before tonight," Andrea said, directing her comment at the president. "First and foremost, we need to review the itinerary in detail. I was hoping we could continue this discussion now in your office?"

Marques Wright leaned in towards Stirling slightly. "Sir, we have our meeting with General Sloane."

Andrea looked at the councilor curiously. It seemed increasingly as of late, the councilor often would monopolize or otherwise engage the president in his own matters, seeming to put his own needs and interests ahead of others.

"I haven't forgotten," he said before looking at Andrea. "We'll set a meeting time to complete this discussion later today. Right now, I have a personal matter to attend to."

"Of course, Mr. President," Andrea replied, formally. She gave the councilor a final side-eye that went unnoticed by everyone.

The elevator doors opened with a silky hiss and Stirling stepped inside alone.

"That's it, then," the president said, providing a close to the conversation. "Marques, clear my calendar after 2PM and set a meeting to review the itinerary. And I'll meet with you and the general shortly."

"Yes, sir," Marques replied in his usual quiet yet smooth tone.

"Perfect." Stirling barely got out the word as the elevator doors closed, happily cutting him off from his advisors and leaving them to their own disputes, distrusts, and disagreements.

AFTER the doors shut, Stirling placed a fingertip on a small square reader recessed into the elevator control panel. This caused a second reader, this one on a display that was shoulder height, to come to life displaying a series of green dots and squares. Stirling stared into the center of the display with both eyes, unblinking, as the green shapes flashed on his irises as a secondary identification measure. His identity was confirmed as the console beeped in affirmation and the elevator began a rapid descent. The control panel quickly showed the floor numbers dropping from floors in the 40s, down past the 30s, 20s, 10s, and finally reaching zero. The elevator didn't stop there, however. Instead, the elevator continued dropping several more stories underground before finally coming to a stop. The doors slid open to a long, straight, and narrow walkway, barely lit with walls and floor carved out of rock.

The elevator doors remained open even after Stirling stepped into the passageway. The corridor was cold and each breath Stirling exhaled lingered heavy in the air before dissipating. The click of his heels echoed off the closed-in walls as he traversed the dark hall, not needing any additional lighting as his keen vampire eyesight more than made up for the shadows that tucked away in the corners along the floor and ceiling.

At the end of the hallway was a heavy steel door with no handles or features. Stirling removed a very weathered antique brass hollow-barrel key from a pocket hidden in the inside lining of his suit jacket. He inserted the key into a steel plate mounted in the right wall by the door and turned it with a metal clank. He pushed gently on the door, and it swung back effortlessly and smooth without a sound despite being so heavy. The room on the other side was wide and rectangular – about the dimensions of a high school gym. The space was fifteen-feet high and carved entirely out of the deep underground rock. Lighting sconces recessed and partially covered in the ceiling offered a gentle glow to the sparse space. The light showed the floor and ceiling to be flat and smooth but the surrounding walls were so dark one couldn't discern if the walls themselves were black or if they were actually deep shadows hiding mysteries known only to Stirling.

There was a single item in the room. Positioned in the middle of the wide rear wall of the chamber was a cylindrical compartment resting waist-high horizontally on a stand composed from shards of obsidian. The stand was illuminated from within by dull bluish lamps hidden among its spiky black rocks. Stirling's footsteps echoed through the large, dark room as he approached the stand.

The room was silent for the longest time, with only the sound of Stirling's own breathing sounding in his ears. He ran a hand along the top of the black compartment, though from this angle it looked much more reminiscent of a casket. The dark chest had rounded edges and was spotless and shiny as if brand new. Stirling moved his fingers along one long edge until he felt an area with a slight impression. The slightest pressure on the invisible button and half of the lid lifted up with a faint hiss then slid aside, leaving half of the compartment open. A dark red glow emanated from within, illuminating its sole occupant.

The remains inside were not entirely human. The creature was certainly human-*oid*, but the remains were twisted and stretched in parts across its chest and abdomen. One arm and one leg were almost entirely missing leaving misshapen, melted stumps making it look as if the limbs had somehow dissolved away. The body was blackened nearly all over and hairless, and covered in scars as if burned in a fire. Large, sickly, petrified boils ran up and down one side of the creature's face and upper body. The hand that remained was curled into itself but the ten-inch long talons that protruded from the fingertips were clearly visible.

The creature's face was a contorted parody of any humanity that may have ever resided within. The jaws were elongated beyond that of a normal human. Its thin, burnt lips were peeled away, exposing nearly three-inch long fangs. Its nostrils were partially melted into the leathery, sunken cheeks on either side. The ears were mostly gone, lost to whatever intense trauma brought demise to the creature.

The body itself, contorted as it was, did not rest flat on the bottom of the casket. Rather, the unholy remnants laid haphazardly atop a set of crispened appendages protruding out of the creature's back. One looked complete as it was as wide and long as the aberration's body while its companion looked to have been torn in half and was partially missing. The "wings" added to the abnormality of the abomination, separating it even further from anything remotely describable as human.

Stirling ran the back of his hand gently along one of the creature's cheeks as he looked into its eyes – eyes that somehow were still vibrant violet pupils despite having not seen life for millennia. The purple eyes would have otherwise still looked alive if not surrounded by dusty, dark red sclerae long since dried-up over time.

"Oh, My Lord, My Almighty, My Master," Stirling said in an almost chant-like mantra. "I vowed to you the Age of the Vampire would come. I not only foresaw this, but I made it happen. It was a long time coming, My Lord, My Master, but time was all we had on our side until the world had the technology to make the promise a reality."

Stirling took a hand and gently gripped the creature's chin as he leaned in close and stared deep into the monster's long dead eyes.

"Soon, My Master, My Almighty," his voice was barely above a whisper as he spoke intently to the dead creature, "I will unite our vampire brothers and sisters from around the world into one. Then our visions of a vampire world will finally be fulfilled."

Stirling's breathing deepened as he looked intently at the creature before leaning forward and kissing the dead, black monster on its exposed fangs. The kiss didn't linger although Stirling relished in a euphoria he felt at such an intimate touch with the creature. Slowly, Stirling moved his lips away from the monster's dry, cracked mouth and gently to its neck. He felt his heartrate quicken in anticipation…then he plunged his fangs into the neck of the dead. Drawing on nothing but dry, dusty essence, the sensation was enough to send waves of hyperstatic warmth coursing through his body as he "fed." After several moments he pulled away and stood up straight, wide-eyed and salivating uncontrollably.

"I wish you could have lived to see this day, My Master, My Holy One. You came to this world for a reason and I believe this is it. You selected me as your Successor, your Chosen One. I was the first of this world upon your arrival to fall under the grace of your kind, the kind of the *vampire*. And for three thousand years I have served you even in your death. And know this, My Lord, My Almighty, I have won this world for the way of the vampire and for you."

Stirling closed his eyes and let out a bloodcurdling inhuman screech that echoed loudly through the chamber as he raised his hands high in the darkness. His claws extended to their fullest and his teeth exposed themselves to their mighty length. His skin rippled and bubbled as he felt his full vampire endorphins course through him. Blood welled in his eyes before finally releasing in thick red trails down his cheeks. More blood simultaneously surged from his nostrils and ears, from the corners of his mouth, and from under his fingernails. He continued to scream in ecstasy as the elation became overwhelming and almost impossible to control. He brought his arms in and dropped to his knees as his body shook and convulsed and quivered and his cries of pleasure slowed to a whisper. His breath remained heavy for several minutes as his body recovered from the throes of the unholy pleasure he had just experienced. The bleeding stopped and his claws and fangs returned to their docile lengths. The room was once again quiet except for the sound of Stirling's own, low breathing.

The vampire president stood and looked again into the coffin at his *master*. He kissed two fingertips then placed them on the fangs of the dead creature.

"Soon, My Master, My High One, the unification of all vampirekind will be complete. Soon, our destiny will be fulfilled."

PRATER

NINE days had passed since I left the kindness and hospitality of Escape Town. It was very nice of them to allow me to stay for the evening, but I sensed some dishonesty among the townspeople. Something about their leader Jim Elliott didn't sit right with me. It seemed as if he would sell the town out in a minute – he just dripped of distrust. Of course, who was I, an outsider with just a few hours to have made that judgment, to determine that of a leader of such a small, tightknit community?

There was one among them, Kasper, who seemed to challenge the duplicity of the leader. His eyes radiated an honesty that far eluded Jim Elliott. At one point he mentioned his wife and daughters, but I never met any of them. When Kasper asked me where I was headed after spending just one night at Escape Town, I felt comfortable letting him know.

"I'm looking for a place called Camp Expectation. You know where that is?"

"Never heard of it." I could tell Kasper really wanted to know more. "What takes you there?" he asked.

"I hear it's south," I said. Unfortunately for him, he'll forever be wondering. "So I guess that's where I'm headed."

I closed the top of my leather satchel that I filled with two water bottles and some food Kasper gave me then slung the bag over my head, allowing the satchel itself to rest on my left hip. I said good-bye to Kasper and a few of the townspeople I encountered on my way out. Jim Elliott did not see me off.

Over the course of the next week and then some I continued across the desert sea of dirt, sand, and brush. Wildlife provided nourishment as it almost always did in the Wastelands – I was particularly lucky one night to come across a red fox. This felt like a prize after feeding mostly on cottontail rabbits for so long (the rabbits just tended to be more plentiful). I was always careful to kill the animal as humanely as possible, despite an inner urge…an inner instinct…to want to ravage and tear into the hapless creatures. I also saw the benefit of taking care to keep as clean as possible. The last thing I wanted to do was to show up among humans covered in dried animal blood because I couldn't control my feeding urges.

On the eve of the tenth day, I saw a fire in the distance. I crouched low to the ground and crept towards it slowly. It was a good few hundred yards away, but my vampire eyesight had no problem focusing in on its details, even through the dark sunglasses that I wore. It was a single, small blaze with just one person sitting next to it. I scanned the darkness around the fire as far as my augmented vision would allow and as far as I could tell the person was alone. In the wastes you could never be too careful of traps and decoys – persons seeming alone and in trouble but who are actually bait. So far, this didn't appear to be the case. Still, I approached stealthily with one sword drawn and held firmly with both hands, maintaining a more squatted position, stepping one foot carefully in front of the other.

The closer I came to the fire and the lone individual, the more the situation felt very familiar. As the distance between us narrowed, details of the person came into sharper focus. He was in his late teens or early twenties and looked like he hadn't bathed in weeks, perhaps months. The choppy cut of his short beard looked to be an extension of the uneven cut of his equally choppy hair. It wasn't terribly cool this evening and the young man had a jacket laying at his side and I could see the torn Led Zeppelin T-shirt that he wore.

I suddenly remembered this person. The young man named Jake I encountered in the barrens three years or so ago. He looked the same. It was a wonder how he had survived so long on his own. When we last met he had come across my fire and encampment. This time, it was the opposite. I hoped he was as friendly now as he was then.

"Mind if I join you?"

I wasn't surprised that the young man about soiled himself from being so startled when I spoke. After all, I was suddenly at the edge of his encampment without warning. The whiteness of his face and the wideness of his eyes were in a petrified state of shock as he jumped around to put the fire between us. His jaw dropped and the nearly exhausted cigarette he was smoking clung momentarily onto his lower lip like the final leaf hanging onto a tree in autumn before falling into the fire. He held up a six-inch knife, trying to come off as if he was prepared to use it (although I seriously doubted he had ever been in a life or death encounter with a vampire, let alone even a fist fight with another person, from the looks of him). I sheathed my sword and held my open hands up in front of me.

"Easy, easy. I was wondering if you wouldn't mind a bit of company."

The knife that was shaking in the young man's hand became more steady. His eyes narrowed as he glared at me from across the fire.

"Hey – those are my sunglasses!"

I admit, that made me want to smile, but I didn't offer to give them back.

"Hey…I remember you." The man lowered his knife and the quiver in his voice settled. "Your name's Prater, right? I remember that. Yeah, your name's Prater."

The young man laughed and threw his arms up and down. He practically hopped as he came halfway back around the fire.

"You prolly thought I was sleeping when you told me your name. But I don't sleep much and I remember you. Not sure if you remember me, my name's –"

"Jake," I interrupted. "Of course I remember you."

Jake sat back in his place next to the fire and grabbed the case of his knife and sheathed it. He held it up for me to see.

"I can't thank you enough for leaving this for me. I can't thank you enough."

"No problem."

"Go 'head and sit down."

I sat right where I was with my legs crossed and rested my wrists on my knees. I stared at the nearby flames as they danced through the shade of the sunglasses I wore – Jake's sunglasses. Jake watched me watching the fire and for several long moments there was only the crackle of the flames filling the silence.

"You've been out here all this time alone?" I finally asked, tilting my head in Jake's direction.

"Uh-huh, yep. Just me."

The young man blinked several times as his eyes danced between me and the fire. I remembered Jake being a bit aloof when we last met, but there was something in his expression that showed the years of loneliness and the scars from constantly living in fear. He bit his lower lip and chewed on it to the point of drawing a tinge of blood. The smell of the human blood (even so tiny and from that distance) instantly infiltrated every bit of me, filling me with an essence I had not experienced for several months – an essence that awakened nerves and fibers in me that I had to fight to control. My nostrils flared and my fangs wanted to show themselves in preparation of a feast. Blood pulsed through the veins of the whites of my eyes as I blinked to fend off the sensations. I took deep, controlled breaths and closed my eyes as the blood in them subsided, returning the sclerae to their normal white.

"I'm impressed," I said softly as I exhaled a deep breath. "I'm sure it wasn't easy."

"Ha! Tell me about it. But here I am. Talking to you on this fine night." He gave me a hard stare. "Who'da thought we'd run into each other again out here? I mean, what are the odds?"

I understood too well what it was like to be alone. By far I'd lived most of the last fifteen years alone. Looking out for just me made every situation easier to end, whether in battle or in the barrens. There was a little part of me though, admittedly, that did seek solace with the comfort of others. I think it brought back a nostalgic warmth of the times when I had friends – well, thought I had friends and those I could trust – until they killed the one person I loved. For the longest time after that I kept to myself. As the years passed, as I would come across other survivors I found ways to be cordial and make good acquaintances – but always for a limited time. Trust unbelonging and relationships unbinding always took over and I would cut ties and say good-byes with no regrets and without ever looking back.

Jake clapped his hands and bellowed another laugh, this one loud enough to cause me pause. It wasn't enough that the fire could potentially bring unwanted visitors but making noise on top of that was an unnecessary gamble. I think he sensed my concern as his eyes settled on me.

"Shhh!" He looked around and pointed out in various directions of dark nothingness. "Don't worry. I've scoped the area pretty good and I tell ya, we're okay here. It's at least seven or so miles to the nearest settlement."

This definitely caught my attention. "What settlement?"

"Place called Camp Expectation."

My expression gave away my thoughts.

"You heard of it?" Jake asked.

I obviously couldn't hide my surprise when he mentioned the place. Without sounding too enthused, I answered, "I've heard stories of Camp Expectation. Not sure if they're tales, truths, or just unfounded whispers. They've just intrigued me."

Jake looked me over again, this time with some suspicion.

"Seems to me you have some definite interest in the place," the young man said.

For some reason, this was a subject I was having trouble hiding my sentiments about. I cleared my thoughts and reset my frame of mind.

"I'll tell you this, Jake. The reason I'm looking for Camp Expectation is my secret to keep, but any assistance you can provide me getting there is most appreciated."

In my travels alone, I had heard people mention Camp Expectation, a place that was supposed to be what life was like in the Old World. Not many seemed to believe it truly existed, though, discounting it as myth or fairy tale. But the more I traveled and the more people I encountered, the more I heard the stories and I increasingly began to wonder if perhaps the whispers were true. Ultimately, though, I had no greater interest in its existence than most others. I was fine fending for myself.

Until the day I heard the leader of Camp Expectation was a woman named Kylee Haddock.

Could it be the Ky I knew? Was she alive? I just felt two women in the barren wastes of this world having the same name to be too much of a coincidence. Before I knew it I found myself actively seeking out Camp Expectation – never having any actual expectation of ever finding it...or her.

Jake laughed again, not quite as loud as last time, but still louder than I cared for nonetheless. I couldn't help giving the dark flatlands and black skies around us a once over, just for my own sake, if nothing else.

"There's worse places you could go," Jake said. "It's about as close to the way life was in the days before the Vampocalypse as you're gonna get. That's word in the desert, anyway."

"If it's so great, why don't you go there?" I asked Jake. Maybe there was something I should know that would warrant me being extra cautious on my approach, if and when I finally came across the place. Jake shook his head.

"Me? Nah, man, I do okay alone." Jake's eyes darted around the tiny encampment. "People scare me almost as much as vampires do."

I gave him a curious look that he immediately noticed.

"I don't scare you?" I asked.

"Nuh-uh, man, something 'bout you is different."

If he only knew.

"So do you know where Camp Expectation is?" I asked outright.

Once again with the laugh. This time it segued into, "Dude, you're heading away from it. It's about seventy-five miles that way."

Jake pointed towards the west, though not directly, and a bit southward – and in a direction completely away from the one I was traveling.

"That direction, huh? You sure?"

"Yep, that's the way." Jake seemed proud. "Beyond the foothills in the distance."

I started to stand as I said, "Then I suppose I better get going."

"That's a good three, four days walk." Jake cautioned.

"I can do it in two. Less, if I don't sleep."

Jake chuckled. "I'm sure you can. Jus' so you know, you're welcome to stay the night here if you want to rest up first. You can always head out in the morning."

My first instinct was to thank him for his generosity and move on but then I thought twice about it. I wasn't in any particular hurry, especially after fifteen years, and waiting one more night – and getting a night of rest, no less – would do good to help recharge for the journey.

"You know what, Jake? I think I'll actually take you up on that."

"Nice!" Jake followed this with a loud "Whoop!" I guessed he hadn't been around anyone in a while, let alone someone he felt he trusted.

And for my part, I felt the same.

"Let me get you something to eat," Jake said as he reached back into the dirt behind him. "I've got some rabbit here that I've been saving for a special occasion. I'd say this is one!"

I held up a hand and cut him off. "I've got it covered,"

I reached into my satchel, which I realized upon this meeting wasn't too dissimilar from Jake's, and pulled out a small rolled up paper bag. I unrolled then opened the bag and pulled out from inside a small plastic bag filled with pieces of meat.

"Red fox."

I'm not sure I'd ever seen anyone's eyes so wide with excitement in my life. It made me happy to share what I had left of the fox with this young man. I knew I would be at Camp Expectation within two days and, even then, I could easily provide for myself under any circumstances that may occur. At least much easier than this young man could.

Jake cooked his pieces of fox on a stick over the flame while I ate mine rare – this somewhat disgusted Jake, though not completely as he was able to laugh it off with, "To each his own, man."

After we ate Jake insisted on giving me some of his rabbit remains but I refused. This was such a genuine person in a world full of rage, anger, death, and deceit. There's been no one I fully trusted in a very long time. And while I never fully trusted Jake, either, out of a matter of logic and survival, the trust I did foster for him was much more than I had felt towards anyone in a long while.

After we ate we decided to take turns keeping watch as the other slept. I decided to let Jake sleep first in thanks for his hospitality.

"It ain't nothin'. You're a good man, Prater. Not many like you around. I'm glad to know you."

These were the last words Jake said to me as he drifted away to sleep almost instantly. I guessed he hadn't had such a secure night's sleep in a long time. There turned out to be only one watch as I decided to just let Jake sleep. As the night crept on, though, I did feel the tiredness come upon me to where

I couldn't fight it any longer. There were plenty of times when I slept alone yet in still somewhat of an alerted state in the event of danger, and this night would be no different. As Jake slumbered on, I eventually closed my eyes as I sat in my lotus position, this time with one of my swords sitting across my lap, and gently nodded off.

The distant glow of the morning breaking in the east brought me abruptly to attention. I instinctively grabbed my sword and rolled backward out of my sitting cross-legged position – where I had slept for who knows how long with my head nodded uncomfortably forward – and into a stance where I was on one knee and my katana was held ready to strike.

My breath was quick as I surveyed the barren grounds around me. The fire was out and thin lines of smoke drifted almost straight up into the calm morning air.

And Jake was gone.

I couldn't help but think this was his payback for me leaving him in the night during our first encounter. I was sure he'd left of his own volition as I would have definitely become aware of any danger, which would have instantly woken me. No, Jake was the one that pulled the disappearing act this time.

I went to the campfire and took a few minutes to further douse the smoldering embers with dirt until no more smoke could be seen. I then stood up and took one last look around the grounds before making my way towards Camp Expectation.

EPISODE 9

CAMP EXPECTATION
PACIFIC WASTELANDS

Z had called ahead to have Dr. Cleary and Annika meet with her and the governor. They waited in the main foyer of Camp Expectation's townhouse hospital in a modest check-in/waiting area. There was a side desk occupied by an office manager who had already greeted Z and Kylee and informed them the doctor would be out in the next few minutes. Rather than making use of any of the cushioned chairs or long couch set in the room, they stood in the middle of the foyer as they waited.

"I had a strange dream last night," Z said to Kylee.

"What's that?" Kylee asked.

Z thought for a moment before starting her account. "It was strange 'cause it seemed so very real, yet not. I mean, more of the circumstances involved in it."

"Tell me about it."

"In the dream we were here, at Camp Expectation, but it wasn't really here. It was much smaller, maybe just three hundred people and felt more like an overgrown campground. You were there, its leader like you are here, but you were referred to as 'Queen' and I was the 'Queen's Hand.'"

Kylee couldn't help but let out a short laugh.

"*Queen?* Not sure I've ever thought that highly of myself. I'm also not so sure that dream deserves the concerned look it's left you."

"There was something else. Something that…left me wondering."

"What's that? Wondering what?"

"In my dream we captured a vampire who claimed to be a half-breed."

"Half-breed?" Kylee repeated. Her tone shifted, growing heavier. "You mean as in half-human, half-vampire?"

"Exactly that." Z paused for a moment before continuing. "I've seen a lot of crazy shit over the years but have never come across anyone, or anything, like that."

Z couldn't quite tell what was going on behind the other woman's eyes. It looked like a mixture of surprise, concern, and melancholy – not any one in particular.

"Have you ever heard of anything like that? Are half-breeds real?" Z asked without addressing the uncertain look in Kylee's eyes.

Kylee held the mixed look for a brief instance longer before she smiled and put her hands on the younger woman's shoulders.

"Governor Haddock," the office manager said, interrupting whatever Kylee was about to say next. "The doctor is ready for you."

Z and Kylee simultaneously turned to see Dr. Cleary coming into the waiting room from an adjacent hall.

"Good morning, Dr. Cleary," Kylee said.

"A good morning it is indeed," came the doctor's cheery reply. "Much nicer than the rains that passed through last night."

"Clearly," said Z.

"It's Dr. Clear-*ee*," laughed the doctor as he turned Z's response into a joke.

Kylee's feigned laughter came across much more genuine than Z's.

"I suppose the two of you would like to visit our latest arrival?" the doctor asked.

"If you don't mind, Doctor," Kylee said. "Is she awake?"

"I'm honestly not certain she even slept at all last night. We finally did get her to eat something and take a shower this morning. She's been pretty quiet, though. Not that we're bombarding her with any questions."

"Let's see her, then," said Kylee.

"This way."

Dr. Cleary led the two women down the hall from which he had just come and to the first door on the left where Annika stood staring out the window on the opposite side into the yellow-gray morning sky.

"Annika," the doctor announced, his voice serene. "Governor Haddock and Z are here to see you."

The sixteen-year old girl remained with her back turned to them, unmoving.

"Would you mind leaving us alone?" Kylee asked the doctor.

"Not at all. I'll be in my office if you need me for anything. Just alert the front desk."

The doctor closed the door behind him as he exited, leaving Z and Kylee with Annika in silence. The ceiling lights were off, with only the light from the window illuminating the twin size bed and single chair and the rest of the sparce room.

Annika stood nearly silhouetted against the window. Her dirty blonde hair was pulled into a pony tail and she wore an athletic tank top that exposed the bandages covering the stitched-up wounds in her shoulders from where they had been punctured by vampire talons. Loose-fitting dark gray sweats went down to the tops of her bare feet. Z and Kylee exchanged a concerned look before Kylee took a step forward. She started to say something but Annika broke the silence first.

"Many scientists had predicted that in a nuclear winter, nitrogen oxide would displace much of the ozone layer that protects us, allowing the harmful UV rays to come to Earth, causing radiation burns that would kill much of the human population. If they only knew that the UV light would actually be blocked, and that vampires would thrive and rule the world."

The looks between Z and Kylee quickly went from worrisome to confused. Annika turned around and faced the women. Dark circles under her eyes underscored hours of tears combined with lack of sleep.

"My sister was, is, was…a scientist," Annika said, her voice dropping lower. "She knows, she knew…all sorts of stuff and would just go on and on to the point I ended up memorizing bits of it."

Kylee offered Annika a resolute look.

"Your sister sounds like a very smart woman," Kylee said.

Annika locked eyes with the governor. "Probably the smartest person I ever knew." She then looked sideways as she added, "I never admitted that to her, though. I wish I had."

Kylee stepped around the bed and offered the girl her hand. "My name's Kylee."

The girl took the hand but there wasn't much effort behind her grip.

"And, of course, you know Z," Kylee continued.

Z held up a hand in a sort of half-wave. "Hello, again."

"Thank you for rescuing me," Annika said softly.

Z smiled, unsure of what to say to the girl whom had lost everything just hours earlier. Sure, Z had saved her from the vampires and from fears unknown, but at what cost? Z always felt she had turned out fine despite witnessing the murders of her family…but had she really? Yes, she ended up a strong, fierce woman but the images and terror never truly went away, and only time would tell how this girl would deal with her own trauma.

"How are you feeling?" Z asked.

"Worst headache ever but the doctor says I'm physically okay."

"Please, sit down," offered Kylee as she padded the upper half of the twin bed with one hand as she sat down towards its foot.

Annika sat down on the bed with her feet hanging over the side. Z slid the nearby chair over next to the bed and sat in it.

Kylee put a reassuring hand on the girl's knee. "You've been through a lot, Annika. It's amazing you're doing as well as you are. I can't say I'd be the same."

Annika drew a deep breath and as she did her chest fluttered as if she had just come off of a long cry.

"I can tell you're shaken but that you're strong," Kylee continued. "Just think about how you were able to dig deep and seek out that inner strength that's kept you alive."

Annika sniffled but no tears formed in her eyes. "I needed to stay strong for my family." She looked at Kylee then over at Z. "What do you think happened to them? Do you think they're dead?"

"I don't know," said Z.

"What do *you* think?" Kylee asked Annika, putting the question back on the girl. "Do *you* believe they're dead?"

"The vampires didn't kill them the first time they took them away," Annika said. "Maybe they didn't kill them the second time, either."

Z looked at Kylee and the return look she received affirmed what she thought. The glances weren't missed by Annika.

"I know about the blood banks," Annika said. "If they were taken to the blood banks then they'd still be alive."

There was the slightest look of hope in the recessed corners of the young girl's eyes that was contagious. The girl radiated as the possibility of her family being alive in the blood banks consumed her. She shot sharp looks between her two visitors.

"I refuse to believe my family's dead until I know for sure. I'll stay strong until I find them and free them. No matter how long it takes."

Kylee took hold of one of Annika's hands.

"Just don't set yourself up too high for disappointment. I know what it's like," Kylee corrected herself as she looked at Z then back at Annika, "we both know what it's like to have our own expectations let us down."

"I have to agree, Annika," Z added. "I know what it's like to lose family at a young age. Mine were slaughtered in front of my eyes when I was four years old. There was no coming back from that."

Annika shot an angered look through Z. "Are you really making this about you right now? Thank you for rescuing me but I don't even know you."

Z tilted her head to the side and took a moment, not wanting to exacerbate the situation.

"I'm sorry, Annika, I don't mean to come across any sort of way. I'm just trying to look out for you."

Annika's eyes softened. A little. "I know. That's fine. I didn't mean to snap at you."

Kylee jumped into the conversation without pause. "I'm glad you're fine with it, Annika, 'cause Z is going to be the one taking care of you, at least for the time being."

"I don't need anyone looking over me." Annika's icy tone returned. "I can take care of myself."

"Yeah?" Kylee said, not quite taunting. "You mean out there, beyond our walls, alone? Somehow I'm not sure that you would last very long. And if you mean in here, in Camp Expectation, then sure, but you still need someone to show you around and help you get assimilated."

Annika paused, thinking, knowing the governor was right. The look on Z's face did nothing but urge her silently to understand.

"Of course," she said. "I get it, I get it."

As the girl's voice trailed off, Z couldn't help but consider the conflicted feelings the younger one must be dealing with. She could see the turmoil behind the girl's eyes, wanting to understand but at the same time struggling to make sense of everything that had happened, and was continuing to happen. This girl was born in the New World and knew nothing of the time before, but she didn't deserve to have everything stripped from her like this. Z decided a change of subject might help the girl clear her mind and refocus on matters besides memories of family and vivid images of their abduction and the death that surrounded them all.

"Annika," Z said, leaning forward in her chair, "do you know who Prater Saxon is?"

"No, personally, not at all," Annika replied without hesitation. Z and Kylee shared a moment of disappointment. "I mean, I did see him from a distance a few times. At least I think it was him. Dressed in mostly black and carried two swords on his back. He always wore sunglasses and at least from what I heard he never took them off as long as he was with us."

Z couldn't help but continue to exchange glances with Kylee as Annika spoke.

"I thought us teens could be brooding but he really ran with it," Annika continued. "And it looked like he hadn't cut his hair in a couple years. Some of my friends said their parents said he was a weirdo."

"Anything else you can think of?" Kylee asked. Her tone was serious yet imploring. "If there's anything else you might remember – "

"My dad said he was coming here."

"Here?" Z and Kylee exclaimed in perfect unison.

Annika looked again back and forth between the two women, whose shared shocked expression was almost comical to the girl.

"This *is* Camp Expectation, right?" Annika asked.

"Right, yes," said Kylee, visibly a bit flustered. Z wondered why this subject seemed to keep Kylee on edge.

"Yeah, my dad said the Prater person was going to Camp Expectation but told my sister and me not to say anything about it, I'm not sure why. Is he here?"

Both women shook their heads. "No," added Z, "we don't even know who he is."

"My dad said he was headed south when he left Escape Town. That was over a week ago."

Z turned to Kylee and said, "That could explain why he's not here. If he headed due south from Escape Town then he'd be off course."

"Is there anything else?" There was an edge in Kylee's voice that only fed more into Z's curiosity about the woman's interest in Prater.

Annika shook her head. "That's all I know."

Kylee put a hand on the young girl's hand and squeezed gently. "You've done good, Annika, thank you."

Annika nodded silently as she looked down and away. There was no thrill or excitement or pride in her demeanor. There was only the lingering sadness as the girl pondered on the fate of family of whom she may possibly never see again. Kylee stood up from the bed and looked at Z.

"Organize a search party based on the estimated trajectory Prater took from Escape Town," the governor said to her master-at-arms. "Let's see if we can find him and bring him here. Maybe we can figure out why the vampires are so interested in him."

"Do you think that's a good idea?" asked Z. "We don't know anything about this person. Just because the vampires are after him doesn't mean he isn't also a danger to us. Do we really want to get involved in whatever game those monsters are playing?"

Kylee stepped around the bed and stood next to Z. Annika looked up and watched silently as the two women continued their discussion.

"I think whatever the vampires want Prater for has got to be something valuable," Kylee said. "And if there's something out there the vampires want but don't have, that makes me want it that much more. I want to bring Prater here before the vampires get to him."

"Aren't you worried the vampires may track him here then?" Z's tone raised a bit as Annika continued to switch glances between the women. "The way they took over and destroyed Escape Town had to be just a small flex of what they are fully capable of. You know I'm always about a good fight but bringing him here could attract the type of attention we've spent years avoiding."

Kylee was about to respond when the walkie talkie clipped to her right hip crackled to life. *"Governor Haddock?"*

Kylee paused for a moment as she and Z continued to stare at each other as if each was baiting the other to speak first. The governor finally brought her walkie up and responded.

"Go for Governor Haddock."

"This is Jackson at gate security. Governor, there's somebody here requesting entry. He's asking for you specifically."

A similar look of concern fell simultaneously across both Kylee and Z's faces.

"Who is it? Have they identified themselves?"

There were a few moments of silence before the gate security officer's voice popped back through.

"He says his name is Prater Saxon."

EPISODE 10

SAN FRANCISCO MECCA
NORTH AMERICA NEW WORLD TERRITORIES VAMPIRE CAPITOL

LOCATED behind several security doors in one of the highest floors of what used to be the Transamerica Pyramid, Dr. Deuteronicus' capitol city laboratories required special clearances to gain access. Icy blue light radiated from the floor while portable light rigs were positioned and shone onto persons and areas in need of illumination. Two sets of surgical spotlights were fixed on the center of the dark surgery room while lights from displays and life monitoring equipment glowed around the room's perimeter. Two medical gurneys, each with very different types of patients, were in the middle of the room.

Ryder Sloane groaned as he writhed in pain from the blackened and still smoking flesh covering nearly the entire right half of his body. The burns from the grenade explosion were too severe for his vampire healing factor to effectively kick in and rejuvenate him. His robotic left half was smudged from smoke and fire that burned hot but did little more than scorch it. Two technicians wearing surgical masks, gowns, and gloves worked gingerly with the burnt and suffering cyborg as he laid back and worked to be still. One of the techs picked a needle up off a stainless-steel side table. The needle and the hand holding it were suddenly under the pressure of the cybernetic hand that squeezed around them.

"No!" Sloane called out. Light wisps of smoke escaped the corners of his mouth, blending in with the smoke rising off his smoldering skin. "No anesthetics."

The tech nodded quickly, grimacing as she fought against the pain of her hand slowly being crushed. To the tech's relief, Sloane released his steel grip and she dropped the needle as she pulled away. She rubbed her newly freed hand, and opened and closed it several times slowly, making sure there was no real or permanent damage.

The other gurney sat parallel to Sloane's with enough space between them to allow doctors and personnel to easily pivot between the two as needed. The patient on this table, however, was naked and rendered almost completely immobile by a combination of metal bars and leather straps that held the frightened man in place on his back. His arms were at forty-five degree angles from his sides and his legs were shoulder-width apart. Streams of sweat flowed off the man's forehead as he looked frantically around the room, trying to make sense of what was happening. Rapid breathing and panicked noises escaped around the edges of the gag that was in the man's mouth and secured by a strap around his head. Two separate technicians watched over the man – one monitored his vitals as the other reached with a cloth and dabbed the sweat off of him.

Dr. Deuteronicus stood between the two tables, each easily within reach as he pivoted back and forth and examined the two patients. The ultrathin vampire had the appearance of a man in his eighties – as he would for all eternity – but moved smoothly and with the spryness of a human a quarter that age. Jonathan Stirling watched the doctor from his place just on the edge of the shadows on the far side of Ryder Sloane's bed as Deuteronicus went from his exams to organizing some tools on a tray positioned nearby. Also in the room was Councilor Marques Wright, Stirling's ever-present personal aide, who stood several feet behind the president, concealed nearly in complete shadow. Unlike others in the room, Stirling and Marques only wore surgical masks as opposed to also donning smocks or gloves.

"Prater Saxon still eludes us," said Sloane.

The usual electronic flange underlying the cybernetic vampire's tone was especially coarse and staticky. He spoke meticulously from the pain in the combination of human vocal cords and electronic compressors that made up his speech. Stirling wondered if Sloane's voice would eventually clear up or if it was permanently damaged. He looked down at his general's burnt face.

"This is a disappointment." Stirling shook his head. "You're my best, General Sloane. I had assumed you would have had the task completed with ease."

Sloane's already audibly labored breathing grew heavier as he seethed. "I will find him. I would still be on his trail if not for my current…condition."

Stirling gave a slight nod in affirmation then looked at the doctor. "We have a lot to be thankful for when it comes to the good doctor here. He was, after all, responsible for making you the beautiful creature you are today." Stirling reached down and caressed the cyborg-vampire's metallic left cheek. "I'm just pleased to know he's able to get you on a fast track to healing."

"Speaking of which," Dr. Deuteronicus interrupted, "I am prepared to take the first slice." Even though he moved like someone much physically younger, his voice was still scratchy and low – unchanged from how it sounded before he was turned. It was only slightly muffled through his surgical mask.

Both Stirling and Sloane watched Deuteronicus as he tenderly took a scalpel with one of the longer curved blades off his equipment tray with one of his gloved hands. The doctor's claws were retracted within his fingers to allow for the surgical gloves to fit. Deuteronicus gestured to the technicians nearest the bound human, and they undid the straps securing the man's head in place. Between the two techs they forced his head to the side, exposing the right side of his face to the doctor, and held it in place.

The scalpel did its work, guided by the careful and skilled hand of Deuteronicus, as the doctor began slowly slicing and peeling away the skin along with a thin layer of flesh from the helpless man's face. Stirling was thankful the man was gagged as the screams he emitted were beyond anything he had ever imagined a human could produce.

"Really, Doctor," Stirling said, somewhat pleading, "can't you shut him up entirely?"

"Unfortunately, Mr. President," Deuteronicus said as he continued his meticulous work, "for the face, we need active skin unaffected by anesthetics. Once we move on to the body we can put him to sleep."

With that, the man suddenly stopped screaming as he passed out. Deuteronicus guessed the pain was just too intense as he peeled the cut skin away from around the man's eye. *Humans, so weak.* He kept a delicate hold of the loose skin he had sliced away from the upper part of the man's face as he nodded towards one of the techs standing closer to Sloane. The technician took a needle from one of the open equipment trays and rushed to the side of the unconscious man. Without hesitation, the tech stabbed the needle deep into the man's heart and pressed the plunger. The man's eyes flew open and looked around wide with shock as his body immediately fell into a violent seizure. The steel bars and leather binds held strong, and the man's body could barely move despite his uncontrollable effort to do so. The technicians continued their strong hold of the man's head as Deuteronicus swiftly and masterfully finished his work, leaving just a thin layer of wet, sinewy flesh as the doctor pulled away the skin from the entire right half of the man's face in a single piece.

"Now, please," Deuteronicus said, "do as the president asked and shut him up."

The technicians repositioned and re-secured the man's head to the table as the third tech acquired a new needle. This one was stuck into the man's left forearm and almost immediately the relentless, gagged screams stopped as the patient fell under whatever drug the vampire pumped into him.

Deuteronicus held the slice of human just a few inches over Sloane's smoking and blackened face as he performed a quick mental assessment and then pulled it away.

"Try not to move," the doctor said, almost as if in warning.

The remaining technician nearest to Sloane lightly sprayed an opaque mist from a palm-sized black vial onto the scorched right half of the cyborg's face. This caused the charred skin to erupt with thousands of tiny black bubbles. Deuteronicus took the newly farmed skin he was holding and carefully placed it onto Sloane's face. The black blisters all popped and released a thick, dark brown fluid that immediately began to meld onto the underside of the thin layer of exposed flesh. A light sizzling sound could be heard and an odor even the vampires tended to find repulsive emanated from the procedure.

Sloane squirmed and hissed as he fought to hold still, battling the sensations as the alien skin became a part of him. Stirling watched, fascinated, as the human skin stretched and shrunk and reshaped itself until it had reformed to look like Sloane's original face. After several long moments of what looked like silent agony from the cyborg, Sloane was able to compose himself as the new face had fully become a part of him, relegating the black scars underneath to a painful memory. Sloane took a moment and turned his head with his new face slowly from side-to-side, then up and around, and contorting cheek and other muscles and rotors to get the skin to feel in place and most comfortable.

"The most difficult part is complete," announced Deuteronicus. "I can continue with the grafting on the rest of the body as the two of you continue your discussions."

"Much appreciated, Doctor," said Stirling.

Sloane looked up at the president as the doctor went to work removing a layer of skin and flesh from the unconscious human's right side.

"You've never told me, Jonathan," the robotic-enhanced voice had smoothed over compared to earlier, "why do you seek this person?"

Stirling looked down at the half-vampire as one of the techs sprayed a large, scorched area of Sloane's side and Deuteronicus laid a sizeable piece of human skin over it. Sloane torqued his body slightly as the adhering processes took effect, though his discomfort was mild compared to when the process occurred on his face. Sloane reached up with his robot left hand and grabbed Stirling's arm.

"Look at me, Jonathan, look what's happened to me. What makes this Prater so valuable?"

Stirling pulled his arm away as he took a couple of steps towards the foot of the gurney. He stopped and scanned the room, and through the darkness he could easily see the barren gray walls with his enhanced vampire eyesight. The banks of monitoring equipment and computer stations stood out clearly as if illuminated by daylight. He looked at the doctor doing his work, the four techs who went about their tasks of assisting and monitoring components of the medical procedure, and his aide Marques standing near the door to the room. He then peered off into a corner of dark nothingness as he spoke.

"You know what I miss? I miss the warmth of the sun. How it feels on my face and on my skin. I miss the blue skies and the seasons. And shadows from bright sunlight. Long, dark, deep shadows. These are the things I miss." He slowly took the couple of steps back to be closer again to the head of the gurney as his gaze dropped down onto Sloane. "This world wasn't meant to be forever scorched and held captive under a never ending nuclear winter. Vampirekind was not meant to have to hide under this blight. Even after three thousand years of hiding and finally claiming this planet for our own, we are still living under the oppressive tools of the humans."

There was a sizzle and hiss as Deuteronicus placed another large slice of skin onto a burnt part of Sloane's side. As this met up with the edges of the last piece the doctor placed, pus oozed up through the seams between them, bubbled over, then evaporated leaving the pieces mended together, though not without a thick scar that would forever act as a reminder of the event that caused it and the pain that followed.

"What do you propose to do?" Sloane followed Stirling's misdirection, avoiding his Prater question. "You can't just stop the nuclear detonations without fear of breaking the ongoing nuclear winter."

"First things first. I must break the code that would allow us all to walk during the day. That would complete the evolution of vampirekind over this world permanently. Then we can break the never ending winter."

Sloane saw an opportunity to bring the subject of Prater Saxon back to the conversation. "And this Prater person factors into those plans?"

Stirling looked again at the surgical technicians who continued to do their work diligently and silently. As was the case whenever anyone was in the presence of the president, there was a sworn secrecy in place that was understood ahead of time. In his thirty years as president, he wasn't aware of anyone who had broken that trust. These technicians, dutifully carrying out their tasks, would be no different, this much he knew. He looked back down at Sloane.

"Prater Saxon is a naturally created half-human, half-vampire hybrid."

Sloane studied Stirling's expression, part of him wondering if the president was joking.

"A *slakeen?*" Sloane asked after a pregnant pause. "Those are a myth. An actual *slakeen* has never been known to exist."

Stirling nodded. "That's been true until some recent information led me to believe otherwise."

"What information?"

"I have contacts overseas who have informed me on good authority that Prater Saxon is indeed a half-human, half-vampire."

An unfocused yet intense look filled Stirling's eyes as he leaned in close to the cyborg-vampire's face.

"The *slakeen* exists and he currently walks this Earth." Stirling's voice was a low growl, and his confidence was sure.

Deuteronicus lifted Sloane's arm and wrapped a wide slice of skin around it. The odor that emanated each time from the pustulating blisters never got any less pungent.

"Are you so certain he has the ability to walk in the sun?" Sloane asked.

Stirling stood upright. "What I'm certain of is the vast knowledge we will gain from research conducted on the world's first known and captive *slakeen*. And at the forefront of that research will be how to make the best use of this hybrid's genetics to help us become the one, true superbeings to have ever existed."

"I suppose you'll be involved with this research?" Sloane asked Deuteronicus.

The doctor stopped from stripping a particularly long and wide slice of skin from the human's upper thigh and looked at Sloane. Much of what could be seen of the human was already void of a layer of skin, leaving bloody exposed swaths of muscle, blood, and bone from head to toe over the right half of the man's body.

"I'm absolutely looking forward to it. I have taken great strides in the last couple of years with biogenetics study and modification. Having a *slakeen* at my disposal could unlock so many mysteries, primarily, the ability to live without fear of natural sunlight."

Stirling let out a short laugh as he waved a hand towards the doctor. "Dr. Deuteronicus is one of the three greatest scientific minds I've ever known. If not for him, you would not be here. If not for he and Mr. Titus, our kind would not have the means to survive the coming millennia."

Sloane waited a moment but Stirling didn't continue.

"And the third?" Sloane finally asked.

"That would have been Geoffrey Appamattox."

"Of course. Creator of the original virus. His expertise could be well utilized for this research."

Stirling shook his head. "With he and his family relegated to the Alcatraz blood banks the bulk of the research is going to fall on our good doctor right here. I have every confidence in him."

Deuteronicus smiled and nodded. "Thank you, Mr. President. I won't let you down, as long as I have a body to actually conduct research on, then –"

Sloane glared at the doctor as he snarled, "I said, I will find him."

Deuteronicus paused a moment as he noticed a ferocity in the cyborg's vampire-robot eyes. He retreated to his work as he meekly stated, "My apologies, I meant no offense."

Stirling laughed again, a little harder this time.

"Gentlemen, easy, please, both of you. The last thing I need right now is for the two of you to be bickering. I already deal with enough of that bullshit between my VP and senator elite."

As if on cue, Marques stepped forward from his place in the nearby shadows and said, "Mr. President, Senator Elite is outside and would like to speak with you."

Stirling looked at his aide, the aggravation rose in him with a determined scowl in the young man's direction. "You should know to tell him I'm busy."

"With apologies, sir, he says it's urgent."

Stirling began to say something but stopped himself, instead releasing a deflated exhale as he nodded. A moment later light from the outside annex sliced through the room as the door to the laboratory hissed aside and the senator elite came rushing in and up to the president as fast as his thick, heavy steps would allow. He hadn't bothered with acquiring one of the surgical masks prior to entering.

"We have a serious problem, Jonathan."

Stirling held up his hand. "Just a moment, Samuel."

The irritation at being made to wait was obvious on the senator elite's face.

"Marques," Stirling went on, either unnoticing or uncaring of Samuel's annoyance. "I'd like you to get in touch with my brother. Get him up to date on the summit proceedings. I'm sure he's also going to want a status update regarding Prater Saxon."

"Anything in particular I should tell him in regard to that last point, sir?"

Stirling shook his head. "All there is to know is that we still don't have him."

"Of course, sir."

"Go contact him while I see what Samuel here needs. I'll meet you back in my office shortly."

"Yes, Mr. President," Marques said before leaving the room.

Light from the entranceway behind the senator elite narrowed into a sliver before completely extinguishing as the door slid shut behind Marques. Stirling noticed Samuel's expression to be an odd mixture of concern and smugness – the peculiarity of which only became more pronounced as the shadows shifted across his face as the laboratory door slid shut.

"Now, what's so pressing, Samuel?"

"We received a report just about twenty minutes ago that the *Harbinger One* has been – for lack of a better word – stolen." The senator elite delivered the news in his usual no-holds barred manner.

The announcement caught the attention of everyone in the room. Stirling inhaled sharply as his body straightened.

"The nuclear submarine?" Sloane asked. "That's one of the boats used for the routine detonations, isn't it?"

"Yes. That is the situation."

Stirling turned to face Samuel full on, his brow deeply furrowed as the already red sclerae of his eyes turned an even deeper crimson. His surgical mask began moving inward and outward more pronouncedly as his teeth grew longer behind it and his breathing audibly deepened.

"When did this happen?" A deep, low grumble underlined Stirling's building rage as he spoke.

"Sometime between 3AM and 4AM this morning."

In an instant Stirling stood practically nose-to-nose with Samuel. The senator elite had seen this rage in the president before but never so close and never potentially directed at him. Still, Samuel stood strong without showing any fear or anxiety as Stirling frothed before him from behind his mask.

"Why. Did it. Take. So long. TO NOTIFY ME?" Each word was pointed and puncutated as Stirling huffed them out. And while at first his tone was barely above a whisper, by the time he reached the end, he was screaming in the senator elite's face, who was spared a shower of enraged vampire spittle by the mask the president wore.

"We've been trying to locate the vessel or determine any trajectory of its course." Samuel looked Stirling dead in the eyes, unwavering as he spoke.

"And?" The single word was back to the near whispered tone.

"It's lost, Jonathan."

For several moments time in the room seemed to stop as no one moved and all eyes were on the president in anticipation of his reaction to the news. In not much more than a blink the president was next to the technician at the head of Sloane's gurney. His claws were at full extension as they perforated the helpless tech's upper arms and the surgical mask did nothing to stop his razor sharp fangs from puncturing deep into the tech's neck. Cold vampire blood showered not only the president but Sloane, who relished drinking in whatever spray came upon him.

A crazed howl came from the president as he pulled his mouth back, tearing nearly a third of the tech's neck away with it. Spitting the flesh aside – which landed on Sloane who grabbed it and instantly began feeding – Stirling then grabbed the already dead technician by the exposed neck cavity that continued to shower dead blood on him and Sloane and tore the head completely off. The body dropped away and Stirling marched back over to stand again in front of Samuel. He held the decapitated head – still wearing its surgical mask, now completely bloodied – up to the senator elite.

"See what you made me do?" he shouted while waving the head by its hair.

Blood from the bottom of the head where the neck used to be splotched Samuel's suit with thick red droplets as Stirling shook it. The president then threw the head across the room with such force it splattered against a far wall in the darkness. He stood facing the direction of the dark as his breathing steadied. Tense moments followed as no one dared to be the next to move or speak. Stirling turned back to the senator elite then looked down at the blood and tissue that had soaked the front of his suit.

"Look what you did, Samuel," Stirling said, calm yet stern.

Samuel sighed as he crossed his thick arms in front of his chest.

"I always felt the humans were being underestimated," said Samuel. "I'm not the only one who's expressed this concern and the need to both be more proactive hunting these rebel groups down, as well as being more violent with them when confronted."

Stirling paced back towards Sloane's side as he wiped the blood from his hands on the front of his already wet, bloody red suit jacket. The senator elite, ever persistent, continued with his criticisms.

"We're now fully seeing the extent of the human resolve. You didn't listen and now here we are."

Stirling said simply, "Enough, Samuel."

The senator elite twisted the corner of his lip as he stopped with his "I told you so's."

"Doctor," Stirling said, his voice stern, "finish your work promptly." He didn't wait for a reply as he looked back at Samuel. "Find that vessel at all costs." The senator elite quietly nodded in acknowledgment.

The door to the lab slid open as Stirling stepped up to it. He was about to leave when he stopped and looked back at Sloane.

"Be sure to *take care* of the remaining technicians once the good doctor is done with you. They've heard more this morning than they need to know."

The three remaining assistants, still shaken from the death of their fellow technician, shared brief, nervous glances as Sloane looked at each of them from his place on the gurney and said, "With pleasure."

EPISODE 11

CAMP EXPECTATION
PACIFIC WASTELANDS

PRATER stood outside Camp Expectation's entrance as he waited on commands from the guards. The double gates were tall and narrow with iron bars that ran vertically every six inches to their iron framework. Heavy steel panels were bolted to the inside of the bars. Small viewports and rifle openings with their coverings currently slid shut were in both gates. Various types of weapons were aimed at him from the guard towers flanking the entrance. From his estimation and vantage point standing alone in the open facing the barricaded entrance there were four automatic rifles (surely filled with silver bullets), two crossbows, and two UV laser rifles, along with a spear launcher and flamethrower. He understood the display of force – one could never be too cautious of strangers.

"Keep your hands raised," a voice from an unknown face said through loudspeakers mounted on the guard towers, "and slowly put your weapons to the ground."

Displaying gentle, obvious movements, Prater first removed his side satchel, pulling its strap over the top of his head then setting the bag gently to the ground. He then reached back with both hands –

"Slowly!" The voice shouted the reminder through the loudspeakers.

Prater made sure to exaggerate his movements as he cautiously removed both of his katana from the X-shaped holster strapped to his back. After setting them on the ground next to his satchel he raised both hands.

"Step forward ten paces," the faceless voice ordered. Prater followed the instructions without pause.

"What brings you here?" the loudspeaker voice asked.

Prater's eyes narrowed as he tried to see which figure nestled in the shadows was calling out to him.

"Is this Camp Expectation?" Prater shouted out to what he suspected were the ears of someone not in the immediate vicinity, but rather, was probably watching from a more secure distance.

"We ask the questions!" came the reply. "What brings you here?"

I'm going to take that as a "yes," Prater thought as he skimmed the guards' shadowed faces. With his vampire eyesight he could make out their features and expressions. An underlying lack of fear combined with the experience of having witnessed who knows how many deaths over the years was evident by the determination in their eyes. If they were going to kill him, his death was sure to just be another in a long, nameless line.

"I'm here to see Kylee Haddock. Is she here?"

The response came with anger, "I said WE ask the questions! Who are you?"

"Would you tell Kylee that Prater Saxon is here to see her?"

A long period of silence followed. Prater could sense unease among the guards. Something was wrong – there was a heightened anxiety among them, yes, but not any actual fear. Still, he wasn't sure what could be taking so long. He considered calling it all off, letting the guards know he meant no harm and would leave peacefully. He also considered simply making a run for it – grabbing his weapons and retreating before matters got out of hand.

A sudden sting on the right side of his neck made him wince. He immediately put his hand up and felt a tranquilizer dart with its needle impaled fully into his neck. As he removed it a second sting like the first hit the other side of his neck. Vertigo kicked in as Prater tore the projectiles away and reached towards the ground for his weapons. He took just one dizzying step towards them before falling.

His sunglasses bounced away as the side of his head knocked against the hard dirt. There was a lazy voice just as the blur of booted feet came into view…before they turned into soft, smoke-like threads that floated away…

"Take him to holding…the governor is waiting for him…"

PRATER moved slowly as he made sense of his surroundings. He looked around with cautious head movements from where he was lying on a plush, purple couch. The room around him was warm and inviting and looked like it could have been someone's middle class neighborhood living room (like those he'd seen in old books and magazines) complete with bookshelves and a fireplace, from before the Vampocalypse. A wide window with partially closed curtains allowed enough natural light in to fill the room with its dull midday glow. The door to the room was closed and there were three chairs matching the couch he was on not far away and facing his direction. Two of the chairs were empty. The chair in the middle was occupied by a woman.

Prater sat up a bit too fast and his head spun. He rubbed his eyes – *Where are my sunglasses?* – and tried to shake the fog from his brain. A moment later he realized his swords and satchel were missing, probably gone the way of the sunglasses. Then he looked at the woman sitting across from him.

"Hello, Prater," said Kylee.

Prater sat silent and motionless. Across from him was the woman he knew as his mother – a person he had not seen in fifteen years, an entire half of his life. He had sought out Camp Expectation in anticipation of her being here and now here she was, and it almost didn't seem real. Thoughts and emotions swirled through him so quickly he couldn't process what to feel. At the same time he tried to get a read on what Kylee was thinking. Her gaunt features were still and unsmiling, keeping her emotions elusive.

"You're alive." The words escaped his lips before he realized he'd said them.

Kylee frowned and a glistening in the corner of one of her eyes led Prater to believe he saw a tear. She nodded briskly and it immediately became obvious she was fighting an entire river of waterworks. She massaged her hands together, displaying an unease that Prater never knew her to show.

"I am," she said with a sniffle.

"I had heard you were here, but I wasn't sure it was true. I mean…all this time…" Prater's words trailed as he looked down and away.

"I'm here, Prater," Kylee said, finding a little more strength in her voice. "I'm alive."

Prater shook his head then looked up slowly until his eyes met Kylee's.

"I almost can't believe it. One of the main reasons I left in the first place was because I thought you were dead. Master Miyamoto told me you were dead."

Disbelief washed across Kylee's face. "That doesn't make any sense. A small group of us got separated from the rest and it was a little over a week after the attack that we came across each other again by chance."

Prater raised his head and full-on faced the woman sitting across from him. "There must have been two groups of Expanse Village survivors," he muttered as he pondered on the situation. "Why would he say he saw you killed and taken away, then? Did you know he told me you were dead?" His tone was slightly accusatory, but not so much that he couldn't backtrack from the weight behind it if needed.

Kylee shook her head rapidly, reinforcing her words. "No, no I didn't. I promise you, Prater. After everything that happened, you were gone. Master Miyamoto told me you left, just like that. He said he didn't know anything else. I had no reason not to believe him. Just like you."

Kylee looked down almost as if ashamed. When she looked back up the woman known around Camp Expectation to always be straight-to-business and stone-faced had changed into that of a concerned parent as she pleaded silently through her eyes at the young man she raised.

"Trust me, Prater."

Prater's expression remained blank. The wheel-of-chance harboring his thoughts and feelings was slowing, with each click of a tab falling into a steady calm rhythm, before finally stopping on emotions Prater seldom felt in his life. He edged forward on the couch as he sat up a bit straighter.

"I trust you, Ky, I do."

Ky. The only person that ever called her that other than Prater was his mother, her best friend, before she died giving birth to him. She hadn't heard that nickname in so long and it was hard not to let long-buried emotions overcome her. It was the only name Prater really knew her by. She never wanted to be known as a "stepmother" despite that being her role for the first half of his life, so she told him to call her "Ky" and for as long as he was with her, he did. They shared a close relationship, and she didn't feel the need to reinforce that with any other name. Now, though, hearing Prater call her that unlocked emotions she tried so hard to keep at bay. She stood up and walked in front of Prater, took his hands, and pulled him slowly to his feet.

Prater was still trepidatious, but feelings wrapped in memories he thought were long gone were starting to get the better of him. He let Kylee help him stand and even though Prater himself wasn't terribly tall, he still could rest his chin on top of the woman's head as she embraced him like a mother lovingly embracing her son. Fifteen years of emotions coursed through Prater and he could feel it flowing through Ky as well. He slowly brought his arms up and held her as he closed his eyes and relished in a warmth and comfort he had not felt in so long and thought he would never feel again. One of his eyes felt a little wet but no droplets formed, unlike Kylee who sniffled as each of her eyes unleashed tears that drew lines of happiness and joy down each cheek. After what seemed too short while simultaneously feeling as though it may have gone too long, Kylee pulled away so they could look at each other, still close enough to hold each other.

"I haven't trusted many people in my life," said Prater. "You were one. Master Miyamoto was another. But now I don't know what to think of *him* so that leaves you as the only one I trust in this world."

Kylee turned to the side as she wiped the wetness from her eyes and cheeks with her fingers then rubbed them away on her jacket. She went and settled back into her soft, purple chair. Prater sat down onto the edge of the couch.

"There's an old saying that time heals all wounds," said Kylee with the familiar strength and resolve Prater recognized from his youth. "But our Earth and this existence have no more time to wait. Fate has brought us back together, Prater. We need to take advantage of this."

Prater leaned forward with his hands clasped together and his elbows on his knees as he found himself nodding along like he used to when he was a child listening to Ky's teachings and musings.

"Is Master Miyamoto here?" Prater asked.

Kylee sighed as she closed her eyes in a long blink. Prater knew what it meant.

"What happened?" Conflicted feelings of both anger and satisfaction clashed within Prater as he pondered on the death of his old instructor.

"He was the master-of-arms here and was killed during an attack on a routine reconnaissance mission."

Prater's retort came quickly. "Did you see his body?" The exchange instantly brought back the memory of when he asked Master Miyamoto if he saw Kylee being killed. "I don't mean to sound doubtful, but I'm sure you understand after what he told me about you being dead…"

"It's fine." Kylee leaned back and crossed her legs. "And not to disappoint you but no, I didn't see the body. It was a report from the survivors of the recon. There were others lost to the vampires on that mission. Their bodies were never recovered, either."

Prater didn't react. He could see Kylee studying him as she tried to figure out what he was thinking.

"Maybe it wasn't what he deserved, but it's what he got." Kylee's words seemed to fall empty on the man sitting across from her.

Prater sat up and looked around the room, first at the empty spaces of the couch on either side of him, then the floor, then the empty chairs next to Kylee.

"Where are my weapons?" he asked, changing the subject and not really acknowledging what Kylee last said. "You know I'm not a threat."

Kylee shook her head. "Of course not. Seizure of your weapons was at the insistence of the current master-at-arms."

Prater couldn't help but let out a short "Hmph."

"Look, Prater," Kylee started as she leaned forward, almost matching Prater's pose, "just because *I* know who you are doesn't mean I can circumvent the rules of this society."

Kylee stood up and went to the fireplace and ran a finger along the underside of the lip of the hearth. There was a click and a panel that had blended seamlessly into the wall above the empty hearth abruptly slid open revealing a wide, dark cupboard. Kylee reached in and from it produced Prater's swords, which she held out to him. Prater immediately stood and grabbed the weapons, practically snatching them from her hands.

"You had them this entire time. You don't trust me." There was no misunderstanding the tone of finality Prater placed on each statement.

"Like I said, the master-at-arms insisted," Kylee continued to explain as she reached back in the cupboard, this time grabbing both Prater's satchel and sunglasses. "And I don't break the rules."

Prater took the bag and sunglasses from Kylee but without nearly as much fervor. He immediately put the sunglasses on. *Feels like home.*

"Maybe your master-at-arms needs to get to know me."

Kylee smiled. "My thoughts exactly."

THE town streets were full of life in a way Prater did not know existed among humans in the post-Vampocalyptic world. Through his travels he encountered mostly small bands of people with the occasional community like Escape Town being very few and far between. The existence of a place like Camp Expectation was never assumed to be real, though, at least not amongst those who continued their daily struggles in the Wastelands. Being here, now, walking through the town that others only dreamed of, he realized the whispers of Camp Expectation never truly encapsulated what life within its walls was like, and the stories could never do the reality justice. The only thing really taking away from the experience was the musty smell leftover from rain the night before.

The building Kylee led them from was an old multilevel elementary school that had been converted into a processing facility located not far inside the main gate. She informed Prater she was taking him to her private office, where the master-at-arms would be waiting, and they would continue their conversation about any additional matters there. As they walked through the town, Kylee described to Prater how it was about two years after he left that the small group she and Miyamoto were in came across Camp Expectation. It was comprised of just a couple of hundred survivors, but they had a good foundation going for a fortified sanctuary hidden away from known vampire activity. Kylee and Miyamoto were almost immediately recognized as great assets and strong leaders to the community and when its governor passed away from cancer another two years after their arrival to the town, Kylee was easily elected to assume the role (Miyamoto had expressed no interest in the position). In the years since, Kylee helped grow the town by executing outreach efforts into the Wasteland, sending missionaries to spread the word of Camp Expectation and to welcome those who would decide to seek refuge there.

"You never worried about word getting to vampires about the existence of this place?" Prater asked.

Kylee shrugged. "You can't worry about those things, just do your best to be prepared. It's vital to provide a haven for survivors, otherwise, what good is all this for?"

Prater didn't disagree, instead reveling in the beauty of life thriving around him. It was a sight he had never seen on such a scale. "You have it pretty good here. There's running water, electricity...I haven't come across any towns this large or with as many amenities."

"We've been pretty lucky. We have wells that are tapped into what's proven to be a reliable aquifer. Power comes from a variety of sources. There are a few working windmills on an old grid just about five miles from here. There's also an old dam on the river but that's closer to thirty miles from here and hasn't proven to be consistently reliable. We have solar panels on some acres not far away. Although sunlight's filtered all the time the panels can still work their PV effect, just much slower. If one part goes down it may affect a portion of the town a bit until power from the other sources either reroute or the batteries kick in. Best part of pulling from multiple power sources is that the town never experiences a full blackout."

The overall comfort Prater was slowly beginning to feel was unlike anything he had experienced in over fifteen years. The sensation was coming on much faster than Prater would have liked. He was still, after all, in a strange place surrounded by strange people – except for one, and that one he had not known in fifteen years. Yet, the feeling was inescapable. Perhaps he had been longing for this feeling for a while and simply had not realized it. Whatever it was made Prater think maybe it could be time to pause his solo adventures and give himself to the comfort of community for a longer term.

"What about food sources?" Some questions lingered as he pondered about his future. "Is the town self-sustaining?"

"We have several animals that we raise for food and farmlands for vegetables. We've so far managed to steadily increase our food production as fast as the rate of population growth. I'm sure you know how scarce food is out there."

"There's more than you might think. The trick can be getting your hands on it."

Kylee half-smiled. "I figure if we can produce and thrive within these walls then many of the people won't have to worry about hunting for their own dinners."

"That's quite contrary to how you raised me." Prater kept his gaze straight ahead, refusing the urge to glance at Kylee occasionally. "I thought you were the great survivalist to impart wisdom to strengthen others both physically and mentally."

Kylee stopped walking, forcing Prater to follow suit. She turned and looked at the young man.

"Things are different, Prater. This world…is different than it was from when I was raising you. And you know what?"

Prater stared at Kylee though he wasn't sure she was aware of the look through the darkness of his sunglasses. That feeling of comfort Prater felt coming on earlier was just as quickly receding.

"I'm different," Kylee said, finishing her sentiment. "The people of this town look to me to lead them to where they can forget about the outside world. I'm the one they expect to maintain this Old World feeling for them so that they can live their lives –"

"As a lie," Prater interrupted coldly.

"What?" Kylee responded with a sharpness in her tongue. "What do you mean by that?"

"Keeping a blind eye to the terrors of what lies beyond the walls is suicide. The world will tear this entire community apart."

Prater paused as a question came to mind. "How is it you've managed to stay undetected all this time?"

Kylee shook her head. "Luck is a large part of it, I'm sure. I'll tell you, though, despite all the rumors you say are floating around out there, it doesn't appear as though the vampires are combing the wastelands, badlands, or barrens searching for this place, let alone looking for any pockets of survivors. Attacks like the one on Escape Town are rather rare. But if luck is what keeps us alive, then I'll certainly accept that with open arms."

As they continued their walk, Prater noticed in the not-too-far distance a long, windowless warehouse that could have easily stretched beyond the ends of a football field. He wondered what could possibly be housed under such a construction that would be of particular use for a town like this in the post-Vampocalypse world. A variety of small passenger automobiles, scooters, motorcycles, and motorized rickshaws scattered throughout the town also piqued Prater's curiosity. They looked to be from the Old World in the days of the twentieth century before the boon of electric vehicles took hold.

"You have a lot of vehicles here. Isn't gas scarce?"

"We manufacture our own. We don't need a lot for our routine needs and our fuelsmith is able to maintain an adequate supply."

Kylee pointed ahead to a white building distinguished by four large concrete pillars that heralded its entrance.

"There, that's where we're headed."

Kylee led them up the stairs and as they approached the two guards who stood on either side of the entranceway stepped sideways in unison and pulled open the heavy doors by their brass handles. The guards bowed their heads slightly then quickly raised them back up as Kylee walked past.

"The master-at-arms awaits you in the council chamber, governor," the guard on Kylee's right said as she walked past.

She nodded in acknowledgement. "Thank you."

After first walking through a small atrium then down a short hall that included two turns, it wasn't long before Kylee and Prater were traversing the narrow council chamber and down the middle of the two rows of six council seats that sat facing each other at the far end of the long room. The gray tile floors seamlessly transitioned to the equally gray stone and concrete walls. Several small windows were cut high in the side walls of the chamber, though most of the lighting came from the half dozen crystalline chandeliers that hung evenly spaced in two rows down the ceiling. Glow from their incandescent bulbs filled the chamber with a warm hue. Z, having been alerted to their arrival, stood waiting at the end of the row of empty council seats, in front of the thirteenth and final seat, Kylee's large governor's chair. Kylee waved away the two guards who stood watch at the back corners of the chamber and they quickly disappeared through doorways nestled inconspicuously along the back wall.

Kylee stopped in front of Z, who had not taken her eyes off Prater from the moment they entered the room. The governor looked back and forth quickly between the two, taking note of Z's cold stare at the man who stood before her.

"This is Prater Saxon," Kylee announced. Prater said nothing as he gave a nod. "Prater, this is the master-at-arms, Zarina Ismagilova."

"Z," the woman introduced herself simply as she studied the man in front of her.

Z took two steps and was so close to Prater she could clearly see the reflection of herself in the sunglasses that hid his eyes and subsequently, a lot of his expression. She stepped to the side and while Prater's head didn't turn, she could see through the side of the glasses that his eyes followed. There was something she found unsettling about this man but she couldn't quite pinpoint what it was. He seemed almost familiar, as if there was an aura about him that she had felt somewhere before. She walked completely around him, staring curiously at the man from all sides.

"Don't be rude to our guest," Kylee said as Z completed her circle around Prater. She scowled at the woman but it went unnoticed.

"Wait," said Z as she held a hand up in Kylee's direction. "There's something…off…but I can't place it."

Prater remained unmoving. "I don't believe we've met." His voice was low and dry, just above a whisper but still with an intensity.

Kylee took a step forward. "Z, there's something you need to know."

"That feeling I've felt before," Z continued as if not hearing Kylee at all. "It's like when I'm around –"

Z suddenly pulled a foot back and was in a fighting stance as she pulled both of her sai from the holsters strapped to her hips. Prater leaped back several feet and in an instant his swords were drawn – one held high and pointed in Z's direction while the other was horizontal in front of his chest. His posture was more crouched than that of Z's, who looked more like a fighter in a ring ready to rumble compared to Prater's stalking pose.

"Z, wait!" Kylee shouted.

Blinded by a white fury that pigeonholed her vision, Z rushed forward with an intensity and rage she only felt when fighting against vampires. Something inside her was telling her this was no exception.

Despite her sai being smaller than the katana swords of her target, Z demonstrated no fear or apprehension as she attacked. Just as she reached Prater she dropped to the floor, sliding feet first and forcing Prater to jump to his side to avoid having his legs wiped out from under him. There was the distinct clang of metal as sword met sai when the combatants passed each other. Z whipped her body around and was on her feet in an instant. She was several steps from Prater, weapons up and ready to attack again. Prater stood upright and stoic, and while he was tensed and ready to act, he held his weapons down at his sides, much more passive than the aggressor standing before him.

As the fight resumed, the two guards Kylee had ushered out of the chamber earlier rushed back in, each wielding their pointed silver spears. Kylee held up a hand that ordered the guards to stand down. They remained in proximity to their governor with their weapons pointed towards the fight, but otherwise did nothing to advance any further.

"Z! Stop!" Kylee cried out in another attempt to quell the battle.

The plea fell on deaf ears as Z attacked again. This time the melee was fiercer as the woman's onslaught of stabs, jabs, swings, and slices were parried or evaded by Prater. The metallic clashing of their weapons echoed off the hard walls of the chamber. Z pressed hard as she moved forward, forcing Prater to move beyond the rows of the council chairs and into an open area of the floor. With each block, Z's anger intensified and her next attacks came with more ferocity. Prater continued to remain defensive and it became apparent to Kylee – to her relief – that he was not interested in hurting Z at all.

The tactic may have been ill-utilized, though, as Z did not let up on her attacks in any fashion. Prater blocked and stepped back, parried and turned sideways, ducked to avoid a stab at his face…and then a flash of metal caught him off-balance as one of his swords got locked in-between the *monouchi,* or main blade, and one of the smaller side guards, or *yoku,* of one of the sai. The tortured scream of metal on metal ripped through the chamber as the sai slid along the katana before finally breaking loose.

A sudden hard hit on the side of his head came from the flat side of one of Z's weapons. Prater's sunglasses clattered to the floor as he jumped back and out of the immediate range of any further attacks. He spit blood onto the floor before looking at Z. He had tried to be calm, patient, and to give this opponent the benefit of the doubt.

That benefit was now exhausted.

Prater adjusted the grip on his weapons as he inhaled deeply. As he exhaled, he couldn't help but bare his lengthening vampire teeth.

"What the *fuck!*" Z shouted. "I knew it!" She glared at Kylee. "You let a fucking vampire into Camp Expectation?"

"It's not like that," Kylee said, desperate for the fighting to stop as she raised her hands toward Z. "I need you to calm down and let me explain."

Z's gaze shot from Kylee to Prater as she exclaimed, "This *is* calm."

"Z," Kylee said, her voice dropping in pitch in an effort to help lower the tension in the room. "You need to listen to me. There's something you need to know."

Z kept her weapons poised towards Prater who stood, unwavering, waiting for the next attack.

"All I need to know is that a vampire has somehow tricked you into letting it in and now I'm going to do something about it."

The rage in Z's eyes was evident as she lunged again towards Prater. Prater planted a foot behind him, swords raised to fight this time, and prepared for the attack.

"Prater's my son!"

Kylee's words surprised both Z and Prater, the latter of whom hadn't considered the possibility that Z didn't already know. But Z was the most surprised and the words stopped her dead in her tracks just as she was arm's length from striking true. She kept her sai poised to attack but withheld the urge to follow through as she took a step back from her opponent. She remained facing Prater, but her eyes shifted between him and Kylee, almost frenetically, as she struggled to process what she just heard.

"He's your *what*? This – this *thing* is your son?" The disgust was thick as it slowly dripped from her words.

Kylee rushed towards Z. Prater was still prepared to fight in the event the entire encounter suddenly shifted again towards the worse.

"Yes, technically," Kylee said, sounding reassured as the tension in the air lowered just enough to be felt. She put her hands up towards Z again as she went on, "and he's just *half*-vampire."

Confusion blanched Z's face and her eyes continued to shift between Prater and the woman whom she suddenly felt as though she knew nothing about.

"What?" Z half-asked, half-stated, as her confusion grew stronger. *"What?"*

Kylee put her hands on top of Z's forearms and began to slowly press them down – with her weapons – to her sides. As Z's arms dropped, the anxiety levels in the room followed suit. While Kylee guided Z's hands to sheath her sai, Prater's movements were similar as he replaced his katanas into the holder strapped to his back.

Z's confusion was no less than it was but the surprise that gripped her had loosened. She finally locked eyes solely with Kylee. Kylee held on to Z's hands in comfort as she turned the younger woman to face her.

"Let's relocate to my office." Kylee looked at Prater then back to Z. "We have a lot to discuss."

KYLEE escorted Prater and Z to her private office, located just steps down a hall off the main council chamber. Prater didn't quite know how Z detected anything about him that clued her in as to what he truly was – perhaps it was an intuition that had developed over years of killing vampires.

As the three of them settled into the office – the governor in her leather chair, Z in her usual seat of preference, and Prater in the remaining seat next to Z's – Kylee recounted to Z how she and Prater's mother were best friends and how, on the day the bombs dropped, Prater's mother was bitten by a vampire while giving birth to him, thereby transforming him into a half-human, half-vampire hybrid. She told about how Prater was left to her by his dying mother and how she not only raised him but helped train him for survival until they went their separate ways when Prater was fifteen.

Through it all, Z was quiet as she listened and processed what she heard. At the end her eyes were left wide and it was all she could do to not have her mouth agape. The expression wasn't coming from simple shock over the tale, but rather, its present-day repercussions.

"And just like that," Z said, intoning suspicion, "we trust he isn't working for the vampires, looking to infiltrate us and capture or kill or do who knows what to us?"

Kylee stiffened as she all but groaned, "Listen, Z, even though I didn't give birth to him doesn't mean I didn't love him any different than his biological mother would have. For fifteen years I thought he was lost or dead, but now he's here," she looked at Prater, beaming, "and I couldn't be any happier."

Z sunk as far back into her chair as she could and gave Prater a sideways look. "I don't trust him."

"Leave the trust to me," Kylee said. Z could tell that was a veiled order from the governor to her to follow along for now, ask questions later. She turned to Prater.

"So, then you. I wonder what makes you so special to the vampires."

Prater sat on the edge of his chair with his forearms resting on his knees. His fingers were folded together and he looked at Kylee and Z with his natural, gray-colored eyes (he had put his sunglasses into his satchel after his tussle with Z rather than putting them back on).

Z was disdainful. "All the more reason he shouldn't be here. If the vampires want him, they could be tracking him."

Kylee looked at Z but didn't respond. She knew her master-at-arms was right, of course, but there was no way Kylee wasn't going to allow her long lost son into the comfort of their town. Whatever troubles he brought with him would just have to be sorted out after the fact.

"They must want you real bad to have leveled Escape Town like they did," said Kylee.

Prater sat upright. "What do you mean?" The words sounded a bit frantic, which was uncharacteristic of him. "What happened?"

Z whipped around in her chair, suddenly more interested in taking part in the conversation.

"Let me tell you what happened," Z said as she adjusted herself to lean more towards Prater. Her expression was serious and her tone was crisp. "Not long after you left, the vampires rolled in, led by a half-robot vampire named Ryder Sloane. And do you know what drew them to that town of innocent people? You."

Z got out of her chair and stood over Prater. "That mechanized abomination said it was looking for you. And they either killed or took to their blood banks everyone! Including…"

Prater could see Z fighting back tears and he wondered what pain was coursing through her. He took on a solemn expression as he looked up at her and tried to convey an unspoken understanding. Z's nostrils flared as she struggled to hold back hurtful words – in addition to her fists – as she turned and dropped back into her seat without adding anything. Kylee reached a hand out in Prater's direction and sat it flat on her desk.

"She lost her adoptive father in the attack."

Prater looked at Z, who sat in her chair but faced the wall away from him.

"Zarina, I'm so sorry," Prater said quietly.

"I told you to call me Z." Her Russian accent was strong as she said the words, underscoring how cold and uncaring she felt towards what she perceived as a fake apology.

"Were there any survivors?"

"There was one," answered Kylee. "A teenage girl."

Prater looked up at Kylee. "Does she know anything about this half-robot vampire?"

Kylee shook her head. "She wasn't able to tell us much."

"What ended up happening with this Ryder Sloane?"

Z looked over her shoulder in Prater's direction. "He's probably back with Stirling. I'm guessing at San Francisco Mecca."

"I would surmise Stirling's the one behind all this," Kylee added. She sat back and lightly bounced her fingertips off each other as she momentarily slipped into deeper thought. "But what would he want with you…"

The words drifted into silence as Kylee said them. As she spoke, she was focused solely on the face of the man sitting across from her and into eyes she had not seen in such a long time. Z looked at Prater, too, but with an air of disgust and no concealment of her distrust. Prater remained wary yet vigilant as he casually looked between the two women, ready to act at the slightest hint of any more trouble from Z. The tension was already heavy and only grew thicker with each passing moment.

A rapid *beep–beep–beep–beep!* abruptly rang from Kylee's suit jacket. Kylee removed the cellphone from her inside left breast pocket and looked at it as it continued to beep. After a moment she glanced up at the two people sitting across from her before answering it by turning on the speakerphone. She set the phone onto the middle of her desk.

"This is Haddock," she said. "Go for code three-one-two-seven."

"*Three-one-two-seven, go,*" came a man's voice through the cellphone speaker. The volume was turned up and his voice was as clear as it was loud. "*Lock-in confirmed.*"

"Security confirmed. Go ahead, Marques."

"*I've located the scientist.*"

A guarded look of excitement dropped onto Kylee's face, while both Prater and Z listened with curiosity.

"That's good news," Kylee said, though her cautious optimism sounded clearly through. "Where is he?"

"*Just as our tips suspected, he and his family have been brought to the banks on Alcatraz. I heard Stirling confirm it himself.*"

The wary look on Kylee's face was gone in an instant, replaced by a wide smile. Prater felt a brief warmth flash through him as he remembered that smile. It was a smile that carried strength yet vulnerability, wisdom yet innocence.

"Good work, Marques." Kylee could barely contain herself as the glee bubbled up within her. "Is there anything else?"

"Yes, the cybervampire we heard about is real. I saw it personally."

"Unfortunately, Marques, I already received an eyewitness account confirming the existence of the cybervampire." Kylee sulked in her seat as she combed her fingers through her hair. "As if we don't have enough to worry about."

"There's one final item, governor."

"What is it?"

"The subject of Prater Saxon came up again, though this time Stirling told the cybervampire why he's been looking for him."

Kylee grew still. She stopped running her fingers through her hair mid-comb and looked at Prater. "What did he say?"

"He said he has it on good authority that Prater Saxon is half-human and half-vampire."

Kylee and Prater looked at each other and Prater instantly felt as though Kylee not only knew more than she was letting on, but that she knew *a lot* more.

"He believes this Prater's blood or genetic makeup holds the key to being able to walk again in the sunlight. He has a doctor lined up to do experiments on Prater upon his capture."

Kylee was silently pondering the news when Marques added, *"That's everything, governor."*

"Thank you, Marques. That'll be all, then."

"Three-one-two-seven, out."

Kylee turned off the phone and put it back into her pocket. She looked at Prater, whose expression had turned skeptical. Z, on the other hand, looked like she was about to explode with anger – a look Kylee was beginning to recognize much too often lately.

"You're working *with* the vampires?" Z shook her head. "And you knew about the cybervampire already? You sent Judge and me to

Escape Town without telling us about that thing first. You got Judge killed!"

Z jumped out of her seat. Prater stood up ready to intervene if Z made any sort of threatening move but the master-at-arms just shook her head and did nothing more than shake a fist at Kylee.

"Lies…lies!" Z stammered at first but quickly focused. "So many lies. It's to the point where I don't know what to believe anymore. What else have you kept from me?"

Prater looked at Z with a surprised expression that carried over when he looked back at Kylee. Kylee sighed as her eyes darted back-and-forth between the two people standing on the other side of her desk.

"Okay," said Kylee, resolutely. She stood up from her chair. "I need to show you both something."

Kylee picked a silver pen up from her desk then turned to face the gray concrete wall behind her. It looked to Prater like Kylee was studying the geometric carvings from the way she ran her fingers along the lines in the middle of the wall. Locating the inconspicuous opening with her finger, Kylee slipped the pen into the hole and turned it. There were clicks and a clang and when Kylee took the pen out of the wall, the concrete door slid away, revealing itself. Kylee looked back over her shoulder at Prater and Z – whose anger had been momentarily quelled by the reveal of the secret doorway.

"Follow me."

EPISODE 12

CAMP EXPECTATION
PACIFIC WASTELANDS

THE room beyond was a bit smaller than Kylee's office. The concrete door had slid back into place, leaving the otherwise black and dark space illuminated primarily by the dozen widescreen monitors arranged evenly across the back wall in rows of three. An ebony counter ran the entire width of the rear wall and was deep enough to accommodate three additional monitors that were undermounted and shone up through glass viewing portals. Three sets of keyboards sat on the countertop, one in front of each undermounted monitor. Each dark side wall popped with various buttons, touchscreen control pads, and dials lit up in rows across recessed processing towers. The room was warm, and the sounds of dozens of invisible electric cooling fans buzzed in the air. Kylee stood in the middle facing the wall of screens, with Prater and Z close behind, who were almost touching because of the limited standing room available.

"Sorry," said Kylee, offhandedly. "This space wasn't really made for visitors."

Z blinked as she shook her head in short, brisk movements while disbelief from the onslaught of secrets filled her.

"I don't know who you are anymore." Z did little to hide her disappointment.

"I can't say I totally disagree," Prater added. His voice was almost a mumble.

Kylee turned around and faced the two people who meant more to her in this world than anyone or anything else. She could see a vague hurt look in Prater's eyes while Z looked away, avoiding any eye contact at all. She took a moment to pause, sighing, to think about what she wanted to say. Nobody interrupted the silence that didn't last as long as it felt.

"This control room is part of an underground military network established in the days leading up to the Vampocalypse."

Z now made quick eye contact as they drilled into Kylee. *"Days leading up?* What the fuck is that supposed to mean? You knew this was all going to happen?"

Kylee stiffened as she shot her own eye daggers back at Z. She was almost a different version of herself than she had been earlier – much more rigid and professional.

"Let me explain. Since there are no longer country borders, the former U.S., Canada, and Mexico work together as the North American Freedom Alliance, or NAFA. We have our own government operating via a handful of bases hidden in the New World Territories along with several substations like this." She turned and pointed at the various screens. "These monitors provide feeds and data from not only our bases but from our substations across the NAFA. Camp Expectation is our cover for this substation. My territory is overseeing parts of the Pacific Wastelands. We work together and communicate via a ghost network based off what used to be known as dark web Internet technology. Some computer scientists much smarter than me were able to set this all up over these last thirty years."

Kylee looked back at Z. "To answer your question, no, I didn't *know* the Vampocalypse was going to happen, but I was tapped to be part of a special project weeks before the bombs went off." Kylee looked at Prater and her eyes softened. "There's so much more."

"Why have you been hiding all of this?" Z asked, sounding frantic as the words spilled out. "Why has the military been keeping this from the people? This should all be shared. The technology, the information we can provide, it can bring strength to the cause. It can help inspire a hope that many have lost."

"Share with the people?" Kylee teetered on mocking in her response. "With whom? Drifters of the Wastelands?" She glanced at

Prater and said, "No offense," before directing her attention back at Z. "Or with encampments and towns run by mini-megalomaniacal rulers like the one at Escape Town and countless others?"

"Why doesn't this military just launch a coordinated attack against the vampires?" asked Prater, entering the conversation.

Kylee shook her head. "The network exists but our numbers aren't great. There are about fifty thousand of us in the entire NAFA. When you're going up against hundreds of millions of vampires, that's a losing battle. We need to be more tactical."

"What about vampires sympathetic to the human cause? Like your spy inside? There are bound to be more like him."

"It's a difficult situation." Kylee addressed both Prater and Z as she answered. "I know neither of you were around before the Vampocalypse, but human leaders didn't always do good things. You wouldn't believe how easily people – good, kind-hearted people who would never think of committing evil acts – how easily they fell in line and did what was asked without question. We're talking horrible acts against humanity."

"I remember you telling me stories," Prater mused.

Kylee shrugged. "Truth is that the last thirty years have been devoid of war, diseases, and famine among the billions of vampires worldwide. Despite being despicable creatures, they've somehow figured out how to thrive as a global society without the problems humans caused at the suffering of other humans. A lot, if not nearly every vampire is perfectly happy being a vampire, preferring the immortality. And a thriving vampire society without human problems is hard to turn away from."

Z rubbed her forehead. "I don't know what to say. Let alone what to think. These creatures don't deserve to live. They took the world away from us." She shook her head in disbelief as her gaze settled downwards. "You're working with fucking vampires," she said under her breath. "And I'm standing next to one."

Prater ignored Z's ranting and leaned his head slightly towards Kylee. "How were you tapped to be part of this?"

The look in Kylee's eyes remained soft as she spoke. "The scientist Marques mentioned, his name is Geoffrey Appamattox. He's the one who created the particle bombs that turned everyone into vampires originally. Prater, before the Vampocalypse I wasn't just a labor and delivery nurse. I had friends who worked at NIOSH who put Appamattox in touch with me."

"What's NIOSH?"

"The National Institute for Occupational Safety and Health in what used to be Spokane, Washington. They conducted secret experiments there that were instrumental in creating the particle that changed humans into vampires."

Z suddenly grabbed Kylee by her upper arms and shoved her back against the counter. All signs of any reticence she was demonstrating were gone. The knives that shot from her eyes earlier became blinding lasers. She was barely restraining herself from tearing Kylee apart with her bare hands.

"That's enough!" Z shouted in Kylee's face. "You're a traitor and don't deserve the death I'm about to bring –"

Prater grabbed Z by her shoulders from behind and yanked her away from Kylee. Z's back smacked flat against one of the recessed banks of processors in the side wall. The systems in the unit kept functioning without interruption, oblivious to the sudden impact to the face of the unit. With his left forearm across Z's neck, Prater reached down with his free hand and quickly grabbed a sai strapped to one of Z's thighs. Its sharp tip was pressed ever-so-slightly into the left side of Z's neck in the next instant.

"Stop this, both of you!" Kylee shouted as she grabbed Prater's shoulders and pulled him back.

Prater and Z continued to stare at each other – unblinking, playing an unseen chess game in their minds as they each tried to guess what the other may not only do next, but then after that, and after that. Prater's arm stayed across Z's neck as long as he could keep it there until Kylee's pulling him away finally forced him to ease back. He kept the point of the sai on her neck – that was until there was enough space between him and Z where Kylee forced her way between them.

With her back to Z, Kylee looked at Prater as she grabbed his right arm and lowered the sai. Prater stepped back as far as the room would allow and handed the sai back to Z, handle first. Z snatched the weapon away and slid it back into its holder.

"It's enough for me, then." Z spat the words and Kylee wasn't sure she had ever heard Z's Russian accent come through so thick. "I'll be leaving. I can't stay here and work with the vampires."

"Z, wait," Kylee said, half-pleading, half-demanding, as she grabbed one of Z's arms.

A red light began flashing near the recessed middle monitor in the counter that caught everyone's attention, casting an intermittent crimson glow across everyone's faces. The surprised looks on Prater's and Z's faces were offset by one of relief from Kylee.

"Both of you, please, give me a moment."

Kylee centered herself to the counter and entered commands in the keyboard. The red light stopped flashing and the twelve monitors on the back wall suddenly worked as one to create a large interconnected single image. Kylee immediately stood at attention as she looked straight at the overly enlarged image of the man facing her.

The face taking up most of the image and staring into the room was hard and intense. He was bald and his skin was smooth, betraying the sixty-three years of life behind his dark eyes. He wore dark green army fatigues with a crest of wings and stars surrounding a NAFA logo on his left breast that was barely in frame. The man was surrounded by a plain, light blue backdrop and with all the monitor images joined as one, the light that shone from the large, combined image significantly brightened the room.

"At ease, Governor Haddock," the man said. His voice was gruff but there was no hint of a New Zealand accent that one might expect from looking at the man.

Kylee relaxed some but still remained more poised than was typical from what Prater and Z knew of her.

"Thank you, general."

"Looks like you've got some visitors."

"Yes, general." Kylee pressed herself against a side counter to provide the man on the screen a better view of the people with her. She pointed towards Z with one hand. "General, this is Zarina Ismagilova, my master-at-arms."

Although she normally would have corrected the introduction to have the man know her by her shortened moniker, Z decided to stay quiet and wait to learn more before saying anything at all. Instead, she looked at the man with the same untrusting eyes she had been showing to Kylee.

Without waiting for any interaction, Kylee pointed towards Prater. "This is Prater Saxon."

The eyes of the man on the screen widened and his face grew large as he leaned into his camera.

"Prater, Z, this is General Oliver Kaur of the North American Freedom Alliance."

Kylee could see a mix of curiosity and delight fall upon the general's face.

"The one and only Prater Saxon," General Kaur said. "I was beginning to think this day would never come. I've heard so much about you from your stepmother."

Z turned to look at Prater now, too, and the shades of distrust on her face were replaced by a sudden curiosity. The way the general said his words it was obvious he knew much more about this human-vampire standing next to her than she did. Still, she remained quiet.

Kylee broke the icy fog that had wafted through the room.

"I brought both of you here right now for this scheduled meeting with the general. I'm sorry I couldn't give you a heads-up. This must all be kept under the utmost secrecy. What you see and hear here stays here as a matter of security for all humankind."

"I'm sure they understand, governor," General Kaur said as he eased away from his camera, providing a more relaxed feel to the room. "Still, I'll leave it to you to deal with any unpleasantries that may arise after this meeting, not that there should be any. For now, there's much to discuss as time is of the essence."

"Wait," Prater interrupted. "What is it you know about me?"

The general harumphed. "You mean your stepmother hasn't told you about…you?"

Kylee stiffened. "I haven't had a chance to fill either of them in as much as I'd like."

"I wouldn't say that," Z countered.

"And more like not at all," Prater added.

"Well, governor, I don't have time to tell stories. I'll leave that to you. Right now, in addition to you having found Saxon, my understanding is you've located Appamattox."

"Yes, general. Our source inside San Francisco Mecca has confirmed he's being held in the blood banks at Alcatraz. I've already begun formulating a plan for rescue –"

General Kaur held up a hand. "That's not going to be necessary."

"Why? What's changed?"

"We have new information that supersedes the Appamattox mission."

Kylee grew more intense as she leaned forward on the counter. "What could possibly be more important than rescuing Appamattox?"

There was a demand in Kylee's voice that the general normally would have addressed, but there were more pressing matters.

"Headquarters received intel that all the top leaders of the vampire world are meeting for a first-time ever summit in San Francisco Mecca. The opening ceremony is scheduled to take place tonight with festivities continuing until dawn. A plan has been executed to ensure none of them make it out of there alive."

Prater exchanged glances with Z, who had become much more invested in the conversation. Kylee's eyebrows narrowed.

"What's this plan?"

"At approximately oh-four hundred this morning, a specially trained team took command of the *Harbinger One,* an *Annihilator*-class nuclear submarine controlled by the vampires. Their mission was to board the submarine and take it to sea and wait until the opening ceremony tonight during which time they would launch nuclear missiles on board to wipe out all of San Francisco Mecca. Further, the missile launch mechanisms that had been specially modified by the vampires were destroyed during the takeover."

"Meaning what?" Kylee snuck in the question as the general paused in his delivery.

"There is a contingency in place that will allow the missiles to be manually detonated on board. This doesn't change the mission, only the method of delivery. Unfortunately, good soldiers will be lost because of it."

"Along with Appamattox." There was a frustration brewing within Kylee that looked as if it was going to boil over at any moment. Her restraint was barely under control. "You can't do this. You must let us rescue Appamattox first."

The general shook his head. "That's a negative. The mission takes precedence. The bomb has to go off tonight."

"Does it, though?" The sudden sound of Z's voice surprised those in the room. "If tonight is an opening ceremony, then there are bound to be meetings for the next few days at least, right? Why not postpone the detonation?"

"Not to be dismissive, Ms. Ismagilova, but we need to stay on track with the mission as planned." General Kaur's oversized image invoked an additional disregard as he literally looked down on Z from the place of his enlarged and elevated image on the wall. "The vampires are surely already attempting to locate the submarine. If they do, or more certainly, *when* they do, if the vessel isn't close enough for the detonation to destroy San Francisco, this will all be for nothing. If that happens, we may never have an opportunity like this again."

Kylee pounded a fist lightly on the counter. "But Appamattox is the one who created the particle and is our best hope of finding an antidote. None of our scientists in any of our NAFA stations have come remotely close to finding a solution."

"I thought all you needed was Prater," said the general.

Now it was Prater who spoke abruptly. "What does he mean?" he asked as he leaned in on Kylee's left in an attempt to make eye contact with her from the side.

Kylee paid Prater no mind as she continued to address the general. "Prater is just part of it. We need Appamattox's know-how to see if it can work. You have to give us some time to get to him."

The general looked at his watch then back up at the trio of eyes on him.

"You have twelve hours before the sub is due to arrive in San Francisco Bay. I can't buy you any additional time, so you have until then to get there and get him out before that bomb goes off."

"It'll take us close to ten hours just to get there. There's no feasible way to pull this off without first formulating a comprehensive plan. We need more time." Kylee was done negotiating. The general had to be more understanding and accommodating.

"Then I suggest you get a hold of your contact in San Francisco Mecca and step up your timeline."

Kylee slapped a palm hard onto the counter. "Dammit, Oliver, you've known me for a long time. There's no reason you can't get me some additional time. This is cutting things too close." She took a deep breath and stood more upright. "I want to speak with President Chief Crowfoot."

A deep grumble resonated from within the general and his lip curled. "President Chief Crowfoot has tasked me with overseeing this mission. And I'm sorry, Kylee, but this is the mission." Kaur's voice didn't sound apologetic despite his choice of words.

"But –" Kylee tried again but this time the general held up a hand as he interrupted her.

"Now's the time, governor. Now's *our* time. We strike first, as soon as possible, without warning." The general lowered his hand

and took a final look at the people in the room. "You have twelve hours. Good luck."

The interconnected visual of the general disappeared and was replaced by whatever individual image each monitor displayed prior to the meeting. With the oversized image of the general gone, the subdued lighting also returned to the room.

Kylee tapped the knuckles of one hand on the counter several times then turned around. Her body relaxed as she sat back against the edge of the counter, but her tone was severe.

"I'm going to need to get hold of Marques right away. Z, assemble a team and prep the motorcade for our immediate departure to San Francisco Mecca."

Z pursed her lips and paused in thought before she responded. Kylee cocked her head to the side as she glared at her.

"You're still my master-at-arms, aren't you?" She added a second time, though less rigid, more pleading. "Aren't you?"

Z crossed her arms in front of her chest. "I am. For now."

"Thank you, Z."

"But you're wanting to take the emergency escape caravan? What'll happen if it's needed while we're gone?"

Kylee stepped away from the counter and stood in front of Z.

"It won't matter if we don't save Appamattox from that bomb going off. The caravan is the best chance we have to successfully make it to San Francisco Mecca."

Z took a breath through her teeth and nodded. She realized Kylee was right.

"Prater," Kylee said, looking at the man she had lost for so long but who now stood before her. She grasped him gently by the shoulders. "There is so very much I need to tell you. I am so, so sorry I've never told you about these things before but there isn't time right now. I have to recontact Marques and work out immediate details. I can't waste a single moment."

Prater's eyes were distant as he looked back at the woman. "Please don't ask me to do anything. This isn't my fight."

Kylee shook her head. "No, no, of course not. You asked about Annika earlier. I know I told you she didn't know much but maybe you can go and just make sure she's okay. You've always had a way of communicating with lost souls. Right now, she's as lost as they get."

Prater nodded. "Sure. I can do that."

"Take a radio with you so I can get hold of you later."

Prater nodded as Kylee returned to her computer workstation.

"We're set for now then," said Kylee.

"There's something I have to know before we head out on this mission," said Z.

Kylee looked back and was again confronted with that look of suspicion from her master-at-arms. "What is it?"

"This agent of yours, Marques. How do you know he can be trusted? Who is he exactly?"

The fact that Z used the word "trust" in the same context as a vampire was a small victory to Kylee. She resisted saying anything that would let Z realize the sentiment. Kylee looked between the two of them several times before her gaze settled on Prater.

"He's my stepbrother." With a deep breath she continued. "Marques was a White House intern before the Vampocalypse who became a vampire like most from the particle bombs that were set off. He was already working with Stirling and maintained his position of trust in Stirling's inner circle as the new vampire world was built. Marques had a brother, Jesse, and they'd always been close but they lost contact with one another in the chaotic days following the Great Turn. Jesse managed to escape being turned into a vampire. He knew Oliver Kaur before the Vampocalypse and went on to be greatly involved with NAFA. Jesse and I met shortly after you left all those years ago. We married two years later."

Here Kylee paused and her eyes dropped.

"We had arranged to have a small wedding at a little abandoned church we found in the Wastelands. There were just a few of us there." Kylee laughed lightly. "It was all just for show, really, I mean, the world obviously wasn't what it was before. We just thought that the feeling of an actual ceremony would help us feel, in some ways, more whole again."

Prater and Z remained silent as they watched Kylee take in a deep breath before she looked back up.

"Jesse was killed on our wedding day. I was knocked unconscious during the fight and when I came to, only four out of six of us had survived. It seemed their primary mission was to kill Jesse and once they completed their task, they left."

The hardest part told, Kylee returned to being more resolute.

"Not long after that, General Kaur was contacted by Marques and he was established as a mole. Jesse had provided his brother the information on how to contact the general directly via secret channels. It was then that Marques pledged himself to the cause for restoring humankind and began providing information to NAFA. Most of it has been pretty useless until now."

Kylee concentrated on Z. "So, if you want to know if I trust him, yes. Yes, I do. I have no reason to believe he isn't on our side. He's always been one of the good ones, but Jesse's murder only strengthened that resolve."

The three of them stood silently for a few moments before Kylee reached out and took Z by her hands. There was no resistance as Z felt a reassurance and warmth in Kylee's tender grip.

"That's all I have to offer. Despite what you may think, I've done all this with my faith in humankind in mind. Nothing else. And I'm not asking you to trust Marques. I'm asking you to trust me. Despite it all, trust *me*."

Z looked at Kylee with a hard stare that didn't soften even when she gave a quick, almost indiscernible nod. It was enough. It had to be. Kylee smiled a silent "thank you" and released her hold of Z's hands.

Changing subjects, Kylee looked at Prater as she said, "It's already been a long morning. Are you hungry? I'm sure there's something on the, ummm, *fresher* side that can be mustered up for you, though it may not be any of your usual fare."

Z pointed at Prater. "*That's* a problem."

Prater assembled a reassuring smile. "There's no problem. I'll be fine, thank you."

PACIFIC WASTELANDS

ABOUT four days walk from Camp Expectation, a lone young man lumbered along a dusty ground already dry despite recent rains. Foothills in the distance beckoned him as he searched for whatever might provide as a makeshift shelter. The day was warm and he had a dirty jacket tied around his waist, over the top of his ragged Led Zeppelin T-shirt. The skeletal remains of sneakers looked more like sandals from the massive holes in them. Still, the nonchalant expression on his face was one of indifference, like he had no cares or bothers in the world.

Jake was twenty-one years old and all he remembered was life in the barren wastes. Born well after the world of vampires took hold, it was just he and his mother surviving on their own. His mother never talked about his father or any other family, and Jake didn't even really know what questions to ask, having mostly only interacted with his mother his entire life. There were fleeting encounters with other lonesome travelers and the occasional small group that his mother would politely interact with, but those times were seldom and they were always moving on, by themselves, into the wide, uncharted world before them. This was how they lived until his mother died of some sickness – she said she thought she had something called "cancer" – when Jake was thirteen. It came on quick and thankfully she didn't have to linger for long. She died quietly in her sleep one night after just a few weeks of the illness. Already well-accustomed to living the life of a survivalist, Jake continued on his own, not needing nor wanting much, content to be by himself.

Jake stopped and looked up at the glow of the sun, obscured by the gray-yellow haze that he always knew to be there. Even though the suppressed glow wasn't extremely bright, for a moment he thought of his sunglasses and wished he still had them.

Sure hope that Prater guy is enjoyin' them!

He pulled his satchel around to the front and opened it. Right on top of everything else was the metallic water bottle he was after. He took the bottle out of the bag and shook it. The quiet sloshing inside made it sound about half full. He twisted off the plastic top then turned it upside down and filled it almost to the top with water. Taking the drink like a shot he stopped and pondered for a moment. His mother had always taught him the importance of careful rationing and the traps of overabundance. One capful was all he needed for the two or three hours, maybe even four if he took it easy and paced himself. It would also help if he could reach the foothills to take advantage of cooler dips and crevasses they may have to offer before moving on to wherever the barrens pointed him next.

Sometimes, though, one capful just didn't seem to be enough. After taking another moment to think again before acting, he went ahead and filled the cap with a second shot of water.

A sudden shove in the back knocked Jake unexpectedly to the ground. The cap went flying out of his hand and when he landed the open water bottle bounced loose before landing with its bottom end propped on some rocks. Jake scrambled forward on his hands and knees to grab it as the remaining water rapidly gushed out and into cracks in the dirt. The ground didn't even look like it got wet as the water disappeared into the dark ground.

"No, no!" Jake cried out as he grabbed the bottle as quickly as he could. But it was too late. All the water save for a few drops had spilt away.

Confused and uncertain as to what happened, Jake slammed the empty bottle against the rocks and a dull echoey thud emanated from inside the metal container. Jake twisted himself around to sit up and see what had knocked him so carelessly from behind…

…to find himself looking up at three vampires glaring down at him with wide smiles that did nothing to hide their salivating, bloodthirsty fangs.

"What's going on, Jake?" The words hissed from the vicious jowls of the creature in the middle.

Jake fell backwards onto his elbows and stared up almost directly into the gray-white orb that was the sun in the sky partially silhouetting the creatures over him. Jake held a hand up to put the sun behind his palm and stared at the vampires through his fingers.

"N – nothing, Kent," Jake stuttered. "You – you know I don't ever have nothing going on."

The one called Kent reached down with one hand, grabbed the knot of tied jacket arms in front of Jake's waist, and effortlessly pulled him up onto his feet. The other two vampires were instantly behind the young man, each holding him by one of his arms. Kent stood in front, still smiling a wide smile.

"You disappoint me, Jake. I have a feeling you got more to say than you're letting on."

Jake shook his head but otherwise didn't struggle. He was far too fragile and weak in comparison to the vampires to put up any sort of respectful fight. Frankly, he was weak and frail in comparison to most humans as well, especially in his current near-malnourished state.

"If there was anything else, I'd, I'd tell you. I would – I would!"

Kent grabbed Jake by his jaw and turned the young man's head from side to side several times then stopped.

"*I would, I would,*" Kent mocked. "I know you would, Jake. You've never let me down. I know that if there's something you've come across during your travels of the Wastelands worth mentioning, you're always certain to tell. You've been instrumental over the years leading us to desert stragglers and small groups of folks that we've been able to add to our blood banks."

Jake shook his head now. "Right! Yes, right. I tell you what I can, you leave me alone. That's the deal."

"Oh, I'm fully aware of our arrangement." Kent squinted and cocked his head to the side. "I need you to think hard, Jake. Is there anything, or anyone, that you have interacted with lately? Anyone to tell us about?"

Jake's eyes were wide as he struggled to process what was happening. The vampire Kent had never acted this way before. Ever since the creature and his companions came across him nearly two years ago, Jake agreed to help Kent by informing the creature of any humans he became aware of in the desert. Kent and his two companions – it was always the same two – would hunt down the humans, take them back to San Francisco Mecca, and take any glory that came from their captures. In exchange, Kent allowed Jake to live. There was something different in Kent's eyes this time, though, and while Jake wasn't really scared, some of the hairs on the back of his neck were raised.

"I'm not here about just anyone," Kent said as he stepped close to Jake. "I'm looking for someone specific. I'm looking for someone named Prater Saxon."

Jake couldn't keep from having his eyes perk open wide at the mention of the name.

Kent stepped even closer to the anxious young man. Their bodies were nearly touching as the vampire, who looked to be a man in his forties, put his face next to Jake's. The creature inhaled slowly and deeply then opened his mouth to fully reveal his wet fangs as Jake shook nervously. Kent lightly dragged the sharp tips of his teeth against the side of Jake's neck, slowly grazing the skin until he worked his way to Jake's ear.

"You know something about this Prater," Kent said in a whisper. His foul breath danced around Jake's ear. "I can hear your pulse quicken and smell your blood as your heartbeat intensifies. Now..." Kent ran his teeth gently against Jake's ear. "Tell me what you know about this Prater."

Jake closed his eyes as he fought an internal battle. All that was good and right in him made him want to protect the kind man he had encountered in the Wastelands, but the sense of self-preservation was overwhelming. Sweat, valuable water his body would normally conserve, began to bead on Jake's forehead. He suddenly felt a razor-like talon stroking his right cheek almost as lightly as the breath tickling his ear.

"Tell me," Kent whispered, enticing, and drawing Jake in. "Tell me what I need to know, Jake. Remember our arrangement…you wouldn't want to break that now, would you?"

Jake closed his eyes tight as he whispered. "Camp Expectation." There was disappointment in his voice. "He's headed towards Camp Expectation."

Kent pulled away and took Jake once again by his jaw and forced the young man to look straight at him.

"Now it seems to me that you might have some affinity for this place you call Camp Expectation," said Kent, almost accusatory in his manner-of-speaking. He pushed Jake's face away, harder than Jake would have liked.

"No, not really." The young man's voice was sullen, defeated.

"I'm curious, then, why you haven't told us about this place before."

Jake looked down and half shrugged. Kent also looked down, but he was shaking his head in disappointment. With a resounding sigh he looked back up then blinked a long blink as he nodded his head. Taking the cue, the vampires holding Jake by the arms forced him down onto his knees. Kent shook his head again though this time while making eye contact with the young man helpless before him. He grabbed Jake by the chin and forced him to look up. Kent thought he saw a wetness in the human's eyes – *Is this man crying?* – and did all he could to hide his disgust.

"You disappoint me," said Kent while shaking his head. "Despite this, I might still let you live."

Kent took both hands and cradled the young man's head and then tears truly fell down Jake's cheeks. The wetness repulsed the vampire as the tears leaked against his hands. He moved his hands along Jake's cheeks and ran his thumbs across the bottoms of Jake's eyes to wipe away the wet. He smiled down at the young man – a sudden contrast from the disgust he did little to hide just a moment earlier.

"Now, my friend, Jake," the vampire said, still holding the young man's face in his grasp, "tell me everything you know about Prater and, most importantly, where is this place called Camp Expectation?"

EPISODE 13

SAN FRANCISCO MECCA
NORTH AMERICA NEW WORLD TERRITORIES VAMPIRE
CAPITOL

THE president's office, located at the top of the former Transamerica Pyramid, was much larger than Jonathan Stirling's old vice president office in the White House so many years ago. This office had individual seats for eight arranged in two staggered rows in front of his oval-shaped obsidian desk. The room was rectangular with a high ceiling comprised of several large, winter-frosted marble tiles with deep crimson-colored veins that looked as if they'd been crafted by drunken spiders. Black wooden beams spanned the length of the ceiling, breaking up the tile pallet. The floor was made of zebra wood planks laid in crisscrossing patterns. Wine red curtains covered the entirety of the wide wall behind Stirling's desk and continued on to cover all of one side wall as well. The opposite side wall was nothing but a single immense floor-to-ceiling, wall-to-wall monitor screen. The fourth wall, behind the guest seating, was an off-white with large paintings that looked like they could have been created by Pablo Picasso fighting through a neo-gothic phase. The two oversized original art pieces took up almost the entirety of space on either side of the office door in the middle.

Brandon Stirling looked more annoyed than troubled. Even though he wasn't at the meeting in person, the shoulders-up image of the president's brother filled the massive side wall screen, making his presence quite imposing. Every tick in the corner of an eye, quiver of a lip, and flare of a nostril was overexaggerated by the enormous image. The thirty-something looking vampire kept his dark hair, beard, and mustache trimmed as precisely as ever. His eyes intermittently focused on Ryder Sloane, who sat in the chair directly across from where the president sat behind his desk. The grafting of the new skin over the burned areas was complete, leaving only the scars of where the edges of skin came together as evidence of the recent surgical reconstruction procedures. The remainder of those in attendance included the president's usual innermost circle: Vice President Andrea McCullough, Senator Elite Samuel Ellis, and Councilor Marques Wright. They sat scattered among the red and black leather seats, which were large and round and were swiveled to partially face both Stirling brothers.

"The lack of progress on capturing Prater Saxon is frustrating, to say the least," said Brandon as he addressed his brother. "Let me use our military resources to find him. I promise it won't take long. Centuries of military experience and I'm just sitting here in NORAD doing a lot of fucking nothing." He drilled his eyes into Sloane. "While your faith in this…thing…is misplaced."

Sloane started to jump from his seat when President Stirling intervened. He lifted a hand towards the cybervampire as he spoke.

"Sloane, stay settled." Stirling took a moment to chew silently at the air then to his brother he said, "Last warning, Brandon. I won't have you disrespecting him any longer."

Brandon sat back in his seat and the shrinking of his face on the supersized monitor helped ease some of the tension in the office. The NORAD commander laughed.

"You can play with your bastardization, big brother. I'll have no part of it."

"Good enough," President Stirling said, satisfied. "We'll hear no more of it then."

The president paused, waiting for an inevitable sarcastic remark from his brother that never came.

"If you're finished I'm certain we can put your military to use, commander," Samuel said, breaking the tension between the brothers. "We seem to have lost a submarine. Maybe you can help us find it."

All eyes were on Brandon as he was strangely quiet for several long, anxious moments, while everyone waited to see how he was going to react. The bellow of laughter that erupted from the monitor surprised everyone, even the president himself.

"You – you lost a submarine?" Brandon managed to wheeze out among the laughter.

"It's not a laughing matter, Brandon," said the president.

"No, it's not," Samuel reinforced. "This was one of our *Annihilator*-class subs. It was stolen by the humans from our base in San Diego and it's carrying live warheads."

A look of alarm replaced Brandon's laughter and the abrupt silence was immediately disconcerting for everyone in the room. Everyone watched the president's brother on the large screen as he went from mocking to boiling rage in an instant.

"First, I applaud you for being able to hide this from me until now. Second, what kind of organization are you running here, Jonathan? How does one just *lose* a nuclear submarine?" Brandon's brow wrinkled and his fangs slung saliva as he spat the words.

Jonathan Stirling pounded a hard fist on his desk and launched up from his chair while growling at the wall screen.

"You will not take that tone with me, Brandon. We may be brothers, but I am the *president!*"

President Stirling's voice was husky and deep and his eyes were as dark red as the office curtains that framed his fury. Those in the room watched their leader, anxious and uncertain of what he might do next in his blind anger. As quickly as it escalated, relief cautiously rolled through the room as the elder Stirling's breathing slowed and his fangs receded from their fully extended positions to more of a casual display.

"Brandon," the president said, his voice calming as the deep red of his sclerae began to reduce in their intensity, "you're here to help with this conversation, not hinder. What's done is done. What we must do now is focus on finding this vessel. I see this as your jurisdiction."

Brandon had also calmed and looked much more accepting of the situation. Samuel and Andrea exchanged a look of what they hoped was not just temporary relief. Sloane had watched the display between the brothers with more curiosity than concern. Marques stayed in his seat, unmoving, taking mental note of everything that transpired as he remained ready for any particular bidding of the president.

"Not the most ideal of circumstances, obviously," Brandon grumbled. "And I'll refrain from explaining how this would not have happened if I had been provided more oversight originally."

"I actually cannot agree with you more," said Samuel. "So much time and resources have been put into building our global vampire society that little concern has been put into locating these pockets of humans. This needs to change."

The president shot Samuel a look that could have just as easily brought violence or death at the utterance of another word. The exchange didn't go unnoticed by Brandon.

"No matter," Brandon said, dismissively, as he rubbed his chin. "I can put together a team to find the vessel. Samuel, have your people get me all the records and information they have on the theft. I want times of day down to the hundredth of a second detailing what happened. I want to know how many humans there were, what they were wearing, how they were armed. I need to know everything – if you know what kind of cologne they were wearing, no detail is too great for you to pass on. I'll have my own people gather maps of the underwater channels lining the coast, but have yours send me anything they may have locally that aren't available on national servers."

"Of course," was Samuel's simple response. He strained to keep from rolling his eyes through the unnecessary details.

"Good," said President Stirling as he sat back into his chair. "Brandon, I'm sure you understand that time is of the essence. There's no telling what these humans have planned to do with that weapon."

Andrea raised a hand as she felt comfortable to interject for the first time in the meeting.

"Jonathan, if I may," she paused as the president looked at her and nodded in acknowledgement. "With this turn of events, maybe we should reconsider the security situation for the summit. Perhaps we should have your brother bring some troops in to help oversee the events over the next few days."

Andrea paused again. The president looked at her but his demeanor and expression didn't change.

"I understand the concern, Andrea, but I don't feel a need for a show of force." The president stopped momentarily and snarled silently as he chewed on nothing. "This summit is a celebration of our accomplishments as a brotherhood and sisterhood of vampires after millennia of repression. We're here to show our vampire family worldwide that we have overcome all obstacles and finally claimed this world as our own." President Stirling's eyes traveled the room before stopping on his brother. "I don't want a show of force to dissuade anyone's perception of that reality."

"And if that's *not* the reality, dear brother?" Brandon asked.

"It *is* the reality, Brandon," President Stirling said, ending the subject.

A sudden beeping from an alarm program on one of the touchscreens flush mounted into President Stirling's black desktop interrupted the exchange between the brothers. Jonathan tapped the button to stop the beeping and a voice came immediately through from unseen speakers in the desk.

"Ryder Sloane has a high priority communication from someone identifying himself as 'Kent'. He says it's of utmost importance and has to do with Prater Saxon."

The president looked at Sloane, needing to do no more in asking for an explanation.

"Before I left the area of Escape Town to come back here, I had ordered several units to canvas the area for any clues to finding Saxon.

Kent is one of my best. Perhaps he's found something of value if he's interrupting this meeting."

Stirling nodded then said to the unknown voice, "Put him through."

The large image of Brandon Stirling shrunk to a tenth of its full size and moved into the upper left corner of the giant wall screen as the rest of the monitor was filled with showing the vampire Kent from the waist up. Sloane stood up as he addressed the newcomer to the meeting.

"I hope you have something substantial to interrupt the president's meeting like this," Sloane warned.

A broad smile flashed across Kent's lips. "Oh, I think you'll be very pleased with what I've got here."

Nearly interrupting Kent, Sloane said, "Get on with it, then."

Without missing a beat, Kent blurted, "I've located Camp Expectation, Prater Saxon's whereabouts."

The surprise statement exploded through the room like a shotgun blast. Sloane rubbed his palms together as he expressed his excitement.

"You're absolutely certain you've located this place?" There was a pride in the cybervampire's voice as he addressed his comrade. "How did you come across this information?"

"Sometimes it's not the methods, but rather, *who* you know," Kent said, still smiling though the expression was more demure. "Some may have thought me foolish for not killing every human every time I came across one, but I always saw the value in forging the types of relationships that afforded me future payoffs. Which means that, occasionally, I get to cash in."

Smiles swept across the vampire's faces as Kent raised his right hand into view of the monitor display – in his grasp was the head of a young man. He held the head by the hair, and the face was long and sullen, with hollow, bloodied sockets where the eyes had been gouged out by Kent's thumbs. The mouth was open and slack and his tongue hung out, white and enlarged from dehydration. The entire head was bloodless, the warmth of human life that used to course through the man having been consumed by the vampires that decapitated him.

"This is my good friend Jake," Kent said. He held the head up to his eye level and he looked into the sagging, lifeless face. "Say 'hello' to everyone, Jake." Kent put the face right up to his transmitter camera, adding a macabre interaction to the proceedings, but not one that wasn't appreciated by those in attendance. Kent pulled Jake's head away as he said, "It seems as though Jake's a little under the weather. He's been pretty quiet since he showed me the way to Prater's whereabouts."

Sloane looked at President Stirling with a satisfied smile, whose own excited expression was what he expected to see.

"Where is this place, Camp Expectation, located?" asked the president.

"Turns out not that far from Escape Town. At least not as far as you'd expect. Less than a couple of hundred miles between the two. I waited until I was able to personally put my eyes on the place before saying my final good-byes to Jake here." With that, Kent carelessly tossed the head off to the side, out of camera view. It hit something off-camera with a thud.

"You should know that this place is larger than Escape Town," Kent continued. "I'm guessing about twice the size."

"The fact that such a large community of humans has been existing without our knowing is troubling," Brandon interjected. "If there is one, there are bound to be others."

"Let's not get ahead of ourselves," the president eased. "Were you able to gauge their defenses at all?"

Kent shook his head. "Not entirely, but there doesn't seem to be any sort of organized military presence or increased defense mechanisms. There's the usual fence and guards, but it looks like a relatively simple town, nothing more, nothing less."

"You'd have no way of knowing exactly what you're running into," Brandon stated, matter-of-factly. "I can offer some of my army to assist."

"No," Sloane said as he stiffened. "Our local forces will be enough."

"I expected you'd be saying that, general," said Kent. "I've already contacted as many of our forces within the vicinity as possible to assemble."

"How many were able to answer the call?" Sloane asked.

Kent smiled. "You will have nearly a thousand at your command here within the hour."

Gasps of delight ruffled through the office.

"I'll have one of our highspeed transports prepped," Samuel offered to Sloane. "It'll have you there about the same time as the troops."

"Perfect." Sloane nodded. Standing tall and resolute, he turned to face the president.

Jonathan Stirling stood up behind his desk and leaned forward on both hands. He pressed a button on one of his inlaid displays and the images of Kent and his brother flipped to where Brandon's became the more prominent face on the monitor.

"Brandon, I agree that General Sloane will handle matters at Camp Expectation. I want you to focus one hundred percent on finding our stolen submarine."

The president's brother smiled triumphantly. "I actually already have an idea as to where it's going."

"Where's that?" the president asked for everyone in the room.

"There's only one logical place: they're headed to San Francisco Mecca to disrupt the summit."

The looks immediately exchanged around the room were in acquiescence of what they already feared but didn't want to believe. Brandon responded as if sensing the anxiety among them.

"We'll begin plotting possible routes and I'll have my best team on it. The sub will be located and once it is we'll retake it and kill the humans inside. Their plan will not succeed."

"Good," said the president. "I look forward to the update on your victory in the matter."

"You should expect nothing less, Jonathan." With that, the image of Brandon Stirling blinked out and Kent's face alone filled the screen once again.

"Marques."

"Yes, Mr. President?" The councilor, having been quiet and observant through all the interactions, immediately came to attention.

"Implement a mecca-wide curfew effective immediately. Notify all authorities and the public that all nonessential personnel are to get home and remain indoors for the duration of the summit. Those with passes to the ceremonies and events may still attend. Aside from that, I expect this mecca to be a ghost town within the next four hours."

Marques cleared his throat. "Four hours, Mr. President? With respect, sir, that's a lot to accomplish within the next four hours. I'm not sure –"

"Not to worry, councilor, the vice president will assist you to ensure thoroughness and efficiency."

Andrea perked up and a sly smile curled the corner of her lips.

Marques blinked as he glanced at the vice president. "I'm sure the vice president has more pressing matters to attend to with –"

Andrea held up a hand. "It's no trouble at all, councilor."

"I really don't mind working on this alone –" Marques began, once again addressing the president. And once again he was interrupted.

Jonathan Stirling seemed to ignore Marques, saying, "I expect the two of you to get started on this right away."

Marques side-eyed the vice president who only smiled in return.

"Of course, Mr. President," Marques said.

The president turned to address the cybernetic general and his comrade on the monitor.

"Bring Prater Saxon to me. Alive is preferable. But dead will do."

EPISODE 14

CAMP EXPECTATION
PACIFIC WASTELANDS

ANNIKA wasn't in her hospital room when Prater arrived. He met with Dr. Cleary who assured him she was fine physically but was certainly under emotional strain. Prater could definitely relate to that sentiment. Annika had insisted on leaving the confines and care of the hospital and had what the doctor felt was an odd request under her circumstances. Prater got the information on where the doctor believed Annika could be found and Prater left.

The area the doctor directed Prater to was a large, empty lot surrounded by a 3-rail horse fence though there were no horses to be seen. The lot was located next to one of Camp Expectation's farmhouses near the edge of the town. At the far end of the just slightly rectangular space was a round paper target tacked to a stack of hay bales. Despite the distance, Prater could easily see the target was unused.

A sudden, heavy *THWANG* cracked the quiet, followed by a swift hiss as air vibrated through the flight feathers of an arrow that met its mark near the center of the yellow dot in the middle of the target. Prater looked at the archer – Annika wasn't too far from him on the near end of the lot, holding a recurve bow. He watched her nock a second arrow into place as she raised the bow and took quick aim. The thick *THWANG* sounded again and the arrow thumped into the target: barely touching the first arrow, but this one was dead center.

"Nice shot," said Prater as he approached the girl at an angle from behind, causing Annika to jump slightly, startled by the sudden visitor.

"Sorry," Prater went on as he entered the lot through an open gap in the fence.

"I didn't expect any visitors." There was an annoyance in the girl's voice.

Prater went up to Annika and extended his hand. She shook it politely.

"You're Annika, I gather?"

Annika didn't nod or in any way acknowledge Prater was correct. "And you're Prater Saxon." She looked him up and down. "Didn't take long for everyone in Escape Town to know who you were. Word travels fast, especially when someone like you shows up."

"Someone like me? Not sure what you mean." A multitude of possibilities barreled through Prater's head. Did she know about him being half-vampire? Did the entire town know?

"Strangers. To the town."

"Oh, of course." Prater made sure not to let out an audible sound of relief. He lowered his sunglasses as he looked at the two arrows in the target again.

"You obviously know what you're doing," he said as he pushed the sunglasses back into place.

Annika retrieved a third arrow out of a nearly full quiver slung behind her back.

"I'm used to using a compound bow but the recurve will do. Just takes a little getting used to."

The third arrow nearly kissed the second as it snuggled in between the first two.

"I suppose you could be a good recreational archer," said Prater, "but from the look of your stance and the accuracy something tells me you've had some training."

Annika's eyes looked proud but still held the underlying sadness of her recent trauma.

"My master believed I was shooting like an Olympian. Not bad, huh?" Annika didn't let Prater respond before adding, "He's probably dead now."

"Yep, probably," Prater said without any semblance of remorse.

The offhandedness of the remark captured Annika's curiosity. "You sound like you don't even care."

"Should I?" Prater shrugged.

Annika squinted and tilted her head as she studied Prater's demeanor. "*Shouldn't* you?" she asked. "My entire town was wiped away. My family and friends are all gone." There was a steadfastness in her voice that to Prater's surprise never leaned towards any grief or anguish. "Don't you feel for them? At least a little?"

Prater paused a beat before replying. "I can't go through this world feeling sad for those who end up lost. I understand you may be sad, or angry, despite your will to be strong. I feel for you and whatever pain you're fighting through. But I can't feel for them."

Annika nodded. "You're right. And in all honesty, right now, I'm not sure if *I'm* even feeling anything for any of them." She swallowed. "I don't know what I'm feeling at all."

Her eyes lowered momentarily before focusing back down the lot at the target. Prater said nothing as he watched Annika let a fourth arrow fly. The arrow knocked others out of the way as it fought for the center space in the middle of the yellow dot.

"Why are you here?" Annika asked while dropping her arms to the side. "Are you here to try and make me feel better? Share stories of your sad, broken childhood to make mine not seem so bad?"

Prater shook his head. "Not at all. The doctor told me I might find you here. Last thing you need is anyone trying to one-up what you've been through. I'm not here to offer you anything. I know you'll ask if you need something."

"I appreciate that." Annika picked up a plastic water bottle sitting near her feet, twisted the top open and took a drink. "So what, then? You here for private lessons? Can't say I'm in the mood for giving any."

"I have some questions about this half-robot, half-vampire you encountered."

Its top twisted back closed, Annika tossed the water bottle aside and grabbed another arrow. She aimed the deadly projectile at the target across the lot then looked back at Prater.

"That bastard is responsible for the fate of my parents."

Without turning to look again at the target, Annika let the arrow fly. It hit the yellow bulls-eye on its edge just shy of the red ring that surrounded it. Prater let out a "Hmph" in acknowledgement of the seemingly effortless feat.

"It was a freak of nature and it was looking for you. And it was willing to do anything it needed to do to find you. So the way I see it..."

Annika grabbed another arrow and aimed it at Prater, nearly point blank into his chest.

"...you're responsible for *everything* that's happened."

Prater wasn't as fast as many full vampires, but he had noticed in recent years his speed and stamina growing beyond that of many, if not most, humans. Taking no chances against an Olympic-level archer, Prater jerked sideways and lurched forward, yanking the weapon from Annika's hands as he rolled to his side then back to his feet. His sunglasses hadn't moved though his hair flopped loosely around his face. He faced the teenager with the arrow nocked and ready to fly at her with the slightest twitch of his fingertips. Annika put her hands up in front of her as she took a few steps away.

Prater loosened his draw on the string as he lowered the weapon. Separating the arrow from the bow, Prater offered the weapon back to its original user. Annika snatched the items from Prater's hands.

"Listen," said Prater. "We've all been through a lot of shit, right? You can hold me responsible but at the end of the day that's not going to bring anyone back."

Annika turned away and focused on the opposite end of the lot. A slight breeze picked up wisps of her dirty blonde hair and brushed them across her face. She let the hair do its gentle caress without sweeping it away.

"You're right." Her eyes drifted past the lot and a high fence line that stretched not far beyond. "I'm just afraid of...being afraid. You'd think in this world ruled by vampires someone like me would live in constant fear. Having grown up in this world and in the protection of others, I've never been afraid. But now those others are gone, and I don't know what I'm going to do."

Prater put a hand out towards the girl but didn't touch her. "Hey, look at me." He paused a moment and when she didn't respond he added, "Annika..."

Slowly, the sixteen-year-old turned and faced Prater. She still managed to hold back any tears from the bevy of emotions flowing through her, not to mention being cried out from the events the day before and forcing herself to move on. The best she could, anyway.

"Annika," Prater repeated her name. He took off his sunglasses as he captured her gaze. "Often the ones who claim to be the bravest are actually the most afraid. Don't let appearances deceive you."

She could see the history of pain behind his eyes as she nodded slowly.

"Yep," she conceded. "I get it."

Prater put the sunglasses back on. "There's nothing else to it."

A quick crackling followed by a beep came from the small two-way radio clipped to Prater's hip.

"Prater, this is Kylee. Come in."

Prater brought up the radio and pressed the comm button on the side. "Prater here."

"Meet us back in the conference chamber. I'd like you to be here as we plan to head out to San Francisco Mecca."

"Got it."

"Is Annika with you?"

"She's here. She's doing fine."

"Good to hear. Bring her with you."

Prater flashed a smile at the young girl who reciprocated the expression, although only slightly.

"We're on our way."

BY contrast to the last time Prater was here, the council chamber was full of life as all thirteen seats were filled with an additional eight people standing as the meeting commenced. Prater led Annika, who had returned the bow and arrows to the townsperson who provided them to her before they left, down the chamber to the far end where the council seats were located. Kylee was in her governor's chair at the head of the council with Z standing next to her. The master-at-arms wore a black tactical vest that was zipped up and snug over a slightly loose all-weather field jacket. Her sai clung strapped to each thigh, with hints of their shiny silver blades pointing down the black SWAT pants that terminated near the ankles of her boots. Z gave Prater a cursory glance before settling warm eyes on Annika.

"Thank you both for joining us," Kylee said as Prater and Annika joined the group.

Kylee wasted no time introducing the newcomers to the meeting. Prater and Annika probably could have had a contest as to who felt more uncomfortable with the attention. They were met with mostly blank stares though a few of the attendees nodded politely. It didn't seem as though anyone knew who either of them was, from Prater's estimation, which put him a bit more at ease.

"This is the task force we've assembled to rescue Appamattox," Kylee continued.

Kylee gestured to specific individuals as she introduced them. Prater picked up on the names provided as an interesting combination of birth names and nicknames as Kylee said them. The first identified was a bald woman with circular tattoos on her head.

"This is Incom. As our communications expert, she makes sure all our comms and transmitters remain in working order."

"I'm also a computer geek," Incom said as she chewed on a piece of gum. "Though there's not much need for that around here."

"Not typically," Kylee said. She utilized Incom's talents for the occasional IT needs in her secret communications room, but not everyone attending this meeting was privy to the existence of that space.

Next was a thin, Asian-American man with short black hair. His clothes were mostly clean except for the scattered oil and grease stains. "This is Wen, he's our fuelsmith. He keeps our rigs gassed up."

Wen held his fists up with his knuckles facing out for Prater and Annika to see. Tattooed across the knuckles of his fingers across his fists were "TWIN" and "TRBO". Wen smiled a wide, proud smile.

"Whaddya think? In honor of my 92 300ZX. Cool, huh?"

"You misspelled 'turbo'." Annika wasn't going to let that slide.

Wen looked at the spelling and shrugged. "Well, it wouldn't have fit if it was spelled right. Kinda like fitting words on a license plate."

"What's a license plate?" Annika asked genuinely.

Wen looked disappointed as he shook his head in response, leaving the question to be answered another day. Kylee continued with the introductions.

"Ecks here keeps his eyes on our recon and scanning equipment. Hopefully we don't run into any surprise visitors, but if we do, Ecks should spot them before they spot us."

"*Ecks* marks the spot," the one called Ecks said as he smiled through the moustache and beard that were the same dark red as the thick hair on his head.

"This is the beast we call Berserker," said Kylee, moving on. "He's an ex-wrestler from the old days. He'll provide additional protection on the journey."

Standing a good head taller than the next tallest person in the room, Berserker was a beast, indeed. He was wide and muscular and wore a cloth mask with cutout eyeholes tied around the top half of his head that very much gave him the look of the ex-wrestler that he was. Loose blonde curls peeked out from under the knot tying the mask together in the back of his head. He looked at the newcomers from behind his mask without emotion.

Kylee nodded at a slim, bald, black man in a dirty T-shirt and khakis. "Elroi is our mechanics expert. He's the one who's kept our vehicles running smooth all these years."

Elroi nodded back in return. "Purring like the kittens they are." His heavy British accent stood out among the others in the room.

"Last for now is Kemena," Kylee announced. "She's our vehicle weapons expert."

"Kemena," said Annika. "That's a pretty name."

The relatively petite yet muscular Hispanic woman with black hair pulled and tied tightly into a bun in the back of her head looked at the teenager.

"It means *strength*," Kemena said as she held up a fist. Her lean bicep flexed its contoured muscle in the light.

"I'm Annika. I don't know what it means."

Kemena only offered a blink to the girl in response before she stepped in front of Prater. She looked him up and down, not just suspicious nor curious, but rather a good bit of both.

"And what was it you go by?" the woman asked with just a hint of a Spanish accent.

Prater didn't move but looked at the smaller woman standing in front of him through his sunglasses.

"Prater."

Kemena leaned in close and almost put her nose onto Prater's chest. Prater frowned as he contemplated what she was doing and even though he didn't sense any danger, readied himself in the event anything went suddenly awry. The gesture was brief and Kemena stepped back almost immediately. Her face pointed down and she looked at Prater through the tops of her eyes.

"You smell...different."

Kylee shot Z a quick, concerned look who only lifted her hands like a gesture of surrender to show she had no intent of doing or saying anything. Kylee gave a low huff of unappreciation before directing herself at Kemena.

"Don't go starting any problems, Kemena. I told you ahead of time we would be expecting these two to join us. They are to be welcomed and trusted at my behest."

Kemena turned sideways then stepped back, keeping her eyes on Prater the entire time, but said nothing else and made no alarming gestures. Potential conflict averted, Kylee went on with pertinent matters.

"You can meet everyone else later," she said to Prater. "We need to get on with the meeting."

"I don't fully understand why I'm here," Prater said.

Kylee stood from her chair and took the few steps needed to put herself in front of Prater. She took a firm hold of his upper arms as her stare pierced into him through the black lenses of his sunglasses. Kylee always knew how to see into him, Prater knew, despite his best defenses.

"You're so good in a fight, Prater. You always were and I'm venturing you still are. We can really use someone like you. This mission is unlike anything anyone has ever undertaken."

Prater shook his head adamantly. "I told you to not ask me to do anything. I don't work for others. It's all I can do to take care of myself."

"Prater, we need you. The fate of mankind needs you."

"This is not my fight," Prater asserted.

Kylee's arms dropped as she returned to her place in front of her seat.

"This isn't the man I used to know," Kylee announced to no one in particular yet to everyone in the room. The disappointment in her voice was heavy. "What's happened to you, Prater? You used to always want to help others. Now all you want to do is look out for yourself?"

Jeanne. Prater's mind was overtaken with images of his love lying in his arms, sputtering her last breaths as their unborn child died at the same time inside her. It was the catalyst that turned Prater to a fulltime life of loneliness. Never again would he put himself into positions of choosing sides and alliances. Never again would he trust anyone other than himself. Never again would he forge friendships and bonds only to end up disappointed and dissolute in a world that never showed care or mercy. Never again.

Prater stared hard at his adoptive mother from behind the black of his sunglasses. He said nothing and made no gestures in response to her question. For Kylee, that was enough.

"My apologies to you all," said Kylee as she addressed the task force poised before her. She gave Prater a cursory final glance. "I truly believed we could count on you, but no matter."

Prater remained silent. He refused to allow himself to be guilted into action.

Kylee resumed speaking to the group. "As I was saying before our guests arrived, General Kaur is holding firm. There's no postponing the nuclear attack on San Francisco Mecca so we must act now."

The principal individuals introduced by Kylee huddled close to the conference table while others maintained more space. Z stood near the table as Prater, followed by Annika, stepped up to stand next to her. Ecks pulled a folded map from his back pocket and opened it up to its full size. The map was from before the Vampocalypse and showed what used to be the State of Oregon and all its major roads detailed by cartographers at that time. Ecks pointed to a black dot in central Oregon and spoke as he traced a thick red line down the map with his fingertip.

"This is us, here at Camp Expectation. We're going to follow this 126 road until we get to highway 97. From there we keep going," his finger fell off the bottom of the map and he turned the map over, revealing a continuation of the roads as they led into northern California, "until we intersect with Interstate 5. Then it's to 505 and finally 80, where it'll be a straight shot to San Francisco." Ecks leaned on the table with his palms. "We're looking at 530 miles of uninterrupted freeway. Some will be smaller roads, but most will be wide and open with several long straightaways. The smaller vehicles won't have an issue getting there on a single tank of gas but the larger ones will need to refuel while on the way."

Wen stepped forward. "That's where I come in. Elroi and I have equipped all the vehicles with quick fueling mechanisms that'll allow them to get fueled up along the way. We'll pull right up alongside and transfer the fuel without even slowing down."

A sudden silence fell on the room as eyes drifted into expressions of uncertainty.

"What?" asked Wen as he scanned the concerned faces. "It'll work. I'm sure of it."

"I don't think you or your refueling rig is the concern," said Kemena. "I think it's the vampires we're sure to face along the way."

Nods and expressions of affirmation fluttered through the group.

"There's sure to be danger along the way," said Kylee. "Vampires can attack at any given time. We can only hope any skirmishes are few and far between." There was a quietness to her voice that conveyed her sincerity of the concern. Her tone became stronger and more resolute. "But that's no different than how we already live life every day. The surroundings will change but we'll remain no less resolute. Humankind has a vendetta to pursue. Today marks the start towards our reclamation of this world."

Kylee could sense some ease creeping back into the air.

"And what do we do when we get there?" asked Z. "We can't just drive into the heart of the city with our convoy and not expect to attract attention."

"Marques has made arrangements to meet us near the 80 interchange with transportation into the city. We'll abandon our convoy and transfer to those transports where he'll be able to get us into San Francisco Mecca."

Scant murmurs circulated as feelings of doubt infiltrated many minds.

"I know many of you are anxious," said Kylee as she addressed the growing sentiments. "I'd be lying to you if I said I wasn't concerned, too. There are so many points where this can go wrong, where this can fail." Kylee straightened herself and she pounded the table. "But we have no option other than to succeed. It's unfortunate that we aren't only fighting against vampires in this but against time itself. We're moving out immediately. We'll meet in the convoy garage in fifteen minutes."

With the meeting adjourned, the motorcade team members quickly began to filter out of the conference chamber. It wasn't long before only Kylee, Prater, Z, and Annika remained. It felt to Prater like Kylee had avoided eye contact with him since her last words to him during the briefing. That feeling continued as she went on to address Z and Annika specifically.

"Z, take Annika and find her a room in Building B. Make sure she has what she needs for accommodations to get her going. She'll be safe there while we're gone. I'll see if –"

"Wait," Annika interrupted without hesitation. "I'm not staying here. I'm going with you."

"I don't think so," said Kylee. "I'm not going to bring someone inexperienced on this mission. Let alone a child."

"But I can help."

Kylee smiled at the girl who squinted in response. Annika wasn't sure if the smile was patronizing or one of genuine concern. She quickly shook it off and looked wide-eyed at the governor.

"I'm a quick learner. I can ride a motorcycle –" Z raised her eyebrows at this " – and I'm good with a bow and arrow."

"This is true," Prater chimed in. "I've seen it. She's damned good at it, too."

"Olympic class," Annika announced unashamedly.

Kylee still had not made eye contact with Prater but he continued with his defense of the girl. "She isn't lying. And since when is age of a concern? I've been alone since I was fifteen."

"This is different," Kylee said, finally looking at Prater. "You're..." Kylee stopped herself and instead resumed her conversation with Annika. "I'm sure you're extremely talented, but regardless, it's your lack of experience that concerns me."

"There's no way you're going without me." A surprising amount of authority boomed from the young girl's voice. "There's a good chance my family was taken to the San Francisco Mecca blood banks and since that's exactly where you're going, I'm going there, too, to do whatever I can to free them. You can't stop me."

Kylee stared at Annika and now she was the one whose eyes narrowed.

"I can't be responsible for you," Kylee said with finality.

"Wait," said Z as she held up a hand. "We determined earlier that I was the one responsible for Annika."

All eyes went on Z – Kylee's with a look of concern as she suspected where this was headed, Annika's with a look of excitement as she suspected the same.

"As the one responsible, I say she comes with me. Otherwise, I'd have no way to look after her. And it sounds like she can be useful."

Z looked at Annika whose face beamed with delight. Kylee abandoned the fight, conceding to Z's argument.

"If Z is taking you on and believes in you, then I do, too. Welcome to the team, Annika."

Annika fought showing any more excitement than she already had, though no one could ignore the broad smile on her face. This was a good distraction from all her recent heartache.

"Z, take our archer and make sure she has all the equipment she needs and meet us at the convoy." Without a breath she continued, "Prater, please stay here a moment."

Z led Annika out of the council chamber and the silence that was left as the doors closed behind them was instantly filled with tension.

"Please, Ky," said Prater as he stared at the woman who raised him and taught him the foundation of who he had become. "Please don't ask me again. This still isn't my fight."

Kylee shook her head as she smiled thinly. It was a smile that did little to veil the worry and underlying sadness in her eyes. She reached over to Prater, slowly, and took one of his hands and cupped it in both of hers.

"Prater, my lovely boy, there's something you should know about yourself. Something I've been wanting to tell you for a long time."

Prater kept his expression in check, showing no emotion, while inside his stomach instantly churned. It was an anxiousness he had never experienced before. This day had been filled with so many revelations and emotions already. He wasn't sure how best to prepare himself for more.

"What is it?" he asked with trepidation.

Kylee gently tapped Prater's hand with one of hers as she continued to hold it. Prater thought he saw a tear form in one of her eyes.

"You can tell me," Prater reassured. "Whatever it is, I'll be fine."

Before Kylee could reply, she was interrupted by Incom rushing back into the room and straight up to her. The communications expert had a finger up to a tiny earpiece and Kylee could feel heightened sense of worry from the younger woman. Prater also noticed the look of concern.

"What is it?" Kylee asked as she released her hold of Prater's hand. Her official posture had promptly returned. "This better be important."

"Governor, there are..." The woman's voice quickly dropped off and a moment of silence underscored her wide, concerned eyes before she continued. "There are vampires at the gate. Their leader demands to meet with you. He says his name is Ryder Sloane."

EPISODE 15

CAMP EXPECTATION
PACIFIC WASTELANDS

IT was almost exactly noon and the truncated glow of the midday sun seemed to hang almost directly over Camp Expectation, illuminating what could have been a scene lifted from an old Western movie. Kylee stood about twenty feet outside the tall, iron gates. On one side of her stood Z with both of her sai held firmly at her sides, not in an offensive stance but ready to move at the slightest hint of danger.

On the other side of Kylee stood Berserker, whom she had asked to come to display some physical muscle. And that he did: at nearly six and a half feet tall, broad chested, and arms as big around as an average man's thighs, Berserker could easily strike fear in those who didn't know him for the gentle giant he truly was behind his wrestler's mask. He stood with his weapon of choice in his hands: a bastardization of an old XL18 flamethrower that he and Kemena had completely reconfigured into a large rifle. The rifle had a large revolving chamber that when fired could either spit out bullets made of super concentrated bursts of flame, or with a flip of a switch shoot a highly focused beam of fire that had a range of nearly two hundred and fifty feet.

Prater had volunteered to go with Kylee and the others to the gate and meet with the vampires, but Kylee insisted he remain in the council chamber.

"Stay here," she had told him just before heading out for the gate. "You're the one he's after. I'm not going to reveal all our cards just yet. Here," she took a microcommunicator earpiece from the outside breast pocket of her SWAT style jacket and handed it to him.

"We'll be able to stay in contact through this. I'm going to leave some additional security outside, just to be safe."

Prater nestled the comm unit into his ear, forced to be content with at least hearing the confrontation between Kylee and the vampires despite not being able to see them.

Despite the standoff nature of the scene, Kylee, Z, and Berserker did not face their uninvited guests alone. Two dozen members of Camp Expectation's security detail lined the top of the walls on either side of the entrance and from the closest guard towers overlooking the scene. Rifles primed with silver bullets, traditional wooden and silver-tipped spears, flamethrowers, and UV laser rifles were trained on the unwanted guests. There would be no way for the creatures to escape so much firepower aimed in their direction.

Facing Kylee, Z, and Berserker from about thirty feet away were just three vampires. At the center stood Ryder Sloane – the end of his new black cloak fluttered gently from a light breeze. His dark hood was pulled up and while this cast his face in partial shadow, the steely gray metal plates that made up the left half of his face managed to somehow still have a sheen about them. The sharp, handsome features of the more human looking half of his face would have betrayed the horror of the metal creature, if not for the blood red eyes, and long, pointed teeth that filled his mouth. Flanking the cybervampire on one side was Kent, Sloane's comrade who had reported the location of Camp Expectation, and on the other side stood a vampire in a red shirt named Gabriel.

"I wish only to speak with the leader of this establishment," said Sloane. The electronic quaver in his voice was unnerving. "Are you that person?"

Kylee moved forward a step to separate herself from Z and Berserker. "I'm Kylee Haddock, Governor of Camp Expectation."

Sloane stepped forward two steps. "I am Ryder Sloane and as a representative of the ruling vampire establishment I have a proposal for you."

Kylee held back a guffaw at the audacity of the creature to proclaim leadership over her and her townspeople in any way. "What's that?"

"It's come to my attention that there is a man here by the name of Prater Saxon. All I'm interested in is him. Turn him over to me and I give you my word we will leave without incident."

Kylee looked over her shoulder back at Z, who subtlety shook her head. She looked back at Sloane and took a deep breath.

"And if we refuse?"

Sloane laughed mockingly then looked straight at Kylee, his red eyes burning into her even from across the distance between them.

"There will be no survivors and the town will be leveled." The bitonal nature of his voice sent chills through the humans who heard the definitively stated words. He raised his robotic hand and gestured to the grandeur of the large wall behind them. "Take a good, long look around you. Go on, please. Because if you don't now, all this will cease to exist. The people will be either killed or taken to our blood banks to live forever feeding the thirst of the vampire."

One side of Kylee's lip curled up. "There will be no bargaining for Prater Saxon."

Sloane shook his head and placed his hands on his hips, causing his cloak to fan out and only increase the creature's stature. "I don't think you understand, Kylee Haddock." The words went from almost playful to a deep hiss. "This is not a negotiation. You will turn Prater Saxon over to me or you will die, and the lives of everyone you are so determined to protect will be forfeit."

"If that's what's to become of it then so be it." The curl of Kylee's lip turned into a full smile. "But I warn you not to underestimate us."

Sloane frowned as he tilted his head gently sideways. "You would let all your people die – you would yourself rather die – all for the sake of one man? One man whom you barely even know?"

Kylee shook her head slowly. "You'll never understand the strength of human resolve. You cheated by using particle bombs to turn humans into vampires. If it wasn't for the bombs you never would have accomplished such domination."

"Domination was always inevitable. The mechanism for getting there was incidental. Technology simply afforded us the means of a mass turn that was never before possible. If technology suddenly provided humans with a way to wipe out all vampires, whether now or if that had occurred before the Vampocalypse, you would take advantage of it. So you cannot judge us when the human race is no different."

The words sank into Kylee and she knew they rang true. Still, she shook her head. "There will be no deal."

The cybervampire turned on his heel and walked back between Kent and Gabriel. The two vampires turned and followed. As the trio of creatures walked away without another word Kylee saw Sloane put a small rectangular device she guessed was a transmitter up to his mouth. Barely five seconds later the voice of one of the guards at the top of the nearest guard tower shouted down to Kylee and the others below. The guard's voice cracked as he couldn't get the words out fast enough.

"Governor! There's a large force approaching over the nearest hill headed directly for us!" the guard screamed as he pointed at the nearby foothills.

All eyes went to the closest hill as hundreds of vampires all dressed in black tactical style gear came flying over the top in such a close formation they looked like an immense murder of crows converging on the town. On the ground were hundreds more vampires running over the crest of the hill and in their direction. While not every vampire possessed super speed, it appeared as though Sloane's army had specifically selected only those with the ability.

Kylee immediately began shouting orders, "Sound all alarms! Battle stations! Drop into defensive positions!"

Several of the guards began shouting at Kylee and her companions to get inside the gate. Z and Berserker turned and ran while Kylee took a quick final look at the three fleeing vampires. A barrage of weapons fired at the creatures – concentrated bolts of laser-like UV rays, silver bullets, and several spears. One of the spears impaled Gabriel through the back and burst from his chest. The motion was quick but was enough for the silver tip of the spear to do its work. Gabriel dropped to his knees, clutching the staff protruding from his chest, as he began to spit up silverized blood. The tip of the spear pierced the ground as his body sagged forward. The shaft of the lance was left coated in silver blood as Gabriel's body slid down the weapon before slumping fully to the ground.

Sloane suddenly stopped running and turned his body sideways so his cybernetic side faced back towards Camp Expectation. He grabbed his cloak with his robot hand and held it up over him as Kent cowered behind, using the cybervampire as his protection. Several bullets clanged and pinged off the metal of Sloane's robot arm and leg, leaving bullet holes up and down his black cloak. One silver bullet dinged solidly off the cybervampire's steel left check, causing his head to recoil sideways, as another grazed the human half of his forehead. Sloane snarled as parts of the flayed skin grew tendrils that reached and closed upon each other, healing the wound as if it was never there. He quickly used his robot arm to harmlessly knock away two spears in succession that were about to strike him. After that, the attention on him was gone as Camp Expectation's forces quickly turned their attention towards the rapidly approaching hoard.

Kylee slipped sideways through the large gates just as they closed to completely seal the town off from the invasion by foot.

"We're going to have to hope the gate and walls last long enough to get the convoy out," Kylee said to Z and Berserker and a few nearby guards who she had come over to meet up with her.

"Wait," said Z, "we're still going to focus on the convoy? What about protecting the town?" Her eyes were wide with uncertainty though she knew what Kylee's response was going to be.

"Z, you saw what I saw. There is no way we're going to hold off a brood that size."

"We're giving up and retreating?"

"No!" Kylee shouted, her emotions were high. There was no time to explain every detail. "Our only chance right now is to focus on saving humanity. We're all expendable for that cause."

Z could only stare at the woman, knowing deep inside that she was right.

"I want the two of you to get to the caravan. We're heading out right away. I'll meet you there in just a minute."

Berserker took a couple of fast steps and stopped and looked back at Z, who was unmoving and giving Kylee a long look.

"Come on, Z," the large man said, his voice deep and bellowing. "We need to go."

Z blinked as she finally gave Kylee a quick nod then turned and left with the big ex-wrestler. As the two ran off the guard nearest Kylee addressed her.

"We may be able to hold off the ones on the ground for a bit, but there's no way for us to fight off that many attacking by air. There's just too many of them."

"Concentrate the bulk of our forces on the gate and be sure guards are stationed all around the top of the perimeter wall to keep watch on all sides."

"And the skies?"

"Carry out my orders." Kylee looked out at the approaching dark cloud. "I'll worry about the skies."

PRATER paced anxiously back and forth just inside the doors of the council chamber. In addition to the uncertainty of what may be happening outside the gates, there was the matter of Kylee saying she needed to tell him something. What could that have possibly been?

She had raised him for fifteen years, sharing her strength and teaching him how to survive. There were surely ample opportunities during those years for her to share with him everything that was important. It seemed now, though, that there was something else – something that brought pain to her eyes and hurt in her voice. A something that Prater hoped she could share with him sooner than later.

Prater listened to Kylee's exchange with the vampires through his earpiece and knew of the pending attack. Deciding he would be more helpful outside the chamber at this point, Prater pushed through the double wooden entrance doors and was met by half a dozen guards blocking his path, each holding an automatic rifle filled with silver bullets.

"Sorry, Mr. Saxon," the guard closest to Prater said as he held up a palm. "We can't let you leave."

"There's an attack coming," Prater said as he held up one hand and pointed it between the guards and in the direction of the gate. "I can help."

"No can do, sir. We've got our orders to make sure you stay here for your own protection."

"There's not going to be any 'protection' from hundreds of invading vampires!" Prater struggled to keep his vampire fangs and talons suppressed as he grew more agitated. Maintaining his composure, Prater said, "And there'll be no one protecting *you* if I need to force my way out of here." The words came out semi-threateningly and he could sense the heartbeats in the guards quicken as nervousness took hold. Still, they managed to stand their ground.

"I'm really sorry, sir," said another guard after swallowing hard. "We wish we could let you by but we can't."

Prater took a deep breath and said nothing as he retreated and shut the doors to the council chamber, leaving him once again alone inside to nervously pace as he waited to hear any further updates. The doors to the chamber were suddenly thrown open. Prater jumped into a fighting posture with both of his katana drawn and ready against what he was sure were going to be vampires rushing in.

"Prater, it's me!" Kylee exclaimed as she raced past him. "I need to get to the security room. Come with me."

Prater followed a quickly rushing Kylee through the back hallways and into her private office. He watched as she scrambled to open the secret door to her security room.

"What are you doing?" he asked. "Shouldn't you be headed to the caravan?"

"I have to enact Camp Expectation's defensive aerial grid or we won't have a chance of getting out of here alive."

"*Defensive aerial grid?* What are you talking about?"

Kylee didn't answer as the secret door slid open. Prater followed her into the dark office and watched as she rushed to one of the keyboards and began typing furiously. The center screen on the wall in front of them displayed a computer-generated blueprint of Camp Expectation. A pulsing red light appeared on each of the guard towers surrounding the town…except one.

"Shit!" Kylee exclaimed as she pounded the counter next to the keyboard.

"What is it?" Prater asked, completely oblivious as to what she was doing though he could tell the fact that the one guard tower not having a red light was an issue.

"One of the sensors is offline. I'm going to have to reboot."

"Offline? Offline from what?"

Kylee seemed to be in a zone as her fingers flowed commands into the keyboard and the monitor with the blueprint flashed and reset to an all-black screen. A series of light blue colored circles appeared in a line in the center of the screen, each spinning and growing increasingly darker. As each circle reached a certain dark shade of blue, it would stop spinning as if "locking" into place. It took several seconds for all of the blue circles to stop and lock then the screen flashed again. The blueprint of Camp Expectation reappeared and one by one, in no discernable order, the red pulses appeared again on each of the guard towers…all except for the same one.

"Come on…" Kylee said quietly as she stared at the screen as if trying to "will" the final light to appear. "Come on." This time she said it louder. "Come on…come on…come on!" Each repeat was said louder and with more intensity than the last, until she finally screamed, "COME ON, MOTHERFUCKER!" while slamming the "enter" key on the keyboard in front of her.

A red light appeared on the final guard tower, much to Kylee's delight. After a few more keystrokes a series of straight red lines appeared between all the towers, connecting each tower with the rest, creating a bright web that shone in stark contrast to the blueprint behind it.

"That's it," Kylee said without explanation.

Realizing Kylee wasn't going to provide any details behind what she was doing, Prater decided to try and change the topic to a matter that to him was just as important.

"Ky, you said there was something you needed to tell me?"

Kylee avoided Prater's eyes and headed for the door.

"There's no time to go into that right now," she said as Prater followed her. "We need to get on the road to San Francisco Mecca before it's too late."

A siren wailed throughout Camp Expectation to signal the oncoming attack. Panic ensued as people ran for shelter. Most ran to the building closest to them while some took the chance to get across town and to their actual homes. There were "vampire shelters" – like Old World bomb shelters – hidden underground beneath many buildings, but there weren't enough to hold the entire population of the town. Many felt the shelters would only delay the inevitable, anyway. With the army of vampires on foot nearly at the front gate and the cloud of creatures approaching from the skies beginning their dive to enter the grounds, that inevitably was about to be tested.

A brilliant blue flash suddenly burst forth from large, oversized mushroom shaped devices mounted on top of each of the guard towers dotting the fenced perimeter of Camp Expectation. Streaks of lightning erupted from the transmitters, intersecting with each other, and instantly creating an intricate electrical web forcefield over the top of the town. The dozen or so vampires that were below the webbing when it formed were lucky – they were immediately disposed of by either spears, bullets, or UV laser rays once they entered Camp Expectation's "airspace". The few dozen that were caught on the electrical plane of the forcefield itself were instantly bisected where the crackling electricity cut through their bodies. And those flying at full speed who were unable to veer away in time to avoid the electrical webbing hit the forcefield. Much of their bodies actually passed through the forcefield, albeit in smaller, fist-sized chunks, as the blue lightning sliced like electronic scalpels through the unfortunate creatures.

Vampires screeched and screamed and called out to each other as they floated above the crackling forcefield below. One of the vampires shouted abrupt commands and the monsters roared and hissed as they swarmed down to the tops of the guard towers and the spotlight-like weapons mounted to them. Try as they might, even despite the efforts of those with the greatest enhanced strength, the vampires couldn't get the electric web-generating conductor units to budge when attempting to tear the devices apart or off their mounts by hand.

A large vampire suddenly shot high into the sky from his position on top of one of the guard towers. Turning around after jetting up several hundred feet, the vampire came screeching straight back down at the guard tower from which it just moments earlier had taken flight. The vampires who had continued to claw, scrape, and pry at the device jumped back and away just as the large vampire crashed its entire body without hesitation into the web-generating device. There was another bright flash – though this time it was from the web-field generator exploding from the impact. The burning, charcoaled remains of the large vampire dropped away from the guard tower and to the ground as the weblike forcefield diminished ever so slightly from the absence of the electrical rays from the demolished guard tower.

It didn't take long for other vampires to copy the maneuver. The creatures streaked downward with their arms pressed to their sides, looking like black-clad humanoid missiles flying towards their targets. It took just moments before the electrical forcefield was completely gone as web generators were destroyed one-by-one from kamikaze-like attacks by suicidal vampires. Nothing then could stop the hundreds of vampires diving and invading from the air. As vampires reached the gate from the inside, despite the best reinforcements Camp Expectation security had to offer, the humans were easily overrun, and the gate was opened.

Ryder Sloane stood at the back of his army and waited, exercising the utmost patience as he watched vampires flood into Camp Expectation. There would be no holding back. No human was going to survive this.

And Prater Saxon would finally be in his grasp.

EPISODE 16

CAMP EXPECTATION
PACIFIC WASTELANDS

KYLEE sprinted across the open pathways and streets to a nearby warehouse as Prater matched stride alongside. Mayhem ensued all around as alarms continued to blare. Vampires swooped down out of the air and would yank humans up and carry them away; callously tear into them with their talons, ripping heads and arms from bodies or slashing into chests and backs to expose gaping, life-ending wounds; or playing aerial tug-of-war as the creatures pulled at appendages in different directions until the bodies finally tore apart. These were but a few of the horrors surrounding Kylee and Prater as they ran. A few unlucky vampires met their demise as Prater's swords neatly decapitated them or the silver bullets from Kylee's pistol met their targets with clean headshots. Nothing could mute the screams of thousands as humans and vampires clashed in an all-out battle around them. With only a relatively small complement of armed and trained fighters to defend the entire town of two thousand humans against a thousand raging vampires, their odds were not good.

Prater recognized the place Kylee took them to as the long, windowless warehouse he had noticed on their walk earlier. One of the townspeople inside quickly closed and locked the door with its sliding bolt as soon as Kylee and Pater burst into the building. Prater was immediately impressed with the size of the space – *garage* was a more appropriate term because of the caravan of ten vehicles parked inside and the odor of grease and oil that permeated the air. On the far side of the line of vehicles, separate from the motorcade, were three long, yellow school buses. All the caravan vehicles, save for Z's purple

Hondamatic CM400 motorcycle, were crazy, mechanical amalgamations of various automobiles, vans, and trucks mashed together. None of them looked like their original models as armored plating, newly mounted weaponry, and other bastardizations showed Prater why Kylee had been so adamant these machines be used to get to San Francisco Mecca. This was a convoy ready for war. The gruff roars of engines and the smell of gasoline and exhaust began to rapidly fill the space as the motorcade fired up. The school buses were not armored and no one appeared to be paying them any attention.

Kylee rushed up to Z, who sat on her bike revving its engine to get it to warm up quickly. Annika sat just behind Z on the extended passenger portion of the motorcycle seat. A quiver full of arrows and the recurve bow she was practicing with earlier were strapped tightly over one shoulder.

"Everybody's ready to go," Z said to Kylee. "We were just waiting on you."

"Good work, Z," Kylee responded. "Let's get out of here."

Z gave Prater a hard stare. "I thought you weren't coming. 'Not your fight,' right?"

Prater shot back a cursory look. A new noise suddenly broke through amidst the sudden untimely tension and the throning of the engines: the sound of vampires banging on the doors and metal roof of the garage as they fought to gain entry.

"I don't think he has much choice in the matter," Kylee interjected to keep from wasting any more time. "Not at the moment, anyway."

She grabbed Prater by the arm and led him towards the vehicle at the front of the convoy – a massive armored semi-truck with a flat roof over its cabin and an oversized hood that accommodated the souped-up and supercharged V12 underneath. The front of the truck was protected by a set of steel bars welded vertically across the width of its large, square radiator grille and headlights. The long flatbed trailer that was attached housed three large weapons on spinning turrets: a spear launcher, a set of dual machine guns, and at the rear, a flamethrower. Townspeople Prater had not yet met prepped and operated each of the turrets. Kylee leapt up into the driver's seat in place of the townsperson convoy member who had fired up the big machine just moments before.

"Get into the battle semi," she ordered Prater, who swiftly complied without question by jumping up into the truck and settling into the passenger seat.

As he settled in, Prater looked over at the school buses that still sat unattended. "What about the buses? Aren't you going to load them up with townspeople?"

The bangs and rattles on the roof and doors of the garage echoed like thunder as they grew increasingly louder. It sounded as if a hurricane was about to tear the roof away over the roaring of the engines.

Kylee kept looking forward as she replied, "There were townspeople tasked with filling the buses in case of an emergency. They must be dead and there's no time for us to reconfigure our plans."

Kylee revved the engine on the long truck and trailer and yanked the air horn pull overhead inside the cabin two long times. A deep, bitonal sound resonated loudly from two horns mounted on top of the cabin facing forward.

"Let's get fucking going!" Kylee shouted with a mixture of enthusiasm and haste as she banged on the steering wheel with one hand.

Kylee slammed the large vehicle into first gear and Prater was jerked back into his seat as they launched forward faster than he expected. They speedily headed towards the large doublewide warehouse sized doors not far ahead – which were still closed and locked as they were rattling from vampires pressing against them desperately trying to get in from the other side. As the truck gathered speed Prater wasn't sure what was going to happen when they reached the doors. Not much ever worried Prater, but a hint of anxiety crept in as their rig only increased in speed as it approached the closed-off exit.

"Ky," muttered Prater. "Ummm…the doors aren't open."

"Not your problem," Kylee stated sternly as she bumped the rig into the next gear.

The sound of the engine powering the semi increased in its intensity as the vehicle gained power and speed. That wasn't the only sound that grew louder, though. The clattering of the metal roofing panels being shaken reached a zenith then immediately stopped as the vampires above finally succeeded in ripping them away. Muted daylight poured in followed by a stream of vampires.

Kylee kept the rig pointed in the direction of the closed warehouse doors as she flipped open a control panel in the center of the dashboard, revealing a small digital display along with a series of analog buttons and switches. A quick flick of a switch and a loud motorized sound emanated from outside the passenger side of the truck. Prater looked at the sideview mirror and watched as an anti-tank Hellfire missile launcher slid out from behind the passenger door and locked into place. He paid no attention to Kylee pressing a button on a touchscreen targeting display on the panel – but definitely noticed the missile that launched from his side of the semi and exploded against the garage doors just as the battle vehicle blasted through the conflagration.

One by one, the motorcade vehicles shot through the fiery opening. Following Kylee's semi was a crimson red BATT UMG personal armored vehicle driven by Berserker. Next was Z's motorcycle, followed by Elroi driving a customized metallic blue 1970 Dodge Plymouth Roadrunner with Ecks riding shotgun; next was Wen with his steroid-injected Nissan 300Z/fuel tanker hybrid; then came Kemena driving what can only be described as a "spear-harpoon rig" mutated from an old hearse. Four other vehicles of varied armor plating and weaponry followed, though the heaviest of the convoy autos were towards the front.

Bursts of silver bullet gunfire, silver-tipped spears, and streams of flame filled the air surrounding the convoy as all defenses were engaged by the fleeing vehicles to ward off the vampires swooping at them from above and racing at them from the sides. These measures did little to help the hapless townspeople, though, who screamed and cried and begged for the safety of the convoy as the vehicles coldly raced by. Kylee looked straight ahead, focused on the mission, but Prater couldn't help but watch as humans fought in vain against the vampire assailants. A nearby woman was nearly decapitated as one of the creatures bit and chewed feverously into the side of her neck. A large vampire rushed up behind a man with its outstretched talons, grabbed him by his shoulders, and tore him in two right down the middle. A man stood alongside the road and tried to get Kylee's attention as they barreled by when a vampire dropped feetfirst and grabbed him not with its steely talons, but with long, clawed toes from its bare feet. The creature rocketed skyward with the thrashing, screaming man in its grasp.

It was then that a sudden sense of direction kicked in with Prater. He surveyed Camp Expectation through the tall semi's windows then settled his eyes on the side view mirror. The town's entrance was getting smaller behind them.

"Where are we going?" he asked. "The gate's back that way."

"We aren't going through the gate. Too many vampires." Kylee's focus remained forward at the road ahead. "Just trust me."

The convoy, still in its straight line, didn't make any turns and was racing towards a blank section of perimeter wall six blocks ahead. On the way townspeople fought helplessly for their lives but the strength and might of the deadly creatures could not be matched. The screams were inescapable and blood stained the streets as people were bitten into, chewed on, dismembered, disemboweled, exenterated, and eviscerated. Those in the caravan focused their weapons exclusively on the monsters attacking their vehicles, leaving those pleading for help to not just fend for themselves but die with the realization of believing their fellow humans drove by seemingly without any care or concern.

The road ahead in front of the perimeter wall suddenly filled with nearly a hundred vampires that dropped straight down from the sky and planted themselves like statues directly in the path of the convoy. Among them were fifty humans, each flanked by two vampires that allowed for no freedom of movement as they were held tightly as hostages on display. And in front of them stood their half-vampire, half-robot leader. Ryder Sloane looked to his right and at one of the captive humans as she cried and pleaded for her life before looking back at the rapidly approaching line of vehicles.

Prater shot Kylee a concerned look. She glanced at him, and he knew he didn't have to verbalize his skepticism. Kylee looked straight ahead again and blared the truck's horn, which caused every vehicle in the caravan to do the same, adding an orchestra of mismatched automobile tones to the pallet of human screams.

"Straight ahead. Full speed!" Kylee's shouts matched the heightened volume of all the noise around them.

Kylee flipped another switch on the semi's weapons console and more clanging and whirring sounded, this time from the driver's side as an M230 chain gun slid out and locked into place behind Kylee's door. It was then that Prater noticed red firing mechanisms built into the steering wheel. He barely had a moment to think more about it when Kylee pressed the fire button.

The M230 roared to life spitting out 30mm caliber silver bullets that tore into the group of vampires ahead of them. The silver went to immediate effect on those that weren't decapitated or otherwise completely disintegrated from the rapid fire of death. Captive humans cried and wailed as they were caught in the friendly fire from the semi, unfortunate casualties in the war between humankind and the undead.

In the middle of all the devastation stood Ryder Sloane, unmoving and defiant as death exploded around him. He stood there, unwavering and glaring at the oncoming battle semi as the spray of silver bullets stopped. In the next moment, instead of the gunfire restarting, a Hellfire missile burst forth and shot immediately at Sloane. The cybervampire snarled briefly before launching vertically as the missile just missed him and exploded into the bullet ridden perimeter wall.

The battle semi crashed through the smoking, burning fence remnants followed by the rest of the convoy. One by one vehicles in the motorcade raced away from the death and devastation of Camp Expectation and into the open barrens of the Pacific Wastelands. The final three vehicles in the convoy weren't so lucky as the vampires were able to organize forces around them before they made their escape. No number of modifications or armaments were enough to stop multitudes of vampires from landing on the vehicles from the air or jumping onto them. For those few who bore the worst of the attacks, the overwhelming numbers of bloodthirsty monsters compared to the few humans on each vehicle made for swift and devastating losses.

Kylee stared intently ahead while occasionally stealing a quick glance at one of the truck's tall sideview mirrors, constantly on the lookout for vampires. Reflected in the mirrors, in the rear, she caught glimpses of the convoy vehicles being overrun. Those at the rear of the motorcade were the easiest to succumb to attack due to not only being the furthest back but also being the smallest vehicles in the caravan. While unfortunate, those initially overrun provided distraction for the vehicles at the fore to get a head start in the race away from the attacking creatures. And though it was helpful, it wasn't enough as vampires were slowly gaining on each of the fleeing vehicles, attacking them one at a time in succession. It wouldn't take long before the creatures made their way to the battle semi in the front. At the moment, though, all there was to hear was the growling of the truck engine and the rumble of the wheels on the road.

"Are we gonna make it?" asked Prater.

The question surprised Prater himself as he knew it was a pointless question to ask. He was just used to being more in control in situations like these. No trust was lost on Kylee but he felt the need to hear an assurance. Kylee's eyes lingered on him for a moment while she continued to drive straight.

"We have to," is all she said with a solemnity that provided no consolation.

A sudden *SLAM!* on the hood of the semi caused the cabin to jerk downwards. Kylee and Prater bounced in the cab as they looked out to see Ryder Sloane standing on the long hood. He stared at the two of them in defiance of the buffeting wind that billowed his cloak around him. Kylee's first thought was to slam on the brakes but that would surely cause the vehicles behind them to crash, and the creature would just be able to fly off anyway. Instead, she reached down the right side of her seat and pulled up a sawed-off shotgun – already pumped and loaded with silver bullets – and aimed it at the cybervampire.

Sloane didn't allow Kylee any time to fire as he easily punched through the windshield of the truck with his robotic arm on the first try, causing Prater and Kylee to shield themselves from flying shards of glass. As Kylee fought to keep control of the rig while simultaneously protecting herself from the glistening splinters, the cybervampire grabbed Prater by his neck and yanked him out onto the truck's hood. Unable to get a clean shot of the creature, all Kylee could do was maintain speed and watch helplessly as Prater grappled and rolled on the hood with his assailant.

As they brawled, Prater found himself on his back with his head hanging off the front of the hood. His satchel slipped away, disappearing over the side then falling under the wheels of the oversized rolling rig. The cybervampire straddled him and Prater's arms were pinned at his sides by the creature's legs. Sloane landed several repeated fists back and forth against the sides of his face. Prater's sunglasses shattered and broke away as his face became increasingly bloodied and bruised. A bloodcurdling vampire screech came from Sloane as he raised his robotic hand high. Prater focused on the dark silver-chrome fist as he prepared to receive another hard punch. Instead, though, the left hand of the vampire opened into a claw-like shape and the fingertips extended mechanically into footlong razor-edged talons.

The first swipe came swift and fast and caught Prater across the right side of his face: around his eye, along his nose, and across his cheek. The cuts weren't too deep, thankfully, but blood still immediately streamed from all of the wounds. Sloane looked down at him as thick, putrid spittle dripped from the creature's mouth and landed on Prater's chin. The monster reset itself and a second swipe came, faster and harder than the last. Prater winced and grimaced as this cut through his black jacket and cleanly flayed his chest with four diagonal slices. Prater screamed outright as a third slash left even deeper cuts across his chest, causing blood to flow from the wounds freely.

The cybervampire was relentless and he pulled his robotic hand up and prepared to strike again. This time, though, Sloane wouldn't be satisfied with another cut. This time, he was going to finish the job he came here to do, and he was going to have the evidence to take back to Stirling to prove the task was finally done. *Alive is preferable, but dead will do,* was the directive. The large steely razor claw came at Prater's face hard and fast, but Prater managed to finally free his arms and bring his hands up to grab the vampire's mechanical wrist. Prater stopped the deadly appendage just as the needlelike points of the razors were about to skewer his face in five ways...

Kylee concentrated on keeping the large battle rig on course as Prater was pulled through the windshield and into a fight on the hood. She still held the sawed-off shotgun and was ready to fire at any time but could not get a good aim of Sloane for a clear shot. Just then, a loud thud banged on the roof of the semi cab. Before Kylee realized what was happening a vampire fist crashed through her driver's side window and grabbed her by the side of her neck. Her unknown assailant pinched hard into the skin of her neck and she let out an uncontrollable high-pitched squeal. In her sudden fit of pain, she unwittingly cranked on the steering wheel of the battle semi – dropping her shotgun in the process – and the large rig jerked abruptly to the right. Kylee quickly compensated, too much so, and as the truck yanked back to the left the wheels on the right side of the trailer lifted off the ground for a brief, heart stopping moment, before slamming back down.

The grip that shot the blinding white pain from the nerves in her neck and through her body released and Kylee saw a body fly off the top of the cab and away to the left as the truck rocked and settled back onto its wheels. The rig swayed and swerved from side to side as Kylee worked to shake off the pain that still almost paralyzed her and, for a brief instant, she forgot about the vampire that had held her just moments before – until one of the creature's hands grabbed the open frame of the broken window of her driver's side door. The long talons held tight as the vampire pulled himself closer to grab the door with his other hand. Having finally fully corrected the direction of the rig, Kylee picked the shotgun back up from the passenger seat and pointed it out her side window.

A deafening screech from the creature resonated through the cabin of the truck as the vampire, the one known as Kent, suddenly tore away the entire driver's side door and tossed it aside. Kylee managed a haphazard shot with the shotgun but missed as Kent slammed his upper body into her fast and hard. She fumbled her weapon and suddenly found herself uncomfortably twisted and practically upside down in the passenger seat. Kylee coughed and wheezed as she struggled to regain the breath that was knocked out of her before the vampire killed her. Kent laughed maniacally as he slid into the driver's seat and took control of the rig. The creature blasted the horn of the semi in uncontrollable glee. Spotting the shotgun down near his feet, Kent grabbed it and threw it out the open doorway.

Prater used the rocking of the truck as it initially went out of control to his advantage and abruptly twisted Sloane's mechanical hand to aim its deadly spikes back towards himself. As the truck banged back down onto all its wheels, Prater shoved firmly with all the strength he could muster and the long, sharp claws of the cybervampire impaled Sloane – three of the deadly points went straight into the human side his own face while the other two stabbed into his neck. With the truck swaying back and forth down the road, Prater applied pressure onto the sharp talons, rapidly working the wounds larger. Cold blood from the creature surged out from around the bloodied spikes and onto Prater's face and chest. As he continued to be drenched in the icy, red shower, Prater's breathing quickened and he pushed the steely points even deeper into Sloane's own face and neck. Blood from the vampire continued to spray down and into the cuts and gashes across Prater's face and chest, mixing with his own blood as it coursed into his wounds.

Prater felt something he never experienced before as a cold tingling sensation shot through the core of the damaged and open blood vessels in his chest and face. Time around him seemed to stop and all his senses abruptly ceased to function. What felt like an eternity passed in what was only two seconds. Everything flashed back to normal and Prater realized once again where he was – lying on his back on the hood of the battle semi with Ryder Sloane above him, who was shrieking from being impaled by his own talons…and blood from the vampire was mixing with his own. An instance of calm coursed through Prater – and the cuts and wounds on his face, along with the gashes in his chest – rapidly closed on their own and healed themselves.

Well, that's new, Prater thought to himself.

With a renewed invigoration, Prater kicked Sloane up and off him – and off the side of the truck. Any feelings of relief never had the chance to manifest, though, as the cybervampire swooped up from over the side of the hood, levitating alongside the truck that had finally fully straightened itself back onto the road. Blood, the cybervampire's own, dripped from his extended steely, mechanical claws, while the wounds in his face and neck closed and healed. Prater leapt to his feet onto the hood, drawing both of his katana as he planted himself strongly against the rush of wind as the rig continued barreling down the road. He stole a quick glance of Kylee as she coughed while fighting to regain her breath from the passenger seat as a vampire drove the rig.

Sloane flew around to the front of the truck; his billowing cloak surrounded him like large black wings. The cybervampire remained upright just beyond the rig's hood, almost as if standing in the air. Then Sloane attacked, lunging forward, and slashing repeatedly with his twelve-inch long steel talons. Prater blocked and parried each swipe from the deadly razors, shifting his footing several times on top of the truck hood. Sloane drifted around to different sides of the hood and continued his ongoing assault. Each attack was stronger and more complicated in execution than its predecessor, but the ongoing clanging of metal-on-metal was testament to Prater stopping them all.

The cybervampire shot around to Prater's right. As he did, Prater shifted his stance and sliced with his swords before launching a sudden side kick that caught the vampire by surprise. Although the force of the kick wasn't nearly full strength when it connected with Sloane's midsection, it was enough to knock the creature further away from the rig and buy Prater the opportunity to leap on top of the cab. His feet securely placed on top of the speeding truck, Prater held his swords tight in each hand, ready to engage. He faced the creature who so desperately wanted to capture him.

"Come and get me, you fucking bastard!" Prater shouted.

Kylee's breathing steadied and she managed to get herself more upright in the passenger seat. She was surprised that the vampire driving the rig wasn't paying closer attention to her as he seemed to be fully invested in the fight that was happening on the hood. Using the distraction to her advantage, Kylee slipped a hand under the passenger seat – the sawed-off shotgun wasn't the only hidden surprise she had stowed away in the battle semi – and discreetly slid a ten-inch silver dagger up the side of the passenger seat and alongside her body out of view from the vampire driving.

She gripped it tight and shifted herself slowly in her seat to gather more leverage for herself. Kent cheered and shouted for his cybervampire leader as he watched the road ahead through the intense fight that played out on the hood of the rig.

"Get that motherfucking human!" Kent shouted as he punched a fist into the roof of the cabin. "Make him cry like that little bitch friend of his that sold him out!"

A blur slashed at the creature's face. He turned away and a sizzling burn streamed across his right cheek as the tip of the silver dagger in Kylee's hand grazed him. The knife created a thin, boiling line where the silver met his skin. Still, the vampire screamed, and blood welled in thin lines along the bottoms of his eyelids. Subsequent multiple stabs from the pointed, silver death came quickly. Kent held the rig straight with his left hand while continuously knocking the dagger away with his right. The defensive cuts and gashes that mounted on Kent's hand and forearm could not heal fast enough to keep up with the number of new cuts taking their place. The creature's arm and hand smoked and steamed as each incision crackled and burned.

Still, the vampire was persistent with his counterattacks and after a hard swipe that finally knocked away the dagger, a swift punch to the bridge of Kylee's nose caused an eruption of crimson from her broken appendage. Kent followed up by digging his claws deep into one of Kylee's forearms, then tearing away so hard his talons created inch-deep gashes that shred her arm open. As blood rushed from Kylee's wounds, Kent swept the dagger up from the floor between them. In a continuous motion, he jammed the point of the blade into Kylee's left shoulder all the way to its hilt. The scream from the level of pain this brought could have shattered the windshield if it had not already been broken out.

"Hey, asshole!" another voice shouted.

"Fuck, what is it now?" Kent grumbled under his breath. His wounds were finally able to work their rejuvenating powers. He didn't have time for more distractions.

Kent looked out the opening where the driver's side door once was and at the source of the new voice. A long, darkhaired woman on a purple motorcycle had pulled up to match the speed of the rig. Kent bared his salivating fangs at her, thinking he would love to have her for a snack once there's a break in the fighting.

The motorcycle increased speed and Kent realized his focusing on the motorcycle driver was merely a distraction as the passenger on the bike came into clear view. He barely had time to register the bow and arrow pointed at him before the arrow was no longer just pointed at him, it was *in* him – straight through his left eye and lodged in his head to where nearly a perfectly even amount of the arrow protruded through the back of his head as was sticking out the eye socket in front.

Kent let out an animalistic snarl as he reeled from the pain. Luckily for him the arrow wasn't silver-tipped but the agony was overwhelming even for a vampire. Still managing to maintain a steady course on the road ahead despite his anguish, Kent reached up with one hand and after a brief pause to suck in a deep breath, he yanked the arrow back out through the eye socket. Blood sprayed out along with tiny bone and brain fragments. The creature began to grow dizzy as the damage to his brain began to take hold.

Any oncoming vertigo or agony from the arrow wound was quickly forgotten as a fresh pain captured Kent's attention: the silver dagger that was plunged up to its handle into his heart. The vampire stopped making noises altogether as his head lobbed weakly to its right and he made eye contact with a wounded, exasperated Kylee who slumped back against the passenger door, blood flowing from the open wound in her shoulder from where the dagger had been. Silver blood bubbled from around the knife and the vampire's chest began to cave in as any bone and muscle structure broke down into a slimy ooze. The effects of the silver as it pumped through the creature's veins turned the entire vampire gray in color. With weak gurgles, Kent's mouth moved like he was about to say something, but then the lower jaw stretched then melted away.

"Who's the bitch now?" Kylee posed as she kicked the rapidly decomposing creature out the driver's door opening.

Fighting through the pain searing through her, Kylee slid into place once again behind the wheel of the semi. The blood pumping from the hole left in her shoulder from the dagger made her weak, but as long as she didn't have to fight any more vampires, she convinced herself she would be good until she could get some help driving and tending to the wound.

Prater's shoulder-length hair whipped straight back from his face as he stared forward into the oncoming wind from his place on top of the racing battle semi's cab. Sloane stood at the end of the hood while his dark cloak fluttered around him, but his body language was far less aggressive than Prater expected as he kept his hands more casually towards his sides.

"You've been a hard man to track down," the creature said as it began to walk towards Prater. His voice was raised to be heard over the rush of wind, boosted by the artificial electronic flange that underscored all his words.

"I'm not here to please," Prater called back.

Sloane stopped walking when he reached the open, missing windshield of the cab. He looked up at Prater on top of the cab. "We don't have to fight any longer, Prater. Come with me and this attack will end. No more of your human friends will die."

"I can't do that, *metalface*."

The cybervampire shifted his weight and Prater could see the creature's chest flex outwards as he inhaled a deep breath.

"I've been instructed to bring you in, dead or alive." Sloane smiled broadly. "And, Prater Saxon, since it's all the same to me, *dead* it is."

The cybervampire prepared to launch himself up at Prater when the partially-melted body of Kent falling out the driver's side door of the truck momentarily captured his attention. Sloane looked back at Prater and floated vertically up and off the hood. The edges of his long, black cloak continued to flap violently in the air as Sloane levitated just a couple of feet off the truck. For a couple of tense moments the vampire stayed in this position as his eyes shifted between Prater and inside the cabin of the semi. Prater kept his eyes peeled on the cybervampire. There was no way he was going to let the monster catch him off guard from such a close proximity.

Sloane suddenly darted away in flight, but not at him as Prater expected. Instead, the vampire took off sharply to his right, quickly pivoted in the air above Z's motorcycle, and shot like a dark arrow with his talons outstretched in front of him into the open driver's side door of the semi.

"No!" Prater shouted. He cursed not being able to fly like other vampires.

Prater sheathed both of his swords and dropped to his stomach. Holding onto a lip that ran along the edge of where the top of the cab overhung the windshield, Prater peered over the front edge to try and get a better look into the cab. Inside, the cybervampire's robotic hand had a hold of the steering wheel while his vampire talons were digging into Kylee's throat. Prater could see blood from puncture wounds in the sides of her neck as she fought with futility and rapidly decreasing strength to break the creature away from her. The creature's dual existence allowed its robotic half to concentrate on driving while the vampire part of him wrestled Kylee with little effort.

Z had raced her bike back up alongside the cabin of the battle semi when Sloane flew inside and grabbed hold of Kylee. There wasn't anything she could do to help by riding alongside. But she knew she couldn't just watch as the vampire tore into one of the only people she ever considered to be a friend in this harsh, unforgiving world. She slowed her pace alongside the battle semi some as she quickly assessed the weaponry on its trailer. Sadly, the townspeople who had been operating the spear launcher and machine gun turrets had been lost to the fight. The flamethrower operator was still battling as she shot long, concentrated streams of fire off the very back of the trailer. Z brought her bike dangerously close to the side of the trailer.

"You said you can drive a motorcycle?" Z shouted to Annika on the seat behind her.

"Yeah!" the girl called back.

"Then take over driving. I'm getting on the rig."

Annika barely let out a "What?" when Z suddenly popped her feet up onto the seat of the bike. Annika quickly slung her bow over her shoulder and leaned forward, digging her fingernails into the bike seat in front of her where Z was just sitting to cling desperately onto something – anything – since Z was no longer available for her to hold onto. Z looked to her right, the wind causing her long hair to trail in the breeze, as she kept balance on the bike and gauged what she needed to do to make the jump. She leaned forward, keeping the throttle steady as she stood a little more upright on the motorcycle.

In the next instant Z was in the air as she launched herself off the bike, causing the motorcycle to veer away from the rig at a slant and start to slow. Annika slid forward on the seat and grasped the handlebars just as the bike began to go into a slight wobble. She didn't realize she was holding her breath until she had tightened her grip of the handlebars and felt the motorcycle seat fully under her. Thankfully it took minimal effort to keep the bike under control, and a moment later Annika was speeding to catch back up with the battle semi, finally letting out her breath as she drove.

As Annika looked at the truck just ahead of her, she saw Z – whose leap from the bike had landed her near the rear of the trailer – working her way towards the cab on the driver's side. The woman suddenly stopped and looked at her, flashed a crooked smile and gave a quick thumbs-up. Annika had never felt so accomplished in her sixteen years as she did just then. And not only did she feel an almost overwhelming pride in herself, but she knew right then that she wanted to be just like this badass woman who was working to save the world while also being responsible for her.

Prater slid himself counterclockwise while lying flat on his stomach on top of the cab. As he did, he spotted Z approaching up the trailer from his left. The two of them caught each other in a glance but made no effort to otherwise communicate any intentions. Prater, while holding onto the top of the truck cab, kicked his feet up to where his body was immediately vertical in the air. He let go of his grip with one hand and twisted his body around like a gymnast, then swung his legs down as fast and as hard as he could, launching himself feetfirst through the driver's side door opening.

Both of Prater's feet landed squarely into the steely left side of the cybervampire, knocking the creature out of the driver's seat and smashing him up against a weak and bleeding Kylee on the passenger side. Without any concern for the rig, Prater carried the inertia of his kick through and landed on top of Sloane himself. The truck immediately careened off the left side of the highway and began cutting uncontrollably across a bumpy field of low grasses. Z had just grabbed onto the frame of the driver's door opening when the truck pulled off road. Her feet slipped off the doorframe and she dangled from the side of the cab as each bump seemed to jostle her harder than the last, steadily loosening her already haphazard grip.

With no way to draw either of his katana, Prater had nothing but brute force to use against Sloane. Lying on top of the cybervampire, who in turn was on top of Kylee and still had hold of her neck, Prater punched and hit with his fists, forearms, and elbows from any angle and in any manner that he could. None of his efforts appeared to do any good as most landed against hard metal. The jostling of the inside of the cab as the truck barreled over rough ground didn't help.

Prater felt the wind get knocked out of him as his body was slammed hard against the roof of the cab by the cybervampire. Pinned against the cab's ceiling, Prater felt Sloane's robotic claws begin to pierce into his chest from the cybernetic hand pressing him violently upwards. As he tried in vain to relieve the pressure holding him, he spotted Kylee trapped under the weight of the cybervampire. Her eyes were barely open and her head lobbed from side to side as the truck bumped along. Blood was everywhere from her broken nose to the lacerations and puncture wounds on her face, neck, and body.

Prater couldn't tell if she was even conscious. The hopeless sight of Ky lying there as the cybervampire continued to squeeze his monstrous talons deeper into her neck caused an unfamiliar sense of panic to begin to set in.

Prater didn't have to be concerned about his predicament of being smashed against the interior roof any longer as the cybervampire exerted all his might and flung Prater across the top of the semi cabin, crashing through the glass of the passenger side door, and disappearing out towards the open fields.

With Prater gone, Sloane looked down once more at Kylee – her eyes were rolled completely back into her head and the blood was pumping out of her neck wounds in large spurts. The bloodsucking creature allowed his thirst to momentarily take over as he plunged his half-robot, half-vampire face deep into the side of her neck. Kylee was too dazed to realize what was happening to her. The cybervampire fed intensely and feverishly for a few moments before pulling himself away and releasing a spinetingling screech. With no further time to waste, the vampire reached up with both hands and grabbed the sides of the passenger door window frame, knocking out some of the few remaining broken shards of the passenger window in the process, as he prepared to launch himself out of the truck in his retrieval of Prater.

"Leaving in such a hurry?"

Sloane looked back over his shoulder and saw Z in the driver's seat, one hand with a firm grasp of the steering wheel, while the other had a tight hold of one of her sai, its point facing down. Before the cybervampire could react, Z stabbed the point of her sai deep into the middle of the creature's robotic left thigh. Sparks erupted out of the damaged area, which increased as Z twisted her weapon, causing all three prongs of the sai to sever steel pulleys and rotors inside the robotic leg. Sloane let out another shriek, though it was out of pure anger rather than pain as he didn't have pain sensors in the cybernetic parts of his body. Daggers of hate shot from Sloane's eyes and tore through Z. To her surprise Z shuddered inside – she had never witnessed so much feral rage directed towards her. Shaking it off, she worked the steering wheel of the rig to redirect the semi back towards the road.

Sloane couldn't waste any more of his time or energy on either of the women in the cab and instead looked back at the open passenger window, once again preparing to takeoff out of the truck. The cybervampire quickly pulled himself towards the window…when a body suddenly filled the opening. Prater stabbed one of his katana in with as much effort as Sloane used in his effort to launch himself out. The sword pierced Sloane's robot shoulder from the top and sliced through sensors and mechanical veins as it channeled deep into the cybervampire's chest.

The steel katana tearing into the vampire did little to slow his momentum and, despite his wounds, Sloane still tried to grab at Prater as he lunged forward. Prater jerked away from the open window while simultaneously twisting and yanking his sword out of the creature – a move similarly demonstrated by Z as she pulled her weapon from the cybervampire's thigh. The movements caused a change in Sloane's momentum that caused the creature to smack his vampire shoulder against the open frame of the broken passenger window. Prater abruptly flung the passenger door open, and the cybervampire bounced and banged through the opening as the truck hit a particularly large bump in the unpaved field.

Prater held himself as far away from the passenger door opening as he could so as not to get caught up with the cybervampire as the creature tumbled chaotically out of the cab. Prater flinched as the vampire claw on Sloane's right hand scratched his chest through the missing passenger window in a final futile attempt to take hold of his prey. Prater watched Sloane spiral and tumble as he fell, before plunging under the large dual sets of wheels of the battle semi. The entire rig bounced as the trailer ran over the flailing creature.

Wasting no further time, Prater scrambled around the passenger door and into the semi cab. He half sat on the passenger seat with Kylee lying loosely in his arms. Her head nodded back and forth and the blood spilling from her wounds wasn't slowing. Prater cradled her and brushed her bloodied, matted hair away from her face as a tear threatened to drop from one of his eyes. He glanced over at Z who split her attention between having eyes ahead while driving and on Kylee. Z's solemn expression was no different than that of Prater's.

Kylee raised a wobbly hand before it dropped onto her chest. Prater urged her to remain still and not exert any energy or stress but Kylee shook her head. Despite her weakened state, she shakily pulled a small, black, rectangular device from one of her jacket breast pockets.

"M–Marques," Kylee's throat sounded full of blood. "Use this to, to contact Marques…"

Z nodded as she took the communicator from Kylee's hand. Any words that came to mind didn't seem important enough to say. Kylee slowly raised her hand towards Prater's face.

"Prater…" His name came out choked and wet.

Prater shook his head and took a gentle hold of Ky's hand. "Shhh, quiet, Ky. We're going to get you help."

Prater knew that was a lie. So did Ky as she forced a tiny smile. The expression was brief as she let out a set of blood-soaked coughs.

"There, there's something…Prater…"

"Stay quiet, Ky, save your energy." Prater stroked Kylee's sweat and blood-filled hair as he continued to rock gingerly back-and-forth with her upper body in his lap.

Kylee's head shook jerkily side-to-side. "No, Prater, no…you need to know some, something…"

"It's okay, Ky," Prater's voice was beginning to sound shaky like Kylee's gestures.

"Something to tell you for…for so, so long…"

Kylee set a bloody hand to Prater's cheek and the two of them looked at each other. The woman smiled an unrestrained, unrestricted smile as all became calm and final in her world. Then her eyes rolled back slowly as her head lulled and followed suit.

"Prater… your mother was… never bitten…"

The words came out in a final breath as Kylee's hand fell from Prater's cheek, leaving a fresh, bloody handprint where she had touched him.

Kylee... Ky... the only woman he had ever known as his mother – no, this *was* his mother as far as he was concerned – was dead. Just like that...she was gone.

Prater's jaw trembled as he struggled with what to say. The reality of her final words settled in, leaving him wide-eyed and unblinking. His mother was *never bitten?* If that's true, what does that mean for who or what he is?

For several long moments the only sound was that of the truck rumbling along.

A look of anguish fell across Z's face that quickly contorted into anger. She smacked the large steering wheel of the truck again and again with the palm of one hand.

"Is this your fight now?" she screamed, demanding an answer from Prater she knew would never come. *"Is it?"*

EPISODE 17

SAN FRANCISCO MECCA
NORTH AMERICA NEW WORLD TERRITORIES VAMPIRE CAPITOL

"A report has come in regarding the assault on Camp Expectation." Samuel Ellis said from his seat across from President Stirling's desk. He looked at information scrolling across a datapad he held in front of him. "The town has been secured. It won't be long before the humans are fully decimated."

"And what of Prater Saxon?" Stirling asked before jawing at the open air. "What's the status of his capture?"

There was a pause long enough for Samuel to give Andrea McCullough – the only other guest in the office, who also sat across from the president – a cautious look.

"A small band of humans escaped in a convoy of highly defended vehicles," Samuel went on as he continued the update. "Prater Saxon was among them."

Stirling took in a long breath as he stood at the side wall where the dark red drapes had been pulled back revealing a large window with a remarkable view of the cityscape beyond. All eyes were on him as he looked out over the immense mecca and fiddled his fingers together behind his back.

"Connect me with Ryder Sloane," Stirling said with an unexpected calm that created more tension in the office.

The president separated his hands and brought them around to his front. He tore his stare away from the city and faced his guests.

He went and settled into the large chair behind his glossy black desk as Samuel completed inputs on his datapad.

"General Sloane's signal is coming through, Jonathan. You can go ahead."

Stirling pressed a touchscreen button embedded into the top of his desk and a 3D display emitter mounted in the ceiling flashed a beam into the middle of the office, centered between Stirling's desk and the guest chairs. A grainy image of Ryder Sloane struggled to come into focus – he appeared to be sitting outside on the ground – but the display was distorted and staticky.

"Holodrone," Stirling called out. "Resharpen image."

The 3D display blanked out momentarily then returned blurrier than before, but instantly sharpened to near perfect clarity. Sloane was indeed on the ground, supporting himself up with his cybernetic arm. His vampire leg was twisted and mangled under him, and his vampire arm hung loose and bleeding from its shoulder.

"Prater evades you *still*," Stirling boiled, making no mention of the cybervampire's condition. "I don't quite know what's going on with you. You've never let me down like this before, Sloane. You're typically so much more formidable."

Sloane stared through the holographic image and into the president's eyes as he said warily, "I shall be in pursuit." The electronic tone that normally underscored his speech buzzed and alternated between high and low pitches, like the squawking of an old transistor radio trying to find a frequency. "I swear to you, he will not evade me much longer."

"No, no. Enough of your fruitless pursuits." Stirling shook his head. The disappointment was evident. "I have a contingency in place to take care of Prater Saxon."

Sloane shook his head – or more like jerked his head in spasmic movements from side to side. "Anyone else you send will do no better. I will capture him!"

Stirling held back a chuckle. "You can barely hold yourself up, let alone chase anyone down."

Sloane continued to look right at Stirling with an anger that told the president the cybervampire knew he was right.

"I'm ordering you to return to San Francisco Mecca," Stirling said. "Fix yourself up and prepare for the summit. Maybe you can do some actual good back here. I've had Marques overseeing implementation of a curfew to shut down the city. I'm sure he can use your help with the security details. The *Red Marauders* will take care of the pathetic band of fleeing humans and bring Prater to me."

"Red Marauders? Their methods can be reckless. Can you trust them?"

Stirling stammered momentarily before responding. "Hopefully more than you."

The cybervampire dismissed the slight. "What of Camp Expectation?"

"That place has served its usefulness. Level it."

Sloane inhaled a labored breath. "I'll see to it right away. Then I'll return and be rebuilt better than before and –"

Stirling abruptly terminated the connection and thereby the conversation.

"I have more important issues in front of me," Stirling said as he nodded to his visitors. "Andrea, my understanding is the final delegates confirmed they are on their way?"

"Within the last ten minutes, yes," Andrea replied. "As long as there are no delays with their arrivals, everyone will be checked in and ready for the opening ceremonies at sundown."

Samuel smacked the arm of his chair. The large man's thick palm made a slap on the leather that caused Andrea to jump.

"Opening ceremonies?" Samuel asked. He inhaled sharply. *"Opening ceremonies?"* He repeated the words louder, more punctuated. "You ended the conversation with your robot toy saying you have more important issues and you want to know about the opening ceremonies?"

The senator elite would have jumped out of his chair if doing so wouldn't have drained all the energy out of him. Instead, he pointed a thick finger at Stirling to drive his point home.

"Need I remind you we have a missing nuclear submarine to worry about?"

Stirling's nose wrinkled and he gnawed at the air. "And need I remind you who is in charge here?" Stirling's words came out with a hiss. "No, the missing sub has not slipped my mind."

"Samuel, you incorrigible, fat fuck!"

Both Samuel and Andrea jumped in their seats as they looked up at the sound of a voice coming from someone they did not realize was in the room. Brandon Stirling was crouched upside down in a dark corner high above. The pointed tails of his black suit jacket hung like flaccid wings of a giant bat, adding to the image of a predator watching keenly over its prey. He was barefoot and the sharp nails of his elongated toes curled around the black crossbeam, holding him as he looked down on the vampire politicians several feet below. The NORAD general released his hold and he dropped onto the office floor, twisting and slamming feetfirst into a standing position in front of the senator elite.

This time, Samuel didn't flinch. Rather, he crumpled his nose in disgust at the vampire standing before him. He pushed himself a little more upright in his chair and shifted his finger at Brandon.

"Shouldn't you be in Colorado?" Samuel asked Brandon snidely.

"I was. Now I'm here."

"There, here, wherever you are, you're in no position to call me names. You may be the president's brother but to me you're nothing but a nepotistic leach who's always relied on Jonathan's intelligence and savvy to get you by."

Brandon looked back at his brother as he forced a smirk and fought against the anger building in him.

"I'm over your incessant complaining and mightier-than-thou views, Samuel," Brandon said while looking away from the senator elite.

The NORAD general peered slowly back at Samuel and took a step towards him. He smacked away the senator elite's finger and leaned in close to where they could feel each other's breath on their faces. They each bared long, salivating fangs in a flex of who harbored greater vampire prowess.

Samuel snarled then said, "And I'm growing tired of you riding on your brother's coattails while the rest of us make our own way. For centuries you've sat back and let Jonathan do all the work while you always have an excuse to get out of any effort. Centuries!"

The rage burning within Brandon grew more evident as his shoulders heaved up and down, accentuating his deep breaths. Samuel looked at Andrea who sat in semi-stunned silence as she witnessed the altercation of these two vampires whom she'd known for over two millennia. She had watched them be angry with each other countless times, but there was something different in Brandon's eyes and the way he was looking at Samuel. Something Samuel didn't seem to see.

"Are you seeing this thing?" Samuel continued as he laughed mockingly and dismissively tossed a hand in Brandon's direction. "Tell me I'm not the only one who's tired of this a-hole getting rewarded over and over and over again for doing nothing. I mean, have you ever known a lazier fucking vampire in all of your exist –"

Brandon was suddenly on top of the much larger senator elite. Pinning him back into his wide seat from his crouched position, the long talons of Brandon's feet dug into the senator elite's heavy thighs. Samuel emitted a mixture of an angry growl and pained screech. Brandon raised his left hand high, baring his claws as he made eye contact with Samuel. Without hesitation Brandon swiped at Samuel's face. Despite his heftier size, Samuel brought both of his hands up in time to grab Brandon's left hand by the wrist just inches from his face. For a moment, a brief smile swept across the senator elite.

It was an expression extremely short-lived as Samuel felt all his breath instantly sucked out of him.

Uncertain of what just happened, Samuel looked down at his body. Brandon's right hand was buried into his chest up to the wrist. He felt the sharp claws sliding deep into him. Any strength or fight he had instantly escaped. He sat helpless as Samuel's fingers of death wrapped around his heart and slowly squeezed. Vampire chemicals shot through him, creating panic, telling his brain and body to do something, but the pain was too much to handle, and the shock to his system rendered useless any reflexes of self-preservation. He tried to somehow *will* his heart to keep beating, to stay strong as the creature upon him tightened his grip, preventing any further heartbeats the vampire muscle attempted.

Then there was an odd sensation unlike anything Samuel had ever experienced as Brandon pulled his hand slowly out of his chest. Samuel felt each artery and vein stretch and pop as his heart was extracted in front of his slowly dying eyes. He tried to say something to Brandon, who continued to stay on top of him as he raised the bloody muscle over his head, but his mouth just moved up and down soundlessly. He held his stare into Brandon's eyes until even that became too much of a strain. His arms fell to his sides, and he felt his right leg twitch just once. His eyelids remained open as his gaze moved slowly sideways and down, then his head slumped forward. All Samuel could mostly see then was the floor and he struggled to keep his eyes open…only his eyes weren't closing. The darkness that gradually dropped like a thick, black curtain was the final call in his nearly three millennia lifespan. Then the eternal blackness took hold.

Brandon still held the heart over his head as bloody streaks trickled and disappeared under the black arm of his suit.

"Well, thank you, brother," said Jonathan. He had remained unperturbed throughout the ordeal. "You certainly did us all a favor."

"Yes, thank you," Andrea added. "I only wish you had done it centuries ago."

Brandon outstretched the bloody heart towards the president, who waved a hand politely.

"Please, it was your kill."

Brandon smiled a wide, crazed smile, then took a deep bite out of the fresh heart. The dead vampire blood felt good and gave Brandon a feeling of renewed energy he hadn't felt in a while. He couldn't immediately recall the last time he had a heart this fresh, let alone from one of his own kills. He just so rarely found himself in a position of feasting on such delicacies as supplies of farmed blood had been of concern for so long, creating a dearth in the availability of fresh kills, even to higher ranking personnel.

Having taken his bite, he looked again to his brother, but Jonathan instead gestured towards Andrea, who took the partly eaten heart from Brandon. While Andrea took her share of the feast, Brandon turned his attention to the lazy-eyed, dead expression on the senator elite. Taking the large, round head in his hands, he gave an abrupt twist and yank and tore it off the dead vampire. As Andrea ate, Brandon turned the head upside-down and plunged his face into the open neck. Once the vice president had her share, which she obviously had found invigorating based on the moans she couldn't help but release, she passed what remained of the heart to the president as Brandon handed her the decapitated head to continue her feast.

Jonathan finished what was left of the heart then took his share of gorging on what remained inside Samuel's head. All three vampires were left with bloody faces and hands from the way they each had animalistically torn into the gory vampire parts. As the euphoria from the feast began to ooze away, the three of them became very quiet other than the sound of their deep breathing. Jonathan raised a bloodstained palm after several silent moments.

"It's a shame to have to work after such a delicacy," he said. His voice was low and sounded lethargic. "Brother, is there any update on the missing submarine?"

"There is," Brandon said as he finally climbed off the dead senator elite. He sucked dripping blood off his fingertips then pulled a handkerchief out of an inside suit coat pocket that he used to wipe his hands as he spoke. "It wasn't easy to gather and develop the intel, but at this point there's near one hundred percent certainty that the attack is meant to be aimed at the summit gathering this weekend. Just as I feared to begin with."

Jonathan took a deep breath and gripped the armrests of his chair. Several pops sounded as the president's pointed claws punctured the leather of the armrests. Without reacting to his brother's obvious anger, Brandon removed his cell phone from his suit jacket pocket and entered a few commands into an app that was synced into the president's 3D virtual projector. The display brought a map of the California coast to life between the desk and chairs. It slowly rotated as a dotted line worked its way from the docks at San Diego and stopped close to San Francisco Bay.

Brandon couldn't resist a devious smile as he continued. "My marine vampires are trained to dive and swim in depths of up to five hundred feet and can hold their breath for up to sixty minutes at a time. Their enhanced vampire sight can see up to a thousand feet underwater in the most minimal of lighting conditions. It didn't take long for my theory to be proven correct as the submarine was spotted not far from the entrance to the Bay."

Jonathan looked understandably concerned. "Why haven't they already been stopped?"

"Arrangements are currently underway to prepare –"

The president slammed a fist onto his desk and stood up. He chewed at the air and let out a muted snarl. "What do you mean? Can't you just send another submarine after it and destroy it?"

"We don't have a fleet of these subs, brother. There's been no need for them since the Great Turn so our underwater naval resources are next to nonexistent. But as I was trying to say, I have a team preparing to attack the sub. Once the soldiers are prepared, the attack will commence and the humans will see their plan fail."

Jonathan paused before commenting. "And the summit will go on as planned. Uninterrupted." There was a definite conclusiveness to the statement that indicated no other conclusion would be acceptable.

"Of course, brother. I assure you this to be the case."

Jonathan let out a loud sigh. "There cannot be any more setbacks. Sloane's failures to bring me Prater Saxon have left me quite, shall we say…aggravated. Don't you disappoint me as well, Brandon."

"Nothing to worry about, dear Jonathan. I told you before that my talents were best suited here. The humans will not succeed in their plans."

EPISODE 18

PACIFIC WASTELANDS

THE battle semi resumed leading the motorcade after reconnecting with the caravan after its offroad detour. In all, seven vehicles survived the escape from Camp Expectation. They drove in a straight line down the four-lane freeway with minimal space separating them. Rolling behind the semi was the 1970 Roadrunner, followed by the tank-like BATT UMG, a heavily-fortified and modified Volkswagen bus, the hybrid Nissan 350Z/mini-tanker refueling rig, and finally the hearse spear-harpoon vehicle. Traveling alongside the battle semi was Annika on Z's '81 Hondamatic. The motorcade rumbled along with each vehicle providing its own unique drone to the symphony of engines barreling down the freeway. The vampires appeared to cease their pursuit following the decommissioning of the cybervampire from the fight. Once their escape from Camp Expectation felt somewhat secured, Prater moved Kylee's body – with the utmost care – into the semi's sleeper compartment.

While the sounds from the wind whipping through the open cabin, roar of the semi-truck engine, and grinding of the road noise were loud, it was the silence that filled the air between Prater and Z that was the most deafening. This went for several minutes as the remnants of the motorcade rolled on towards San Francisco Mecca. Prater stared out the open passenger window while Z's gaze remained steadfastly straight ahead. There were a couple of moments when Prater started to say something and on one occasion stole a quick glance at the stone-faced woman driving the semi.

Instead, he sat quietly, pondering as he replayed the events in his head. Each moment was ingrained within him like frozen capsules of time – stark reminders of the loss he witnessed…and suffered. He wondered over and over again what he could have done differently, what he could have done to save Kylee, to save his mother.

A distant boom captured Prater and Z's attention. Prater leaned out the passenger window and looked back. In the distance far behind, a large mushroom cloud ballooned into the sky. The explosion wasn't large enough to be nuclear but it was clear that a weapon had been detonated to level Camp Expectation.

"I should have never come here," Prater murmured.

Z remained visibly still though she jumped a little inside from Prater's sudden words. She glanced sideways at him then quickly refocused on the road.

"It wouldn't have made any difference," Z said. Her solemnity was evident.

"Now the only woman I've ever known as my mother is dead. All because I led the vampires straight to her."

Z let out a breath. "It's not your fault. It was only a matter of time before they located Camp Expectation. It was inevitable."

The silence between them returned and the cabin was once again consumed by the sounds of the wind and road noise. Z looked out to her left and was happy to know that Annika was still riding alongside on her motorcycle, unharmed from the attacks. The silence continued for another couple of minutes before Prater suddenly spoke up again.

"Yes, this is."

"Yes what is?" Z asked.

"My fight." He looked at Z and this time when their eyes met, they shared a look of strength. "This *is* my fight now."

THE vampire lowered the binoculars that only sharpened his already extra keen eyesight then ran a hand over the top of his bald head. The creature lightly scratched his gray and black goatee – still stained red with blood from a recent feed – as he stared across barren roads and brown grasses and small desert shrubs. Hillsides rose in the distance and even further were the peaks of foothills that led up to mountainsides. He wrinkled his nose as he sniffed the air. There was nothing to be seen or heard here.

The vampire walked from where he was standing in the roadside grass and back to his Harley-Davidson motorcycle that sat parked in the middle of the street. This creature known as Snoweyes – nicknamed as such due to his irises being completely white save for a fine outline ring of black – put the binoculars into one of the side saddlebags mounted at the rear of his bike then pulled out a pair of dark Wayfarer sunglasses and put them on. He then picked up the black and red leather vest – his "cut," emblazoned on the back with the logo of the Red Marauder Motorcycle Club – from the motorcycle seat and put it on over his crimson-colored T-shirt. Mounting the bike, Snoweyes kickstarted the machine and it roared to life with a throaty growl.

Without looking back, Snoweyes raised a hand and flicked a forward gesture before starting down the road. Behind him, the rumble of nearly a hundred more Harleys driven by vampires, many with vampire passengers on those with double seats, all wearing matching Red Marauder cuts, shook the ground as they moved on behind their leader. The red headlights of the motorcycles looked like angry cyclops eyes as they thundered forth to seek out and intercept their prey.

ANNIKA

I wonder if this is what it was like as a 16-year old in the Old World. I mean, obviously there weren't vampires, at least like there are today. But the orphan part. I wonder if it used to be any easier. Maybe there was more love and support – at least I hope there was. Here, everybody's an orphan, so it's everybody for themselves.

Why did my parents bring me into this world? Was it for a sense of normalcy for a life long gone? I'm happy to be alive...I think. My parents would tell me stories of what the world used to be, back when there were blue skies, green trees, and sparkling oceans. They would show me photos but they didn't mean anything to me. It made me sick to hear about a world with beauty and love, filled with people who cared about each other. Why would I want to know about that? What good did it do to show me those pictures? I often felt as though it was torture over anything else. I suppose, though, my parents got something out of sharing those memories. And even though I would tell them I enjoyed their tales, inside, I sometimes hated hearing about them. It was a world I never knew and will never know.

Flatlands and barrens with sprouts of green and sparkles of yellow and red flowers that somehow managed to defy the odds greeted us in deserted stretches of barrens following our escape from the cybervampire. Dead farmlands and wide open spaces alternated lining the many miles of the desolate road until we entered into the rolling foothills of nearby mountains. The highway winded up and through the hills, providing glimpses of snow in the distant higher elevations. I had never seen snow before and for a moment I allowed myself to get lost in a piece of nature that I was happy to see wasn't lost in the post-Vampocalypse.

We passed through the remains of a small town – let me correct that, it was more of a tiny town as it looked to be comprised of barely a dozen old, small buildings that lined either side of the two-lane road – where anxiety ran high for a potential vampire attack. Thankfully, none came. From there the highway expanded into four lanes with a center divider. The foothills were once again in the distance and the wide open plains provided solace in that any incoming vampires would be easily spotted well before they reached us. By contrast, the occasional overpasses we drove under brought the nerves back as they provided many corners and shadows for the creatures to be hiding in as they waited for us to pass.

It was during a long, straight, boring stretch of road when I suddenly saw water ahead. I wasn't sure where it came from but a glistening pool of water covered the entire road. For some reason we weren't slowing down but as we got closer, the "water" disappeared. I blinked hard and didn't know what to think. I would later learn that these tricks of vision were called "mirages." There was so much to discover about the world outside the walls of Camp Expectation. Something else I was in awe of were "dust devils," little sand tornadoes in the wastes. Nature was filled with wonder, indeed, and I was filled with wonder as I took it all in.

Churches. There were so many small, abandoned churches that lined the highway or were easily spotted in distant fields. It didn't matter if the road was two or four lanes, if we were in rolling foothills or wide open spaces, the churches were always there. Lifeless, without any signs of having been occupied for decades. I wondered what their gods thought of all this. If there is a god, I wonder whose prayers it decided to fill and whose it decided to ignore. I'm not a religious or praying person, but it doesn't hurt for me to occasionally ask for a little help in keeping my family alive until I'm able to save them. This is the only prayer I hope god answers.

Our motorcade drove on. We rounded a corner and a lake appeared, brown water with small white breaks on its rippled surface. Running alongside the lake, bordering marshy, green swamplands was a set of train tracks. There was a train sitting there, also apparently broken down and abandoned for many, many years. I estimated close to fifty cars connected together, rusty and overgrown with foliage as the Earth slowly consumed it over time. A hill beyond suddenly brought on a vision of a cloud of vampires flying over, darkening the skies and filling the air with their horrid screeches.

I blinked and nothing was there — just my imagination running rampant as I tried to stay sane in all this craziness.

For some reason seeing the occasional abandoned cars hit me kinda hard. There weren't many of them as most had been cleared by vampires in the thirty years since the bombs dropped. But those left behind made me wonder about the stories. Were there families with children? Were they taken away by vampires? Are they out surviving on their own? There used to be generations within families where stories were passed down. Now everybody's story is the same — they all start thirty years ago, are filled with blood and pain, and end as survivors living on nothing but hope.

"Welcome to California" the sign read. A "state," one of fifty that used to be part of the "United States of America." We drove through some sort of old border inspection station (empty and abandoned, of course) and eventually entered an area of more foothills called Shasta National Forest, with Mt. Shasta resting in all its glory in the not-too-far distance. I had never seen such a majestic sight of a mountain so large in my life. Its snowcapped peak beckoned me and I hoped I could one day see what it was like to stand at its summit, on top of the world. I found it odd how warm it was outside despite having snow so relatively near.

As we approached the halfway point in our journey I had the excitement of watching Wen, the fuelsmith, and his refueling rig in action. The tank on the rig trailer wasn't like a full sized semi, being much smaller and secured onto the flatbed trailer in front of the customized refueling mechanism. It was a cool piece of machinery the way it pulled up alongside another vehicle and extended its fueling contraption — a hose on the end of an easily maneuverable and extendable pole — without decreasing speed in the slightest. The receiving vehicles were already outfitted with devices that provided easy connectors for the hose. Wen's assistant drove their rig while Wen himself went out to the open air of the trailer to work the fueling apparatus that was positioned behind the cab of the truck along with a large oblong tank filled with gasoline. Wen flashed me a grin and thumbs-up when we made eye contact as I watched from my position driving Z's motorcycle close to the fueling vehicles. There was a degree of nervousness from feeling more vulnerable to attack during the refueling, but no attack came.

I think it was about this time we started getting too comfortable on our trek. It had been nearly four hours since we fled the Camp Expectation attack and the desolate, barren roads didn't do anything but help feed complacency. I was stupid to think the vampires had stopped chasing us. I was stupid to let myself feel safe. But, really, what else was I to think?

EPISODE 19

PACIFIC WASTELANDS

"WE should reach San Francisco Mecca in about four hours," Z announced. "That'll put us there close to around eight o'clock tonight."

"The refueling while on the road was impressive," said Prater. The tension between them was all but gone. "Can't say I've ever seen anything like that."

"We're lucky to have the knowhow among us to create these rigs."

The journey over the hours following their escape was uneventful, if not still stressful and filled with the anxiety that fear of the unknown brings. Many of the miles traveled were long straightaways lined with the trunks and sticks of what used to be lush, forest-like trees that did nothing to provide any sense of safety. A large right curve around a hillside brought the caravan glimpses of Shasta Lake on their left. The area managed to maintain a picturesque quality in its own way despite the mottled skies and gray-brown water. A steep foothill covered in barren tree remnants acted as a barrier on their right while a sheer cliff dropped off on their left. Z shifted downward and the rig slowed as it maneuvered the bend in the road. The interstate ahead curved back to the left and onto the top of a long, double-deck, truss bridge that spanned the lake. The motorcade continued in a line as the vehicles maneuvered the turns, except for Annika who kept alongside the driver's side of the semi. Z grabbed the microphone of the truck's CB radio from its cradle on the ceiling of the cab and relayed a warning to the others in the convoy.

"Be extra cautious," she said. "Keep eyes all around but especially in the air. We're going to hit the bridge as hard and as fast as we can."

The semi led the caravan around the next bend in the freeway and onto the straightaway atop the over 3500-foot long bridge. Z pushed the truck to try and rebuild optimum speed after pulling out of the bends in the freeway. The vehicles were totally exposed as they crossed the open air of the four-lane bridge far short of top speed. Travelling down the middle of the two lanes on the right side of the interstate, the motorcade was separated from the other two lanes by a concrete barrier. The bridge, unsurprisingly, was barren just as much of the road since leaving the old Prineville area and up until this point had been. Still, an uneasy feeling settled into Z as she focused on the open bridge deck ahead, determined to get to the other side and out of the danger zone as quickly as possible. Everyone's eyes remained alert and skyward just as Z had commanded. Even Z herself couldn't help from taking constant glances upward in anticipation of vampires flying in from above to take advantage of their vulnerable position.

A lingering look to the skies didn't prepare her for a sudden thump that shook the rig. Looking ahead, Prater and Z saw not just a few but dozens of vampires scuttling and scampering out from around the sides of bridge like an army of insects swarming on its prey. The semi plowed through several of them, but vampires were immediately throwing themselves under the front wheels of the truck, sacrificing themselves and forcing the rig to slow as additional numbers formed a group in front of the vehicle. The truck was brought to a standstill a little over halfway across the bridge due to the sheer numbers of vampires swarming around them. The trailing motorcade grinded to a halt in line behind the battle semi.

Annika slowed the purple Hondamatic she was riding as soon as she witnessed the first vampires crawl onto the highway and get crushed under the drive of the semi. Their broken and mutilated bodies were spit out from under the weapons trailer attached to the truck. Their bones creaked and cracked as their healing factors rapidly rebuilt themselves, closing their wounds, giving them immediate strength to continue fighting. Annika knew of the vampire healing abilities but had never heard of nor witnessed any happening so fast before. She quickly cut the bike sharply around the back end of the semitrailer as she avoided rolling and tossed vampires bodies, narrowly slicing through the space between the trailer and the Plymouth Roadrunner that screeched to a stop not far behind.

The purple Honda motorcycle shot out the right side of the semi and Annika found herself about to collide with a vampire standing directly in her path. With no time and space to stop she cut the handlebars sharply to her left and dropped the bike onto its side. Annika rolled away onto the hard pavement as the motorcycle slammed into the legs of the vampire, knocking the creature down and sliding and grinding over the top of it. The weight and inertia of the crashing bike was enough to completely rip the face off the vampire before coming to a halt on a blood-streaked pavement.

Annika's chest ached as she struggled to regain her breath and fought through the pain she felt all over after tumbling onto the road. She laid face down, coughing and wheezing, and slowly brought her hands to her sides to prepare to push herself up. Shock replaced any adrenaline as she was suddenly yanked up off the street by the back of her neck. Lifted in the air by the unknown assailant, Annika kicked as she clawed at the hand that had a strong hold of her. She pulled in vain at the long, firm fingers wrapped around her neck – the vampire hadn't sunk its talons into her but that didn't make her situation any less dire.

Despite her efforts, Annika couldn't tear away the vice grip the vampire had of her. The creature turned her in the air and they faced each other as Annika looked down at the monster. Already short on breath, her new circumstances prevented her from taking any more air in. The creature smiled as he held her up proudly like some sort of trophy. The vampire let out an ear-piercing screech and its mouth opened wide, exposing a mouthful of sharp, venom-soaked teeth. Annika's vision dimmed as her final breaths escaped her. Unable to inhale any further, she watched as the face of the monster that had her grow blurry and out of focus as a dark tunnel slowly closed upon it.

A bright glimmer of steel suddenly flashed in front of Annika's eyes and she found herself dropped onto the street. She shook her head and coughed as she sat sideways on the road rubbing her neck. A shadow fell on her, and she looked up certain to see the face of her doom…

Prater was there with a bloody katana in one hand. It was then she noticed the decapitated head of the vampire that had hold of her lying a couple of feet away on the road, staring at her with the same thirsty look it had just moments earlier – though now the life behind its eyes was vacant. A hand came into her line of sight as Prater offered to help her to her feet, a gesture she happily accepted.

"Are you okay?" asked Prater.

"As much as I can be." Annika's voice was understandably shaken.

"We need to clear a path so the caravan can get through," said Prater.

Annika blinked rapidly as she nodded. The battle around them was swiftly ramping up in intensity and she did a quick check about her, feeling around her back for her bow and arrows. She somehow still had her quiver of arrows strapped across her back but she had lost the recurve bow when she tumbled in the crash. Thankfully, the weapon was on the ground not far from her and just a few feet from where her crashed motorcycle lay.

"I'm gonna head towards the front of the rig," Prater continued. "Follow me and watch my back."

Prater started in the direction of the front of the motorcade. Annika followed, snatching her bow up off the ground and immediately turning to face behind them, rapidly drawing and firing an arrow as a vampire came over the side of the bridge and ran to within just a few feet of her. The creature's head recoiled back as the arrow lodged through the middle of its forehead. With the vampire having fallen so close to her, Annika was able to get a clear view of the monster. To Annika's dismay the vampire was a girl who looked to be no older than her – they could have been classmates or maybe even friends in another life.

Annika's parents had always told her learning the skills she has would help in a fight. They also did their best to convince her that the fight would surely come one day, though she would have admitted that a part of her believed it would never come. But this was that fight, Annika knew, and it would either be the first such fight of many or her last. Until now, she always had her family to protect her. She was the youngest, the baby, the one with the most life yet unlived to lose. But those protections were gone and there were no assurances anyone was going to be there any longer to protect her. She was still growing up, but the last few days matured her in ways she never fully anticipated.

Annika carefully stepped backwards as she kept watch for any other vampires that may approach from behind them. While she had an arrow nocked and ready, she had to be discriminate with them as their amount was much more finite than many of the other weapons being used in the fight. As she moved, the back of her foot tapped against Z's Hondamatic, signaling her to sidestep the fallen bike. She glanced down at the motorcycle as she walked by. Somehow the throttle was stuck fully open and the back wheel was spinning rapidly as the engine screamed. The crushed and partially mutilated body of the vampire it had struck was still under it and the creature was still alive.

Despite its face having been torn off, the creature tried to raise a hand towards Annika as she stepped around the grotesque scene. As it did, the hand was snagged by the back wheel of the motorcycle as it spun at full speed. The vampire's hand and arm were jerked hard by the wheel as the creature's talons became entangled in its spokes. Much of the skin and flesh stripped away from the vampire's arm as it was sucked into the rear drive chain. Bits of the creature shot through the mechanical workings of the damaged motorcycle and the wheel came to an abrupt stop. A loud pop followed and a plume of smoke shot straight up out of the bike's engine. The monster would have screamed if it wasn't already gurgling a bloody yowl.

As Annika looked towards the rear of the caravan, she saw others fighting off vampires as they came up from under the side of the bridge. Looking down the line, Elroi was operating a machine gun mounted to the back of his Plymouth Roadrunner almost directly behind the front seats. His gunner had been lost during the escape from Camp Expectation, so he had taken over, spitting silver bullets at those unlucky enough to find themselves in his sights. Berserker had his modified flamethrower secured to the top of his civilian tank, spewing fire in controlled streams. Incom and Ecks each operated a UV laser rifle on opposite sides of the heavily armored Volkswagen bus. Wen and his fuel rig assistant, a young man who called himself Sparks, fended for themselves with M16 rifles spraying silver bullets. And finally there was Kemena who worked the hybrid spear-harpoon launcher on top of the modified hearse while the hearse's driver took shots with their own M16.

At the front of the fight, Z stood on the long hood of the semi battle rig, stabbing and slicing with both of her sai at any vampire that dare come too close. On the ground to her right, Prater was cutting away with both of his katana. Despite fighting valiantly, most of their efforts were nullified as it was difficult to strike true in the mayhem, and many of the vampires simply immediately healed from their non-fatal wounds and remained in the fight. Regardless of any micro victories, their efforts felt fruitless. It would only be a matter of time before the numbers overwhelmed them and their efforts were extinguished.

SNOWEYES stood at the end of the bridge, facing the front of the melee, far enough away to be safe from the fight. Behind him the Red Marauders' motorcycles sat empty as their owners and occupants participated in the thick of the fight. Although the vampires far outnumbered the humans, the fight was not yet clearly on the side of the abhorrent creatures. Snoweyes was able to tell their numbers were slowly decreasing.

The undead motorcycle gang leader looked to his right at the vampire standing next to him, the only other one not partaking in the fight. Argo was Snoweyes' second-in-command and the club's sergeant-at-arms. Standing six-foot four and a lean but very muscular two hundred ten pounds, Argo was a commanding figure even if he wasn't necessarily the largest. He had a dark brown mustache that rounded down into a thick beard, all framed in a dense lion's mane of hair. Standing shirtless with his arms crossed, the dark, diamond-patterned tattoos around each forearm looked like wide vambraces but were nothing but ink and design. Argo rarely entered the fray of a battle, which was no different than their leader Snoweyes, but when he did he was sure to not only win, but win decisively.

Snoweyes raised his left hand and made an arc in the air, ending with an open palm stretched straight out that he closed twice. Argo nodded and pulled a flare gun from a holster at the base of his back. Aiming the pistol straight up, a bright red flare went up with a loud poof. And while everyone noticed the flare, it did nothing to pause any fighting. Snoweyes maintained his watch of the battle as Argo holstered the flare gun without any emotion.

PRATER slid one of his katana out from a dead vampire's forehead as the flare went off. Just as the creature was about to drop seemingly lifeless onto the street, Prater brought his other sword around and decapitated the monster. He glanced up at the exploding flare then at Z who was still on the semi-truck hood next to him fighting away.

"What do you suppose that's for?" Z shouted down to him.

"Not sure," Prater yelled back as he took on another attacking vampire.

"Ohmigod," Annika called out to get their attention. "Look!"

Prater's gaze followed where Annika was pointing towards the back end of the motorcade. But what she was pointing at was past the harpoon trailer, beyond the fighting, and past the end of the bridge. While the freeway curved to the right, what had Annika's attention was on the foothill that butted up against the interstate.

Driving down the hillside was a vehicle unlike anything any of them had ever seen. Looking like an oversized excavator from hell, the bulk of the machine was over four-stories tall with a boom that reached nearly twice that height. The behemoth drove on two sets of immense track rollers as it effortlessly plowed its way through the skeletons of long dead trees covering the hillside. The metal beast was all black and accented by red gears and piping. Tall exhaust ports shot intermittent plumes of flame straight into the air as if the mechanical creature was breathing fire. Two large cranes extended up and away from behind the controller's cab like giant metallic antennae stretching high into the sky. Attached to the end of the excavator's large boom arm and in place of the traditional bucket was an immense set of steel jaws modeled on vampire teeth. The oversized contraption opened and closed like a creature eager to taste prey and, even more terrifying, red fireballs flared inside of the large "mouth" as if it was a mechanical demon.

Prater and Annika watched as they were momentarily paralyzed in awe of the excavator rolling up behind the harpoon trailer at the tail end of the caravan. The tractor chains chugged the behemoth along swiftly for such a large machine and clanked loudly as the tracks met the pavement of the freeway. Even though the mechanism was already obviously extremely large, its actual enormity became apparent as it pulled up in contrast to the trailer. The tractor treads themselves were as tall as a two-story house and easily straddled the concrete center lane divider. The monster took up nearly all four lanes of the freeway when it finally stopped advancing. Its jaws-like bucket was large enough to comfortably hold a locomotive engine. The excavator stopped behind the harpoon trailer with its boom extending its mechanical mandibles high.

Kemena maneuvered the two longest stick controls in the middle of a line of several that stuck up from a control panel mounted on the floor. She spun her 360-degree turret in the direction of the motorized monstrosity and immediately pumped several long, silver spears at the attacker. The hearse's driver stood on the flatbed next to the big turret, emptying magazines of silver bullets at the menacing steel beast, attempting to strike the excavator's driver's cab. The cab was tiny compared to the rest of the machine and remained safely protected behind the large boom. Bullets did nothing but leave superficial scratches on the steel where they glanced off harmlessly.

"Aim for the joints and hydraulics on its main boom!" Kemena shouted to the hearse driver.

As the driver adjusted their aim and did their best to shoot at the constantly moving and shifting boom, Kemena adjusted one of the shorter control sticks in front of her and the feeding mechanisms of the turret clanked and shifted. She tried to steady her breathing as she took much more careful aim this time, using the crosshairs sight display of the turret to focus on the large hydraulic cylinder on the lower arm, or "stick," that extended to the giant maw preparing to bear down on them.

Kemena squeezed the trigger once and it wasn't a spear that shot out of the turret this time but a harpoon with a steel cable in tow. The harpoon impaled the cylinder at its base where it was attached to the boom. Kemena cranked on various controls and the cable pulled tight which caused the boom and its deadly mouth to go off-kilter compared to the direction they were originally swinging. The entire excavator sputtered and the flame from its exhaust ports shot higher than ever. Shifting another of the turret's control sticks caused the cable holding the harpoon to recoil and pull the boom arm sharply down towards the highway.

The immense excavator made a screeching, piercing noise like a wounded animal and for a brief instance it looked as if the machine may be mortally wounded. The screeching then turned into a deep, loud bellow and the two large "antennae" that were sticking up into the air bent and came crashing onto the freeway, impaling their tips into the concrete. The large boom suddenly yanked the opposite way and the harpoon cable snapped like a taut string.

While the harpoon end yanked away while still stuck in the boom cylinder, the broken steel cable recoiled backwards with a loud metallic *TWANG!* and Kemena had to duck to avoid being decapitated by the loose end that shot back in her direction. Unfazed, she shifted the turret and fired another harpoon, but the jaws-bucket swung and knocked it away before it made contact. The huge metallic mouth continued its movement and stopped right over the middle of the spear-harpoon hearse. Kemena and the driver fired spears and bullets with no effect as the immense steel jaws quickly slammed down and snapped shut onto the hearse, crushing the turret along with Kemena and the truck's driver within its mechanical bite. The metallic behemoth raised its black, steely maw and the large antennae sticking into the road helped to stabilize and balance the excavator as it continued to raise the broken hearse high. Fire and smoke pumped out from within the black jaws of the large beast as the vehicle burned inside the closed apparatus.

Prater maintained an eye on the destruction unfolding while fending off vampires from his place at the front of the motorcade. He cut and slashed but unless he got a clean decapitation or stab to the brain, the creatures would, save for regrowing any lost limbs, heal quickly and continue the attack. Behind him Annika did her best to eradicate those she could from a distance with headshots from her bow and arrow, though less than half her shots struck their targets because of their unpredictable movements. And while she continued to use her arrows sparingly, it wouldn't be much longer before she ran out. Z, meanwhile, kept fighting from her place on the hood of the truck, poking and stabbing with her sai as creatures came at her from multiple directions.

Prater and Annika pivoted as they battled and Annika ended up with her back to the passenger side of the semi. Annika watched as Prater sliced the top of the head off a vampire rushing at him, which provided a very brief break in his fight. He looked back as the giant, black excavator raised its huge metallic jaws wide, releasing the final burned and broken remains of the harpoon trailer over the bridge rail and into the water below. Prater was certain he saw a charred and blackened corpse tumble out among the burnt rubble. Then the machine began to advance upon the refueling rig and armored Volkswagen bus – the vehicles had maneuvered to be side by side on the bridge during the fight.

"We can't let that thing take out any more of us.," said Prater. "I'm going to go stop it."

"How?" Annika sounded on the edge of panic. "What are you going to do?"

"I'll figure it out when I get there."

Prater looked up briefly at Z who had heard his announcement and glanced down at him. She gave him a brief nod in-between strikes at opponents. Prater didn't take the time to acknowledge the gesture and instead leapt up onto the weapons trailer of the battle semi, deciding it may be safer to run on top of the vehicles rather than beside them as he made his way towards the back of the motorcade. He slashed and hacked at the vampires in his path, but never engaged fully as he ran as fast as he could at the monster excavator.

Annika watched him take off and in her distraction was caught off guard as a vampire rushed at her from the side. She swerved her bow and arrow in the creature's direction, but the distance was too close and the vampire was too quick for her to get off a shot. Pressed with her back against the battle semi she went to swing the bow at the monster like a club when Z dropped down behind the creature while driving both her sai – held together with both her hands – into the top of the creature's head. The force of the strike drove the vampire onto the road with its head open and bleeding from the fresh holes plowed into it.

Annika gave Z a crooked smile of relief with a knowing "Thank you" in her eyes. Z flashed back a similar smile, but her eyes were saying, "Fuck, yeah."

SNOWEYES continued to watch the skirmish silently from his place at the end of the bridge. He stood resolutely and emotionless with his hands clasped and resting comfortably in front of him. To his side, Argo stood with his arms crossed and fire in his eyes. Snoweyes removed his sunglasses and the white irises cut through the yellow-gray of the air surrounding them. He looked at his sergeant-at-arms and could tell the larger vampire was eager to join the fight.

Argo maintained his staunch posture and forward stare but let out a grunt in acknowledgement of his gang leader's recognition of his desire to enter the battle. Snoweyes said nothing but raised a finger and pointed in the direction of the combat. This broke Argo's icy posture as one side of his mouth curled up and he uncrossed his arms. Throwing his hands to his sides, eight-inch long claws jutted out of his fingertips and he let out a snarl as he snapped together his mouthful of razorlike fangs. A moment later the sergeant-at-arms was running full force towards the conflict – an uncontrollable embodiment of rage ready to tear into each and every human until he reached his target: the president's prized Prater Saxon.

EPISODE 20

PACIFIC WASTELANDS

THE path to the excavator may as well have been a mile long for the amount of peril in Prater's path. The battle semi-trailer had no human survivors to operate its weapons, leaving Prater forced to cut and slice his way past three vampires that each blocked his path but barely slowed his run. Upon reaching the tail end of the trailer, he leapt onto the hood of the Plymouth Roadrunner. Elroi was still firing away from the vehicle's machine gun, spinning it in all directions, as he managed to keep many of the creatures at bay.

"Take that, you bloody, cocksucking vampires!" the bald, black man shouted. His heavy Cockney accent punctuated each syllable.

Prater ran around the backside of the rotating machine gun mount and dropped onto the ground in front of the BATT UMG civilian armored carrier. He pressed himself against the grill of the heavy vehicle as a stream of fire from Berserker's modified flamethrower passed not too far overhead. The heat of the flame was instant and kept the creatures at a relative distance – at least for the moment. Once the jet of fire moved past, Prater jolted around the side of the oversized combat vehicle and positioned himself between the Volkswagen van and Wen's bastardized 350Z. He arrived just in time to see Wen's assistant Sparks get dragged from the refueling rig platform by a vampire. The young man kicked and screamed as he was taken and thrown over the side of the bridge – bringing his cries of protest to an abrupt halt. Wen was either oblivious or indifferent about the casualty as he continued spraying silver from his M16 at anything that dared try and get too close.

Prater stared up at the immense excavator towering above them like a dark dragon from another world. He needed to come up with a plan on how to attack the machine before the beast began its next attack. He only had moments to decide what to do.

ARGO sprinted across the bridge with the speed of a cheetah. Ahead, the vampires were dispersed among the various vehicles in the motorcade as the resolve in the humans proved to be greater than anticipated. Z continued her victorious reign atop the semi engine hood. Argo knew he would have to catch this one by surprise.

Z stabbed a vampire through the side of its head just as it was about to impale her sides with its claws. As the creature dropped dead and slid off the side of the hood, Z glanced over her shoulder towards the front end of the bridge. She barely registered the large, dark shape that launched towards her full speed as it leapt off the road, grabbed her around the waist and lifted her into the air, then slammed her back against the edge of the empty windshield frame of the semi cab. Her body went limp in the creature's arms and in a continuous motion Argo raised the woman over his head then slammed her onto the hood of the semi on her back. Both her sai clanked loudly as they bounced off the truck and onto the highway. Argo straddled the unmoving woman and raised a claw high as he prepared to tear into her.

"Z!" screamed Annika as she watched from where she stood between the battle semi and side of the bridge.

The shirtless, musclebound creature looked at the young girl and the two locked eyes. Argo snarled and spittle sprayed as he snapped his teeth. Annika brought up her bow and took aim.

This was her last arrow.

She was about to release the string when the red-eyed monster bellowed then leapt away in the direction of the excavator, followed by the surrounding vampires in earshot of whatever animalistic command the creature just exclaimed. The young girl let out a sigh of relief as she lowered her weapon, finding herself in a break in the fighting due to the sudden departure of the vampires around her. She slung the bow around her shoulder then used the steel bars masking the radiator grille on the front of the truck to climb onto the large hood. She knelt beside the unconscious woman and put her cheek near the woman's face, looking for any signs of life. Z wasn't moving but thankfully was still breathing. Annika's lip quivered as she found herself suddenly shaking and crying hopelessly, unsure of what to do or what was going to happen next.

SWEAT poured off the large man who called himself Berserker as he worked his flamethrower, catching vampires up to two hundred feet away with concentrated streams of fire that caused several to plunge themselves into the lake below. Many eventually worked their way back into the battle, blackened and scarred, but still healed well enough to continue fighting. His wrestler's mask was soaked with perspiration but still managed to keep the sweat out of his eyes. Beads of sweat rolled off his bare shoulders and down his bare back, drenching the tank top stretched over his upper body. The tall, broad man unleashed yelps of rage as he worked to increase the vampire body count.

A vampire, the largest he had yet seen by far, landed on the ground in front of his civilian tank. He watched as the creature – with his big hair and big muscles – glared up at him before grabbing the front of the large BATT UMG vehicle under its metallic front bumper. Then, much to Berserker's surprise, the vampire began to pull and strain and, through immense effort, lifted the front of the five-ton vehicle off the ground. Berserker detached his flamethrower from its mount and pointed it in the direction of the powerful creature. Fire shot out randomly as he tried to aim at the vampire but couldn't get the creature into view as the front of the BATT UMG continued to rise higher. Berserker tumbled backwards as the vehicle flipped completely onto its roof with a loud grunt from the vampire.

Argo took several deep breaths as he shook his arms to recover from the strain and effort he'd just exerted. He marched forward towards the upside-down vehicle and around to its back end, fully expecting to see the big, masked man who had been wielding the flamethrower to be dead underneath. To his astonishment, no one was there.

"Looking for me?"

The deep voice surprised Argo and the big vampire turned around and looked up at the man standing on top of the upside-down armored vehicle. The large human still had his flamethrower and it was aimed right at him. His nose wrinkled like that of a rabid wolf, but he didn't have the chance to make a sound before a white-hot stream of concentrated flame blasted into his chest. He screamed and recoiled backwards as fire blasted his body. Stumbling to his side, Argo finally tumbled over the side of the bridge. An audible splash was heard as the big creature fell into the lake.

Berserker smirked to himself. That was easier than expected. Sounds behind him caught his attention and that was when he became aware of the small group of vampires that had followed their large, long-haired leader. They were engaged in a fight with Elroi and the machine gun he operated from the top of his Plymouth Roadrunner. Believing Elroi was holding his own, Berserker climbed down from his overturned BATT UMG and rushed to the side of the bridge where the big vampire he set on fire had fallen. Looking to the water far below turned up nothing.

The sound of a "thump" behind him caught Berserker's attention and he turned around to see the big vampire – his thick hair was singed and smoldering while his chest was black and scarred from healing after being blasted by the fire stream. The creature exhaled a thick cloud of smoke then abruptly snatched the flamethrower out of the ex-wrestler's hands. With a mighty scream, Argo tore the weapon apart in two then discarded the pieces over the side of the bridge.

Berserker only smirked and, with the imposing creature staring at him with rage just a few feet away, reached up and tightened the knot to the tattered scarf he wore around the top half of his head.

"That's how this is gonna be then?" his deep voice taunted the vampire as he raised his fists. *"Mano y mano?"*

Berserker was physically both a bit taller and some wider than the vampire facing him though the creature was clearly much stronger. But that didn't matter to Berserker. The man had never backed down from a fight and this wasn't going to be the first. He took a heavy, hard swing with his right fist and landed the blow squarely on the left side of Argo's face. The vampire barely flinched. Berserker quickly followed with a hard swipe with his left fist and again Argo didn't react as he took the blow.

With a snarl the vampire gave a double-fisted punch squarely into Berserker's chest, launching the big man backwards like a cannonball until his back smashed against the bridge guardrail. The ex-wrestler shook his head and laughed casually to himself. He'd taken similar hits during his pro wrestling days...but this one did smart more than he could remember. Despite the discomfort, he was glad the creature didn't decide to grab him. After seeing how the vampire effortlessly tore his flamethrower apart, he knew the key to surviving would be to not allow the monster to get a hold of him.

"Well, now we've got a fight," Berserker grumbled as he quickly got to his feet.

The vampire had not moved and was still ahead of him. Curiously, it seemed to just be watching him. Berserker didn't waste any time analyzing the situation and took off running at the creature as fast as he could in the few steps they had between them. The vampire stood still, broad chested and with his arms out to the sides, prepared for battle. But instead of attacking again with his fists, Berserker launched himself into the air, brought his knees immediately to his chest, then slammed both feet in an outstretched straight forward kick into the chest of the creature.

The vampire may have been stronger, but it wasn't immovable. As Berserker dropped onto his back on the road, Argo stumbled backwards before tripping over the dead and blackened remains of one of Berserker's earlier flamethrower victims who did not survive. The vampire shook his head as he got onto his hands and knees, facing away from the big human who just felled him. A human who Argo was certain would not live much longer.

As he stood, Argo heard the human taunting him from behind, "*Red Marauders?*" the human said with disdain, referencing the logo of his motorcycle club inscribed in a bold red and black tattoo across his upper back. "What a joke. I've fought bigger and badder during my amateur wrestling days."

Argo shook his mane so that it completely covered the artwork. He turned and faced the human with a look of contempt that matched the human's scorn for him.

"We shall see," said Argo, his voice low and husky.

Argo launched himself in full sprint towards Berserker as the ex-wrestler did the same and the two behemoths went straight at each other. Argo outstretched his arms as he made a grab for Berserker's upper body. Berserker, though, had other ideas as he again propelled himself into the air, this time twisting himself sideways, and the two large bodies connected like a cross before the ex-wrestler wrapped himself around his target. Despite getting caught off guard once again by the style of the attack, Argo was still ready as he only took a few steps backwards before he planted his feet and grabbed at the human entangled around him. Easily pulling the weaker opponent away, Argo lifted Berserker high in the air straight overhead, then used a wrestler's finishing move of his own as he slammed the man face down onto the highway, breaking several of the man's ribs in the process.

Berserker wheezed as he tried to catch his breath. He'd suffered broken ribs before – it was all par for the course. He just needed a moment to compose himself…a moment that would never come as he was abruptly yanked up by claws that dug painfully into the back of his neck. Lifted high in front of the creature, Berserker looked down at his attacker and into the eyes and at certain death. The man was helpless as the vampire's other powerful hand poised to deliver what was to be the killing blow. Berserker kicked and squirmed as he tried to grapple with the powerful grip holding him to no result. He continued to stare down at the creature, fighting away his fear and suppressing any pain, vowing to himself to keep eye contact with the thing that would finally take the fight out of the great and mighty Berserker.

AS he stared at the gigantic excavator towering over him, Prater knew he had to get to the relatively tiny control cab of the machine. That would be his only chance of disabling the monstrosity and to save Z, Annika, and others who may still be alive. As the large boom of the toothy bucket prepared its next attack by rotating and raising high, Prater was able to spot the open-aired cab mounted to the fore of the giant compartments holding the engine, pump, and drive assemblies. He looked at the immense steel treads and wheels and determined they were too large to provide a viable way for him to climb up the beast. As the boom positioned nearly directly overhead, Prater realized its next target was the van next to him – and immediately knew what he needed to do.

The giant mouthlike claw descended and grabbed the Volkswagen in its colossal jaws. The van, while heavily armored, was no match for the power of the metal death machine as it crumpled like an aluminum can between the steel monster's teeth. The humongous claw raised with the broken and damaged van in its grip. Ecks and Incom miraculously scampered out from inside the large metallic jowls, tumbling to safety just before they were raised too high off the ground to survive the drop.

Prater climbed around and perched himself on top of the giant claw as it rose up and away from the bridge. Holding onto the large arm of the excavator so tightly his hands quickly grew sore, Prater rode the long stick that held the deadly bucket as it raised higher and higher into the air. The long mechanical arm of the death machine nearly straightened as it extended into the sky. Flames erupted from within the metallic mouth as the Volkswagen van was incinerated before its molten husk was dropped over the side of the bridge. Prater felt the heat from the exploding van as he worked his way around the thick links attached not far from the bucket then onto the large cylinder itself that acted as the primary hydraulic controlling the steel mouth of the beast. Once his feet touched the base of the bucket cylinder, he immediately leapt onto the next piece of the machine – the stick cylinder – as he continued to make his way towards the cab. His next maneuver would be the most precarious: sliding down the near vertical boom itself.

Prater realized he had forgotten to breathe – and even then, he wasn't sure how long that had occurred. Nothing else mattered except getting to the controls of the machine. The large mechanism was already pivoting to line up over its next victim: Wen's 350Z refueling rig.

The vampire sitting at the controls of the goliath excavator was an older looking man – he looked to have been in his upper 60s when he was turned – balding on top except for wisps of white hair that fluttered in the breeze of the open air cab. He wore a set of round sunglasses that would have had him mocking the look of a maniacal scientist if it wasn't for the leather Red Marauders cut he wore over a long-sleeved, white shirt. He yanked forward on one yoke while pulling back on another and the large mouth of the bucket opened wide as it prepared to eat the doomed 350Z directly below.

The creature let out a half-cackle, half-yowl as he slammed on the controls to grab the defenseless refueling rig. A sudden blur came swinging in through the windowless opening in the side door of the cab and a hard slam from the bottoms of booted feet connected with the side of the vampire's head, knocking him against the opposite side of the small cab.

Prater was on top of the creature in an instant, grabbing the back of his collar and slamming his face several times against the front dash before the dazed vampire could react to what was happening. Finally having his senses come about him, the vampire gripped the dash with his talons, digging them into the hard plastic. He looked at his attacker and growled – just as Prater shoved one of his swords up through the creature's chin and out the top of its head. Wasting no time, Prater slid the weapon out and replaced the bloody blade into its back scabbard. The cab was barely large enough for Prater and the vampire to share the space, but not large enough to allow Prater to easily work the controls with a corpse in the way. He grabbed the body with both hands and with a mighty heave shoved the dead vampire out the opening where a front windshield would be.

Pulling on one of the controls, the boom arm moved the bucket away from Wen and his 350Z but not the way Prater expected. While the jaws avoided grabbing the refueling rig, it quickly dropped onto the freeway, digging into the road as it skid across the opposite lanes, thankfully away from Wen and the others. Prater adjusted the joysticks and took a moment to get a feel of how the giant excavator worked. There weren't many controls, but the entire contraption was so huge that the corresponding movements felt sluggish, which was the biggest adjustment as Prater tried to get the machine to feel more natural and intuitive.

Once he tamed the immense beast, Prater looked down at the road and at Wen who raised a fist and looked to shout an exclamation of either triumph or excitement – or possibly both – Prater couldn't quite tell from his elevated distance. Prater reached up and worked a couple of additional controls and the large stabilizers that were rooted into the freeway lifted and returned to their spot as overhead antennae. Then, ever so slowly, Prater was able to get the gargantuan treads to move the immense machine. He wasn't trying to get anywhere in particular, rather, he was still getting the feel of the controls. Experimenting, he pivoted the machine first to the left, then to the right. Flames shot high in hot, red columns from the exhaust pipes pointing into the air as the massive metal monster bellowed under Prater's control. He couldn't help but smile as he moved the gigantic claw of the excavator forward, ever so slowly as he considered his plans, looking to end this fight once and for all.

BERSERKER tried kicking out with his legs in a final, desperate effort to break free from the vampire's deathly grip of the scruff of his neck. He was weak and tired from the fight, and nothing he did was going to stop the creature from taking his life. He wasn't sure if the outstretched talons of the vampire's other hand were going to tear his face off, rip his heart out, or who knows what other demonic atrocity it was capable of.

And still, Berserker kept his eyes locked on those of his would-be killer. The creature finally thrust its other hand forward and Berserker flinched as the razor-sharp talons came at his face...

A bloody pointed tip of a steel weapon burst out from the vampire's forehead. Vampire blood splattered across Berserker as the weapon retracted from the creature's mortal wound, and for a brief instant Berserker thought he could see clear through the vampire's head. The ex-wrestler dropped to the freeway as the dead vampire released its grip and collapsed dead onto the road.

Berserker partly sat up and partly lay on the road as he rubbed at the blood coming from the wounds in the back of his neck where the vampire had held him. He wheezed loudly and his breathing labored through the mass of broken ribs. His ability to breathe at all was a test of endurance unto itself. Still, though, he was alive and grateful for whoever just saved him.

Looking up into the eyes of Z, his savior, Berserker let out a weak, "Thank you."

Z's reply was cut off before it even began. She could only watch as a vampire, bald with a goatee and wearing Wayfarer sunglasses, landed behind Berserker. The creature grabbed the large ex-wrestler from behind with one hand on his neck and the other on a shoulder. With a mighty shriek the vampire pulled his hands away from each other – tearing Berserker in half nearly clean down the middle. Blood splashed Z as she could only stand in shock of the abrupt carnage she witnessed. Over the years she had dealt with vampires of varied strengths and sizes and their ways of killing and none of them fazed her. These over-the-top theatrics served their purpose, though, of striking a fear in her that was unfamiliar. But fear would not rule her this day.

Slashes from Z's sai came rapidly and Snoweyes leapt back in retreat of the deadly swipes. The vampire cut to his left and was about to attack when a loud, metallic screech from above captured everyone's attention. Eyes scanned upwards to the sight of the large excavator claw hovering above them. Fire shot up from the machine's tall vertical vents like white hot tornadoes swirling into the sky. The gigantic, black machine seemed alive as its gears grinded, servomotors buzzed, and hydraulics hissed.

The vampire snarled at Z before unexpectedly grabbing her underneath her jaw and lifting her up – not just off her feet but high into the air as the vampire took off in flight. Z clawed at the creature's iron grip to break free but realized she would drop to her death at the height they had already achieved. She figured she was being taken away to ultimately end up in the blood banks. But rather than flying away from the fighting, they flew closer to the giant excavator –

specifically its huge, metal-toothed maw that was swinging about like a Tyrannosaurus rex snapping at its prey.

Terror began to take hold as Z realized they were flying right at the opening of the giant claw. Z reignited her fight to be released. She preferred to take her chances in the fall rather than inside the certain death of the monster excavator. Her struggles got her nowhere and she found herself flung right into the steel jaws just as they were drawing themselves closed.

Z barely shot through the narrowing gap of the huge claw just before it snapped shut with a loud metallic *CLANG!* She tumbled and bumped into the middle of the apparatus, coming to a stop as, much to her relief, the entire contraption also stopped moving. She sat up quickly, figuring any vital injuries would make themselves known. None did. Taking a quick look around it was like she was in a cave, except it was hot and smelled of burnt rubber and steel…and flesh. A sliver of light slicing through the dusty air caught her attention. She sprinted to the front where there was an opening a few inches wide where the two halves of the mouth and steely teeth met and interlocked. Peeking through the opening, Z could see the ground from the downward tilt of the bucket. A fall from this height would certainly kill her. Still, she had to think of a way out – and fast before the internal fire erupted or she was dumped out against her will. The next instant, though, she stumbled and fought to stay on her feet as her steel prison moved downward – though to what ends, her imagination raced unsuccessfully to predict.

PRATER stopped the giant claw from moving the moment he witnessed Z drop into it. He paused a moment hoping she would be able to get her bearings after being flung so violently inside, then lowered the boom and bucket towards the ground.

Distracted by Z's sudden predicament, Prater didn't detect the vampire flying at him like a rocket from the windowless opening on his right. The creature grabbed him with both hands and turned him in a dizzying spin before slamming his back against the joysticks and control panel. Acting quickly, Prater dodged left and right to narrowly avoid his attacker's claws digging into his sides. Each thrust of the lethal talons smashed through the plastic and metal dashboard behind him, destroying several controls and rendering them useless.

Prater landed several quick punches into the bald, goateed vampire's face, knocking the creature's Wayfarers off in the process. Prater immediately noticed the vampire's white irises – empty voids of expression that were somehow more disconcerting than the all black irises of some vampires he had seen. In the next moment the two of them were smashing through the cab's side door and flying skyward. Far below them, sparks began shooting around the control panel before wisps of smoke floated up from behind several of the excavator's panel and gauges.

The giant boom lurched sharply upward, returning to the height it was originally at when Z was initially dropped into it, then came to a sudden halt. Z was balled up and lying on her side as she was jostled at the mercy of the machine. The roaring echo of grinding steel sounded throughout the inside of the claw. She tucked her head in and covered her ears to try and deaden the deafening noise. A new sound took over as the steel echo diminished. Looking up Z saw a large circular hatch slide open near the center of the roof of the claw revealing a dark and foreboding opening. A bluish glow flooded the space around Z as a pilot light inside the dark turned on with a hiss. Panic immediately set in as it occurred to her the entire place could be filled with fire any second. The next moment, though, the pilot light extinguished and the opening resealed itself.

Z wasn't sure what caused the flame device to retract but she wasn't going to wait for it to make another appearance. She raced again to the slim opening at the front of the claw and tried to push her body through the largest gap she could find between the interconnected metallic teeth. It was a fool's attempt, she knew, as she could barely get the width of one arm through, let alone her entire body. She slammed her fists against the steel as she released a scream of frustration. Looking up and down the immense, dark space she couldn't see anywhere to go to escape. Her only thought was to check the entire length of the claw to see if maybe, just maybe, there was an opening somewhere large enough for her, though even then she wouldn't know what to do once she got through as the certainty of falling to her death would likely occur. With little else to go on, Z began her search for the unlikely opening, poking her arm through every few feet as she gauged whether more of her body could fit through.

Prater grappled with the vampire as they flew in a large circle around the excavator. The creature had hold of Prater through his black jacket as the vampire's talons dug into his chest. Prater landed a few solid headbutts to the white-eyed vampire's nose but it barely bled. As they came around the front side of the gigantic boom and stick of the excavator, Prater thought he saw a hand jut out from between the jaws of the bucket and then disappear. Then he noticed the hand again a few feet further away and took some solace in knowing Z was okay – at least for the moment.

As they continued their rapid flight, Prater took in more of the enormous machine from their angle high and above the behemoth. The two large truss-style stabilizers were folded up and back looking less like antennae this time and more like the bent hind legs of a grasshopper. The gigantic boom was nearly vertical and the stick supporting the bucket was almost completely horizontal as it reached out and away from the body of the colossal, black, insectoid-like machine.

Prater stopped wrestling with his captor and instead drew one of his katana from over his shoulder. With a single thrust he stabbed the creature in its side so perfectly the tip of the blade came out the creature's opposite side almost exactly in line with its point of entry. The vampire screeched, practically deafening Prater, and they entered a nosedive towards the long bucket cylinder mounted to the topside of the stick. Prater twisted his blade forward and back while it was still inside the creature, which only made the monster continue to wail. Then the two of them crashed onto the giant cylinder.

As they broke away from one another, Prater kept hold of his sword as he and the vampire fell away and slipped down opposite sides of the large, black cylinder and landed a few feet away from each other on the flat, but slightly downward tilted, top of the stick that held the bucket of the excavator. Prater got right to his feet and as he did, he could feel the puncture wounds in his chest from the creature's claws healing. Standing on the long arm of the machine, Prater was on the lower end of the declined stick looking up towards the vampire who stood staring at him, heaving and huffing with rage. The area wasn't very wide, just about ten feet, and there were no rails nor any other modicum of safety. The giant cylinder that controlled the stick hung overhead. Immediately behind Prater were two large side links that helped connect the front of the hydraulic cylinder to the stick itself.

The vampire was suddenly flying straight at him with its arms outstretched and the sneer of a demon on its face. Prater brandished both of his katana as he kept his feet steady in anticipation of the attack. Just as Prater went to swing at his airborne assailant, the vampire flipped and went from coming at him headfirst to feetfirst. Prater still slashed at the creature's legs but the unanticipated maneuver through off his attacks and most of the force of the double-footed kick still slammed against his chest. Prater stumbled backwards and his back smacked against the hard black steel of one of the side links before he toppled onto his stomach into the space between both large links. Before he could get up, the vampire was on top of him, yanking him to his feet by his neck.

A distinct buzzing and crackling sound came from the excavator cab as the control panel continued to spark and fry. The large boom abruptly swung again as the long stick the combatants were on began to drop. The claw at the end raised up as it opened, exposing the insides of the contraption to the filtered daylight, then stopped.

Z was again tossed about though she quickly got to her feet and raced to the front of the open jaws. She looked down at the ground that was still too far to jump but she knew she had to use this opportunity to escape the steel trap. She began to climb up and between the large spikes of the lower "teeth" of the claw when everything moved again, and she bounced along the hard steel floor and all the way to the rear of the apparatus.

The unexpected erratic movements from the boom and stick knocked Snoweyes off the machine, with Prater still in his grasp, and the two tumbled through the air as the vampire fought to gain control. Before he could initiate flight, though, Snoweyes slammed inside the large open claw as the contraption jerked around and scooped the vampire and his captive out of the air. Unable to keep hold of his prisoner, the creature rolled hard one direction as Prater tumbled away from him.

The jaws began to close once again but again stopped with a few feet wide opening between the two halves – a space easily large enough for someone to work their way through. Although the claw provided an opening to escape, getting to it was going to prove challenging as the entire excavator began to rotate on its giant treads and the boom jostled around unpredictably. There was also the matter of the vampire squaring off against them.

Prater and Z had their weapons drawn to fight as the world around them began to sway. Adjusting quickly, they used the momentum to their advantage and leapt off the shifting steel floor to fly through the air to slice and stab at the vampire who was using his flight powers to try and remain in the center of the open space around them. This proved to be difficult as the unpredictability of the claw left Snoweyes bouncing off its metal sides regardless of his efforts – all while evading the deadly attacks by the humans rushing through the air past him. Snoweyes had his sharp talons extended to their fullest and the space echoed with the pings and clangs from when his organic razors would clash with the steel wielded by the humans.

After several dizzying displays of back-and-forth aerial acrobatics that looked like a choreographed ballet between three highly skilled warriors, one slice of Prater's sword went deep into the vampire's side as Z pierced the creature clear through one of his thighs with a plunge of her sai. The trio of combatants tangled in the air then fell together to the metal floor. Snoweyes snarled and snapped his jowls loudly as he grimaced in pain. Swinging his long claws in blind rage at the humans, the vampire sliced a deep gash into Prater's left shoulder. Prater fell away from the creature and rolled onto the floor, his blades clanging and echoing as they bounced inside the steel claw.

The entire contraption stopped moving again and the combatants each took a moment as they gathered their breaths and, in the case of both Prater and Snoweyes, allow their wounds to begin to heal. The dark space turned blue and a sound familiar to Z caught everyone's attention. They all looked up to see the pilot light exposed high above them. This time, though, the mechanisms didn't immediately reverse themselves and close. Rather, a new sensation filled the large open space around them – the odor of gas fumes was quickly filling the air.

Prater took off running towards the opening at the front of the claw. Z was right behind him. With his wounds less severe compared to those of the vampire's, Prater was easily able to immediately sprint for his life. Snoweyes, on the other hand, lost a lot of blood from his injuries, and even a vampire could only lose so much blood and still fully function. The white-eyed creature was slower to his feet and although the stab wound in his leg was healing, the nature of the hole having gone through the front and all the way out the back of his thigh was proving to be painfully troublesome as he attempted to run. The deep slice through his side wasn't helping matters as he winced and had to keep his body bent forward to try and alleviate the pain as his organs worked hard to rebuild themselves.

Reaching the front of the partially closed bucket, Prater and Z sheathed their weapons and began climbing up onto the large claw teeth, high enough beyond their thick metal bases to where they could take advantage of the opening and balance themselves on the precipice of the immense metal contraption. Looking down was not for those wary of heights and proved there was no path for escape. Looking up, though, revealed the teeth to the top half of the claw, hanging down like giant black steel stalactites just a few feet above. Prater was the first to reach up and, despite the almost impossible angle of how the upper claw teeth were positioned in relation to where they stood on the lower bucket, managed to get his hands around the topside of one of them and pull himself up. Swinging a leg up and over he found himself laying lengthwise on the top edge of the upper claw, breathing heavily from the strain and anxiety that came with the precariousness of his position. Looking back down into the lower half he saw Z as she was beginning to pull herself up.

Prater reached down to her and shouted, "Give me your hand!"

The two grasped each other's wrists and held strong as Z pulled up and stood with her feet between the teeth of the lower claw. With another hefty tug Prater yanked Z up and off the lower maw. She held onto Prater's arm tight with both hands and prepared to swing a leg up onto the top of the top claw – when a vice-like grip squeezed around her ankle so tight she thought it was going to break. She looked down and there was the vampire with the white eyes, holding on for his life and attempting to pull her back down.

A deadly tug-of-war ensued and Z screamed partly from the strain of trying to pull herself up while kicking as violently as she could to knock the creature away from her, and partly from the stress in her arm and leg as they felt like they were going to be pulled out of their sockets. A loud hiss sounded from inside the bucket and the smell of gas grew stronger than ever. Prater and Z shared a quick look of desperation.

There was a loud *POP!* from inside the claw just as Z landed a strong kick to Snoweyes' face. The vampire's grip slipped but he still managed to hold onto her ankle with both of his hands. But it didn't matter as a white-hot plume of flame shot from inside the jaws. Normally the contraption would have been completely closed for the incinerator to take full effect, but in the excavator's damaged state the claw was left partly ajar, and flames shot out in all directions, engulfing the vampire in the process.

Despite his head and body being consumed by fire, Snoweyes continued to pull himself and climb higher up Z's leg as he placed one smoking death grip over the other. Flames worked their way up his arms and towards Z's leg. Z could feel the heat as she continued to kick and scream at the creature to let go of her.

Another loud hiss and pop from inside the claw was immediately followed by a second blast of flame. Hotter than the last, the fire that shot out instantly turned much of Snoweyes' body to thick ashes. The blackened and charred vampire's lower body looked intact, though his legs began to flake and dissolve away into the air. The ashen state consumed the vampire up to his neck, leaving just his head and one arm as a blackened and seared reminder of the terror that gripped Z.

Prater looked down at the monster that still had hold of Z's leg in desperation with its one remaining grip. He and the vampire locked eyes and Prater watched as the creature's white irises turned black then cracked along with the rest of its face. A final kick from Z and the ashen remains dropped away, part into the lower bucket of the claw and part into the breeze that surrounded them. Prater quickly helped Z get to the top of the upper claw and even though their perch was still relatively unstable, they took a moment to breathe and experience a momentary relief from their ordeal.

And momentary it was, as loud crackling and bursts – the worst yet – erupted from the excavator control cab. Prater and Z looked down at the cab from their elevated height and watched as smoke poured from the control panel and a fountain of sparks shot straight up, hitting the ceiling of the cab and fanning out like a bright electric umbrella. The entire cab of the excavator then exploded sending metallic sparks and shards in every direction. Prater fell on top of Z as hot fiery fragments rained upon them. The entire bucket they were standing on began to shudder once again, though this time not because the boom arm that held it was swinging, but because the entire excavator itself began to pivot and move.

The immense treads clanked to life as the big machine jerked at an abrupt angle and launched at a speed unexpected of such a large piece of equipment. Wen looked up from where he sat in the driver's seat of his refueling rig – just as the right tread of the excavator clipped the back end of his vehicle. The part-350Z, part-modified trailer was quickly dragged under the tread. Though Wen tried jumping to safety, his own car door slammed against him and pulled him backwards with the rest of the vehicle. The excavator barely stuttered as it rolled over the refueling rig, causing the half-full fuel tank to explode. Incom and Ecks fled from the new devastation and joined Elroi by leaping onto the back of the Plymouth Roadrunner.

The giant death machine rotated again and went full force into the nearby side guardrail of the bridge. The concrete and steel that made up the barrier crumbled like a sandcastle under the weight of the excavator, doing nothing to slow the machine from plummeting over the side and towards the water below.

Prater leapt up and pulled Z in tight to his body as he launched the two of them off the rapidly teetering excavator bucket. The fall and tumble against the road was greater than a mere human could handle – but Prater was no mere human. He kept a strong hold of Z as they bounced and rolled on the pocked and pitted battle damaged concrete with Prater absorbing almost all the impact. They stopped rolling just as the last glimpse of the black and steel death-bringer disappeared over the side of the bridge and thundered in a loud splash into the lake below.

Prater laid on his back with his eyes closed as each laborious breath reminded him of the broken bones throughout his body. At least that pain distracted him from the bleeding lacerations on his hands and face. He cautiously opened his eyes and saw Z looking down at him. Her warm and heavy breath felt good against his face, reassuring she was alive, as he still held her tight. He could see an amazement in her eyes as he felt the cuts on his face healing themselves and knew that she was in awe of what she was witnessing. Internally, he felt his bones moving and cracking as they reset themselves and fractures mended. It was all terribly uncomfortable and Prater continued to look into the woman's eyes as his body healed, doing little to hide his grimaces and winces.

After several silent moments Z rolled off Prater and onto her side, exhausted and relieved as the battle had ended and they were surrounded by silence. Prater turned his head to the side, equally relieved, and saw an unexpected sight: the Wayfarer sunglasses that had belonged to the snow-eyed vampire, somehow not only intact, but not even scratched.

And despite all the death and destruction they had just endured, Prater smiled.

EPISODE 21

SAN FRANCISCO MECCA
NORTH AMERICA NEW WORLD TERRITORIES VAMPIRE CAPITOL

JONATHAN Stirling stood in the center of the large, circular stage constructed in the middle of Wearh Arena, the largest stadium in the San Francisco Mecca area. Located just three miles from the capitol building, a large portion of the city was leveled to allow for the building of the 90,000-seat facility. The roof of the black and silver stadium was comprised of over five hundred interconnected, hexagonal, two-way mirrors that allowed for a view of the skies from within the facility but reflected the muted sunlight from above. In each of the four corners of the stadium floor stood a tall vertical truss containing lighting rigs and speakers used during any number of vampire entertainment events.

This was to be the location for the opening ceremonies of the first-ever Global Vampire Summit occurring that evening. Right now, it was early in the afternoon as Stirling completed his walkthrough of the facility, ending on the newly constructed stage. Hundreds of technicians and decorators buzzed like bees choreographed in a hive as final preparations took place. No one could afford for any detail to go wrong during the ceremonies – mistakes would be paid for in blood. Commands and responses echoed through radio transmitters, light rigs around the stadium were tested, security checkpoints and patrols were reviewed.

Stirling looked up and admired the thousands of seats, imagining they were each filled with the most attentive of attendees watching him and hanging onto his every word as he led his people into the next stages of their New World. He could already hear the symphony of cheers as those in attendance chanted his name as their now and forevermore ruler.

"Do you hear that, Andrea?" Stirling asked with an air of triumph already resonating in his voice.

"Is it the sound of your well-deserved success?" Andrea asked coyly.

Stirling's gaze lifted upward. He watched as the two-way glass overhead went completely black on cue from a technician's order. This drastically darkened the entire stadium but was immediately offset by a deep red lighting that glowed from behind long horizontal panels across the fronts of the enclosed second-level suites that lined the arena.

"You know me too well," Stirling said. One corner of his mouth curled up in a half smile.

"We still should be careful, Jonathan," Andrea warned. "The humans are growing increasingly bolder. I must admit I have some reservations after General Sloane's failures."

Stirling's triumphant tone disappeared as he glared at his vice president. "Not you, too, Andrea? My brother recently disposed of one problem." The killing of the senator elite was still fresh on everyone's minds. "Don't tell me you're giving up on me as well?"

The stage gradually began to rotate – a test of another feature that would be put on display during the ceremony later and a taste of what ultimately was to come for the spectators at the evening's festivities.

"Not at all, Jonathan." Andrea's voice softened some.

As the stage continued to slowly turn, several rectangular hatches slid open around the circumference of the round platform. In all, twenty-three dark openings appeared in an already black stage. A wooden cross emerged from each opening attached to a rising metallic arm that lifted them to just above the head height of the vampires.

"Crosses?" Andrea raised one eyebrow. "I'm not sure about this religious imagery, Jonathan."

Stirling grinned at the vice president. He paused to chew at the air, then said, "They serve a purpose. Trust me."

The stage slowed its rotation then stopped. The banks of lights positioned around the stadium flashed random test patterns. Stirling watched it all with both scrutiny and pride. He knew what he was witnessing was but a fragment of what the ceremonies would have in store for the spectators here in just a matter of hours.

"Excuse the interruption, President Stirling."

The new voice caught Stirling off guard and the president turned abruptly to face its source with baring teeth and a narrowed brow. He was put at ease when he realized it was Marques who commanded his attention. The inches-long talons that were prepared to tear out the heart of any unwelcomed presence receded into his fingers as Stirling took a few deep breaths and firmly squeezed the councilor's shoulder.

"You must be more cautious, young man. In times like these one can never be too careful. I'd hate for you to see an untimely end."

Marques had managed to maintain his composure despite momentarily being the target of the shallow, dead eyes and rage of the president. Stirling grinned a devil's grin at him.

"I have some updates for you, sir. I've just come from seeing General Sloane. His transference is complete and he is recuperating quickly. He'll be available to you within the hour."

Stirling grunted as he looked away. "I hope the upgrade is worth it. This will be his last chance with me."

"Of course, sir. I could tell he was distraught from his failures at bringing you Prater Saxon." Marques' voice dropped as he completed the statement.

Stirling sensed something was amiss. "What is it, Marques? Spit it out."

"General Sloane isn't the only one who has failed at capturing Saxon. We've received a report on the Red Marauders."

The two vampires stared at each other in silence. The look in Marques' eyes was telling, while the lack of any expression in Stirling's face caught Marques off guard.

"The humans are still headed this way then." Stirling didn't need to ask. "Prater Saxon is still with them."

"That is the belief, yes," Marques answered.

The president let out a long breath as he paced slowly between the councilor and Andrea. He stopped and silently snarled with his nose in the air while biting at nothing. Andrea watched quietly from her place on the other side of the podium. The president's gnawing gestures were something that had slowly developed over the last few years though she never knew what caused it. Stirling never openly acknowledged the mannerisms and no one had ever asked.

"If I should say so, Mr. President," Marques continued, "they're sure to be targeting you and the global vampire leadership. This aligns with your brother's beliefs that the stolen submarine is headed this way. For your safety and the safety of all the summit attendees I recommend we concentrate all our security here, in and around the stadium. Your well-being and that of the delegates is paramount." Marques studied the look in Stirling's eyes as his words set in. Then he continued, "I'd even go as far to say that everyone else is…expendable."

Stirling crossed his arms as he looked out over the crowd of the tens of thousands he imagined would be watching later in the evening. He narrowed his eyes as his mind raced through various scenarios of capturing Prater Saxon and the evening's opening ceremony festivities, meticulously weighing out the priority of one situation over the other in his mind. Marques stepped up behind the president, slowly, until he was just a breath away. The councilor's voice was low and quiet when he spoke next.

"I'm sure your anger over the Prater Saxon situation runs deep. Your desire to apprehend Saxon is palpable but there are more immediate matters at hand. You should stay focused on tonight's summit. Saxon can wait."

Stirling considered the circumstances silently for several moments before he looked back at Marques. "Yes, of course. The safety of the dignitaries and those in attendance tonight should take precedence. Concentrate security in and around the stadium for tonight's festivities. Reduce the surrounding areas to minimal patrols and keep this area on high alert."

"Excellent, Mr. President. I'll take care of it."

"And the curfew is already in place?"

"Yes, sir. The streets are already almost completely cleared from north of the Golden Gate Bridge to just south of the old San Jose District."

"Good, good. With the streets empty it'll be easy to remain focused solely on the arena."

Andrea took in the interaction between Stirling and his aide with curiosity. Stirling seemed to place a lot of confidence in Marques' assessment of the situation…though something seemed a bit "off" in her estimation. Maybe it was Marques' body language or his lowered tone of voice, or both. She made sure, though, to keep any thoughts to herself. For now.

"Was there anything else, then, Marques?"

"No, Mr. President, thank you. Excuse me while I carry out the orders."

Stirling turned his eyes back to the empty stadium seats as Marques left the stage. Andrea watched the councilor disappear down a set of steps that ran alongside the elevated stage before she addressed the president again directly.

"Excuse me as well, Jonathan. I'm going to ensure all the commodities are prepared for the ambassadors and their entourages."

"Thank you, Andrea," Stirling said. He looked at her with eyes wide a proud grin. "This is our night. Our celebration is long overdue. It's too bad Samuel didn't live to see this day but I'm happy that you did."

The president and vice president bared their fangs at each other with fiendish grins and the vice president turned and exited the stage via the same stairs Marques used just moments before.

ANNIKA

THINGS *grew strangely quiet around the front of the battle semi once the big-haired vampire left, taking the other vampires with him. I could still hear the fighting going on further down the caravan but around me, where I was, the air fell still. I looked down at Z as she lay still on top of the truck's hood. It was a struggle at first, but I managed to regain my composure. I thought about my archery training to help my breathing as I wiped away exhausted tears. Although I was calmer, I still wasn't sure what to do now. Assessing my surroundings there were several severed parts of vampires that were beyond regeneration – a sight that brought more relief than revulsion. On the ground next to the truck were Z's silver-bladed sai, stained red from the blood of the undead.*

Turning my attention back to the woman who was my new guardian, I gently shook Z while quietly calling out to her. It was a struggle, but I managed to keep my cheeks dry of tears that threatened to return as at first I saw no response at my attempts for revival. Then without warning Z suddenly came to, abruptly sitting up with a loud gasp. I had to jump back to keep our foreheads from colliding. Z coughed as her senses flooded her and I pulled her close and held her tighter than I had held onto anyone in a long time.

"Thank god you're alright!" I couldn't help exclaiming my excitement. I quickly put a hand up to my own mouth realizing I was louder than I meant to be. A quick look around kept me at ease as no vampires seemed to have been alerted by my sudden outburst.

Z gave in briefly to the hug but pulled away quickly. "Where's Prater?"

"At the back of the caravan trying to take out that excavator."

"I've gotta go help him."

I felt suddenly conflicted. "Z, I don't know what to do. I'm – I'm scared." The words came out shakily – I know I can be emotional and tend to be transparent with my feelings but admitting these feelings out loud made me feel like, well, a kid.

Z took a firm hold of both my shoulders. "Good. You stay scared. That's exactly what you need to be. You know why?"

I know the confused look on my face answered her question.

"Because fear is what's going to keep you alive. If you aren't afraid, you get careless. You think I'm not afraid?"

My mouth opened like I was going to say something, but I didn't know what. I just shook my head.

"Trust me, I am." Z quickly looked around. "Now let's find a place for you to wait until I get back."

Z ushered me to the sleeper cabin of the semi cab. The space was bigger than I expected but still unremarkable other than the built-in bed and a storage cabinet. I lay down on the bed and under the circumstances it didn't bother me that I was lying next to Kylee's body. I had my bow and arrow next to me – my last arrow – and Z covered me with a brown blanket before closing the blackout curtains that separated us from the driver's cab.

And there I waited, breathing quietly, as I listened to the sounds of the battles in the distance. Booms and crashes mixed with blasts from various types of weaponry echoed around me in the dark. I tried to imagine Z and Prater fighting their way to victory but the battle sounds went on and on – signaling no quick end to the fighting. As the combat raged, I squeezed my eyes tight and put my hands over my ears. I had had enough. I just wanted it to all stop.

Then it suddenly did. And that was even scarier.

The newfound silence made me more panicked as I immediately realized I didn't know what the quiet meant. Did we win or lose? If we won it most likely wouldn't be too long before Z came and got me. But what if we lost? What if the next hands to pull the blanket off my head aren't human?

As the seconds and minutes of stillness mounted, I found myself growing more scared. The longer it was until Z came for me, the more I became convinced we didn't win and that I was going to be discovered by the vampires. I did my best to keep my breath still – but couldn't help but scream when the blanket was suddenly yanked from my head.

And I was immediately pulled tight into Z's comforting arms.

Z quickly told me what happened and described how after the death of the motorcycle club leaders the remaining vampires seemed lost as they appeared to lose purpose or focus or both. Those that remained were either relatively easy to dispose of or fled off the bridge and up into the surrounding hills. Once our rapid reunion was done, we immediately began heading out of there. We weren't much of a motorcade anymore as there were just six of us and two vehicles remaining: the battle semi, which carried Z, who drove, Prater, and myself, and the Plymouth Roadrunner with Elroi, Incom, and Ecks. We made our way to the end of the bridge and were at close to full speed as the war semi launched its remaining Hellfire missiles at the dozens of motorcycles gathered on the road waiting for riders that would never return, before then easily plowing through the fiery, smoking remnants.

Our journey towards San Francisco Mecca continued, taking us out of the mountains and foothills that gave way to open farmlands, grasslands, and wide spaces with sparse trees. Some of the roadside farms had the decaying bones of livestock on them – their owners either long dead or long gone. I'm guessing many of the animals didn't necessarily fall prey to vampires but instead died of neglect, starvation, or dehydration after their owners vanished, and that made me sad in a way this crazy world hadn't already.

Massive grain and food silos were visible along points of the freeway. The majestic silver and white cylindrical structures looked more like miniature industrial complexes among the barren wastes what with the pipes, containers, and tubing that surrounded and connected them all. The silos themselves used to be kept clean and pristine but many now were defaced with anti-vampire graffiti symbols and propaganda.

Another type of farms we began to see were massive solar farms. I wouldn't have thought they would be of much use in a nuclear winter but I suppose if they got some sunlight then they could still harness at least some energy.

My heart sank as a huge cemetery revealed itself along the side of a stretch of the freeway. There must have been thousands of white, unmarked crosses. I wonder who would have taken the time to bury all these people? Or maybe there weren't any bodies buried there at all and the crosses were just markers to commemorate the dead…or undead.

Much of the remaining journey was, thankfully, uneventful, and any tension there may have been between Z and Prater earlier was gone. They did fill me in on the events of the battle during the drive and from the sounds of it, they built a good bond through the fight.

We lost precious time from the battle on the bridge and it wasn't going to be much longer before sunset. We seemed to be making good time despite the delay as we traveled west on the final stretch in the direction of the dropping sun as we edged closer to San Francisco Mecca. As we grew nearer the outskirts of the immense megalopolis, the communicator device Kylee had given to Z as a direct line to Marques beeped.

Marques directed us to meet with him at a discreet rendezvous point, a few miles off an unmarked dirt road exit. It was an old, rundown, and long abandoned gas station convenience store parking lot. There wasn't much else around except for distant rolling hills covered in ground level brush and a few nuclear winter defying trees. There were a few others with him and they arrived split between two sleek, black, electric vans. After some very brief introductions we were moved from our very conspicuous, very loud, you-can-see-us-coming-from-ten-miles-away vehicles and to one of the vans.

"You're late," Marques said to Z, dryly.

"We were delayed by some of your…" Her eyes traveled to each of the vampires who had accompanied Marques. "…comrades. Most of us didn't make it. This is all that's left."

I could tell that Z was very suspicious of Marques and the vampires with him despite whatever earlier reassurances Kylee may have tried to give. Marques attempted to instill some confidence with Z.

"There are so very few of us dedicated to the cause," he told her. "Despite many having revulsion towards their existence, the hunger and love of quenching the thirst overrides it all. Not to mention the promise of immortality. It's an addiction. Then there are those like me though, just to be *transparent, I too am addicted to the thirst. There's no denying that. But my heart and dedication is for the greater good and what is right, and that's returning this world to humans. Rescuing Appamattox is key to that plan."*

Marques imposed upon all of us how time was of the essence. He gave Z a small transmitter earpiece that was strictly tuned to a frequency where she could hear updates on the pending nuclear strike by the submarine as it entered the bay.

"General Kaur has indicated the detonation is expected to occur shortly after 9PM. This communicator will keep the general in contact with you. He's agreed to at least provide you updates when possible. And this," Marques said as he handed over a palm-sized datapad, "has schematics of the blood banks. You'll be able to use this to navigate to where you need once you enter the facility."

Z nestled the transmitter into her ear and activated the palm pad with one hand. Satisfied with what she saw after briskly swiping through a few screens, she put the datapad into one of her tactical vest pockets. Marques continued with his instructions. He gave us a heads-up about a curfew in place and to not be surprised by the lack of visible life and movement throughout the streets as we made our way. Our vehicle was not unlike any of the other government vans operated by the vampires and with travel restricted strictly to police and government business we should easily make our way unnoticed.

"Take the van to the north end of the Golden Gate Bridge and down to the old Lime Point Lighthouse. An unattended boat will be waiting for you there. Approach Alcatraz Island from the west side. There are guard towers on the east side that'll do periodic spotlight sweeps of the west shore. Expect a few guards to the entrance near the base of the old main cell building, along with another four inside the facility itself."

"Only four?" Z was skeptical.

"History's on our side. Nothing like this has ever been attempted so security is minimal. They'll be caught completely by surprise. Aside from that it's mostly scientists and technicians in the main building who have no interest in security matters. You'll need to be quick, though. By the time you get to the island you'll barely have an hour until the detonation."

Before we left, there was a final, somber matter to attend to. Marques' "people" carefully took Kylee's body with the promise that she would be handled with the utmost care and that they'll dispose of her respectfully. There were no long or heartfelt "goodbyes" from either Prater or Z despite their close relationships with Kylee – no tears or touching farewells. Of course, I don't know what either of them was feeling on the inside, but on the outside, it all came off as just business. I wasn't sure if this was good or bad…or just sad.

As we piled into our respective vehicles, Marques went up to Prater and I couldn't help but witness their interaction.

"I guess we're related in a sense," Marques said.

Prater gave an almost imperceptible nod as he said, "Kylee told me about you." There was a pause before he added, "She said there was something important she needed to tell me. Do you know what she was talking about?"

Marques shook his head. "I wouldn't be sure, no."

Prater said nothing else before he entered the van. There wasn't time to get into a deeper conversation. A few final pleasantries were exchanged before we left.

This was all so surreal and so crazy. I can't believe how upside-down my life had become in just a matter of a few days. I never thought I would be a warrior in a fight like this. Yet here I was, part of what had to be the greatest rescue mission in the history of humankind. But I have to admit that even though the mission is to rescue Appamattox, I can't ignore that all I really, really wanted was to rescue my family. I'm certain they're there. Despite having just one arrow left, I was going to do everything I could to get to them and free them.

I can't wait to see my family again.

EPISODE 22

SAN FRANCISCO MECCA
NORTH AMERICA NEW WORLD TERRITORIES VAMPIRE CAPITOL

COUNCILOR Marques Wright pulled into the private parking garage located directly underneath Wearh Arena. He maneuvered the government issued electric, black van quickly through the concrete garage. The rubber of the tires squealed on the smooth concrete floor, echoing like banshees through the structure. The garage was lit as well as one would expect an underground parking garage to be lit with overhead lights spaced enough to leave dark areas in the corners and ceilings. After making a final turn, the van drove past several vehicles of the same color, make, and model before parking in one of two specially marked empty stalls near a set of elevators.

The rendezvous with Z and her party had gone as quickly and smoothly as he had hoped, but Marques wasted no time rushing back to the stadium as soon as possible. He had told various stories to different people depending on who they were in the political and societal hierarchy to hopefully keep anyone from wondering where he was or what he was doing. There was no time to spare with all the buzz surrounding the evening's festivities and, as a personal aide to the president, Marques already needed to be in multiple places at once as he oversaw some of the final preparations. He was able to use that to his advantage as he crafted various lies to mask his true intentions.

The humans had followed Marques for several miles before they each went their separate ways. Marques dropped the vampire accomplices who had accompanied him off at an inconspicuous shelter operated covertly by a small, local group of vampires pledged to the human's cause. They took Kylee's body with them and would cremate her in a simple, yet reverent ceremony before scattering her ashes in nearby barrens of the Wastelands.

Hurriedly exiting his van, Marques went to the unremarkable and dimly lit foyer where two sets of elevator doors waited side by side. He placed his palm on a scanner that opened the doors on his left. He was about to rush in when he was stopped by the presence of someone exiting the elevator.

Andrea McCullough immediately stepped out the doors, forcing Marques several steps backwards as they moved out of the small foyer and back into the large, cold garage.

Marques drew in a quick breath. "Vice President McCullough, you surprised me. I didn't expect you to be here."

The vice president placed a strong hand on his shoulder.

"These final moments leading up to tonight's summit are crucial, Mr. Wright," said Andrea. "And no one seems to know where you've been for over the past hour. I want you to help me understand why the president would allow you to disappear for so long."

Her voice was smooth in a way that Marques wasn't exactly sure how to interpret. Was she trying to convince him to remain calm? Or was she trying to demonstrate an accusatory tone?

"I'm not sure what you mean, ma'am, I haven't disappeared." Various excuses flipped through his mind like lines of computer code racing down a screen before settling on one. "I've been following up on complaints surrounding accommodations for some of the attendees, if you must know."

Andrea stared intently into Marques' eyes and the councilor looked back, unwavering. The vice president's bloodshot, emerald eyes narrowed before she turned and took several steps away from the councilor.

"You left with two vehicles and returned with only one." Andrea looked back over her shoulder at the empty parking space next to Marques' van. "What happened to the other van?"

Marques grew visibly angry and he raised a finger to the vice president. "Are you spying on me?" he spat, deflecting from her question. "The president won't stand for this."

Andrea fully faced Marques again. "I think what the president won't stand for is your lying and sneaking around."

Marques glared at Andrea, unblinking. The fortitude that had built within him over the years to see humanity restored no matter what ultimate price he may have to pay fueled his presence of mind. He casually moved his hands from his sides to slightly behind himself and the deadly claws hidden in his fingers gradually extended, doubling the length of his gaunt fingers. Decades of lies and deception had all led to this point. He couldn't allow anyone – let alone the vice president no matter her position or stature – disrupt the cause now.

"Madame Vice President, I'm going to have to insist that you change your tone with me. I don't appreciate what you're insinuating."

"And I'm asking you again why you took two government vehicles out of the mecca and returned with just one."

Marques didn't immediately answer. Andrea folded her hands in front of herself and held her arms close to her body. One side of her mouth twisted upwards in a self-confident smirk.

"I know you're up to something, councilor. I'm going to find out what that is."

Acting before Andrea could make a move, Marques launched himself forward – his outstretched hands with their deadly, spindly talons all aimed at the vice president. He was going to do whatever was needed to keep the human's plans a secret even if that meant killing one of the highest positioned officials in the vampire world. The moment Marques moved, though, a large black shape swooped in at incredible speed and cut him off from his target.

Tall and metallic, the object stopped with a blur and a loud *CLANG!* and stood like an obsidian monolith between them. Marques took a wary step away from what he at first thought was a casket-like object when he realized it wasn't any sort of container at all. The councilor shuddered as the front of the object separated vertically and began to unfold and extend outwards to the sides. As the wings revealed themselves, the monster's true nature was exposed.

The cybervampire Ryder Sloane hadn't simply been upgraded, rather, he received a completely new existence. As the batlike wings extended – slowly and meticulously as if the creature underneath was emerging from a cocoon – they looked to not be entirely mechanical as the "arms," joints, and bat "fingers" that stretched to their outer edges looked more like glossy spider legs, and the wing membranes looked like densely intertwined black spiderwebs. The body showing underneath was no longer half-robotic, half-vampire. Nearly all human and vampire remnants had been wiped away and replaced as the only part that resembled the old Ryder Sloane was his head.

Nearly a foot taller than Marques, the unveiled body was completely humanoid in shape, though it was actually very far from being human, or even vampire. A black-chrome, insect-like exoskeleton made up the entirety of the body. Several openings with reinforced plexiglass coverings showed muscles and sinewy veins intermixed with robotic gears and motors, along with more shiny black parts. His heart and lungs could be seen through clear plates in the exoskeletal ribs and breastplate as they pumped and heaved and did their work to help keep the biomechanical menace alive.

Slowly and gently, the unfolded and fully extended wings revealed their true majestic span reaching nearly fourteen feet from tip to tip. The view of Andrea and the elevators behind the cybervampire became obscured as the oncoming creature filled his field of vision. The heavy bangs of Sloane's steel feet echoed throughout the garage as the unholy visage trod towards the councilor. Marques was prepared to take on the vice president or any other normal vampire, but the aberration coming steadily towards him was anything but normal.

Marques had to act both fast and first – this he did by throwing a hard, quick punch with his right fist, intent on shattering parts of the plexiglass shell shielding the creature's heart. But while

Marques was quick and he believed he had the element of surprise in his favor, he grossly underestimated the speed of the cybervampire. Sloane's wings snapped shut in front of him, closing him off from the councilor. And Marques immediately realized that the edges of the wings that met vertically in the middle were razor sharp.

Yanking his arm back in reflex, Marques winced in pain as he held the bleeding stump of his forearm close to his body. In the next instant, the wings separated, and Sloane slammed both of his robotic skeletal fists into Marques' chest, sending him flying several feet through the air until his back slammed against one of the garage's concrete pillars. The councilor slumped to the hard floor and the cybervampire was instantly over him. Marques looked up while spittle and blood dripped down his chin. He coughed from internal injuries that his healing factor were slow to rebuild. The councilor recoiled as the cybervampire dropped a hard foot onto his chest – not quite a stomp but more than enough to put pressure on already broken ribs, bruised organs, and his struggle to regain breath. Attempting to fight through the pain, he grabbed and clawed at the creature's metallic foot with his remaining hand but was useless in relieving any of the pressure forced down on him.

"You won't win," Marques choked out the words. He managed to crack a smile through his agony as his battered organs and torn skin and muscles struggled to regenerate.

Marques was certain the robotic general was going to crush him under his foot or otherwise deliver a death blow but instead the creature's wings folded back behind him. The cybervampire looked over a shoulder as a new shadow moved out from around one of the other nearby pillars.

"I think this will be all we get out of him," said Sloane. The new body of the cybernetically enhanced vampire was very different but the deep, electronic, underlying flange in his voice remained.

Marques' eyes grew wide as he saw who the new shadow belonged to: President Jonathan Stirling. Andrea became visible again as well and she held a mixed appearance of glee and anger.

"You see, Jonathan?" Andrea asked as she and the president walked over to stand next to Sloane and his writhing captive. "My suspicions are always right."

"I'm disappointed, Marques," Stirling said as he looked down at what was his trusted aide.

"I wish my intuition on this had been wrong, Jonathan," said Andrea. Her eyes held an expression of pity as she looked down at Marques. "I would have never figured you to be sympathetic to the human cause. I admit that despite it all I'm surprised by this."

Marques glared up at Andrea as he continued to struggle.

"I'm not," Stirling said, surprising Andrea. "You see, loyalty towards the humans runs in his family."

Andrea's mouth dropped. Any semblance of pain in Marques' face was replaced with shock.

"Yes, councilor. You think I don't know about your brother?" Stirling gleamed.

"I don't know what you're talking about." The words Marques hissed said one thing but the look on his face betrayed him.

Stirling's voice was low. "I'm sure Jesse believes differently."

The shock gave way to a look of defeat as Marques' eyes dropped. He had convinced himself for years that no one, let alone Stirling, knew of his relationship to Jesse. It was a fool's belief. He should have realized that it was only a matter of time before all the truth came out.

"You…killed my brother?"

"Let's just say watching the life slowly slip away from his eyes as he cried for his life on his wedding day was especially satisfying."

"But then why…"

Stirling huffed then struck a smarmy grin. "As they say, keep your friends close, but your enemies closer. And you, my dear Marques, are most definitely not my friend."

The president squatted down to bring him more face-to-face with the man pinned to the garage floor.

"Let me offer you a deal. Tell me the exact plans and targets of the humans and I'll let you go. You leave the North America New World Territories never to return. That simple."

Marques knew a lie when he heard one, especially one told by the president. Decades of working closely with the man allowed the councilor to pick up on many of Stirling's nuances. Although, maybe in this instance Stirling wasn't even bothering to hide any deception.

"I'll die before I tell you anything." Marques mustered a strong defiance in his tone.

"Then you admit you know something that's worth dying for," said Andrea as she looked down at Marques from over the president's shoulder.

Stirling took Marques by the chin. "This is your day of reckoning, Marques. Know who you truly are and where those loyalties should lie. You have a chance to be a hero for all vampirekind. I suggest you think about that." He leaned in as close to the councilor as he could. His voice fell to a soft yet compelling whisper. "Why are the humans heading this way? Especially with their plans involving the nuclear sub? Are they on some sort of suicide mission?"

Marques smiled a mouthful of teeth outlined in bloody edges. Then without warning he spat bloodied spittle into the president's face and laughed. Stirling didn't recoil. Instead, the president calmly closed his eyes while pulling a handkerchief out of the inside pocket of his suit jacket. He casually wiped the vile wet off his face then coolly tossed the kerchief aside. Then Stirling stood and his calm resolve was more terrifying to Marques than the outburst he expected.

"I trusted you all these years and this is how you repay me. Through this betrayal."

Stirling nodded at Sloane who returned the gesture. The cybervampire looked down into the defiant eyes of the helpless councilor. Stirling and Andrea watched together as Sloane raised one of his razor-edged wings. The cybervampire was about to strike when the president interrupted him.

"Not his head."

A break in Marques' defiance showed as his lower lip began to quiver. He stared up into the one vaguely "human" eye of the cybervampire, one of the few human traits still visible on the mostly mechanical monstrosity. There was the distinct *shing!* from one of the bladed wings as it sliced high and around in a wide, fast arc. An even louder and more resolute *CLANG!* followed as the steel of the wing met with the concrete floor of the garage. Then again, again, and again.

Marques wailed from a deep, intense pain unlike any he had ever known. He looked down at his body and the cybervampire foot that had him pinned down was gone, replaced with a bloody mess of his eviscerated midsection. He locked eyes with Stirling as he shouted and cried into the dead expression of the president. A severe lightheaded and wooziness kicked in as his innards struggled to regrow and rebuild, but such a severe wound would never heal, and he would bleed out completely in the process. Already the organs in his upper body began to slow and fail and he wished the cybervampire had cut his head open to make for a quick and painless death. Now this slow death left him with nothing to do but hurt until he hurt no longer. His tears and cries stopped of their own volition…even his body's way of expressing pain had shut down. Dying silently, he watched as Stirling and the vice president walked away.

"You're not going to kill him?" asked Andrea as they approached the elevators.

"Better to let him bleed out." The president smiled. "More painful that way."

The heavy, clanking footsteps of Ryder Sloane stopped behind the president.

"What of the mission to track down Prater Saxon?" the cybervampire asked. "I must be allowed to redeem myself."

The trio stopped walking as Stirling addressed his general. "In good time, General Sloane. We must play this carefully. For now, I do believe all attention must be on tonight's summit in the event the humans make some sort of play there. The doors are set to open shortly for the public to take their seats. We don't have much time until the festivities begin."

Stirling's eyes drifted to the blood dripping off the edge of one of the cybervampire's wings. "Clean yourself up and meet us upstairs."

Sloane nodded and then took a few loud, metallic steps before he flew away – headfirst, wings back – into the shadows of the garage. Stirling and Andrea took one final look at Marques, laying pitifully as he gasped and choked on his dying breaths, before entering the elevator.

A janitor would be sent down later to shovel up the remains.

EPISODE 23

SAN FRANCISCO MECCA
NORTH AMERICA NEW WORLD TERRITORIES VAMPIRE CAPITOL

THE sun dropped below the horizon and darkness engulfed the Bay. The lights inside Wearh Arena went out and the 90,000 vampires in the stands rose to their feet as they screeched and wailed with excitement in anticipation of the festivities. One by one the deep red lights lining the second level suites illuminated in synchronization with music. The symphony was comprised of swelling orchestral strings in minor tones combined with punches from synthesizers and drums, all played live by musicians in a pit that lined a third of the outside of the round stage. The crowd quieted as each panel lit up until the only sounds in the stadium were the melancholy tones from the orchestra. Once all the red suite panels were lit, lights and virtual projectors illuminated from the vertical trusses rising from the stadium floor and a new and much more elaborate light show took over, one that contained laser beams and, most impressively, lifelike 3D images projected in the air over the stage and as large as the stage itself.

The first image was that of the Earth, a big blue virtual marble half the size of the stage, floating and slowly rotating in space. A small light – tiny in relation to the size of the planet – streaked in and orbited half the planet before expanding larger and growing brighter until it took over the entirety of the Earth image, turning it into a bright, burning sun suspended in the middle of the stadium. The realistic quality of the images elicited thousands of gasps and "oohs and aahs" of excitement from the crowd.

The sun shone only for a few moments before morphing back into the Earth rotating in all its beauty and splendor. A hush returned to the crowd as they watched small, glowing, red dots appear on the virtual globe, most along the eastern seaboard of North America, before several others appeared in a wave that traveled west. As the Earth continued to rotate, more and more of the glowing discs appeared all over the sphere until they each expanded and combined together, transforming the planet into a huge, red orb.

The red glow dissipated and the blue/green Earth returned once again. The peace and tranquility were brief, though, as smoky white contrails appeared from several nations, creating crisscrossing streaks around the globe, which turned into small, white circles that rapidly spread devastation across the lands. More and more of the white streaks appeared, faster each time. Within moments the small, white circles and streaks became indistinguishable as they coalesced into large, white swaths and splotches that consumed the world.

The audience watched eagerly with anticipation as the white globe remained unchanged for several moments as the orchestra continued to play. Finally, the white on the globe began to slowly dissipate to reveal the world underneath. Gone now were the bright blue of the seas and oceans, the green of the forests, and the white of the snow. Everything that was vibrant and luminous was now shades of yellow, brown, and gray. One would expect the crowd to fall silent in shock at the sight of the scarred New World, but rather it brought forth the loudest applause yet with everyone on their feet, shouting, and clapping their approval and appreciation of what the world had become.

After nearly two straight minutes of cheers and ovation the dull, decrepit world dissolved as the music stopped and all lights in the arena went out, leaving the stage in complete darkness. A hatch slid open in the center of the circular platform and white smoke billowed out along with a bright beam of white light that shot straight up to the ceiling of the arena. Music returned, quiet at first, then building in a swell that culminated in a ceremonious yet macabre theme heralding the entrance of Jonathan Stirling.

The president rose from under the stage, through the smoke and bathed in the light that continued to shine straight up through the square glass platform on which he stood. The entire stage began to rotate as Stirling made his dramatic entrance to immense applause. He was dressed in a slim-fitted suit of all black with blood red accents that ran from his collar, along the edges of the lapels, and in thin, irregular lines down his arms and legs that evoked images of veins branching through his limbs. He raised his arms with his palms reaching out wide and a smile only slightly less beaming than the intense light that bathed him. It was several moments before the rotating stage slowed to a stop and the light beneath the platform was replaced by spotlights shining down from the light towers. The music stopped and the crowd quieted as they retook their seats. President Stirling needed no other introduction.

"What you just witnessed was a history of the world, our world, and how we came to be."

Stirling's voice was picked up by high-intensity directional mics mounted to the four audio/lighting towers in the corners of the arena so there was no need for any physical microphones on his person, allowing the president to walk and speak completely unrestrained. He looked out towards all areas of the arena as he talked to the audience, ensuring everyone felt as included and welcomed with his words as possible.

"The next chapter in our steps to total independence will be to eliminate the need for the nuclear winter that is vital to our survival. I promise you that I will pioneer the future and crack the code to once again allow us to feel the warmth of the sun on our faces as we did when we were human, without fear of death or harm from the deadly rays that have long taunted and tempted us. I shall soon hold the key to this existence and once I do, I shall share it with the world!"

Knowing full well this speech was not only being delivered to those in attendance but also to a televised global audience of nearly five billion vampires, the applause of those in the arena felt almost paltry to Stirling. Still, he smiled, making sure to look directly into spaces he knew the live cameras were hidden. He raised his hands and gestured for the crowd to return to quiet.

"I am happy to know that the support for this inaugural Global Vampire Summit is not only from those of you here with me tonight, both in person and virtually around the world, but also from the very highest authorities of our existence. Please join me in not only thanking, but welcoming, our global vampire leadership, gathered in-person, together, tonight, for the very first time!"

A long, curved stand with six wide, high-backed, thrones made of gold frames inlaid with large, red diamonds, and with deep purple velvet cushions rose along one edge of the stage. The riser took up a third of the circumference of the platform and provided several feet of space between each of the occupied royal chairs. Stirling introduced each guest-of-honor as a spotlight highlighted them in their luxurious seat one at a time: President Yaromir Volkov of the Union of Soviet Vampire Republics, Prime Minister Sienna Taylor of the EuroAtlantic Federation, Paramount Leader Keung Yao of the AustrAsia Territories, King Mbarek Zewde of the Africa Vampire Alliance, and President Pablo Gallardo of the South America National Assembly. Each of the dignitaries were adorned in attire native to the local vampire cultures they represented.

In the sixth seat was Vice President Andrea McCullough, dressed in a dark red business suit with large, black buttons and a skirt hemmed just above her knees, with matching pencil-thin stiletto heels and a wide brimmed hat with black lace that draped across half her face. The audience applauded with each introduction, with the loudest praise being saved for her, the local representative.

After again calming the crowd, the president continued, "But tonight is about much more than just politics. This is a celebration of you, my brothers and sisters, a celebration thirty years in the making. Tonight, we celebrate our total domination and victory over this Earth! Welcome, everyone, to the first ever Global Vampire Summit!"

The riser with the global vampire leadership remained still while the stage began to rotate again slowly and the live music resumed. The twenty-three hatches hidden around the edge of the stage slid open and moans emanated from the dark spaces, foreshadowing the horrors to come. Out of each opening rose a wooden cross and secured to each cross by thick, steel braces at their ankles and wrists was a human, or at least something that vaguely resembled human. Each of the crucified was utterly emaciated to the point where it was a wonder any of them were still alive. But alive they were, as evidenced by their labored squirms and groans of pain. Their inhumanly thin states weren't their most disturbing trait, though.

Each victim had been expertly and meticulously skinned from head to toe and their sexual organs had been cleanly surgically removed, leaving nothing more than horrifying, bloody masses of muscle and sinew that made it almost impossible to distinguish the men from the women…or the boys from the girls. Their mouths were sewn shut and their eyes had been removed, leaving nothing but black, soulless sockets. A person would have screamed in terror at the sights. The vampires, however, all screamed with delight.

The stage stopped rotating and Stirling invited the VIPs to join him in the center of the platform. As his guests made their way towards him, dozens of vampires swooped in overhead, screeching and carrying sets of heavy, steel chains. With every two vampires, their chains terminated in metal hooks that impaled a human being, stripped bare and suspended by nothing more than the curved steel going through their arms, chests, backs, and shoulders. There were close to two dozen men and women in this predicament – naked while crying and screaming in pain from the hooks suspending them and the fear of whatever worse circumstance was about to come.

Spotlights captured the twisted faces of pain and terror on those trapped and struggling in the air much to the thrill of the tens of thousands in attendance witnessing live along with the billions watching remotely from around the world. The music quietened to almost nothing as the vampires glided in a circle over the stage all in the same direction. The captives continued to scream and struggle save for a few who passed out from the shock and pain. Gradually, the music began to get louder again and the vampires flew a little bit faster.

Louder and louder the immense crescendo of the instrumentation grew as faster and faster the vampires soared overhead. Then, as the orchestra reached its peak, the music abruptly stopped, as did the collective screech from the vampires flying above. All spotlights shone on the creatures and their captives circling in the air as a tension momentarily filled the stadium.

Stirling raised his hands above his head and clapped twice. An unseen microphone picked up the sound of the clap and amplified it. Recognizing their cue, each set of vampires abruptly split apart and flew away from each other while still gripping their chains. There was no resistance from the helpless humans as they all were instantly ripped apart in the air, simultaneously exploding and looking like two dozen bloody fireworks. Though, in this case, the fireworks had the subsequent effect of showering blood, flesh, and innards onto the party below. The crowd went wild over the display but not as wild as the dignitaries who dropped into an unholy, uncontrollable feeding frenzy, writhing on the blood-soaked stage, sucking on the bowels of the dead, and exchanging wide-open mouthed kisses and tender bites on one another's necks and wrists as they gave in to their hungers and desires. Quickly, though, their tender bites became stronger, and vampire leaders gushed their own blood onto each other. They tore away their bloodstained clothing and gave fully into each other, at times bringing themselves to the brink of death – then allowing their wounds to rejuvenate and rapidly heal – from the combination of sex and violence they all welcomed together.

The audience salivated and hailed their leaders from the stands as they witnessed the feast and orgy that transpired as the world watched. It didn't take long, though, for many in attendance to give in to their own primal desires, kissing and biting and feeding off each other's blood – some just a little, others taking it further, too far, by tearing entire chunks of flesh out of their brethren as they feasted. More and more blood began to flow in the stands as more clothes were shed and the decadence spread throughout the arena.

Stirling had casually and silently stepped away prior to the feeding, opting instead to watch from an edge of the stage accompanied by Ryder Sloane. He smiled, satisfied in the flawlessness of how the opening ceremony was progressing, as his vice president and the vampire leadership continued to give themselves to the euphoria erupting through the stadium.

EPISODE 24

SAN FRANCISCO MECCA BLOOD BANKS
ALCATRAZ ISLAND

THE small, black electric-powered boat hummed near silently on the smooth surface of the dark waters of San Francisco Bay. The night air was quiet and the waters calm. The journey from where they found their boat waiting at the Lime Point Lighthouse didn't take long, though longer than anyone in the boat would have liked. In addition to their approach being so quiet, they had the added benefit of cruising under cover of fog that steadily increased in thickness as they made their way towards the island shore. While the haze grew heavy, it never fully obstructed their view as they navigated their way and beached the boat onto a gravelly part of the island.

With their weapons drawn, Z led Prater and Annika, along with Elroi, Incom, and Ecks, from the black shore as they crept to the south end of the main building. The guard towers and lights were on the northeastern side, where the boat dock was located. They easily evaded a single casual sweep from a roaming searchlight as they crept up to the building and around its east side. No one appeared to take notice of their approach.

The covert group crouched as they raced up to and around the corner of what used to be the main cellhouse but was now laboratories and prep units for any humans in need of special attention prior to being placed into the banks deep below. The triangular shaped black building that Z's digital reader identified as the primary prisoner entrance – their current destination – came into view. The area wasn't very well lit and Z was having trouble determining how many guards were at the doorway. The group dropped back and crouched low as the searchlight swept the area again. As the light passed, Prater took a quick peek around the corner and at the entrance. His hybrid vampire eyesight provided a grainy yet bright view of the situation.

"Two vampires standing guard," Prater said quietly to the group.

"Not much security at all," Z said in a near whisper. "Just like Marques said."

"So far, anyway," added Elroi.

"I've got 'em," said Incom as she moved in front of Prater.

Using the corner of the building, the communications expert steadied herself as she brought her UV laser rifle up to her shoulder. She looked over at the nearest guard tower with the searchlight, which was several yards away down towards the boat dock and made sure the light was facing well away from them. Refocusing on the guards, she wrapped her finger around the trigger and took aim through the night vision scope mounted on the rifle. The vampires were dressed in all black uniforms with their heads and faces fully exposed. They had no weapons – their deadly talons and venomous bites would be enough against any human who dared step foot on the island.

But they weren't enough against the quick, expertly-placed laser bolts that bore hot UV light concentrated holes in their heads. Two quick shots and both vampires dropped dead to the ground. All eyes in the group went back to the guard towers and to a silent collection of relief as no alarms were raised. The nearest searchlight was still serenely making its way around as Z led the group in a hurried line along the side of the main building and into the now unguarded entranceway of the triangular shaped prisoner entrance. Moving into the wide, dark entry, the group found themselves inside a freight elevator. The lighting inside was so dim it may as well not have been on at all. Prater took in the details – or lack thereof – with ease.

"No buttons or controls anywhere," he announced quietly.

A steel gate came down and closed off the entranceway. Everyone stumbled on their feet to keep balance as the elevator lurched into an abrupt descent.

"Four...five..." Ecks murmured as the elevator continued to move.

"What are you doing?" Annika asked.

Ecks held up a finger to the teenager to stave off any further interruptions. "...six...seven..."

The elevator slowed to a much more cushioned stop in contrast to its sudden start.

Ecks stroked his red beard. "Seven stories underground is what I'm guessing."

"Mm-hmm," Elroi concurred.

A steel gate nearly disguised in the low light opposite the entranceway clanked open. A chill filled the elevator that drew tiny clouds of anxious breaths from its occupants. Generators droned steadily in the distance. No one stepped out of the freight car, instead staring into the almost completely dark hallway that greeted them.

"Are you sure this is the only way?" Incom asked in a hushed tone.

"The only way in or out," Z acknowledged as she studied the digital schematic of the facility on her datapad.

Z led the group rapidly through the near dark using the map to guide her. Prater was just a step behind, followed by Incom and Ecks. Annika was next while Elroi covered the rear. A bend to the left was up ahead, lit just barely brighter than the dark gray hue of the corridor.

"This entire compound is under the seabed of the bay," Ecks muttered in awe. "An absolute master feat in engineering."

"Too bad it's all going to be destroyed within the hour," said Elroi.

Z stopped when they reached the turn in the hall. She cautiously glanced around the corner then pulled back, pressing herself against the wall. There was an unusual odor from down the corridor, like the rancid smell of freshly butchered meat. She looked again at the digital reader then addressed the group.

"After this turn is a short passageway that opens to what looks like some sort of staging area and the primary warehouse. And…on my god…"

"What?" asked Prater.

"According to this, the holding area is ten stories deep and filled with human blood pods."

A louder than desired gasp escaped Annika that was quickly shushed by Z.

"We need to get to the control room on the opposite side of the stage," Z said. "That's where the controls are to free Appamattox."

"And my family," Annika added.

Z and Annika locked eyes and Z blinked. She was about to say something when a series of soft beeps from the comm piece snug in her ear took away her attention. A voice came through the moment she tapped a button on the device.

"*Zarina, do you read?*" General Kaur's voice was surprisingly clear through Z's earpiece.

"I'm here," Z replied.

"*Just a quick update. The sub is on schedule as planned and is due to reach target ground zero in forty-seven minutes.*"

"Forty-seven minutes," Z repeated. Her eyes darted quickly at the shadowy faces around her.

"*Appamattox or no, that bomb is going off, Zarina. I'll check back shortly with another update. General Kaur out.*"

"Let's move," Z said as she took the group around the corner…

…and bumped into a vampire guard who was about to round the corner itself. Two additional guards walked behind it – both of whom screeched as they witnessed Z stab both her sai into opposite sides of the lead vampire's head. They immediately separated as Z pulled her weapons from the creature, allowing it to drop dead in front of her. The vampire on the left lunged at Z, who darted to her right to avoid the attack. Prater was there and lopped the vampire's head off with a single slice.

The remaining vampire didn't attack but instead turned and took off in flight back towards the stage. Elroi didn't appear to even think as he raised his large gun in the direction of the fleeing creature. Precise aim wasn't necessary as the projectile that shot from his bazooka quickly expanded into a net made of thin silvery strands. The vampire was fast, but it couldn't outpace the speed of the trap as the net caught the airborne feet of the creature then rapidly enshrouded the entire body. As the vampire tumbled and rolled across the dark stage the silver strands constricted and sizzled into the flesh of the creature. Singed and smoking pieces of the monster popped through the irregularly stretched openings in the lattice, leaving vampire pieces across the black stage like a trail of breadcrumbs on a dark forest floor.

"Nice work," said Incom.

"Yeah," said Ecks, "but I wouldn't be surprised if that doesn't catch some attention."

"According to Marques there should only be four vampires inside here," said Z. "That took care of three." Without pause she added, "Let's keep moving."

Z had the group halfway across the stage when spotlights blasted on, nearly blinding them. Beyond the spotlights, all the lights in the entire complex popped on, exposing the vast expanse. They paused momentarily as they couldn't help but take in the sheer enormity of the space. Rows upon rows of countless black pods hung from steel tracks that ran the full depth of the depot. An overhead klaxon began to blare in an intermittent pattern, echoing through the cavernous facility, as Z gestured with one hand to keep them all moving.

Sets of black, biomechanical insect-like legs shot up out of the dark stage without warning, reaching and grabbing for the human invaders. The spindly limbs were confined to established spots on the stage and everyone who escaped the appendages did so as a matter of luck due to where they happened to be standing. Everyone except Ecks. Incom shouted out to their ensnarled teammate. She went to grab one of Ecks' arms that reached out between the tall legs that imprisoned him, but pulled back as the tips of the appendages shot silky, weblike strands at their captive while simultaneously starting to spin. The silver spear Ecks was carrying caught up in the webbing along with the rest of him as the legs rapidly spun and wrapped pearl white strands around and immediately immobilizing him.

The rest of the team was helpless to stop the cocooning they witnessed. Annika was trying to calm herself after screaming at the initial shock of what she saw happening to Ecks. Z grabbed the teenager by an arm and began to practically drag her across the stage.

"Everyone get to the control room now!" Z commanded.

The group reached the far side of the stage where the control room – a small room with glass walls barely large enough for three occupants and filled with computers and monitors – was built out of an exposed rock wall. The glass door to the room was closed and locked and the single vampire inside – *Number four,* Z thought to herself – seemed to taunt them through the glass windows that ran floor to ceiling on the room's three exposed sides. Everyone was crowded around the booth and Z was about to try and smash one of the windows with the butt end of the handle of her sai when she noticed a reflection in the glass. She looked back just as five vampires flew in from the darkness of the far end of the cavern and landed on the stage behind them, rabid and breathing heavy, snarling through elongated fangs, and flexing their sharp talons.

The band of humans turned to face their new adversaries, weapons drawn, ready to fight.

"Hold them off while I get into the control room," Z commanded.

A new movement from the stage momentarily caught everyone's attention as the pod enveloping Ecks was carried away by hoses and chains to take its place among the countless others in the cold blood bank facility. With that, any trace of Ecks and the spindly appendages that cocooned him were gone, and Z knew there would be no time to try and rescue him. The distraction was fleeting and the pod had barely lifted off the stage when the adversaries returned to their standoff. Just then five additional vampires flew in and landed among the first five.

"We're well beyond *just four more,*" said Prater.

SAN FRANCISCO BAY

BRANDON Stirling stood in the middle of the Golden Gate Bridge, on its west side, looking out past the strait and towards the black ocean beyond. The darkness was cushioned by the haze of gently rolling fog under the glow of the lights that illuminated the iconic bridge. The air was still and the evening was cool and quiet from the lack of vehicles and pedestrians stemming from the curfew and areawide lockdown.

Brandon was barefoot and dressed in a skintight, black wetsuit like the fifteen other vampires who stood with him lining the side of the bridge. He glanced at a small digital datapad strapped to his left wrist then back out at the black water. Just then a barely audible splash from over a hundred yards out marked the point where a dark figure jetted up out of the bay before arcing towards the bridge and landing steps away from Brandon. The vampire wiped his long, wet hair out of his face as he stepped up to the president's brother.

"I see it," the creature reported to Brandon. "Just about two miles out and rapidly heading this way."

Brandon's lip twitched and he suppressed a snarl. "Good work. We're running out of time. The closer it gets the more damage it can do. We need to intercept it before it gets into the bay."

"Yes, sir. This way," the vampire said as he leapt over the side of the bridge, launching himself out and away to hit the icy cold water nearly two hundred and fifty feet below. Brandon immediately followed, who himself was followed by the fifteen vampires with him. Their talons fully extended, the creatures screeched and howled through mouthfuls of razor fangs until their sounds were cut off as each plunged deep into the black water.

Larger, faster, and stronger, the special underwater ops vampires selected by Brandon for this mission were not ordinary vampires. As if made for the water, these could hold their breath easily for up to an hour underwater at depths of up to nearly five hundred feet. Their keen eyesight allowed them to see close to a thousand feet in the deep, sometimes more when lighting conditions were optimal. One of their most effective traits was the ability to locate items underwater through an echolocation not unlike those of dolphin. Like their brethren who could fly, these creatures could propel themselves underwater through an unseen, self-created kinetic energy that allowed them to move in whatever direction they wanted without the need for exerting any physical movements.

Brandon was evolved in the same ways as the special team he now led, having learned of the abilities many centuries before. It wasn't until the Vampocalypse and Great Turn that he became aware of many others with the same abilities, and it was then that he began recruiting those he could to his army. The team had been tested under controlled environments as part of their training, but this would prove to be their first actual assignment as a full unit. Brandon did not anticipate failure.

The vampires moved with their arms pinned to their sides, looking like black arrows in the chilly, dark water, and unaffected by the freezing cold or the currents. The scout with the long hair was in the lead, followed closely by Brandon, then the others in a fanned-out pattern. The accuracy of their sonar proved to be instrumental in the tracking and location of the submarine as it traversed the waters up the coastline, before it got too close to the city. Brandon was eager to finally let loose on the humans. Those in the stolen vessel would not only pay the ultimate price with their lives, but their loss would stand as testament to those who would dare defy vampirekind.

EPISODE 25

SAN FRANCISCO MECCA
NORTH AMERICA NEW WORLD TERRITORIES VAMPIRE CAPITOL

PRESIDENT Stirling rejoiced in the exhibition of blood and flesh transpiring on the stage and in the stands before him. His fellow vampire leaders were almost indistinguishable from one another as each was soaked head to toe in the blood of their feast and from each other, and the wails they released were born from a combination of lust, pain, and sex. Nearly all of the attendees in the stands had followed similar suit and the rising cacophony of thirst-quenching moans had achieved a tandem rhythm that reverberated through the arena.

After watching for a few minutes from just offstage, Stirling stepped onto the edge of the stage itself and a podium emerged from under the platform to greet him. The lights focusing on the bloodstained banquet dimmed and spotlights shone on the president. The music stopped and, after several moments of languishing moans from the stands, the crowd quietened and all that could be heard were the muted cries from the tortured captives hanging from the crosses surrounding the platform.

"I am so happy to know that my fellow leaders have been satisfied and you, you my vampire brothers and sisters around the globe, you too have been satisfied in the feast your eyes have just ingested."

Stirling dove right into his speech without salutations or fanfare, making sure to make eye contact with those on the stage as well as with the various cameras aimed in his direction. He occasionally smiled a thin smile but mostly maintained a serious expression, along with a tone of voice that was strong and assertive and knew just when to accentuate the right words or phrases to solicit timely applause from his captive audience.

"The blood of those who give their lives to our cause is cherished. While there is no peaceful coexistence between human and vampire, the human contribution to our eternal livelihood does not go unrecognized." Scattered, polite though unconvincing clapping popped through the crowd then quickly stopped as the president continued. "Tonight we see nothing but light as we move forward to a new day of true, global, vampire domination. Only together, my brothers and sisters, unified as one," he rose a fist slowly into the air as his voice crescendoed, "under one governing authority, can we forge our way into the future!"

Stirling waited for the cheers that had inevitably greeted his words to die down.

"This summit and the convening leadership you see before you is the final step to the one, true way forward for our kind. We shall move ahead with urgency for there is much to accomplish. We shall right any wrongs of our vampire ancestors and the word 'vampire' will become synonymous with life and posterity for all eternity." He looked out and raised both hands to the crowd. "You are all here as eyewitnesses tonight as I show you the way, the way forward in my unity of all." He slowly brought his hands in front of his chest and intertwined his fingers together. "Beginning tonight we all start anew, united under one guide, one banner, one way for us all!"

Another round of applause shook the stadium as Stirling waived his clasped hands in the air back and forth on either side of his head. This time he egged the crowd on to continue their applause and he finally began to hear it. It was quiet at first as sole voices among the thousands of cheers were easily overpowered, but relatively quickly, the voices changed and the words from those in attendance became more clear.

"Stirling! Stirling! Stirling!" The president's name echoed through the arena as it was chanted from the lips of the tens of thousands in attendance, tenuously at first, but very quickly strengthened to a level of frenzy never witnessed by any of the global leaders before in their own territories. A few curious looks fell the bloodied expressions of the ambassadors but no one said anything as the president continued. Chants of his name muted as his supporters hung on to his every word.

"As I stand before you all, addressing the world, know that those who dissent or who are not with us shall be forever sentenced to the black sleep of nothingness and will not see the light of the eternity that awaits. Of this I am most certain, and promise you shall be judged and your finality will be cruel."

Stirling stopped looking out among the stands and communications monitors that were beaming his speech globally and instead focused solely on the leadership before him. Slowly they each stood from their feeding and fornicating positions on the stage, more and more curious about the president's words and his meanings. In the silence that occurred the moans of the skinned and agonizing humans on the crosses were all that filled the air.

"And so, you shall all witness a future that begins now. As each of you know, our Vampire Scriptures tell us that if one vampire takes the life of another, regardless of circumstance, the victor earns the spoils of the dead. Tonight, brothers and sisters, shall bring the ultimate display of this law." Stirling paused and smiled, and for the first time during his speech it was a full, wide smile. "And I intend to be so very, very spoiled."

While Stirling was speaking, few paid attention to the small drone that floated through the stadium just above the heads of the humans attached to the crosses encircling the stage. Just as the president said the final words of his speech, an intense crimson flash from the drone bright enough to momentarily light up the entire stadium stole everyone's attention. There were exclamations of surprise and amazement from what some thought was simply a light show, though most in attendance knew exactly what it was.

As the fluorescent red snow fell upon the stage, the shackles binding the flayed humans to the crosses opened and the twenty-three tortured souls dropped to the stage. They had already begun to change from the effects of the particle bomb – their fingers became sharp, pointed talons as fangs tore through the black strings that sewed their lips together. The sounds that came from their freed mouths was anything but human. Immediately driven by the carnage in the middle of the stage, the blind newturns, guided by the euphoric scents escaping from the bloody and naked vampire leaders, advanced upon them, ready to quench their newfound thirst. The chant of the crowd calling Stirling's name resumed as they cheered and watched the global vampire leaders fight for their survival. It immediately became apparent that the numbers of newturns were too great for the vampire leaders to handle and one by one they succumbed to the new feeding frenzy that overtook the platform.

During the melee Andrea was able to somehow break free and she stumbled away from the new blood orgy. She staggered and grabbed onto Stirling's podium to keep from falling. The vice president looked into Stirling's eyes and the kinship she had felt with him for centuries was gone, replaced by a cold stare she didn't recognize.

"Jonathan," Andrea bloodily spit the name out, exhausted from fighting.

Stirling couldn't tell if the blood dribbling from the corner of her mouth was hers or someone else's. For that matter, he couldn't tell where any of the blood she was covered in had come from. He just stared at her, unmoving physically and unmoved emotionally as she spoke.

"What, what are you doing?" The fatigue in her voice was thick.

Stirling stepped around the podium and put an arm around the woman who could barely hold herself up. From this new angle he could see deep wounds in her right side pumping out blood in rhythm with her heartbeat. The smell of the freshness coming from her tempted him to take part in the feast himself, but even though tonight was about him, he needn't take time at this moment to join the ecstasy and bliss proliferating the arena. He pulled the vice president close to his chest, holding her tight to keep her from collapsing as she let go of the stand.

"I'm sorry, my dear," Stirling said to her as he kissed the bloody, matted hair on top of her head. "I have loved you in ways over the centuries that you will never know, but there is no place in this future for you."

The president held Andrea out from him by her upper arms as he looked into her pained expression. She was tired and her will was gone. She knew that fighting was useless. She was surrounded by chanting Stirling supporters, the global vampire leaders were all as good as dead, and the presence of Ryder Sloane just offstage over Stirling's shoulder solidified her fate. Her eyes half-closed from the pain and exhaustion that screamed at her but she managed to muster up a final moment of resolve.

"Fuck you, Jonathan," Andrea hissed before spitting a combination of saliva and blood onto the president's face.

"Charming," was the only word he said before he abruptly ripped the vice president's arms out of her sockets.

Andrea's screams were ongoing as Stirling pierced his talons deep into the sides of her chest, breaking through ribs and puncturing her lungs. Yanking her close the president took a large bite out of the side of her neck, then another and another, leaving her head barely attached as it flopped sideways and held on only with a patch of skin and a few tendons and thin pieces of muscle. Not yet dead, Andrea looked at Stirling, at her demise, and then felt herself get flung back into the bloodthirsty feasting that was occurring in the center of the stage. Slick, sinewy, flayed bodies were on her in an instant, and as her head was finally torn completely away from her body, Andrea lost consciousness as she welcomed the final death that followed.

SAN FRANCISCO MECCA BLOOD BANKS
ALCATRAZ ISLAND

PRATER took a curt swing with one of his katana and the head of the vampire nearest him went flying over the edge of the stage and into the ten-story abyss. Incom did her best to make use of her UV laser rifle, but the close proximity of their attackers made it difficult for her to get open shots at vampire body parts not protected by armor. Annika stayed shielded from the fight as much as possible next to Z as the older woman punched at the glass door with the pommel end of her sai. The thick glass was resilient and she knew no more time could be wasted. The overhead klaxon continued to sound its recurrent warning.

"Elroi, I need you!" Z shouted.

"In a jiffy, love, I'm busy at the moment!"

Elroi stepped between Prater and Incom, knocking Prater aside in the process, as he brought his weapon up – having reengaged the machine gun portion – and began spraying silver bullets in several directions as if the weapon was guiding him rather than the other way around. Six of the remaining nine attacking vampires dropped with a multitude of lacerations, gashes, and various dismemberments coming from the silver that shot into them. Silver oozed from their wounds as their damaged flesh smoked and burned. Elroi continued to fire, spinning around and blasting several bullets into the glass control booth – being careful to aim high so as to not damage any of the equipment inside – shattering its walls completely. He saw Z rush to confront the creature inside as he continued to turn and face back across the stage.

As Elroi spun, his plan to blast the final three vampires ended when his weapon let out the familiar but unwelcome *click, click, click* of being out of bullets. The vampires, cowering in various dark corners around the cavern, were emboldened by the empty clicks and rushed to attack the infiltrators. Prater stabbed and slashed at his attacker, initially keeping it at bay, as Incom's UV rifle was knocked out of her hands. She suddenly found herself grappling on the floor, desperately trying to avoid the sharp claws and snapping jaws of the creature on top of her.

The third vampire, the largest one remaining, ran at Elroi on the final empty click from his weapon. The Brit was no match to stop the weight of the creature as it launched the full force of its body at the smaller man. Elroi found himself on his back, screaming in pain from the two sets of talons digging deep into his chest, and immobile from the weight of the monster on top of him. His machine gun and bazooka net launcher were useless as they lay out of reach from where he dropped them when he was hit. He did have one desperate idea, though. Rather than continue struggling to force the heavy vampire off of him, he slid a hand between him and the monster on top and strained to pull an item from his utility belt – one of the electric net capsules for his bazooka launcher. Freeing his hand from the struggle, he held the capsule out to the side and the creature glanced at it with a hint of curiosity beneath its raging growl.

"Take this, you ugly motherfucker!"

With that, Elroi smashed the ignitor pin end of the capsule against the side of the vampire's head.

Nothing happened.

The creature screamed angrily and dripped venomous drool onto Elroi's face much to his disgust. Out of panic and desperation, Elroi slammed the capsule rapidly and repeatedly against the vampire. The creature opened its mouth wide and Elroi's last thought before the capsule detonated against the hide of its head was that his entire face was about to be taken in a single bite.

The net enveloped most of the vampire and some of Elroi's upper body and head as it exploded onto them as they lay wrestling on the ground. The silver mesh of the net went to immediate work on the vampire. The creature rolled as it struggled to break free, entangling the net around both itself and Elroi in the process. The vampire's talons were still deep in the man's upper body, and Elroi's blood loss was already to the point where immediate medical treatment was needed if he was going to survive…treatment the British mechanic knew was not available. As the silver dug into the monster on top of him, he could feel, for a fleeting moment, the silver coated, dissected bits dripping onto his body. A coldness rippled through his body as the net constricted tighter and tighter. Then there was just darkness.

Incom's situation wasn't much better than Elroi's – though while the monster that had her pinned to the ground didn't have its claws buried in her (yet), she had no weapons to help with her struggle, and she could feel fatigue setting in. The day had been long and full of fight, and while she still had some strength left in her, she wasn't sure how she was going to get out of this predicament. She tried in desperation to kick and push but each snap of the jaws at her face inched closer. With the next bite she felt the tips of fangs graze her cheek, not enough to break skin, but enough for her to know that her luck was just a second or two away from running out.

Cold blood splashed across her face as the creature's head was ripped away from its shoulders. The weight of the monster's body fell on her and she had to blink rapidly to get the vampire blood to clear from her eyes so she could see what happened. Prater was standing over her. Impaled to the end of one of his swords was the head of her vampire attacker – Prater had skillfully impaled the base of the creature's skull then used leverage and a quick cut of his other sword to slice the head off, showering Incom in the creature's blood in the process.

"Sorry about the wait," Prater said. "I was a bit preoccupied."

Prater glanced at the nearby floor and Incom's eyes followed to see the vampire Prater had last fought with lying there – its head was attached but split cleanly vertically down the middle. Prater stepped away from Incom and disposed of the decapitated head stuck to his sword as Incom shoved the vampire carcass aside. She accepted Prater's open hand to pull her up off the floor.

"Incom, come help!" Z shouted from the control room.

Incom rushed to the control room while Prater wiped his swords across dead vampire bodies before sheathing them. Incom entered the booth – if it could still be called that as its walls of glass were completely shattered leaving an empty framework with counters and banks of computers – and stepped over the dead vampire with a hole in the middle of its forehead to join Z and Annika at the primary control panel. There were three monitors in the control booth, two of which showed constantly cycling readings of vital signs of the thousands of captives held in the facility. The third provided the primary user interface and was flashing a large ACCESS DENIED in red letters inside a box across the middle of the screen.

"You're the computer expert," Z said to Incom. "Can you crack this?"

"I can try," Incom said. She was already entering commands into the keyboard. "Give me a few minutes."

"We don't have a few minutes."

"What about his family?" Incom asked as she began the search for their target, though she already knew the answer.

"Just the professor." Z glanced down at Annika who failed to notice the look.

Incom was practically salivating as her fingers flew across the console. This was it – she was in her element, finally, after so long. The blaring alarm echoing through the facility silenced.

"There, that's better," Incom said. "Now I can think."

"Can you turn the heat up?" Annika asked. "It's freezing in here." She wasn't entirely serious, of course, but at the same time she wouldn't have minded if there actually was a way to make the place warmer.

Incom was hard at work as Prater and Annika kept watch for any other vampires that may appear. To the relief of those who survived the fight, no additional vampires had shown up, but it was certainly not a matter of *when* they would arrive but rather, how soon. Z was looking on anxiously when the transmitter in her ear beeped.

"Zarina, come in, this is General Kaur."

"I copy, general, what's going on?"

"Some disturbing news. Here in HQ we've tapped into the live feed of the vampire summit and President Stirling's speech. It's more diabolical than we thought. Stirling just slaughtered all the world's top vampire leadership and the vampires seem to be going crazy in support worldwide over it."

Z stammered, unsure of what to say.

"What is it?" Prater asked.

Z held a finger up in response as she addressed the general.

"Maybe this can buy us some time," Z said. The words came out before she even realized it.

There was a long pause and Z began to wonder if she had lost connection with the general.

"That's a negative, Zarina," General Kaur said, breaking the silence. *"The mission continues as planned. The bomb will be detonated as scheduled."*

"What?" Z couldn't help but shout, surprising everyone in the booth and making Annika jump. "We have a chance to save not only Appamattox but so many others! One of my team was taken just moments ago. He and the others aren't beyond saving." She resisted the urge to look at Annika as she spoke.

"We can't do that. This is our opportunity to wipe out the entire vampire leadership – and that means Stirling and his top cabinet and advisors. The fact Stirling did some of the killing for us is just bonus."

"Just delay the attack at least by a few minutes. Even if it's just five or ten. Any bit helps."

"This is our first step towards reclaiming our world, Zarina. Nothing is going to stop that."

Annika was suddenly by Z's side. It didn't take much to gather what was being said between Z and the general despite not being able to hear what he was saying.

"Please," Annika pleaded, projecting her voice towards Z's earpiece. "It's just a few minutes."

"I'm not going to say this again, Zarina. The detonation goes on as scheduled."

The definitiveness in the general's voice was dismaying. Now Z did look at the girl beside her and she could see the hurt in her eyes...eyes that Z, despite her own childhood history and upbringing, felt had seen way too much for someone so young.

"You're fucking crazy," Z said. Her tone was low but she knew the general would have still heard her just fine. His response, though, was unexpected.

"Hold, Zarina, we're getting something in here on another channel."

Z could hear several voices talking all at once in the background but couldn't make sense of what anyone in particular was saying. The volume of the vocal exchanges raised alarms in Z's mind but even that didn't prepare her for what the general said when he returned.

"Our strike team on the sub has reported incoming vampires."

"What do you mean, 'incoming vampires?'"

"Vampires have located the sub and are attempting to board it."

Z shook her head in disbelief. The confusion on her face was echoed in the looks of Prater and Annika who were only hearing half the conversation.

"I'm sorry, general," Z said. "It's –"

"With the sub under attack our timeline is nullified."

"What does that mean?" Z asked the question, fearing the answer.

"The strike team is going to delay the detonation but only in the interest of getting the sub as far into the bay as possible to do the most damage. But there's no way of knowing how quickly those vampires are going to infiltrate the sub."

Z put a hand up to her ear with the transmitter in an effort to mute herself as much as possible from the general. She leaned over towards Incom.

"How's it coming?" she asked in a whisper. "We're running out of time."

"It's coming." Incom smacked her gum loudly as she concentrated without missing a beat on her nonstop inputs in her frantic search.

Data was flying so rapidly across multiple applications on the monitors that Z wasn't sure what was system generated and what Incom herself was entering. Annika watched intently, carefully studying every entry and keystroke. It didn't look as if there was a single point where a "search" for Appamattox could be done. Incom's efforts involved a combination of manual searches by name and visual searches across schematics. The effort appeared cumbersome at best.

"Just about got it narrowed down…" Incom's words tapered and she popped her gum.

Z released a quick, near-panicked sigh. "Okay, general, we just need enough time to release Appamattox and get to safety."

"I suggest you all get out of there now. I can't guarantee your survival.

"But –"

"God be with you, Zarina."

"There is no god, general. You should know that."

"That's all then, Zarina. General Kaur out." There was a brief crackle of static then the transmitter went quiet.

"Motherfucker!" Z couldn't help from voicing her frustration.

"I found him!" Incom exclaimed, bringing some much needed good news.

"Hurry, hurry!" Z shouted. Annika couldn't help but echo the words as she felt overcome with excitement.

"It'll take just a minute for the tracks to sort him out and bring him to the stage."

"Just hurry," Z said, now more calm, though not any more reassuring. "That nuke's gonna go off any minute. We may already be as good as dead."

SAN FRANCISCO BAY

BRANDON Stirling followed beside and just behind the vampire who had located the sub as they channeled their way through the dark waters. He narrowed his eyes and focused on a large, black shape ahead, moving like a leviathan through the deep at full speed in their direction – the *Annihilator*-class submarine *Harbinger One*. The vessel was traveling fast, but the mutated vampires would be able to temporarily keep up, at least long enough to reach their target points on the vessel. Brandon slowed his strike force just enough to provide a series of hand signals that notified the team to break into predetermined groups and initiate their individual missions.

Four vampires were responsible for destroying the scopes and communications equipment on top of the sail; four were tasked with infiltrating the sub through the torpedo tubes; five, including Brandon, would enter through the forward escape hatch. The final four had what Brandon considered to be the most important task of all: dismantling the massive propellers. The vampires adjusted their speeds and trajectories and made for their assigned areas.

Brandon smiled to himself. The humans would not succeed today.

EPISODE 26

SAN FRANCISCO MECCA
NORTH AMERICA NEW WORLD TERRITORIES VAMPIRE CAPITOL

STIRLING rejoiced in the glow of adulation poured upon him by the stadium crowd. The unholy decadence transpiring on the stage and in the stands was slowly winding down, but it would take a lot more to quell the lasting excitement that saturated the arena. The lingering stench of blood and sex filled the air and the floors were stained with the lifeforce of the dead. The live music thrummed on in the background, slowly transitioning selections in a minor key, adding to the gruesome atmosphere as the scenes played out like a grand play on a world stage – which was exactly what Stirling wanted.

The president was about to address the crowd when an aide rushed to his side and, begging his pardon, requested he step offstage for a moment. Stirling smiled and waved to the crowd from behind the podium before stepping out of the spotlight and into the shadows just offstage. There a communications officer awaited along with Ryder Sloane. The cybervampire stood tall and poised with his shiny black metallic wings folded around him, leaving only his head exposed.

"President Stirling," the officer began, "I beg your understanding of my reporting this untimely news."

"Just out with it, officer," said Stirling.

"Alarms have raised at the Alcatraz blood banks. We've attempted to reach security on site but have been unsuccessful."

Stirling's eyes darted around the dark of the offstage area, looking at nothing as his mind raced. The sounds of small servomotors buzzed next to him as Sloane adjusted his posture as the cybervampire's focus on the conversation intensified.

"It's sure to be the escapees from Camp Expectation," said Sloane.

The cybervampire sounded more matter-of-fact than theoretical. Stirling grumbled low in agreement as he wrung his hands.

"Prater Saxon is certain to be with them," Sloane went on.

Stirling set a palm on the glossy, smooth wing of the cybervampire.

"Go, general," said Stirling. "This is your time of retribution. Get Prater Saxon and bring him to me."

Sloane nodded then took a couple of steps away from the president. His wings retreated behind him as he prepared to launch himself into the air.

"Yes, Mr. President. I shall return with Prater Saxon, this I pledge to you."

Stirling's mouth twisted as he said, "Or don't return at all."

Sloane gave the president a subtle nod then barely looked ahead before shooting straight up into the air. All eyes were on the biomechanical vampire as he streaked up and out through an opening located in one of the highest walls of the arena. His wings folded back like a falcon attacking its prey and there was a collective gasp at the sheer speed at which he launched himself and exited the stadium.

SAN FRANCISCO MECCA BLOOD BANKS
ALCATRAZ ISLAND

AN extraction track slid into place in the high ceiling overhead along with massive sets of spools of chains with hooks that rattled and clanked as they lowered the eight stories to the row containing Appamattox's pod. A set of small rails folded out from the pod holding rack and connected with the chains, securing the hooks into place. Appamattox's pod slid across the rails and locked into the hooks. The rails detached and the pod was raised by the clanking chains up to stage level where it anchored against a locking mechanism on the extraction track. The pod was three-quarters of the way back from the stage but immediately began sliding forward as soon as the pod locked into place.

The entire process felt like it was going painstakingly slow though it was obvious the mechanisms were moving as quickly as they were meant. Everyone watched helpless under the pressure of the unknown time constraints as the pod clanked toward them.

Incom and Annika remained in the control booth while Prater and Z awaited the arrival of the pod from the stage. Annika was feeling the cold of the cavern more and more and the constant reminder from being able to see her breath wasn't helping. The control panel in front of Incom suddenly flashed red and a wretched screech erupted from the track as the pod shuddered and stopped. It was still a good hundred feet away.

"We have a problem!" Z yelled from the stage.

"Fuck!" Incom smacked the counter next to the keyboard. "Working on it!" But she already knew there was probably no chance of her keyboard commands doing anything to free the mechanism electronically.

Annika rushed out to the stage while Incom continued her work. "What happened?"

"Track's jammed," said Z. "Not sure what happened."

"Maybe I can climb out there and knock it loose," said Prater.

"You're crazy," said Z. "One slip and you're done. You may be one of them but you can't fly."

"Do you have any better ideas?" Prater asked.

"I do," said Annika.

Z and Prater looked at the girl who held up her bow.

"I have one shot left," Annika said. "I can use it to knock the pod loose."

Prater and Z exchanged a quick look.

"It could work," said Prater. Z nodded.

"Okay," Z said. She looked intently at Annika. "Take the shot. And make it good."

"Uh-huh," Annika said, almost dismissively.

Annika was already getting into a mental zone as she nocked her last arrow. She held up the bow, steadying her aim as she took a deep breath. This was the shot of her life. Everything she had learned from her archery lessons had come to this. She stood up strong and straight, pulled gently back on the string, and slowly exhaled. Her frosty breath lingered in the cold air in front of her then quickly dissipated. She let the arrow fly.

A clang echoed as the arrow met with the connector holding the pod to the extraction track. The arrow fell into the depths of the cavern below...and to everyone's relief the pod resumed moving towards the stage.

"Great shot!" Z exclaimed as she held the youngster.

Incom joined the others as the pod was lowered with a heavy thud then left standing vertically on the stage. The chains detached and receded into the extraction mechanisms overhead. Wet, slippery sounds combined with a deep gurgling, followed by coughing noises came muffled from within the casing. There was a light hiss as the pod separated down the middle. The body revealed underneath was cocooned head to toe like a large chrysalis waiting to expose its long-gestating contents to the world.

The silk that made up the cocoon was hard and strong despite countless pinholes covering nearly every visible area. Prater and Z gently eased it out of the pod and laid it face up on the floor of the stage. The only substantial opening in the cocoon was around the area of its mouth. Prater stuck his fingers through the gap and grabbed its sides in an attempt to tear the cocoon open. The strange silk would barely flex and would not tear. He drew one of his swords and, as Z held the opening as wide as it would go, carefully guided its tip into the gap and slid the blade up over the face, then down the remainder of the body, slicing open the morbid prison.

The cutting complete, Prater sheathed the blade then he and Z pulled away at the cocoon, exposing the man underneath. Geoffrey Appamattox would not have been recognizable to anyone who knew him. Even Incom wondered if this was the same person whose image appeared on one of the monitor screens in the control room when she located him. Of course, thirty years had passed, but the man, thin and frail but not entirely emaciated, looked two decades beyond his actual sixty years, having lived half his life as part of a factory for the preservation of vampires. His hair was matted, gray, and stringy, and a matching beard that had gradually grown over the years touched the middle of his chest. His clothes were wet from humidity and perspiration and were shredded and torn from the hundreds of blood draw, life support, and monitoring needles that had punctured them. His body was mottled with bruises and droplets of blood dotted his skin from where the needles had pierced his every reachable inch.

Prater helped Appamattox sit up as the man coughed and tossed his head from side to side, working to grow accustomed to regular air again – both on his skin and in his lungs. He coughed some more then ever so slowly pried his eyes open. These were the eyes of a man who had not seen light in three decades and the pained expressions he made showed he was going to need some time to adjust to the surroundings of the real world.

"Professor Appamattox?" Z asked with haste as she knelt next to the man and leaned in close to him. "Are you Geoffrey Appamattox?"

Prater put a hand on Z's shoulder and nudged her away. Z recoiled with aggravation.

"Easy, slow down," said Prater. "He's just woken up from a very long sleep."

Z grabbed Prater's hand and shoved it away. "How many ways do I need to say that we have no time? That nuclear bomb, which is probably only a hundred feet away from us for all I know, is going off any moment now. We need to get Appamattox out and away from here as fast as we can."

Prater glared at the woman, piercing her with the knives he shot through his sunglasses.

"I understand that," he said. "But our mission is to save Professor Appamattox, and if we end up harming him in the process, or worse, then this will all be for nothing and we may as well kiss our asses goodbye."

"I'm Geoffrey," the man said in barely a whisper, though it was enough to silence Prater and Z's squabble.

"Pleased to meet you, sir. I'm Prater."

Appamattox swallowed hard, forcing the action, and chose to slowly blink in response.

Z leaned back in. "I'm Zarina, that's Incom." She gave a fleeting glance around and realized Annika wasn't immediately with them. "I do apologize for the haste, professor, but a nuclear bomb is about to go off and if we don't get out of here, then as Prater said, we may as well kiss our asses goodbye."

Appamattox blinked in response again but this time added a gentle nod.

"I'll take care of the professor," Prater said. "You get Annika and we'll get out of here."

Z looked up and down the stage but didn't see Annika anywhere. "Where is she?"

Prater pointed at the far end of the stage. "There, in the control room."

Z rushed to the control room where she was met by an overly excited Annika. Sweat was beading on the girl's forehead and she had an almost impossibly huge smile. Her fingers trembled as they hovered over the keyboard in front of her. On multiple monitors there were images of three people and their pod locations in the blood racks. Even though Z didn't recognize the faces on the screens, it was easy to realize who they were.

"I found them," Annika said as tears filled her eyes. The words were quiet but they grew stronger as she repeated them. "I found them. I found them!"

Z grabbed Annika by the shoulders and turned the girl to face her. She wanted to pause, to plead silently with her eyes because the words felt impossible to say…but there simply was no time.

"Annika, we have to go. It took too long to get Appamattox as it was. I'm so sorry."

Tears instantly gushed down the teenager's face as it twisted into anger. "But they're right here! I found them. There's time. I *know* there's time!"

"Annika, there is *no time*. There's a good chance we won't make it out of here as it is." Z's tenor went from pleading to demanding. "We need to go. Now."

Annika shook her head aggressively as she struggled to break free of Z's grasp. "No, no. You go! I'm gonna stay and free them and we'll get caught up."

Z gave the girl a stern shake. "If we leave you you're as good as dead. We're taking the boat and you won't have any way to get off this island."

Annika's voice grew strained as she grew more frantic. "We can swim! We'll make it."

Z framed Annika's face in her hands. "Are you listening to yourself? Appamattox can't even walk. You expect your family to *swim*?"

Annika's eyes flipped to the screens as she looked from face to face at each of her family members. She pulled herself away from Z and leaned in close to the images, rapidly shifting her attention from one to the next. In her mind she heard each of them pleading to be freed, to not be left behind. Maybe if she couldn't free them all…

"At least one!" Annika pleaded. "Let me save at least one!"

Z yanked the girl by the arm and whipped her back around to where they again were eye to eye. "Would you quit being so goddamned emotional? Do you want us to all die because of you?"

Annika pulled herself away from the older woman's grasp. "Are you kidding me? Did you just say that?"

Z's patience was exhausted. Before Annika could object, Z scooped the girl up and tossed her over a shoulder. Holding her tight while the girl kicked to be freed, Z exited the control booth and started across the stage.

"I'm sorry but we don't have time for this. I'm not letting you die here."

Annika stretched her arms and hands out towards the control room as she was carried away, watching as the faces of her family on the monitors got smaller and smaller in the distance that rapidly grew between them. She pounded on Z's back in agony and cried out in protest but her words fell on deaf ears. Z showed no signs of slowing despite her best efforts to force herself loose, and Prater and Incom ignored her as well as they all rushed towards the freight elevator together. Her thrashing grew stronger with each step Z took further away from the control booth. A stream of free flowing tears abandoned Annika's wet cheeks as she was carried into the elevator. The fight abruptly abandoned her as the freight elevators closed and Z finally set her down. Dropping instantly to her knees as the elevator began to ascend towards the surface, Annika put her face in her hands and sobbed uncontrollably. She shook off Z's feeble attempt at consolation when she felt the woman's hand on her shoulder. Reconciliation might come, eventually, but now was definitely not the time.

The elevator came to a halt and Annika knew there was no turning back. Fighting any further would do no good right now. She would have to take that battle up again later for a more immediate fight was about to present itself.

The freight elevator doors opened and the group headed towards the glow from the exit ahead that led to the open air of the island. Incom was in the lead with her UV rifle firmly in her grasp, followed by Z, Prater holding Appamattox in his arms, then Annika. But the freedom they expected to find did not greet them as hoped. Incom was the first to exit the short corridor to the open island and she was immediately snatched into the air by a vampire that swept out of nowhere and took her high into the foggy night, never to be seen again. Her UV laser rifle dropped to the ground as her screams faded away into the dark, outlasting any image of her disappearing into the mist.

Prater stood in the glow of the spotlights that flooded them, cradling the barely conscious professor in his arms. Appamattox still could barely keep his eyes open as his struggle to regain some semblance of strength continued. With the professor in his arms, Prater was currently of little use in battle. The vampires could easily scoop him and the professor away before he had a chance to think twice. The only reprieve he felt, however slight, was the fact that aside from the vampire that took Incom away, only three others greeted them. Surely there were more vampires in the offices of the main building nearby but Marques appeared to have been right in that they showed no interest in a fight. To Prater's immediate left, Z stood with both of her sai drawn and ready. Maybe she could hold her own in a three-to-one match, but Prater wasn't entirely confident in those odds, not after everything they'd endured.

The vampire in the middle of their greeting party stood out the most of the three. Unlike the others, this one wore a business suit rather than the uniform of an Alcatraz guard. Mr. Titus held up a hand with his palm facing towards the humans. His claws remained elongated and his fangs were exposed but his demeanor was relatively relaxed.

"You cannot take him," Mr. Titus said with both confidence and authority. "I won't let you."

"You won't have to."

Annika's words were somehow even more authoritative than the vampire's as she suddenly stepped out from behind Z and Prater, wielding the UV laser rifle Incom had dropped. The sixteen-year old screamed with hate, anger, and all the emotions within her as she released a barrage of lasers at the trio of vampires. The teenager took no aim and paid little attention to exactly where the shots went as long as they were in the direction of the creatures before them. Cold agony lent a cutting edge to her cries that would have sliced into the monsters as effectively as the laser beams if they could. As the surprise and subsequent confusion among the creatures diminished, the aftermath of the scene presented itself.

All three vampires lay dead. Two with massive UV laser injuries to their faces, heads, and hands – defensive wounds as the suddenly surprised vampires held their hands up in reflex only to become scorched and scarred beyond recognition. The third – Mr. Titus himself – was disposed of by Z. The vampire's decapitated head was impaled on the end of one of Z's sai. His eyes were partially rolled back, his face sagged, and his mouth opened and closed in slow, mindless movements that were either from silent, dying protest or simple reflexes of the already dead.

Prater, still carrying Appamattox, Z, and Annika quickly ran to the dark eastern side of the island where their boat waited. Z already had the electric vessel running by the time Prater set the professor comfortably down. Annika sat in the back of the boat, keeping herself as far away from the others as possible. With imminent danger from vampires temporarily at a halt, the hum of the engine and the splash of the water as the boat broke across the glasslike surface of the bay were the only sounds anyone could hear...aside from the muted whimpers of a girl who was still grappling with knowing her family was so close to freedom, but who would never again see the light of day again.

SAN FRANCISCO BAY

BRANDON took his place with the others huddled around the forward access hatch of the submarine. Using all their combined strength they pulled and pried on the steel door. Initially it was solid from the water pressure and inside latch securing it in place, but slowly, the hatch began to budge. The movement was nearly imperceptible, but it was there. Employing a rhythm to their concentrated repeated effort led to another very slight shift in the door. It wouldn't take much longer before they would pull the hatch free, spilling water into the submarine and gaining them access.

The group assigned to the torpedo tubes used their obscene strength to pry open the launch silos, flooding them, then followed the tubes down to eventually force their way into the torpedo room. From there they would make their way to the missile silos, flooding compartments and killing any humans along the way. The vampires working on the sail scopes and comm equipment on top of the submarine didn't have to be concerned with gaining entry; rather, they began to forcibly bend, torque, and break the sonar and radar equipment, along with the communications and data masts. With little resistance, the sub's comm equipment was easily rendered useless. Once all the topside apparatus was destroyed the group would enter the sub through the forward escape hatch, following Brandon's group as they infiltrated the vessel and tracked down all the humans inside.

Those assigned to take out the submarine's propeller, not unlike their vampire comrades, carried no technology-based weapons. As was typical *modus operandi* for the vampires, their weapons were themselves. The four creatures exerted all their might as they shot themselves through the black water around the backside of the quick traveling sub, then approached the giant twisting screw driving the vessel at enough of an angle so as to not get caught up in the submarine's wake vortex. They positioned themselves around the enormous propeller and on cue from their subgroup leader, the vampires carried out their assignment.

A cloud of bloody vampire parts shot into the giant wake of the submarine as all four vampires simultaneously launched themselves into the rotating screw. The massive propeller heaved and churned as parts of the creatures got caught inside the hub and components that were designed to drive the device. The giant aluminum blades sputtered and slowed, before coming to a choppy stop.

As the efforts of Brandon and his team reached a zenith, the forward escape hatch ripped open and water poured into the exposed enclosed hold. The vampire with the long hair jumped down and tore open the secondary hatch at the bottom which was accomplished with much greater ease. Water began to flood the small room below and Brandon and the rest of his group entered the sub and the rapidly flooding compartment. They quickly moved into the next room and sealed the door behind them, securing the flooding compartment. Once they were all in and joined by the team tasked with taking out the comm equipment on top, they would break through the hatch to the next room: the control and operations center. Any resistance from the humans would be in vain.

The massive, black vessel slowed and stalled and began to list. Brandon realized the propeller team had done its job. With the propulsion system destroyed and the vessel slowly filling with water, it would only be a matter of time before the submarine sank and settled to the floor of the bay. But Brandon wasn't going to gamble on that being enough to deter the humans from their mission. He still had the task of ensuring all resistance aboard were killed. Once that was accomplished, he would be able to report back to his brother that the threat was neutralized, and take his place as second-in-command in the new vampire world.

EPISODE 27

GOLDEN GATE BRIDGE
SAN FRANCISCO MECCA

Z, Annika, and Prater, still supporting the weakened Appamattox, approached the side of their escape van, waiting undisturbed right where they left it on the dirt road parked at the steps to Lime Point Lighthouse. Z opened the side door of the van and Prater gently set Appamattox into the nearest rear passenger seat. Annika stood to the side with her arms crossed, no longer whimpering but still unable to keep tears from rolling down her cheeks, as she looked back across the bay and at Alcatraz Island. Her family was there, under the bay, and the powerlessness she felt made her chest feel cold and heavy.

The yellow glow from the lights on the Golden Gate Bridge washed the area in a dim amber through the hazy fog that blanketed the entire Bay Area. The red-orange towers of the iconic suspension bridge stretched high into the evening sky, their tops transforming into silhouettes in the thicker fog that hung higher in the air.

A shadow suddenly flashed across the dirt road and the van, causing everyone to look up. The shape of what looked like a large prehistoric bird disappeared into the foggy blanket surrounding the nearest bridge towers.

"What was that?" asked Annika, equally distracted by the shape despite her sorrow.

"It's the cybervampire," said Z, her eyes scanning the dark, foggy skies.

With Appamattox secured by blankets and a seat belt, Prater stepped away from the van with his eyes also searching the surrounding mist for any sign of the creature that stalked him. He took a few quick paces away from the van then looked back at Z.

"I'll take care of this," Prater said. "I'm the one he's after. I'll stay and distract him."

"You can't stay here," Z asserted. "That bomb's about to go off."

"*This* is my fight. I'll make it out of here if I'm meant to."

"That's a shitty take." Z spat the words at Prater with disgust.

Annika walked up and stood near Z.

"Look," said Prater, "if I go with you and we get attacked, it's possible none of us will make it away from here in time. If I stay I can distract him to buy you enough time to get away."

"You're going to die," Annika said, morosely.

Prater focused solely on Z. "You know you won't be able to force me to go like you did Annika." He didn't mean that to be spiteful but he noticed the reactionary hurt in the girl's eyes. He looked back at Z. "And you're wasting time."

"Goddammit," Z said, dismissively, as she went and opened the passenger door of the van. "Let's go, Annika."

Moments later Prater watched the van spin its tires on the dirt road, kicking up a cloud of dust that added to the hazy soup already hanging in the surrounding air. Traction quickly kicked in and the van sped away into the night with its valuable passenger and, Prater hoped, to safety.

With the van gone, Prater rushed to the rocky hill lining the dirt road. His gaze stretched up the sheer, rocky hillside to the bridge deck at the top. He hoped to reach the top while acting as bait for the cybervampire regardless of where he was on the ascent. To make it to the empty street at the top he would have to climb the side of the tall hill then scale a vertical base support for the bridge deck itself.

The fog grew noticeably thicker as Prater made his way up the hillside. It wasn't long before the dark, prehistoric-shaped silhouette crisscrossed overhead. Prater was far enough away to not hear any sound, which made for an eerie surrounding atmosphere. He felt as though he was so visible on the hill and didn't understand why the creature hadn't yet attacked. Was it taunting him, advancing the already dangerous cat-and-mouse game to an even more treacherous level under the pressure of the ticking time bomb in the bay?

The answer came swiftly and violently as the cybervampire crashed into him out of nowhere, smashing his body against the rocky slope. Spikes from the creature's fingertips pierced his shoulders from behind, shattering his scapula, using the wounds as handholds as the cybervampire scraped and bounced his helpless, raggedy body along hard dirt and rocks of the hillside as they shot upward. Jetting beyond the top of the hill, Prater – adrenaline pumping and feelings of pain from new lacerations and scrapes on his face and hands, not to mention broken ribs notwithstanding – reached up and back with both hands and grabbed the creature's head. Holding tight, he jammed his thumbs into the cybervampire's eyes and pressed as hard as he could. The cybernetic eye was strong and resilient, but Prater felt a sickening squishing and pop as one of the creature's last remnants of humanity, its remaining "human" eye, dissolved away.

Prater suddenly found himself released from the vampire's grasp as the creature flew up into the dense fog. Unnerving shrieks pierced the night as Prater fell from a height he could not determine from the haze surrounding him. Salvation came unexpectedly, if not painfully, as Prater slammed face first against a vertical brace connecting one of the main overhead suspender cables to the bridge deck. He somehow kept hold of the large, round brace as he rapidly slid down, falling away onto the pavement of the barren freeway just as he reached the bottom.

Prater wasn't sure how long he laid there on his back, staring up into the dark haze of the foggy sky. His vision was blurry in one eye from popped blood vessels and he realized he didn't know when he lost his Wayfarers. He fought to regain steadied, deep breaths as his body healed his wounds. The road was quiet save for his strained breathing, giving no indication of how near or far the cybervampire might be. After spending no time than absolutely necessary, Prater forced himself to his feet despite not yet being fully recovered. He couldn't afford to be caught off guard by the creature again.

Standing in the middle of the bridge deck, Prater looked in the direction the van had fled, hoping the cybervampire hadn't decided to abandon him and pursue the others instead. He then turned and looked down the length of the over mile-long bridge in the direction of the megacity beyond. Even with enhanced vampire vision, Prater could only see close to fifty feet through the thick foggy haze ahead of him.

A heavy, metallic thud came from the bridge deck just beyond Prater's vision. The faint sounds of unseen gears and rotors emanated from the fog, followed by a dull, rhythmic clanging as robotic footsteps advanced towards him. Prater drew both his katana and stood with the swords out to his sides, ready to move in whatever way he may need depending on how the creature may attack.

An attack didn't come, though, at least not in that moment. The footsteps continued to get closer, not too slow, but steady. Then as if curtains were being drawn back on a stage, the fog parted to make way for the semi-vampire, mostly robotic, abomination. The cybervampire's wings were folded back, not exactly non-threatening, but not displaying any aggressive posturing. His arms were at his sides and his stride remained constant until he stopped about twenty feet in front of Prater.

The two stood facing each other under the amber glow of the Golden Gate Bridge lights saturating the fog around them. The confrontation was little about posturing as the two simply stared at each other, combatants inexplicably entangled in the theater of the post-Vampocalypse. Prater couldn't help but wonder what the creature may be thinking, but he didn't take the curiously calm moment for granted as he kept strong grip of his weapons and remained prepared for any attack.

SAN FRANCISCO MECCA
NORTH AMERICA NEW WORLD TERRITORIES VAMPIRE CAPITOL

"MY vampire brothers and sisters, at no time in our three thousand year history has there been a more important day than today. I promise you that from this day forward each moment will be dedicated solely to your wellbeing. Gone are the days of fractured missions and disparate focus. There shall now be a single direction, propelled by a singular bold vision for all vampirekind. Those who sacrificed themselves tonight did so that the rest of us may live in greater security and prosperity. They died for all of you. They died for all vampirekind."

Applause and appreciation answered President Stirling's words as the stage slowly rotated through his closing speech.

"The architects of the new vampire world will labor and toil with boundless energy and enthusiasm as we pave our way forward. Under this unified direction, we will stand strong. Under this unity we will have eternal peace. Any faction of resistance will be destroyed without regard. The machinations involved are delicate but as long as we keep unity in mind, the future we desire will not only be a vision, it will be reality. We shall never look back, and we shall not forget the ravages of war and disputes of the past, of the stench and sneer of humankind, nor of innocent vampires lost over the ages to an inferior species. We now represent power over this world and all others are subservient. The mad men that hunted us in the past will not remain unchecked as our hunters become the hunted."

The president raised a fist in a demonstration of might.

"Vampirekind shall represent the pinnacle of power over the Earth. History shall look upon us as the true keepers of this world, and we shall move into the future with strong hands and fiery focus. This world is yours, my brothers and sisters, and I shall now and forevermore rule these riches for you to consume as vampirekind for all eternity."

Music fitting of a victor's lap struck from the orchestra as fireworks shot high, visible through the stadium's two-way mirror-paneled ceiling. With the festivities coming to a conclusion, many attendees began to empty from their seats. An automated announcement reminded those leaving that a curfew was still in place and to head home immediately following their exit from the stadium.

Stirling had barely come offstage when an aide stepped in front of him. The aide stood upright and stiff at attention, arms pinned to his sides, his jaw firm and angled upward slightly. His eyes gazed in the same inclined angle as his jawline, resisting any urge to look directly at the president.

"Can I help you, Mr. Grady?" Stirling asked, sounding a bit exasperated. The day had been arduous, in all likelihood still had several hours to go, and his attitude did nothing to hide the fact he really didn't need something new added to an already full plate.

"Mr. President, if you don't mind, I need a moment with you in private."

The president led the aide down a short corridor off the side of the stage and into a small makeshift office – his personal private space for use before and during the evening's ceremonies. The room was well lit but otherwise sparse, providing not a lot of extra space beyond themselves and a couple of small pieces of furniture. The aide closed the door behind them then stood at attention.

"Go on," Stirling said, choosing to partially sit on the edge of the small desk built into a side wall rather than in the chair sitting nearby. He clasped his hands together and let his arms hang casually in front of him. "Relax, Mr. Grady. Tonight is a night of celebration. Now what's so important?"

Grady looked directly at the president with an intensity in his eyes.

"Mr. President, our local security advisors completed some calculations and have determined there's a concerning risk."

"A risk?"

"Mr. President, there's a good possibility the submarine the humans have commandeered has made its way into the bay. If they get close enough and detonate the warhead on board, the blast would destroy the entire city, including everyone here along with it. Even in the best case scenario, if the blast zone wasn't to actually reach us, the detonation would cause significant earthquakes and tidal waves that will level the city. Either way, it's not safe here, Mr. President. It's been advised to take you out of the city and get as far away as possible in the event any of this occurs."

The actual possibility of the humans succeeding in their mission hadn't seriously occurred to Stirling.

"My brother has the matter under control, I assure you. He and his task force will stop that submarine before any damage can be done. I'm sure there's nothing to be frightened of, Mr. Grady."

"I must ask that you reconsider, Mr. President. The security advisors have faith in their assessments and –"

Stirling bolted upright off the desk and took the few steps available before he stood directly in front of the aide. The smaller man struggled as he maintained a sliver of decorum in front of the president. Saliva dripped from the tips of Stirling's fangs as he leaned closer to the aide before he spoke.

"And I put my faith in my brother, Mr. Grady." Stirling's voice was airy with a slight raspiness. "Do I sense that you do not? Because it would be a shame if anyone questioned the intentions of my brother or anyone in my regime."

The aide resumed his stiff posture. "I don't question any intentions, Mr. President. No one does."

"I just pledged to lead all vampirekind to a prosperous future and now you expect me to run? I don't think so, Mr. Grady."

Stirling stepped away and even though the aide didn't look visibly relieved, Stirling could feel the man's heartbeat gradually slowing from its near explosive rate. The president's voice was calm and silky as he continued to speak, quite in contrast to his darkening tone just moments before.

"There is no need to create panic. Everyone is to maintain their positions. The curfew is set to continue through the night. This will help keep calm amongst our citizens. My brother will be successful commandeering the sub and everyone in the city will be none the wiser."

"Of course, Mr. President."

Stirling's brow grew pointed and he took a moment to briefly chew sideways at nothing. He wasn't precisely certain the aide agreed with or believed everything he said but it would have to do. Now was not the time to second guess the intentions of others.

"You're excused, Mr. Grady."

Stirling watched the aide leave then closed the door behind him. He turned and leaned his back against the door and released a long sigh. He went to the desk and took the cork off a bottle of human bloodwine that was calling to him. He took two long steady drinks, emptying half the bottle in the process. Setting the bottle back on the desk he sniffed as he wiped red stains from his lips with the back of his hand. Glancing around the office at nothing, Stirling finished the bottle then smashed it against the floor.

He let out an aggravated snarl before tearing the office door open and breaking into a determined walk down the corridor on the other side.

GOLDEN GATE BRIDGE
SAN FRANCISCO MECCA

IT was quiet, a near dead silence save for the sounds of waves gently lapping against the nearby shoreline. A cool chill was in the air, with steady breaths adding to the haze of the fog floating over the deck of the bridge. Prater and Sloane stood about twenty feet apart in the middle of the road facing each other in their tense standoff. Despite the quiet of the air around them, Prater could hear – and, of course, feel – the creaking and cracking of his body healing. Cuts and scratches sealed themselves shut as the flesh mended and skin regrew.

He discovered early on that his rapid healing was not comfortable – actually the opposite as it could be rather painful – but he was grateful for the newly acquired ability.

"You know I'm not going to let you take me alive," Prater said, disguising any of the pain.

Ryder Sloane cocked his head, amused by the statement. Blood that drizzled from his damaged vampire eye socket was beginning to dry. The eye itself did not regrow.

"Delivering you to the president dead isn't ideal," said Sloane. He drew in a deep breath that caused electronics unseen behind the exoskeleton to buzz quietly. "But if that's the case then so be it."

"Before we resume our fight," Prater interjected. "I've gotta know, why are you so set on getting to me?"

"You are the mission ordered by the president. He's been wanting you for a very long time. I'm just a method to achieving those means."

"But why me specifically?"

"The reasons for the president's desires are inconsequential to the mission, which is to acquire you and bring you to him."

Prater couldn't help but let out a light chuckle. "But you can't seem to get me, right? All your efforts so far have led to the deaths of many others, but yet here I stand, unbroken, ready to fight as I always am."

Sloane took a single heavy metallic step forward. "It's just a matter of time, Prater Saxon. This is a game you have played well but are destined to ultimately lose."

Prater looked out to the bay in the direction of the black Pacific Ocean beyond. After a brief moment he turned his attention back to the cybervampire.

"Maybe that's the problem," Prater said. "Maybe you've been looking at this like a game when it's not a game. This is real life." He paused before adding, "Either way, you were never meant to win."

"There's no logic in that statement. I am destined to win. If I was fated to lose, we wouldn't be having this conversation now."

Prater adjusted his posture and his body tensed, ready to fight, with one foot in front of the other, both swords raised like they were extensions of his fists. He heard bones in his shoulder crack as the final rejuvenating pieces set back into place. He gave a quick shrug of both shoulders and cocked his head as his adrenaline began to flow.

"Then maybe it's time to end this conversation," said Prater.

"Perhaps it is," said Sloane.

The cybervampire rocketed headfirst with his arms and claws extended forward as Prater ran at the creature, his swords poised and ready. Just as the two combatants were upon each other, Prater dropped and rolled to one side, slicing up with both swords as the cybervampire streaked over him. The blades bounced and clanged harmlessly against the creature's exoskeleton, sparking as they went. The monster twisted upright and landed on the ground with the already familiar clank of the metal feet slamming onto the road. Prater rolled up onto his feet, and the two found themselves facing each other again, closer this time, and on opposite sides from where they started.

They went at each other again, both on their feet, and when they met Prater wasn't needing to evade the cybervampire's metallic claws, but rather it was the forward edges and tips of the creature's black-chrome wings that were slicing and stabbing at him. Prater spent his time blocking the onslaught with his katana and wasn't able to direct any strikes of his own. Several attacks and blocks occurred and Prater found himself slowly stepping backwards as part of his defense. Without warning the cybervampire changed his attack and instead of striking with his wings, he instead swept them back swiftly and planted a sudden, unexpected side kick into Prater's chest. The steel foot slammed into Prater, cracking ribs anew, and sent him flying backwards before ending on his back on the hard road. Despite his predicament he held strong onto his swords as he bumped and scraped along the street.

Prater let out a loud wheeze as he took in an uneven breath and the pain of what felt like a thousand steel splinters exploded through his lungs. As his body began the healing process, Prater hoped for a moment of reprieve from the fight that didn't come. A shadow dropped upon him as the cybervampire landed with his feet straddling him with his wings spread wide. Prater took alternate swipes with his swords but the creature's wings moved in fast, smacking his futile strikes away and sending his weapons flying out of his hands and clattering well out of reach.

Sloane reached down and drilled his talons into Prater's chest, eliciting a scream that Prater couldn't help but let out. Leaning in close, the black hollow socket of the missing vampire eye added to the ominous presence of the creature. The glowing red sphere that floated in the darkness of the functioning robotic eye orbit looked Prater over. When the creature spoke, his mouthful of knives could have easily torn most of Prater's face off and he would have been defenseless to prevent it.

"My objective is complete. I'm taking you to the president and his wishes shall finally be fulfilled." The words were deliberate and spoken with the satisfaction of someone who had just consumed their favorite meal, though luckily for Prater, that wasn't the creature's objective.

Prater staved away unconsciousness as his struggle for breath continued. He was violently yanked to his feet and his body continued to scream inside as it strained to heal itself through the blitz of injuries. The cybervampire pulled his face in close again and Prater could smell hints of whatever synthetic fluids the mostly robotic creature needed to function. The odor wasn't simply vile, it was inhuman.

"Your time is done, Prater Saxon. You now belong to us."

*** Priority Brief ***

**NORTH AMERICAN FREEDOM ALLIANCE
DEPARTMENT OF HUMAN RESOURCES COMMAND**

*** **CLASSIFIED DOCUMENTATION:** *EYES ONLY* ***

**FROM THE DESK OF: GENERAL OLIVER KAUR
SUBJECT: OPERATION TWILIGHT FURY**

Additional details have been received regarding the status of Operation Twilight Fury.

At approximately 2053: The vampire submarine *Harbinger One* entered San Francisco Bay and passed under the Golden Gate Bridge and nearby Alcatraz Island, approaching the San Francisco Mecca shoreline and intended target. Up until this time, Operation Twilight Fury had proceeded without further incident since commandeering of the vessel, with Directive AA-17 the primary directive.

At 2117: Transmissions from Special Ops Team Bloodforce Four confirmed that vampires had attacked the vessel, disabling several key systems. Although primary communications were disabled, encrypted messages were able to be transmitted from a datapad networked through NAFA dark web Intranet.

2123: Flooding of multiple compartments on board the *Harbinger One* confirmed as vampires made their way through each compartment of the vessel. All propulsion systems confirmed destroyed. Irrevocable damage to the submarine determined to be sustained, and the submarine began to sink.

2137: Final transmission. The *Harbinger One* settled on its side on the bottom of the Bay as vampires were monitored moving through each compartment, barely ahead of the flooding waters. The door to the missile control room where a member of Special Ops Team Bloodforce Four processed the codes to manually detonate the warheads on board was closed and latched. The door was heavily reinforced and provided the last defense to protecting the Special Ops Team member working to detonate the warheads.

2141: It is believed that it was at this time that vampires breached the missile control room. Resistance status unknown as the transmission was disrupted. It was at this time that a large nuclear detonation was registered from beneath the waters of San Francisco Bay. Total destruction of the *Harbinger One* presumed along with zero possibility of survivors.

Additional details will be provided as further developments are reviewed. For now, the complete and absolute destruction of San Francisco Mecca is being reported through all public vampire broadcast outlets.

Operation Twilight Fury is considered accomplished.

*** End Brief ***

EPISODE 28

SAN FRANCISCO MECCA
SAN FRANCISCO BAY AREA

AS the fight between Prater and Sloane raged; as Z and the others continued fleeing as fast as the van could drive away from the city; as the vampires in the mecca remained locked away behind the curtain of the curfew; as Brandon and his team fought for control of the submarine; and as the humans inside the sub reached the zenith of their resistance, they detonated the bomb.

A split-second, muffled boom was followed by a brilliant flash underwater that illuminated all of the surrounding bay. An immense irradiated dome of water vapor and spray erupted like the head of a giant mushroom from the bay with Alcatraz Island, the Golden Gate Bridge, and the shore all less than a mile from the blast zone. Plumes of hot, fiery devastation followed, shooting out in all directions from the spray dome. For several moments the night became day under the light of the blast as an unnatural glow cast itself on the city and the entirety of the Bay Area. The sudden change in the air surrounding the explosion created a vast vacant expanse that continued to take over the area, gradually freeing much of the bay from the hazy gray blanket of fog.

As the light gradually diminished into nothingness, it was replaced by a deep, throaty rumble from deep within all of the Bay Area. Almost immediately the entire city and surrounding area began to rock and shake from the growls of an earthquake that sprung to life, triggered as a result of the explosion. The spray dome and plumes continued to stretch far away from the blast zone but they were joined by waves in the water taller than many of the buildings in the nearby city. The ground continued to shake and the waves grew steadily larger as they stretched towards the shore.

The damage that ensued easily dwarfed the San Francisco earthquakes of 1906 and 1992 as the ground trembled for close to a full six minutes before finally stopping. Very few buildings in the city limits of the mecca survived, leveled by the violent and unending vibrations of the ground beneath them. Many who may have been lucky enough to survive the collapse of structures around them found themselves under several feet of water as waves rushed in, one after another, pressing further and further inland, leaving only the tallest of the city's famed hills dry at their pinnacles.

The great vampire capitol building, the largest structure in all of North America, swayed and rippled. Black glass cracked and broke as shards sprayed the streets below. The grand passageway connecting the two towers of the building high in the sky broke into several pieces that plummeted to the ground. As the ground continued to shake, both buildings did little to withstand the destructive forces that caused them to bend and sway and ultimately crumble into dusty, smoking piles of their former grand selves.

The pods carrying humans in the blood bank racks under Alcatraz shook and many, if not most, broke away from their chains and crashed to the ten-story deep floor. More and more pods fell, and quickly a pile of split and shattered pods began to create a hill of broken and bloodied cocoons. Crimson fluids leaked from the silk-wrapped bodies as they spilled out and tore away from the needles injected into them. Annika would never know that her parents and sister were among those who ended up in the pile.

The blast from the underwater nuclear blast less than a mile away continued to wreak havoc as the immense, dark, rock walls of the cavernous facility formed deep cracks from their tops down. As Alcatraz Island itself crumbled and dissolved away as a result of the combined assault from the nuclear blast, ensuing shockwaves, and earthquake, water rapidly made its way from the cracks in the ceiling and walls. A few drips suddenly became a deluge of rain from above and waterfalls along the walls. Computers and monitors in the remnants of the control room exploded and sparked as water worked into electronics and power supplies. Moments later all the power blinked out, turning the cave into a pitch black void with only the sounds of creaking chains and rushing water left as a reminder of what the place once was.

The Golden Gate Bridge, so majestic against the backdrop of the bay, was also no more. The two grand Golden Gate towers shuddered from being so close to the explosion yet managed to stay erect, though the entire bridge shook and swayed from the detonation and subsequent quake. Several of the vertical braces snapped loose and the large, main suspension cables that ran the length of the bridge crashed partially onto the twisting and galloping bridge deck as the rest fell into the water. Moments later the bridge deck itself broke apart causing large chunks of steel and concrete to splash into the bay. Most of the street ended up underwater. All that was left were the two towers and jagged pieces of the bridge deck that clung onto them.

The black van racing northward away from the city was buffeted as it was nudged by the outermost edge of the largest shockwave from the nuclear explosion that rolled across the land. Z and Annika were witness to the light that flashed throughout the Bay Area, along with seeing the initial spray dome and blast plumes in their sideview mirrors, but other than being shaken from the vibrations stemming from it all, they were fine. Appamattox remained in his barely conscious state but managed to give a weak thumbs-up on one hand when Z glanced back to check on how he was doing.

The submarine had done its work, Alcatraz and the blood banks were gone, and San Francisco Mecca was in ruins. Anyone caught in any of the destruction zones did not escape and did not survive. In those moments, thirteen million human souls who had been transformed against their will into vampires were wiped out. That was thirteen million souls who would never have the opportunity to become human again. Thirteen million souls who used to be human, who had no choice in their lives or their ultimate destinies.

In this, the landscape of the war between humans and vampires was changed forever. But those in the know of what happened harbored uncertainty – would it be humans or vampires who benefitted most from the event? Only history would know.

And history was far from being written yet.

EPISODE 29

GOLDEN GATE BRIDGE
SAN FRANCISCO MECCA

PRATER struggled for breath as he attempted to pull the cybervampire's claws out of his chest with no success. His newfound healing abilities were useless as long as the vampire's talons stayed in him. He tried punching and kicking at the creature but his blows struck mostly metal and did no damage. His strength was seeping away and each of his blows did more to weaken him than damage the robotic vampire.

Then there was the boom from underwater and the illumination as night artificially turned to day, lighting up the entire bay along with the Golden Gate Bridge. Spray from the blast showered down upon the bridge deck, prefacing the destruction to come. The initial shockwave from the blast shook the entire bridge as if the structure was struck by a gigantic hammer.

Prater and the cybervampire each looked out in the direction of the boom and blast. A few short seconds later the bridge was slammed violently by the shockwave. Both Prater and Sloane were knocked sideways off their feet and the cybervampire lost grasp of his prisoner as they rolled along the bridge deck. Prater used the opportunity to grab his swords as he tumbled, pulling them in tight to his body as he bounced along the vibrating street.

Sloane wrapped his wings around himself like a black metallic cocoon and he let the sudden shaking take him where it would. As the initial vicious vibrations gave way to more of a sway of the bridge decks, Sloane unfurled his wings and he instantly saw his target nearly fifty feet from him on the shaking and cracking bridge deck.

Prater was on all fours sheathing his swords as he fought through the pain of his body healing itself. The focus of his fight then shifted to standing up on the buckling bridge deck, though the twisting and tilting of the concrete beneath him was rapidly increasing. Prater needed to get off the bridge as fast as he could. He tried to run but more limped and zigzagged on the street as the road under his feet began to bend like rubber. He may have had some advantage of slightly enhanced speed and strength from being part-vampire, but those abilities were negated by the shuddering of the surface under his feet. Still, he pressed on as quickly as he could, making his way haphazardly towards the end of the bridge. His feet stumbled over themselves on the bending street, making him look like a drunk trying to make their way home on foot after a long night out. Adding to the deadly obstacle course, several of the tall, steel, vertical support posts broke away from the main suspension cable and began slamming onto the street around him.

Prater was thrown about the twisty, turvy bridge deck as he rushed towards more solid ground. In some instances the natural sidestep Prater was forced to perform on the galloping deck floated him to safety; in others Prater had to jump or duck and in one case slide across the pavement to avoid the falling posts. As if facing a final trial in some crazy real life videogame, just as Prater thought he outmaneuvered the last falling suspender, the massive main suspension cables that gradually lost support as each vertical suspender fell got to where they could no longer remain hanging over the bridge and themselves smashed onto the bridge deck like giant longnecked prehistoric beasts toppling to their deaths. As all the cables came down, the power went out on the bridge, draping the bridge in a curtain of darkness. Prater's vision immediately adjusted for the sudden blackness and his pace was uninterrupted as he raced on.

The end of the bridge was in sight with just a dozen or so more stumbling steps to go. Any elation Prater may have felt from the proximity of returning to the safety of more sure-footing was suddenly stolen away as a body smashed into him from behind. Hard, metallic arms wrapped around his midsection and whisked him into the sky. The bridge deck under Prater's feet crumbled and disappeared to the black waters far below as he was grabbed – the cybervampire ironically saving his life as they sailed into the sky.

A droning *whump! whump!* of the creature's flapping wings underscored the distress Prater felt as they fled from ground zero. The creature snapped and snarled his deadly fangs just a breath away from his right ear. Prater kicked and hit the cybervampire any way he could manage in a struggle to break free. The harder he fought, though, the stronger the cybervampire tightened its grasp. The creature was not about to lose his prize this time.

Prater had other ideas.

Taking a quick study of the cybervampire's forearms crossed in front of him, he saw the long exoskeletal parts that provided framework for glass coverings, under which he could see humanlike muscles and veins combined with tiny mechanical piping and tubes. He tried to pry away the glass casings but they were installed too flush and tight into the creature's arms. Looking beyond the forearms there were servomotors and small robotic wire casings at the elbows and wrists that provided free movement.

Exposed servomotors and wire casings.

Without an additional thought, Prater smashed as many fingers as he could from both of his hands into the bare elbow joint of the cybervampire's right arm. Tiny sparks and pops came from the joint as Prater pinched and pulled on unprotected wires. The right arm instantly fell loose and powerless at the elbow as power was disrupted to the creature's forearm. Despite the cybervampire still having hold of Prater with his other arm, the sudden change shifted the creature's balance. They tilted in the air and Prater began to slip loose. The cybervampire tried to adjust his grip but only succeeded in causing Prater to slide closer to freedom from his grasp.

For a brief moment Prater caught the gaze of the cybervampire's robotic eye – just before he slipped out of the creature's hold entirely and fell nearly a hundred feet into a thick grouping of trees lining the dark, barren highway that traveled northward and away from the devastated mecca. Branches and limbs cracked and broke under the weight and inertia of Prater's body but did enough to provide a slight semblance of cushion before he was deposited face down onto the hard ground. His healing factor – at this point it was more of a perpetual *rehealing* factor – was certainly working overtime.

Prater lay unmoving for longer than he liked but not nearly as long as he really wanted. He pushed himself up onto his knees then finally fully to his feet. His movements were slow as he continued healing from his wounds. There was no need for abrupt movement until necessary. Scoping his surroundings he was on the wooded side of a wide eight-lane highway, a relic of the days before the Great Turn. Highways like these were still used but the amount of traffic on them was a mere fraction of what it once carried, and tonight none at all due to the curfew. From its size, this particular highway had to be the main road leaving the mecca, though Prater wasn't sure how far away they were from the city. From where he stood he could only see a relatively small section of the highway, maybe a quarter mile in each direction, before turns in the road eliminated any further views.

Prater had barely started walking along the side of the freeway following the northbound lanes when he heard the familiar flapping of wings rapidly approaching. Realizing the sound was suddenly upon him from behind, Prater dropped flat onto his stomach. The cybervampire flew over him, screeching as his extended talons just scraped against the swords strapped to Prater's back. Prater leapt to his feet and drew his steel blades as the creature landed in the freeway lane next to his, facing him. It wasn't hard to notice the cybervampire's right arm hanging limp at the elbow, a testament to the creature's vulnerability. The cybervampire folded his wings behind him and the two combatants again found themselves in a stare down not unlike the moment they shared on the bridge before initially engaging in their fight.

"This fight is finished," said Prater. "There's no reason to keep going."

Ryder Sloane stiffened and took several deep breaths as he considered his response. The claws on his remaining usable hand flexed slowly in anticipation of their final battle.

"The president says you hold the key."

"The key to what?" There was a strain in Prater's voice as he kept his anger burning at the subsurface.

"What is with all this?" asked Sloane. "A final *tête-à-tête* before I take you in?"

"*Take me in?*" Prater mocked. "Take me in where? Your city is destroyed. Your president and all your leaders are surely dead." He waved a sword at the creature staring at him. "You have no mission! Why are you continuing this fight?"

Prater kept careful watch of the cybervampire. He couldn't tell if the creature's demeanor changed but it did seem to be standing a little less straight.

"I am a weapon," Sloane said but his voice had less of an edge, a bit less authoritative. "I do have a mission. This is what I know."

"You're being controlled, brainwashed maybe, even. But you don't have to be. Listen to yourself now." Prater kept his katana raised but did soften the tone in his voice. "Something's different."

Sloane tipped his forehead towards Prater. "The mission is all I know."

"I don't think that's true." Prater's voice gradually grew more assertive as he allowed an air of superiority to creep in. "I'm guessing you used to be more of a complete vampire...more of a complete *human*." He knew he was taking a big chance with that particular word choice. "Think hard. I'm sure your human memories are in there somewhere."

"I have no such memories. The mission is all I know."

"Search yourself. Think. I'm sure those memories are in you. You just have to try –"

"I have no such memories," Sloane repeated. The deep underlying electronic flange in his voice became more pronounced. "The mission is all. I. Know."

The cybervampire flung himself at Prater – his wings were pinned back as the creature moved, a blur in the night, eliminating the close distance between them in an instant. Prater jumped to the side, swiping with both katana as he evaded the attack and a loud *CLANG* echoed in the dark. They both looked at the road between them and there lay Sloane's severed right forearm – Prater had managed to cut the appendage away during their brief exchange.

Sloane attacked with fury, interchanging swipes with the razor edges of his wings with stabs from their pointed wingtips. Prater blocked and parried with both of his swords, barely evading death with each move. Some of his defense was with both katana in unison with the blades parallel to each other, while others were demonstrated independently with the swords slicing and cutting intricate individual movements.

The cybervampire broke off his attacks and shot twenty feet up in the air then immediately came straight down at Prater. He would have smashed Prater into the ground with both of his robotic feet if Prater hadn't leapt back and out of the way at the last moment.

I guess the mission now is to just kill me, Prater thought.

Prater jumped at the cybervampire with a spinning round kick while simultaneously slicing his blades through the air. Sloane was forced to put his wings up as a shield and Prater pulled the kick at the last moment but still brought both swords hard onto the wings. Sparks erupted as metal met metal. Prater rushed behind the creature and jumped onto his back as the wings unfurled. The cybervampire screamed a banshee's scream as he tried to shake Prater off by fiercely jolting his body and flapping the wings. From his position on the creature's back Prater could see how the wings were attached to the exoskeleton by large joints in the area of the shoulder blades.

With the cybervampire's initial, albeit brief, attempt to shake Prater off failed, Sloane flew straight up again, this time with Prater clinging to him from behind. Prater held strong with his legs wrapped around the waist of the creature. He quickly sheathed one sword while at the same time jamming the tip of the other into the attachment joint of the cybervampire's right wing. He twisted and torqued the blade with both hands and drew more sparks from the monster. The cybervampire's right wing fell loose and useless, leaving the weight of maintaining their lift on the remaining wing and Sloane's preternatural ability of flight. Sloane maintained the upward direction, though they began to spiral due to the off-balance coming from the damaged wing.

The sword in Prater's hands suddenly snapped leaving half of the blade stuck in the wing joint. He couldn't resist a quick frown – then jammed the jagged, broken remainder of the katana up to its hilt into the right temple of the creature. The scream that came from the cybervampire was unlike anything Prater had ever heard – human or vampire. It was a guttural growl mixed with the surrendering cry of someone who had witnessed their own death – all punctuated by the bass of the electronic robotic undertone in the cybervampire's voice. The two combatants plummeted together, intertwined, back towards the ground. Just before they hit, Prater pushed himself off and separated from the cybervampire, causing he and the creature to go tumbling in different directions. He had the broken half of the katana in his hand, having pulled it out of the creature's temple as they separated.

The adversaries rolled and bounced on the freeway lanes, though Sloane's landing was much louder from the clanking and clattering of his exoskeleton skipping across the asphalt. He jumped immediately to his feet but the broken wing was debilitating his movements as it hung behind him at an unnatural angle. Its weight and the way it slung low and dragged on the road slowed him down as he turned around to face Prater. His cybernetically enhanced vision was partially blackened from a failing optical core that resulted from Prater having impaled his head with the broken katana blade. When he completed his turn he noticed too late that Prater was already upon him. An onslaught of hard punches alternating with strong side and forward kicks greeted multiple parts of his exoskeleton.

Pure adrenaline drove Prater as he pressed on and on and the cybervampire, though metallic and larger than him, stumbled backwards. Through the melee Prater extracted his other sword and began using that in tandem with the shortened broken blade to attack the creature. A sudden strong swipe from Sloane's good wing knocked Prater off kilter and he tumbled to the road. The broken katana blade bounced away as he rolled, barely keeping himself from being sliced and cut from the good blade still in his hand.

Sloane felt the processors in his brain – the ones left undamaged from when the broken blade pierced his temple – reroute commands and was able to automatically eject the broken wing from his back. A buzzing shot through his brain, causing him to wince and make a face as if to cry out – though no audible sound emitted from his twisted silent scream. Anger coursed through the cybervampire as the only emotion he could process, and he half-skipped, half-ran at Prater. His mission was in front of him – the man who was so elusive all this time, slipping through his grasp no matter how tight he squeezed – and he was not going to let him get away again. He would complete this mission. He would kill Prater Saxon and bring him to the president.

Prater got to his feet just as the cybervampire was upon him and before he could do anything the creature knocked his remaining katana out of his hand, slicing open his forearm and the top of his sword hand with deep gashes in the process. Prater yelped then he found himself entangled with the creature and tumbling onto the highway. The gladiators punched and hit each other as they rolled. Sloane's deadly claws swiped as his spiked teeth snapped. As they fought the cybervampire ejected his remaining wing which allowed the battle between them on the ground to intensify. Prater felt fresh cuts on his face and hands as he and the creature battled. The monster seemed to make more effective contact through their brawl and he could feel blood coming from gashes on his body too numerous to count.

As they grappled and rolled, a new, unexpected advantage wound up in Prater's possession. Then Prater swiped and struck hard against the side of Sloane's head – not with his fists, though, but rather with the robotic forearm that he had severed from the cybervampire earlier in the fight. The metal on metal of the exoskeletal forearm smacking against the full robotic side of the creature's head let out a loud clanking echo – over and over again – up and down their dark segment of the freeway as Prater repeatedly pounded on the monster. With his enemy dazed and the non-robotic, vampire portion of the creature's face bloody and puffy from bruises, Prater turned his attention to the creature's midsection. Three strong bangs with the metallic forearm against the cybervampire's chest shattered several of the glass coverings protecting the creature's steel ribs and live organs.

Sloane strained to look into the face of his attacker with his slowly failing robotic eye. Prater tossed the broken forearm aside then reached into the creature's chest, forcing his fist through the mess of wires and bloody veins to put his hand in the cavity holding the monster's heart. Sloane didn't flinch or move, defiant despite internal pain sensors erupting into overdrive.

"It doesn't need to end this way," said Prater as he reached up with his free hand and wiped blood that dripped down his face from a deep gash across his forehead, a wound that like his others was working to heal itself.

"There is no other way…for this to end." Sloane forced the words through damaged processors that caused his voice to buzz and crackle. Its mechanical flange resonated deeper as he spoke.

"I can tell you're afraid. Stop this. Stop all of this. Let me try and help you."

"You…cannot help me. You…are the objective. You are…my mission. You…are the key."

Prater felt himself growing anxious. "The key to what?" He repeated the question, louder, spitting the words directly into the creature's face. "The key to WHAT? Tell me what you know!"

Sloane released a low cackle. "Chaos…is all there is. Nothing can change…that. Humankind…is doomed."

Prater banged a fist against the creature's upper chest with his free hand. "Please just stop this. Stop the killing. Stop the chasing. There's no reason for any of it anymore. You've lost."

"It doesn't matter…if I win…or lose. Someone…will always be after you."

Prater cocked his head and exhaled sharply. "Last chance."

"You are my…mission. My mission…is all I know."

Prater squeezed his hand that held the cybervampire's heart. He felt the cold, undead organ implode under the pressure of his grip. He watched as the electronic red orb floating in the dark of the creature's cybernetic eye socket blinked. Just as it began to fade the dying robotic vampire laying before him let out one final laugh…a laugh that didn't echo but faded out as the cybervampire's final motors, processors, and internal applications all shut down.

All but one.

There was an odd beeping, faint at first, that persisted despite all the cybervampire's functions seeming to have terminated. Leaning in closer to the creature, Prater could hear the beep was originating from inside the monster's head – and was growing not only steadily louder, but increasingly faster. Deciding this didn't sound like anything good Prater jumped up and off the cybervampire and sprinted down the highway away from the creature as fast as his battered body would allow. He wasn't fast enough to escape as the cybervampire exploded. The blast slammed into Prater's back like a semi-truck and carried him thirty feet in the air before depositing him onto the hard asphalt. Fresh scrapes and cuts adorned his face as his body slid to a stop.

Prater wasn't sure how long he laid there – a familiar sensation as of late. The night was quiet and the air was cool and Prater didn't remember the last time he felt so relaxed despite his injuries and circumstances. Eventually, he rolled onto his back. The sensation of his body healing all over cradled him in a reassurance that he would soon be as good as new. He just had to give it a little time. So he stared up into the dark sky. Where he was exactly and how far away anyone might be was anyone's guess. Closing his eyes he gave in to allowing his body to heal and he drifted away into a plane between sleep and unconsciousness.

The distant hum of a vehicle approaching on the highway captured Prater's attention but he wasn't sure if it was real or within a dream. Fighting to open his eyes and bring himself out of the semi-unconscious state he was in, Prater thought twice as bright lights from headlights washed over him. Voices echoed his way, strong and familiar. As he finally pried his eyes open a shadow blocked the light of the vehicle and a silhouette that started as a misshapen mass in his unfocused gaze became more defined as the footsteps drew nearer. The person stooped down next to him as if examining him. The hint of Russian accent in the woman's voice left no question as to who it was.

"Well," said Z, "Looks like you were meant to make it out."

EPISODE 30

SAN FRANCISCO MECCA
NORTH AMERICA NEW WORLD TERRITORIES VAMPIRE CAPITOL

IT'S *been advised to take you out of the city and get as far away as possible in the event any of this occurs…advised to take you out of the city and get as far away as possible…get as far away as possible…*

The words of his aide, spoken to President Stirling just a couple of short minutes earlier, replayed over and over in his head as he made his way through private corridors directly beneath Wearh Arena. His personal driver greeted him at his town car in the stadium parking garage. Stirling dismissed the driver as he himself slipped into the driver's seat of the all-black, four door, electric powered sedan. The car hummed through the private garage with its rubber tires squeaking on the smooth cement floors. Two turns and a short incline later and the vehicle exited the stadium and sped towards the capitol building just a few empty city miles away.

Into the garage of the capitol building, parked, and to the elevator – Stirling was there in practically no time. Down, down further than anyone's credentials other than the president's himself would allow, the elevator dropped. At the bottom, out the doors, and through the cold hallway to the steel door, there was no time to waste. The familiar "clang" as the door unlocked. Into the large, dimly lit room with the dark walls. Securing the door behind him. A sigh of relief.

Stirling took a moment to gather himself as he rested with his back against the door, breathing heavy. That moment was barely taken when the room began to quiver and shake. His eyes darted around the space and specifically at the high ceiling looking for any signs of damage – there wasn't any he could see, at least not yet. Without hesitation, Stirling bolted across the increasingly shaky room and draped himself across the shiny, dark casket that sat resting on its pedestal, prepared to try and protect it from any threatening damage.

It felt as if the shaking was never going to stop. Stirling kept cover over the chest and while the room remained intact, wisps of dust flaked away from the smooth rock-carved walls and ceiling creating random trickles and loose threads that dissipated harmlessly in the air. The power faded twice – causing the blue lamps shining from the floor and onto the obsidian casket stand to dim each time as well – before going out permanently. The shaking persisted and Stirling clung ever tighter to the top of the casket in the dark. Finally, many long, endless minutes later, the trembling subsided and stopped. Emergency power generators kicked in and the lights turned back on, returning the room to its original ghostly atmosphere.

Stirling lay across the chest until he felt confident the principle tremors had stopped. There were sure to be aftershocks, but there was no reason to be concerned about those until they actually occurred. He finally stood, clenching his fists at his sides while again surveying the room. The expression on his face was harder than the rock walls that surrounded him. The room had survived and so had he. Most importantly, though, as far as Stirling was concerned, so had the casket.

Stirling reached between two of the stylistic obsidian shards supporting the casket and located a hidden button. A singlewide doorway in the shadowy wall immediately behind the president revealed itself as a panel slid away. The snug room on the other side was barely more than a tiny closet. Its black-as-night environment was disrupted by illuminated lines from recessed control panels, computer monitors, and touchscreens. A single seat – a chair crafted solely for the president – sat in the middle of the digital array.

Stirling took the seat in his one-person war room and quickly entered commands into a satellite monitoring system. The corresponding display showed a satellite image of the greater San Francisco Bay Area that under the blanket of night provided few details aside from a large swath of darkness. And that was the problem – the image should have been filled with millions of lights illuminating the buildings and streets even though most were currently empty. Stirling zoomed in closer to more clearly see finer details in and around the capitol building.

Jonathan Stirling had personally witnessed more than his share of unfathomable events during his three thousand year life, but he had never seen anything like the devastation shown in the images displayed now on the screen. Multiple fires helped illuminate the local destruction in the dark. The bulk of the sprawling megalopolis that was San Francisco Mecca was completely leveled. No building survived the combination of nuclear blast and subsequent earthquake. Fathomless black fissures branched from the San Andreas fault system and stretched their demon-like fingers through the blackened landscape with no care or consideration. There were absolutely no signs of life – not a single vampire could be seen staggering among the ruins.

Stirling snarled as he sat seething in his chair. He had killed the vampire leadership himself, sure, but seeing his entire capitol city destroyed was not something he had ever fathomed. In the next instant he was struck with the realization that his brother was dead. Brandon obviously failed in his mission to stop the humans from setting off the bomb. After three thousand years, his brother would truly be missed. But that fool's braggadocio had finally gotten the better of him. And now was not the time to mourn.

Stirling would have to take stock of which of his most trusted survived. For certain he knew at least Deuteronicus had lived as after his most recent work on Ryder Sloane's modifications, the doctor had requested to retreat to his private laboratories. These were in a secret location far away from San Francisco Mecca and known only to the doctor, Stirling, and a handful of others who worked closely with Deuteronicus. Stirling knew the doctor's experiments were crucial to the future of vampirekind, much of which would be instrumental once Prater Saxon was finally – *finally* – in his custody.

The opening of a new application on the computer monitor directly in front of him activated a tiny camera built into the workstation and Stirling saw his live image staring back at him from a corner of the screen. Stirling sat fuming, considering the situation for several minutes in complete silence. A quiet resolve eventually washed over him and it was then he knew what he needed to do. With a few quick keystrokes his image was networked into the global vampire broadcasting systems. With a growl and sneer that exposed his vampire venom dripping fangs, Stirling addressed the world.

"What we have just witnessed was an unparalleled tragedy. San Francisco Mecca has been destroyed. The core of our government has been shattered. These heinous acts by the human animals make it obvious they are organized and dangerous. None of us are safe. None of *you* are safe. My own brother, my sweet Brandon, is dead. If our opposers can strike this close to me then they can easily get to each and every one of you. Make no mistake, every human wants us dead and is an enemy to all vampirekind. Human sympathizers are just as dangerous and are no different than the humans themselves. Hear my words now as they fall upon the world. As your one, true leader, I vow that all humans and any who support them will suffer the ultimate consequences. You will be sought out and found. You will be tortured. You will be slaughtered. None of you will survive the oncoming holocaust of humankind. From this moment, this is war."

The words spilled out, unplanned and unrehearsed, guided only by fury and rage. All around the world, eyes were glued to screens as Stirling's short but effective speech resonated throughout all of vampirekind. In the hours, days, and weeks that followed, groups and teams of vampires, organized most through official authorities while others were formed of vampire vigilantes, began to take action as those in Stirling's crosshairs were identified. Handfuls of suspected, though often never proven, human sympathizers were dragged from their workplaces and homes then tortured and murdered in every unique way imaginable. Every incident played out in the public, in front of coworkers, family members, and friends, and broadcast over the vampire telenetworks. Hordes of screaming and chanting vampires often cheered on the violent ends to which their vampire brothers and sisters met, even when loved ones or relatives were involved.

Masses of vampires spread into the barrens and wastelands in operations of a scale never before employed, with the express intention of locating any and every human possible, whether in towns, villages, or campsites, or lone individuals wandering the desolation between meccas. As humans were discovered, many were taken to the blood banks – those were the lucky. The unlucky found themselves physically assaulted and violated in ways their nightmares never could have imagined, all to the satisfaction of the vampires that took advantage of them, before eventually becoming food to their captors.

NORTH AMERICAN FREEDOM ALLIANCE
HEADQUARTERS
UNDISCLOSED LOCATION

GENERAL Kaur watched the vampire president's speech from his private office in its undisclosed location, flanked only by his innermost advisors and aides. Everyone sat silent as they witnessed the vampire leader's proclamation. The general saw the anger and hate in the creature's eyes and he knew to expect vengeance. The true war between humans and vampires was about to come.

SAN FRANCISCO MECCA
NORTH AMERICA NEW WORLD TERRITORIES VAMPIRE CAPITOL

HIS speech concluded, Stirling sank in his chair, still enraged but helpless at the moment to do little else. Turning his attention to a set of readouts on a side monitor, he completed an entry into its keypad and a list of names populated in a list down the screen. Stirling highlighted a particular line and expanded its information. The president sat quiet as he stared at an image of Ryder Sloane and a readout that read:

PROJECT: CYBERVAMPIRE Mark XIV
STATUS: OFFLINE
CONDITION: SELF-DESTRUCT (FINAL OPTION)

Stirling pressed his fists to his eyes and shook his head. Venom seeped from his fangs and pooled on the workstation desk in front of him. He tried to control his breathing as his anger only intensified. Not stronger towards the humans, however, but at another target.

Prater Saxon. I don't think you understand your true value. You will be found and you will fulfill your destiny for vampirekind, I promise you.

Stirling's mouth cracked and snapped as his jowls jutted out and his already long fangs grew longer still. His cheekbones sharpened and creases in his brow deepened into a vicious scowl. The red of his eyes burned the fires of hate as he released a deep, raspy growl.

Count your days, Prater Saxon. You will be captured soon. Even if I have to come after you myself.

EPISODE 31

OSAKA PREFECTURE
JAPAN ISLANDS MECCA

SINCE the Vampocalypse, nearly all of the Japanese island of Honshu had evolved to become not only one of the largest vampire meccas in the AustrAsia Territories, but in all the world. Osaka sprung to special prominence, becoming the *de facto* capitol of Japan Islands Mecca, and it was in the penthouse of the tallest high-rise in all the city that the Japanese governor, or *daimyo*, of the Osaka Prefecture territory watched from the comfort of his private suite. He sat in shadow in his wide and tall black leather chair, silhouetted with his back to a large bay of crystal clear windows. Flanking the daimyo were two of his aides, both Japanese as even in the post-Vampocalypse the islands maintained an ethnic homogenous society. On one side stood a man in a dark suit and sunglasses and on the other was a woman in a sleeveless, all-white suit and matching gaiter. Both were similarly shadowed in front of the sun setting beyond the glass behind them. The sky was afire in deep reds that stretched through the atmosphere like plumes of flame, all the more pronounced from the nuclear winter particles saturating the air. Lights of night life were unfolding in the buildings and streets far below and as far as the eyes could see, though the daimyo's eyes were focused on the monitor screen on the wide, blood red desk in front of him as Stirling's speech ended.

With the video feed gone to black, the Japanese leader's attentions were drawn to a scene unfolding in the office in front of him. A lone light shone down from the high ceiling, basking the rest of the office in darkness and hiding the actual size of the suite that in full illumination would reveal itself to be the size of a large executive conference room. Black marble tile covered the floor and the space was completely empty of furniture save for the desk and chair in front of the window. At the center of the light shining down was the live show the daimyo was watching before being interrupted by his advisors and Stirling's speech.

Three female vampires, their true ages unknown although they looked to be the human equivalents of barely twenty years old, were naked and intertwined. They bit and sucked without consideration of where their mouths touched as their silky bodies slithered and twisted into inhumanly impossible shapes. Trails of blood drew maroon colored webs onto their skin. Their sighs and moans filled the room as they gently and supplely partook and devoured each other.

"Stirling's move to eliminate the global vampire leadership was surprising though not totally unexpected," the daimyo said in Japanese to his aides. *"The destruction of San Francisco Mecca seems to have only increased his ambitions. I'm sure it's no coincidence, though, there was no mention of Prater Saxon."*

"It does seem unusual," said the male vampire standing beside the daimyo. *"I would have thought Stirling would announce a global bounty on finding him."*

"I don't think Stirling's that smart," the daimyo huffed. *"If he was, he would have seen his failures before they occurred. He's sloppy in his methods."*

"His methods have positioned him as the leader of all vampirekind. That shouldn't be discounted as he should not be underestimated."

"I know of the potential dangers involving Stirling, I assure you."

Never at any time did the daimyo or his two comrades take their eyes off the blood and lust-filled show transpiring in the middle of the room. The daimyo stood and walked slowly around his desk as he continued speaking. The two who stood by his chair followed as they took a "front row" view just outside the edge of the spotlight of the violent sex show unfolding before them.

The daimyo continued. *"Considering the information I leaked to him about Prater Saxon, I'm certain Stirling will remained focused on finding him."*

"His focus is misguided, if so," the male aide said, continuing their conversation. *"With the humans showing such great potential for harm, any deviation from that threat is sure to weaken Stirling's viability as an effective leader."*

The daimyo crossed his arms comfortably in front of him. *"This is the opportunity I've been waiting for to present itself. It's time Prater learned the truth about where he came from. He needs to know what makes him so important. We must get to him before Stirling does."*

"The yakuza is ready for the order," said the woman aide as she interjected herself for the first time into the conversation. Her voice was low and raspy and her words were spat with an edge as sharp as the single katana strapped to her back.

"Stirling's ambitions have helped flesh him out," said the male comrade. *"That should make it easier to track him down."*

The daimyo tilted his head sharply and his neck cracked loudly, momentarily overtaking the moans and ecstasy of the women in the spotlighted circle in front of him. He then took off his suit jacket and handed it to the male vampire. Next to come off was his already unbuttoned suit vest, followed by the white button down shirt underneath.

"With Prater in our hands," the daimyo said as he made himself shirtless, *"Stirling will be forced to realize that his murdering of the global vampire leadership was a mistake and his undoing. He has only created instability in the vampire hierarchies that will ultimately allow us to present our full potential."*

The daimyo stepped towards the bloody theater in front of him. As he did, the bright spotlight shining down chased away the shadows that had enveloped him starting at his bare feet then moving up his still suited pantlegs, before shining bright off the chiseled musculature of his abdomen and chest, then fully illuminating his salivating fangs and face.

Rin Miyamoto smiled as the vampire women on the floor in front of him, their naked bodies punctured and lacerated all over, crawled to him and while one began to remove his pants the others began to lick and lightly bite his toned midriff.

"And we shall make this world ours."

Miyamoto barely said the words before he dove into the flesh and blood of the women before him. The three female vampires squealed with delight as they took part in the frenzy of bloodstained sensuality that the daimyo gave himself into. The daimyo's two aides stood silently watching as the women gave in to their leader – and continued watching as unaffected observers as a realization washed over the women. The scene quickly turned from lust and gentle customary vampire bloodletting to one of brutality and death as Miyamoto began tearing large chunks of their flesh out with his teeth and gouged deep into their bodies with his extended talons. Their screams echoed through the large, empty office suite, much to the glee of the daimyo and his companions, as Miyamoto devoured the women in ways unimaginable to any human.

PRATER

QUESTIONS. So many more questions than answers. The questions I was suddenly left with over the past few days opened emotional wounds that weren't as easily patched as those under my newfound powers of healing.

Why did Master Miyamoto lie to me about Ky's death? I had known Rin Miyamoto for so long and had no reason to ever question him. He was always such an honorable man. In some ways he was the father I never had – not that I needed that type of figure in my life. Ky plenty fulfilled any parenting roles needed to prepare me for the cruelties of the world. But now Ky was gone. It was essentially just a whim that put me on the path to finding her in the first place. I had thought about her often, but to actually seek her out after so many years wasn't something I had genuinely considered until I heard her name spoken out of nowhere by a stranger. Then our reunion felt like anything but, and ultimately our time together was brief. And now she's dead and I'm left pondering over her final words to me.

I'm still in a daze from her telling me my mother was never bitten. If she was never bitten, then how am I part vampire? That's a side of me I've never questioned – the tells have always been obvious. But Ky had told me about how it happened during my birth and though it wasn't a subject that came up often, she never wavered from that account. But now I'm left questioning what or who I am exactly and what that means for my future. The cybervampire told me I was the "key." I can only suspect that maybe the secrets of my origins and me being the 'key' to some greater vampire plot are somehow interconnected. Maybe General Kaur can shed some light on the mystery when we deliver Appamattox to him. That might be a longshot but for now it's the only shot I have to take to hopefully solving that mystery.

Then there's that voice that calls out to me. I used to think it was a woman's voice as it sounded deeper being so distant. But as the voice has become more clear, it's sounding more like a girl's voice – something closer in tone to Annika's than Ky's or Z's. I'm always left shaking my head, though. This world is dark and crazy, and I can only hope this voice isn't evidence of the insanity of the world creeping in and slowly consuming me.

Or maybe I've just been crazy all along and not realized it. Until answers come, if they ever come at all, I'll continue to survive each day as I had been, looking out for myself first and foremost, with one weary eye ahead and one eye in constant watch of the dangerous world around me. Lessons learned over the past few days is that I can't trust humans the way I thought I could, even loved ones, and maybe there are vampires that can be trusted some after all. Trust, though, can be like a thin sheet of glass — it may be crystal clear between those involved but it can be easily shattered. And no amount of trust will ever change one general sentiment, despite it being a part of who I am.

I fucking hate vampires.

EPISODE 32

PACIFIC WASTELANDS

SUNLIGHT, muted as it was, shot golden-gray crescents through the gaps between the curtains and into the small front sitting room of the one bedroom motel room. After retrieving Prater from his fight, Z drove as fast as she could through the night without stopping to get as far away from the devastation of the mecca as possible. They drove for hours, far beyond the reach of the diminishing aftershocks of the bay earthquake. Z headed northeast as they sped away from the flattened mecca, and had moved off and away from the major freeways. She maneuvered the interconnected side streets and remained off of any of the main thoroughfares that, considering the recent attack, may be drawing vampire traffic towards the destruction. They were well into the afternoon of the day following the attack on San Francisco Mecca when, on a long, barren stretch of road somewhere in the desert far past a sign welcoming them to an Old World territory called "Nevada," they came across an old abandoned single story of interconnected motel units. It was there they decided to finally stop and take temporary refuge while they tried to get some rest.

Prater sat on the couch and Annika was at a small kitchenette table with her face in her hands, weeping as she had on and off since being dragged away from the blood banks under Alcatraz. Z walked out of the bedroom, closing the door gently behind her before joining Prater in the small living room area. She looked tired with dark circles under her eyes and her tousled hair pulled loosely back but still carried herself strong. A single, low wattage light hummed from the middle of the ceiling, barely doing more to light the room than the slivers of illumination coming through the curtains.

"How's the professor?" asked Prater. He was tired, too, but his wounds had healed and he felt as healthy as ever. His clothes were frayed and torn from his battles yet he made sure to keep his katana on his back – always prepared for a fight.

"Sound asleep," said Z. "Some bedrest is going to do him some good. We're going to need to get him some nourishment. I'm sure he's going to wake up hungry for real food."

Prater looked up with some concern at Z from where he was sitting on the sofa. "What we *need* to do is figure out a way to get him to General Kaur or someone who'll know what to do with him."

The sound of a stool crashing caught Prater and Z's attention as Annika shot up from her seat in the tiny kitchen area and rushed up in front of the Russian woman, red-faced and with cheeks wet with fresh tears. Z didn't flinch but also didn't put up any defensive posture despite Annika's face being just inches from hers.

"I could have saved them!" the teenager screamed while droplets of spit spattered on Z's face.

Z blinked then wiped the wetness away from her cheeks. "And we'd all be dead right now. You and every member of your family included."

Prater stood and put a hand on Annika's shoulder. "She's right. We wouldn't have escaped the blast zone if any extra moments were spent in those blood banks. I'm so very sorry, Annika."

The girl glanced at Prater, her face just a bit softer, then glared back at Z. She knew they were right but it didn't take away any of the pain or the feeling that Z was still responsible despite what would have been. She stammered for a few moments while continuing to give Z a death stare, then stomped back to the kitchenette, reset the stool then sat back down, crying.

Z started to move towards the girl when Prater held up a hand and gave her a light shake of his head. Z stopped and nodded. She understood Annika just needed some time to herself so she redirected her attention back to Prater.

"Why are they after you?" she asked. "What makes you so special?"

Prater shook his head as he turned away. A crack of decayed sunlight split down the middle of his face. Prater let out a breath.

"I don't know. Kylee wanted to tell me something before she died." He looked back over his shoulder but couldn't quite see the Russian woman standing just out of focus behind him. "Now I'll never know what that was."

"Maybe you aren't meant to know," said Z. Her tone was soothing. "Whatever it is, you haven't known it all this time. Maybe it's something better left to the unknown."

Prater turned around and when he did Z was standing close to him. She put her hands around his shoulders and pulled him even closer. Prater welcomed the warmth even if his return embrace was loose and not quite as fulfilling. He did close his eyes, allowing himself to ease into the comfort Z was offering.

Prater?

Prater suddenly pulled back. He was immediately in a defensive stance and one hand reached up and back and took hold of one of the katana handles. His eyes were wide as he looked around the room in search of the source of the female voice that just penetrated his brain.

"Did you hear that?" Prater asked. Both Z and Annika were looking at him with wide eyes and concern.

"Hear what?" asked Annika.

"I didn't hear anything," said Z while shaking her head.

The air in the room suddenly grew thick and everyone's hair began to lift weightless as static electricity surrounded them and a low, directionless hum filled their ears. A loud *POP!* sounded as the incandescent light bulb in the overhead fixture exploded. Annika screamed. Prater and Z each ducked and covered their heads as tiny glass shards rained upon them from the broken fixture.

Prater? Can you hear me?

"There!" Prater shouted. "There it is again!"

Prater looked at Z and Annika – who had rushed back and was clinging closely to Z – hoping for some reassurance he wasn't the only one hearing the voice but only received confused looks in return.

Before Prater could ask anyone again about the voice, the static in the air gave way to flashes of purple lightning that cut through the entire room. Prater and Z stared at the lightning that surrounded them all with both alarm and curiosity while Annika looked nothing but terrified as she cowered from the flashes, despite the bolts doing no harm whenever striking any of them.

"What's happening?" shouted Annika.

Z held the girl tight but this did nothing to stop Annika's abbreviated cries.

As the frequency and density of the lightning strikes intensified, a white glow began to fill the room. The light had no specific source, seeming to appear from everywhere at once. Objects in the room began to wash out in a white fog as the glow intensified. Annika screamed louder.

Then they were gone – Prater, Z, and Annika blinked out of existence – along with all of the mysterious light.

Seconds passed…*one…two…three…*

The crescent of filtered sun peeking between the curtains was the only light in the room.

…four…five…six…

The room sat empty and quiet as if none of them were ever there.

…seven…eight…nine…

In a sudden reversal, the room was instantly awash in a blinding white glow that reduced to purple lightning. The supernatural light dissipated, along with the deep hum and static electricity that accompanied it, leaving the room quiet and still.

Prater and Z stood in the middle of the small living room area, looking far less disheveled. They were dressed neck to toe in clean, formfitting, black tactical gear with their weapons securely strapped to their bodies where they had always been. Prater removed the thin-rimmed, round, mirrored sunglasses he was wearing and rubbed his eyes as he looked down at the floor. Z dropped her head and collapsed onto her knees with her face in her hands and wept.

Annika never returned.

TO BE CONTINUED

ACKNOWLEDGEMENTS

I would like to give many thanks to some very important people, starting first and foremost with my readers, supporters, fans, and followers. This is mostly a labor of love on my part, but knowing you all are out there and enjoying the ride along with me means so very much and makes the journey worthwhile. Next, thank you as always to my publisher, Amanda Rotach Lamkin, and the entire Line By Lion team! 2024 represents 10 years of us working together. I'm so very honored to be part of the LBL family.

A few other well-deserved thank yous go to Rachel Roland, my personal editor, who keeps me grounded, especially in our ongoing war with commas; Thomas Lamkin, Jr, who's part of LBL but deserves a special shoutout for the always amazing cover art; Don Snowden, for the beautiful map illustration; and to my personal friends who allow me to repeatedly turn them into characters in my books, only to creatively kill them off every time like Kenny in South Park.

VAMPOCALYPSE II is the first sequel I've ever written. For those of you who read the first book, thank you so much! I achieved most of the expectations I set for myself with this story, and I can only hope it meets most of yours as well as the next chapters in the adventure are revealed in the pages before you.

I did a couple minor retcons in this from Book One. For one, I now reference Prater's weapons as specifically being katana. In addition, the "epilogue" at the end of Book One told by Zarina I framed in this book as being an account of a dream rather than reality. As with many stories, ideas morph and change and I felt the direction I took in Book Two is better suited to the overall story.

This is the longest novel I've written, and it originally began much longer. I carved away a solid six or seven chapters excising, among other things, entire sequences detailing the humans commandeering of the vampire submarine, additional attacks by the Red Marauders on the fleeing heroes, and a chapter describing the origins of Ryder Sloane. Some of these ideas may be repurposed and used later, but I'm considering putting *The Ballad of Ryder Sloane* up on my website at some point. If it's not already there by the time you read this, stay tuned!

Finally, what happened to Annika? I'm not going to reveal that here, but suffice to say, Prater, Zarina, and Annika have become part of a much larger universe. More to follow!

VAMPOCALYPSE II: VENDETTA
Written between August 19, 2022, and December 17, 2023
E.S. Brown
April 6, 2024